D1554677

TWISTED FATE

THREE STORIES
of SUSPENSE

♦ TRACI HUNTER ABRAMSON ♦
♦ GREGG LUKE ♦ STEPHANIE BLACK ♦

Covenant Communications, Inc.

Cover image: *Winter Sunset behind Beautiful Trees* © Yuri, courtesy www.istockphoto.com and *Tortured Surface* © Glitschka Studios

Cover design copyright © 2014 by Covenant Communications, Inc.

Published by Covenant Communications, Inc.
American Fork, Utah

Printed in the United States of America
First Printing: June 2014

20 19 18 17 16 15 14   10 9 8 7 6 5 4 3 2 1

ISBN 978-1-62108-533-1

HUNTED

◆ TRACI HUNTER ABRAMSON ◆

For Christina and Lara

Acknowledgments

THANK YOU TO THE INCREDIBLE people at Covenant who continue to help me follow my dreams, especially Samantha Millburn for your continued support and guidance. Thank you to Rebecca Cummings, Jen Leigh, and Kathryn Brown for your input through the revision process. And finally, thank you to my amazingly talented friends Stephanie and Gregg for being willing to journey on a new adventure with me.

Chapter 1

SHE WAS GOING TO DIE this time. She was sure of it. Reagan pressed back into the corner of the living room, wishing she could make herself invisible, clasping her arms tightly around her legs.

Her dark hair was matted from sweat and tears, and she could taste the blood from the last time the back of Laith's hand had connected with her cheek. A slight breeze carried the scent of fall through the open window and into the dingy three-room cabin, but the fresh air couldn't hide the underlying smell of dust and despair.

Her mother had promised this time would be different. Her mom had been so convinced that this latest in her string of loser husbands was going to make their lives better. If only she had known how bad things were really going to get.

The colonel looked over the paper he held in his hand, his dark hair cut short, his military uniform perfectly pressed. He looked like he should be in an office somewhere instead of in the middle of the woods. Reagan recognized the sergeant stripes on his sleeve but had never dared question why Laith always called him Colonel. He motioned toward Reagan, causing her to shrink farther into the corner. "What about the girl?"

"I'll take care of her." Laith didn't even look at her, dismissing her with a vague gesture, like she was some piece of trash that needed to be taken out to the curb.

"Make sure you do. She's seen too much." The colonel turned and gave her a hard stare. "She knows too much."

Laith's voice took on an edge. "I told you I'd take care of it."

Reagan bit back a sob. The heavy crate of automatic weapons in the middle of the sparsely furnished living room was proof that she wasn't the only one about to die.

How could her mother have missed this? She could understand not knowing that the colonel was a criminal in the making. After all, who would expect a marine sergeant to be involved in a plan to hurt his own countrymen? Laith, on the other hand, was always talking about guns when he wasn't complaining about everything and everyone.

"Help me load this into my truck." The colonel motioned to the guns.

The two men circled the crate so they could heft it together, then maneuvered it out the front door of the secluded cabin. Reagan looked up to find herself alone. She thought of what these men were planning, what they were capable of. Something bubbled up inside of her, something resembling anger.

She had a choice. Cower in a corner knowing that the next few minutes would be her last or fight to stay alive.

A surge of resentment and adrenaline made the decision for her. She wasn't going to let Laith decide her future for her. She wasn't going to die like her mother. Afraid to reconsider her choices, she forced herself to stand. Despite the throbbing in her ribs, she limped across the room to the back door.

Footsteps sounded on the gravel driveway, followed by a shout. A sudden sense of urgency overwhelmed her. Without looking back, she burst through the door, refusing to let the pain stop her.

As she stumbled across the yard, she let a yelp of surprise escape her when a gunshot rang out and sent bits of bark flying. She ducked behind a tree and gasped for breath. Whatever emotions had been swirling inside her were quickly replaced by terror.

Footsteps crunching through the fallen leaves grew closer, and Reagan's will to survive eclipsed everything else. Her heart beating wildly, she pushed away from the tree and ran.

* * *

Jill Valdez stood on the back deck of the rented cabin and stared at the wild clash of colors. Fall made the Virginia countryside look like God had painted a glorious masterpiece for everyone to see. If only she didn't feel like God had turned His back on her.

Five years of trying to have children and more medical tests than she could count had brought her to this point. She had tried everything: prayers, trips to the temple, blessings. Nothing had worked. Nothing had given her the answers she had so desperately wanted. Now she had to face reality, the one she had been avoiding for so long. She would never be a mother.

The doctors had presented the finality of that fact more than two months ago, but she still struggled with the news. Only days after that last doctor's appointment, she had returned to work as a second grade teacher, and three of her coworkers had announced the exciting news that they were pregnant. A number of others had discussed their latest challenges of daycare and giving up their summer freedoms with their children to come back to work.

Jill had remained silent, feeling more and more alone. She tried hard not to be resentful. After all, it wasn't that she begrudged these women their chance to have families. She just wanted to join their ranks.

Her husband, Doug, didn't say much, but she knew he was equally disappointed. He seemed to have gotten over the initial shock more quickly, almost as though he was determined to readjust their life plans so they could leave this chapter of disappointment behind them. She suspected he had already resigned himself to the likelihood that they would remain childless long before the doctor had given them the final test results.

Jill, on the other hand, had stubbornly clung to every shred of faith that something could change their circumstances, right up until the doctor had told them all hope was lost. Of course, hope wouldn't have been lost if surrogacy or adoption was a possibility, but Doug refused to consider either alternative.

Paid surrogacy was illegal in Virginia, so that route was highly unlikely, and every time she tried to broach the subject of adoption, Doug would shut down the conversation. For the first time in her marriage, she felt like there was a huge chasm between them, and neither of them could find the bridge to cross it.

This weekend away had been Doug's idea, a chance to recapture some shred of the relationship they had once shared before doctor visits and fertility treatments had consumed their lives. The foundation was still there. She knew it was. In those rare moments when she could forget about their lack of children, her marriage was wonderful. She simply couldn't quite bring herself to envision a life with only the two of them for the next fifty years.

She had seen Doug with his nieces and nephews and had always appreciated how he could get down on their level to play ball or a board game. She had spent the past seven years teaching other people's children and now she had no hope of ever teaching her own.

The door behind her opened, and she turned to see Doug step outside. He wasn't smiling; his face looked almost dangerous with his mouth firm and his dark eyes brooding.

"Are you okay?" Jill asked.

Doug answered her question with one of his own. "Are you still mad?"

Her stomach clenched as she prepared for what would likely be a repeat of the adoption argument. She had promised herself she wouldn't bring it up this weekend, but how could she hold all of these tumultuous emotions inside? Why should she have to?

"I'm not mad. I just don't understand you right now." Jill folded her arms across her chest. "I know you have so much love to give. I don't know why you're so unwilling to consider adoption."

His jaw clenched. For a moment he didn't answer her, but finally he said wearily, "You aren't going to let this go, are you?"

"I've tried, Doug. I have. I just don't know how to take a dream that's been a part of me since I was a little girl and set it aside. It's bad enough that we can't have our own kids, but it's hard to accept that you're choosing to keep us childless."

He shook his head in obvious frustration and turned his attention toward the trees.

* * *

Doug tried to understand where Jill was coming from. He wasn't blind to the turmoil this ordeal had put her through, but he kept wondering when she was going to come to terms with reality. He imagined for a moment what it would be like to add another person to their family, someone who would come to them through circumstance rather than genetics.

He struggled against the idea of adoption, but not because of the reasons Jill thought. He had no doubt that they could make room in their hearts and their lives for someone else, even if it wasn't their own biological child. He just worried about whether they could handle the baggage that might come with a child who had been unwanted, abandoned, or even neglected and abused.

As an FBI agent, he had seen all too often the emotional scars imposed on children born to parents who didn't want them or who weren't in a position to care for them properly. For weeks he had wrestled with the idea that maybe he and Jill could make a difference in a child's life, but his prayers continually left him searching for an answer that wouldn't come.

He heard a rustle in the leaves that sounded oddly out of place, and he scanned the surrounding woods. "Did you hear that?"

"What?"

Doug heard it again. A crunch of leaves the wind hadn't caused. His hand shifted instinctively to rest on the gun holstered in the front of his waistband. As an FBI agent, he was required to be armed at all times, even when on vacation. The sound grew louder. "Something's out there."

"It's probably just . . ."

Doug held up a hand, signaling for her to be quiet. He listened closely, trying to determine if the footsteps were human or animal. Then he heard it. The unmistakable sound of a gunshot. "Go inside," Doug said urgently, drawing his gun. "And stay down."

Jill didn't argue. She quickly hurried inside as Doug rushed down the stairs to take cover behind the nearest tree. That was when he saw her.

The girl couldn't have been more than twelve or thirteen, her dark hair tangled, her eyes wild with fear. One of her arms was wrapped tightly around her ribs as though she was trying to control the pain centered there.

She stumbled forward. Another shot sounded, and bark flew off the tree beside her and leaves rained down to the ground.

Doug's training kicked in, the instinct to protect dominating. He shifted so the girl could see him and motioned for her to continue toward him. "Hurry. It's safe here."

The girl stopped, clearly caught between whatever was chasing her and the unknown now standing before her. She looked back, terror still shining in her eyes. Then, after only a brief hesitation, she altered her course toward Doug, running as fast as she could manage.

She was nearly to him when he noticed a flash of color through the trees. Taking preventative measures, Doug shifted and fired once at a nearby tree in the hope of scaring off the girl's pursuer.

The figure in the woods quickly ducked for cover. Doug motioned for the girl to go inside. He waited until she was nearly to the door before shooting once more high into the trees. Then he pounded up the steps and dashed into the cabin.

The girl was on the floor, pressed against the wall below the window. Jill was crouched down a short distance from her, her cell phone pressed to her ear.

"Stay down," Doug said, listening for any other signs that the girl's pursuer was approaching. "Jill, are you okay?"

She nodded. "I called 9-1-1. The police should be here any minute."

The words were barely out of her mouth when Doug heard the distant sirens. Cautiously, he moved to the window and peered out. Whoever had been chasing the girl wasn't visible now. He ducked back down and turned to look at the girl.

"Are you okay?"

She looked up at him with the oddest expression. For a moment, Doug wondered if she spoke English. Then somehow, he understood. It wasn't the words that were foreign to her. It was the question itself. She was one of the broken children, unfamiliar with the concept that someone would take the time to see her, that someone might actually care.

Chapter 2

JILL WAITED UNTIL AFTER DOUG went outside to meet with the local police before she turned to the girl. Her own heart was still pounding with adrenaline, but she managed to keep her voice calm as she spoke. "Everything is going to be okay."

The girl's eyes were bright green and wild with fear, her lip bleeding and swollen from what appeared to be a blow to the face. Her narrow frame shook with each breath, and Jill suspected she was in a state of shock. "What's your name, honey?"

She didn't answer, but her eyes darted to the window above her.

"Don't worry. My husband will make sure that whoever was out there won't hurt you." Jill stood and closed the distance between them, crouching down in front of the girl. "My name is Jill," she offered. "That's my husband, Doug, out there. He's with the FBI. You can trust him." She hesitated, waiting until the girl looked at her once more. "You can trust me."

"Reagan." She shifted slightly and winced. "My name is Reagan Bower."

"Where does it hurt?"

Her shoulder lifted slightly.

"Can you tell me who was chasing you?" Jill asked gently.

Tears filled Reagan's eyes. "Laith and the colonel. They were going to kill me."

"Why?" The question popped out of Jill's mouth before she could censor it. She tried to keep her voice calm when she continued. "Why would anyone want to kill you?"

"Because I know too much." Warily, she looked at Jill, multiple emotions visible on her face. "They're going to shoot people. Lots of people." Reagan drew a deep breath and winced again in pain.

"I think we need to take you to the hospital and make sure you're okay."

"No! They'll find me. I can't let them find me," Reagan insisted with absolute certainty as her face paled with another rush of pain.

"It'll be okay. We'll keep you safe."

Reagan leaned weakly back against the wall. "Please don't let them find me." Her voice faded to a whisper.

Jill continued to offer assurance, but less than a minute later, Reagan's eyes glazed over and then fluttered closed.

* * *

Doug stood a few yards away from the emergency room so he could talk on the phone without being overheard but still keep an eye on the entrance.

He dialed the number for Hector Flores, one of his fellow FBI agents. "Hector, I need a favor."

"I thought you were taking a few days off," Hector said in his easygoing tone.

"Not anymore. I had an incident at the cabin, and I was hoping you could do some background for me."

"What kind of incident?"

"The kind that involved a young girl being chased by someone who wanted her dead."

"A young girl? Who is she?"

"Her name is Reagan Bower. Can you see what you can find out about her? She said one of the men after her is named Laith."

"I'll see what I can dig up."

"Thanks." Remembering Reagan's panic about someone finding her, he added, "The girl is worried about being found, so we need to keep this need-to-know."

"You got it," Hector said. "I'll see what I can dig up. Give me the name of the hospital, and I'll head down there. It sounds like you could use some backup."

"I'd appreciate it." Doug gave Hector his location and headed for the entrance. If he was lucky, maybe the girl would be awake by now and could tell him what was really going on.

* * *

Reagan sat silently on the edge of the hospital bed. Everyone kept asking her questions, but she didn't trust these people. How could she be sure they wouldn't send her back? Then she saw Jill, the blonde woman who had tended to her when she had first arrived at the cabin. She remembered the way Jill had promised to keep her safe, and she wanted desperately to believe her.

"How are you feeling?" Jill asked, her voice sounding genuinely concerned.

Reagan wasn't sure what to say. Her ribs still hurt from her latest beating, but she was used to the beatings. Laith often used his fists or the back of his hand to remind her who was in charge. The nurse had offered her painkillers, but Reagan had refused them. She didn't take pills, and she wasn't about to start.

Fresh, white bandages covered most of her arms. Her race through the woods had resulted in an array of shallow cuts and scratches. Those were minor in comparison to what would have happened had she not run away. She still could barely believe the colonel had told Laith to kill her.

She pushed that memory aside, not able to face it. Mustering up her courage, she forced herself to ask about her future. Her voice wavered. "What happens now?"

"Where is your family?"

"I don't have a family."

Jill stepped forward. "Can you tell me what happened to them?"

"The doctors said my mom overdosed." Reagan said the words, but still wasn't quite able to believe them. She knew her mom had always taken lots of pills for her depression, and she'd always known when to stop. But three months ago, she hadn't stopped in time. Reagan had come home from school and found her passed out on the couch. Only that time, her mother never woke up.

"What about your father?"

"I never knew my father."

"Who's been taking care of you?"

"I was living with my stepfather, if that's what you mean." Reagan's eyes hardened. "But he never took care of me. He's the one who wants me dead."

"Laith is your stepfather?"

Slowly, she nodded.

Before Jill could ask any more questions, Doug appeared in the doorway, his expression serious. The way he looked at her, Reagan guessed he had been listening to her talk to Jill, that he had been spying on them.

"Is everything okay?" Jill asked him.

"I just talked to the doctor. He said that child protective services has been called." He looked right at Reagan, and she shifted uncomfortably. She wasn't used to people looking at her and acting like they could really see her. He continued. "Since you don't have any family to speak of, you'll be put into foster care for now."

"No." Reagan shook her head vehemently, panic welling up inside her. "Please don't let them take me. He'll find me." She pressed her lips together and forced herself to draw a breath. "And if he finds me, he'll kill me."

Doug looked at Jill now, and Reagan thought she saw something pass between them, like they were talking without actually saying any words. Jill nodded, and then Doug stepped forward. "I might be able to work something out so you can come home with us. Would that be okay with you?"

Reagan didn't know what she'd been hoping for, but she definitely hadn't expected this. She stared at Doug, not sure what to think of him. His eyes were dark and direct, the hard planes and angles of his face making him look dangerous. At least he didn't have that evil vibe like the colonel.

She shifted her gaze to Jill, a little surprised to see the hopeful expression on her face. Not able to figure their angle, she drew a breath and forced herself to ask, "Why would you want to help me?"

Jill's voice was direct and sincere. "Because we can."

Doug's expression remained serious. "There is one catch. When we get home, I want you to talk to me. I want you to tell me everything you can remember."

She considered the alternative and slowly nodded her head. "Okay."

* * *

Doug waited in the hospital lobby, already second-guessing his decision. What was he thinking, taking in a thirteen-year-old girl? He lifted his eyes heavenward. This was exactly the reason that he *didn't* want to consider adoption—a child who clearly had a ton or two of emotional baggage.

Her mistrust of men in general was obvious, though Doug had to admit he felt a small sense of satisfaction that he appeared exempt. She wasn't as comfortable with him as she was with Jill, but from what the police had told him, so far, she had refused to talk to anyone besides them.

A middle-aged man wearing a dull brown suit and holding a well-worn briefcase approached. "Mr. Valdez?"

"That's right." Doug stood, accepting the hand the man offered.

"I'm Brian Wendall with child protective services. I'm here to take over Reagan Bower's case. The nurse said I needed to talk to you before they could release her into foster care."

"There's been a misunderstanding," Doug told him. "She'll be staying with me and my wife for the time being."

"This is highly unusual." He frowned and drew a file out of his bag. He looked over the thin file. "According to our records, her stepfather was granted guardianship after her mother died." He looked up at him now. "Has anyone made any effort to contact the stepfather?"

"Oh, I've definitely made an effort to contact him."

Brian looked up at Doug, confused. "Am I missing something?"

"If you haven't been told that she's in the hospital because of injuries sustained from her stepfather's abuse, then yes, you're missing something." Doug tried to keep his frustration out of his voice but knew he wasn't succeeding.

Brian's brow furrowed. "I thought the minor was in an accident."

"It was no accident." Doug drew out his identification and flashed his badge. "Maybe it will help smooth out the process if you check the little box that says the minor is in protective custody."

"I understand you want to help," Brian said, his tone placating. "But my job is to make sure the minor is in a safe environment. Just because you have a badge doesn't mean you're the best choice."

Doug bristled at his words. He couldn't say why he was so determined to fight for this girl, but something deep in his gut, something he couldn't explain, pushed him to dig in his heels. "She trusts us. That makes my wife and me the best choice."

Brian gave Doug a haughty look. "Are you approved foster parents?"

"No," Doug said, his eyes meeting Brian's. "But we're keeping her."

"Mr. Valdez, you can't just decide to take over guardianship of a minor child."

"Actually, this badge says I can," Doug said, even though he knew he was severely stretching the truth.

"It doesn't work that way." Brian held up the file in his hand. "If you want to apply to be her temporary guardian, I'm sure you can petition the court. In the meantime, she needs to come with me."

"You're not taking her." Doug's resolve strengthened. He drew a breath, reminding himself that he needed this man on his side. "Look, we both want the same thing. We want Reagan safe. Until we know more about her stepfather and his whereabouts, she needs to stay in protective custody. I would really appreciate it if you could give me a few days to find out what really happened today. After that, we can reevaluate the situation."

The man frowned again, clearly considering. "Even if the FBI wants to maintain custody for now, I'll still need your contact information, and we'll have to schedule a home visit."

Doug nodded, but Reagan's earlier concern that her stepfather would be able to find her if she went into foster care also resonated through his brain. He took the paper the social worker handed him.

The thought popped into his head that this man didn't really need his personal information since Reagan was technically in protective custody. Rather than filling out his own phone number and address, he wrote down the information for FBI headquarters.

He supposed he should at least give the man his direct line at the Washington Field Office, but someone at headquarters could patch through any calls from him. Besides, this would ensure that no one would know which FBI office he worked at. If anyone did try to search for Reagan, the only thing they would find would be a web of misdirection and secrecy.

"I'll give you a call on Monday," Brian said as he took the paper back from him. "Here's my card if you need anything before then."

"Thanks."

"Good luck." Brian gave him a skeptical look. "I have a feeling you're going to need it."

* * *

"What was I thinking?" Doug muttered as he climbed into bed beside his wife. Jill had already settled their new charge into their guest bedroom and seemed fine with this unexpected situation. Personally, he felt that rather than go to sleep, he should be standing guard outside of the girl's room to make sure nothing else happened to her. He kept his voice low when he added, "We're not equipped to look after a teenager."

Jill rolled onto her side and propped herself up on her elbow so she was facing him. "Doug, we were just talking about adopting. Then, not an hour later, Reagan showed up. Maybe it's fate."

"We were arguing about adoption. I certainly wasn't agreeing to it, especially not to adopting a teenager who has been living with some kind of criminal."

"*She's* not a criminal," Jill stated simply, "and it sounds like she doesn't have anyone. Maybe she's supposed to be here."

"Jill, I can't do this with you right now," Doug said wearily. "This situation is stressful enough without having you badgering me about the size of our family while we're trying to care for Reagan."

Jill's voice grew defensive. "I only want to help her."

Doug put his hand on hers, and his voice gentled. "I know you want to help, but promise me you won't get too attached. We have no idea what we're dealing with."

Jill was quiet for a moment. "Did you notice how she wouldn't talk to anyone but us?"

"Yeah." Doug reached over and turned out the light on his night table. "I noticed."

Chapter 3

"DON'T YOU ANSWER YOUR PHONE?" Hector said by way of greeting when Doug opened his front door to find his partner on the other side.

"Sorry. I turned it off last night when I was at the hospital, and I don't think I remembered to turn it back on." Doug motioned him inside. He pointed at the thick file in his hand. "What's that?"

"The file on the girl." Hector handed it to Doug. "Apparently, social services has been monitoring her for a while, but they've never had cause to remove her from her home."

"How did you get this?"

"After I called to let child protective services know we were keeping her in protective custody, they put me in touch with her caseworker," Hector said.

"Then why did he give me such a hard time last night about us releasing Reagan over to CPS?"

"Who?"

"Brian Wendall. He caught up with me in the waiting room last night when I was waiting for Reagan to be released."

"Something's not right here." Hector shook his head. "Reagan's caseworker is a woman named Marla Duncan. She's the only person from CPS who was at the hospital last night."

"Then who is Brian Wendall?"

"Let's see if we can find out." Hector retrieved his phone from his pocket and dialed the number listed inside Reagan's file. Doug listened to the one-sided conversation, unable to decipher anything from Hector's one-word answers. As soon as Hector hung up, he shook his head. "Social services hasn't ever heard of Brian Wendall."

"Let's assume for a minute that it was Reagan's stepfather or this colonel she was talking about who came looking for her. How did he know she was there?"

"He might have just played a hunch. You were in a rural area, and that was the only hospital around."

"Or someone could have followed us there. The road to our cabin was the only way out." Doug shook his head. "I'm not sure what this girl is involved with, but it sounds like someone is pretty intent on getting to her."

"Did you give this Wendall guy any information that would help him find her? Or you?"

"He has my name, but I put down the address and phone number for FBI headquarters."

Hector's eyebrows lifted. "He might be able track you down through DMV or property records."

"No, he won't," Doug said. "I haven't changed over my driver's license since I moved here from Florida, and we're renting our house."

"That's lucky."

"It's not luck. It's habit. After working for so many years with witness protection, I make it a point to separate work and home."

"That explains why the higher-ups signed off on Reagan staying here." Hector glanced toward the kitchen, where Jill was busily making pancakes. "What about Jill?"

"I didn't give him Jill's name, and she hasn't changed her driver's license either. Something about the guy rubbed me the wrong way. I guess now I know why."

Hector nodded. "Look, I know the girl has been through a lot, but we really need to know what she knows."

"She promised to talk to us this morning. I'll let you know as soon as I find out anything. In the meantime, can you run a check on Brian Wendall?" Doug retrieved from his wallet the business card the fake case worker had given him. "Here's the information Wendall gave me. Maybe we can track him down through his phone number."

"I'll see what I can do."

"Thanks, Hector. I appreciate it."

"Talk to you later."

* * *

Reagan sat at the kitchen table, her hair still damp from her shower, the thick terrycloth robe Jill had given her wrapped tightly around her. She had read about places like this in books, seen them on TV, but she hadn't really believed people lived like this until now.

It wasn't the house itself, although the townhouse was definitely a lot nicer than the various apartments and trailers she'd lived in over the years. There was something else about it, almost like there was some warm feeling in the air. She couldn't quite put it into words, but it wasn't something she had ever felt before.

Not a single pill bottle was visible anywhere, nor could she see any empty beer cans or liquor bottles littering the tables or countertops. She didn't even see a single ashtray.

Her eyes swept the room, and she noticed a couple of tennis rackets leaning against the wall next to a wire bucket filled with tennis balls. A pair of shoes lay haphazardly beside it, thick white socks tucked inside them. The kitchen was clean and tidy, except for several books stacked on the corner of the counter, a notebook and pen lying beside them. She also noticed the green ceramic frog cookie jar. She knew it was a cookie jar because Jill had pulled the top off when she had given her a snack last night before she went to bed.

A bedtime snack. That was another thing she had heard about but had never before experienced.

Everything about these people was foreign to her. She had expected Doug to question her when they arrived at their home last night, but Jill had given her something to eat, shown her to her room, given her clean oversized pajamas to sleep in, and told her to get some rest. She had promised Reagan she would be safe and insisted they could wait until the next day to talk.

Reagan had stood just inside the bedroom door for several minutes, trying to listen to Jill and Doug talk, but all she had heard was someone playing the answering machine and some bishop asking to meet with them. She couldn't recall ever meeting a bishop and wasn't quite sure if she could picture what one would even look like.

When she had awoken, she'd ignored her hunger pains that had resulted from sleeping so long. Instead, she opted for a shower in an effort to erase any lingering traces of her life with Laith. Now she was sitting here in the sunny yellow kitchen, her stomach full and the scent of pancakes lingering in the air.

"Do you think you can answer some questions for me now?" Doug asked from his seat across from her.

Reagan instantly stiffened. She didn't like thinking about her yesterdays, about the years of taking care of her mom while trying to avoid whatever man was currently hanging around the house. She didn't want to remember those last three months in the dusty cabin while Laith saw her only as someone who could put a meal on the table for him while he plotted and planned to hurt people. She especially didn't want to think about how she had dashed out the back door when Laith and the colonel had hauled a crate of weapons outside to the colonel's truck.

She forced herself to look at Doug. He had a way of looking at her that made her want to squirm in her seat, but she had promised she would try to tell him what he wanted to know. Her mom had taught her to always keep her promises. "I can try."

"You said yesterday that Laith was going to shoot lots of people."

Reagan nodded.

"Do you know any details? Can you tell me about it?"

She drew a deep breath and let it out. "The colonel was helping him plan it."

"Plan what, exactly?"

"There are other people who think like they do. They have guns." Her eyes darkened. "Lots of guns."

"Have you seen the other people who think like them?" Doug asked.

"Yeah. They come to the cabin to practice shooting."

"How many were there?"

"I saw three besides Laith and the colonel. One of them is named Wendall or something like that. I don't know about the other two."

"Brian Wendall?"

"That might be it." Reagan wasn't sure if it was a good thing Doug knew Wendall's full name or if it was a sign that something bad was going to happen. "How did you know about him?"

"Just tracking down some leads." Doug shifted gears and asked, "Where are they planning on using these guns?"

"Some party." Reagan struggled against the memories, wanting to help Doug but not wanting to relive those moments when Laith and the colonel had tried to enlist her in their plans. "I saw a picture of the hotel the party is supposed to be at. I could see the Washington Monument in the background."

"Do you think you would recognize the hotel if you saw it again?"

Her shoulders lifted. "Maybe."

Jill slid into the seat next to her. "Did Laith or the colonel say when they were planning this attack?"

"I know it's soon, and it's supposed to be on a Saturday night."

"Is there anything else you can remember?" Doug prompted.

Reagan nodded. "They said something about being in costume."

"Did they say why?"

"Something about blending in. They said no one would know their guns were real if they were all in costume."

Jill looked up at Doug. "Halloween is in a few weeks."

"I'll have Hector run a list for me of costume parties in the D.C. metro area." Doug picked up the cordless phone on the counter and dialed a number. "I'll be right back."

Reagan watched him walk out of the room. Jill stood up and moved over to the sink, where she began loading their dirty dishes into the dishwasher. Reagan stayed where she was, not sure what she was supposed to do. Before her mom had died, she'd spent most of her time hiding in her room with the handful of books she had managed to collect from the used bookstore in her old town.

Sometimes, if Laith wasn't home, she could watch television, but usually, her mom said it was too loud. When Laith was around, the last thing she wanted was to be anywhere that he could see her.

Reagan eyed the books on the counter, a tattered version of *Little Women* topping the pile.

"I washed your clothes last night. They're in the dryer." Jill pointed at the stacked washer and dryer in the far corner of the kitchen. "Go ahead and get dressed, and we can go run some errands."

Apprehensively, Reagan stood and did as she was told. When she returned a minute later, dressed in her old jeans and T-shirt, her battered tennis shoes in her hand, she asked timidly, "Where are we going?"

Amusement and humor sparked in Jill's eyes. "Shopping."

"Shopping for what?"

"Clothes. Shoes. Whatever we need so you can feel at home here."

Reagan goggled at her. "You're buying me new clothes?"

Before Jill could respond, Doug came in and sat down in a chair, leaning over to retrieve the tennis shoes in the corner. "I'll come with you."

"You? Shopping?" Jill laughed. "This should be good."

Reagan stared at her, not sure what to think of the playful tone or the spontaneous laughter. Bracing, she shifted her eyes to look over at Doug, waiting for him to scold Jill for talking to him that way, or worse, for his eyes to go dark and mean when his hand lifted. But Doug just tied up his laces like it was no big deal.

She looked back at Jill, daring to ask the question, "Doesn't he like to go shopping?"

"Oh, no. He doesn't go to the mall." Jill shook her head. She leaned closer to Reagan and whispered, "Of course, we do have his handcuffs around here if we need them."

Jill's humor was contagious, and Reagan barely resisted letting out a giggle of her own. She sat down to put her shoes on. Then logic made her ask the simple question, "If you hate shopping, how come you're coming with us?"

"I just want you to be safe. We haven't found Laith yet, and I don't want to take any chances."

Her stomach clenched at the straightforward admission. "Oh."

"I'm sure it will be fine," Doug assured her. "The hospital where you were treated is three hours away from here. It's just my job to make sure you stay safe. Besides, Jill loves to torture me with this kind of stuff."

"Come on," Jill said lightly as she motioned toward the door. "It will be an adventure."

Chapter 4

JILL LED REAGAN THROUGH THE mall, Reagan's eyes focused on the floor rather than on the window displays. The few times Jill had asked her opinion on a piece of clothing, Reagan had simply shrugged as though she was afraid of expressing her opinion. She couldn't tell if Reagan really didn't care what she wore or if she was afraid of asking for too much. Either way, Jill was determined to make sure the poor kid had something to wear besides the raggedy pair of jeans and the T-shirt she showed up in.

After two hours of unsuccessful shopping, they followed the scents of grilled meat, Chinese food, and french fries to the food court, where they grabbed a quick lunch. While they ate, Doug pulled out his cell phone, undoubtedly to see if Hector had called with any new information. Jill suppressed a smile when Doug grumbled to himself about forgetting to turn the phone back on after they'd left the hospital the night before. He turned it on and listened to a handful of messages, but from his expression, she guessed that none of them gave him the updates he'd been hoping for.

After they finished eating, they headed back toward the stores. Now refueled, Jill was ready to make some progress whether Reagan was ready for it or not.

"Let's go in here." Jill pointed at a large department store. She could almost hear her husband's groan. She hadn't been exaggerating when she told Reagan that Doug hated shopping. Anything he couldn't buy online, he figured he could do without.

Jill led the way to a rack of jeans. "How about these?"

When Reagan responded with her typical shrug, Jill started selecting several pairs that looked like they would fit. She then moved over to a rack of plain T-shirts.

"What's your favorite color?"

Another shrug.

Jill picked up another assortment and handed a stack to Reagan. "Let's have you try these on so we can figure out your size."

She led the way to the dressing room, Doug taking up a guard-like post a short distance from the entrance.

For the next hour, Jill collected samples of clothes from the racks in the juniors department and kept up a constant parade of shirts, pants, skirts, and dresses to the dressing room. As she might with her second graders, she gave Reagan choices between two or three alternatives, gradually coaxing her into giving her timid opinion. When Jill was finally satisfied that Reagan had the basics, she led the way to the shoe department.

Doug followed along silently, carting their purchases as they moved from shoes to accessories to pajamas. When Jill started ushering Reagan toward socks and underwear, both Doug's and Reagan's cheeks colored.

Fully aware that Doug's presence would continue to make Reagan uncomfortable, Jill turned to him and said, "Doug, why don't you take all of that stuff out to the car? I'm sure we'll be fine for a few minutes by ourselves."

Clearly eager for an escape route, Doug agreed. "Okay. Where do you want me to meet you?"

"How about the bookstore?" Jill nodded toward Reagan. "I'm sure Reagan could use some books or magazines to keep her occupied."

"Okay." He made sure his cell phone was still on. "Call me if you need me. Otherwise, I'll see you there in fifteen minutes."

* * *

Doug loaded shopping bags into the trunk, shifting them so the shoe boxes wouldn't get crushed when he closed it. The large boot box clunked with Reagan's muddy tennis shoes that she had put in it, the new boots now on Reagan's size-eight feet.

Doug was just walking back into the mall when his phone rang. He saw Hector's name on caller ID.

"Hey, Hector. What's up?"

"We have a problem," Hector said, tension in his voice. "I set up a couple of alerts to make sure no one tried to track you down since you gave that fake CPS guy your name."

"Yeah. And?"

"One of them just popped. Someone ran a background check on you last night."

Doug thought over his personal information in an effort to identify any vulnerabilities. When they had first met, Jill had been rooming with a witness he was assigned to protect. Because of their association and his determination to keep both his witness and then-girlfriend safe, he had set up a trust to pay his expenses. His lease and his utilities went through the trust, in essence making his home a safe house. He drove a government car so there was nothing to trace back to him there. Besides, if someone had figured out what car he drove, they could have traced the GPS and found him last night.

Then he thought of his cell phone, the only item that was listed in his own name. He hadn't remembered to turn it on until he'd checked for messages when he was eating lunch with Jill and Reagan.

"Do me a favor and run a GPS trace on my phone. See what you can find."

"I already did," Hector told him. "I can clearly see that you are in Tysons Corner right now."

"Great," Doug muttered, instantly looking around for any perceivable threats. "Can you back trace my history to my house?"

"No. When I set the alerts for you, I had the cell phone company clear your history. Since you didn't have your phone on last night, I don't think anyone could tie you back to your house. At least, not unless you take your cell phone home with you while it's on."

"Where are you right now?"

"I'm heading your way. I'll be there in five to ten minutes. I thought you might need some backup."

"I appreciate it." Doug caught a glimpse of a familiar face. Striding toward the department store, where he had left Jill and Reagan, was the man who had claimed to be Reagan's social worker. "Hector, hurry. We have a problem."

* * *

Jill rolled her eyes when she pulled her ringing cell phone from her purse to see her husband's phone number displayed on the touch screen. "Two minutes late, and he's already wondering where we are."

As soon as she said hello, Doug responded with a tense, "Where are you?"

"Sorry. There was a line in the lingerie department. We are just leaving now."

"No, don't." Doug's tone made Jill stiffen.

"What's wrong?"

"I think someone is here looking for Reagan. I want you to take her back into the dressing rooms."

Jill listened to Doug outline his plan as she steered a bewildered Reagan toward the closest dressing room in the women's department.

"What's wrong?" Reagan asked the moment Jill hung up.

Jill considered censoring her answer. After all, she didn't want to traumatize the girl any further. The wariness in Reagan's eyes swayed Jill to trust her with the truth. "Doug saw someone here that was asking about you at the hospital."

Terror flashed in her eyes. "They found me."

Jill reached out and put her hands on Reagan's shoulders, partially as a gesture of comfort and partially to hold her in place so she couldn't dart back out of the dressing rooms. "Doug has a plan. I need you to trust him," Jill said firmly. Her voice softened when Reagan's terrified eyes shifted to look directly at her once more. "I need you to trust *me*."

Reagan sucked in a deep breath and let it out with a shudder. "What do I have to do?"

"You can start by going into one of these dressing rooms so you're out of sight. I'm going to go out and get some clothes for you to change into."

"But we already bought a bunch of clothes."

"Yes, but they're all in the car. Doug doesn't want you wearing your old clothes out in the mall in case someone might recognize you," Jill explained. "And I think I can find an outfit that will help you look older. I want you to look like you're someone else."

"Okay." Reagan looked at her doubtfully, but she stepped into one of the open dressing rooms.

"Just stay in there. I'll be right back." Jill walked to the edge of the dressing room, hating that she had to leave Reagan alone even for a minute. She looked around, noticing a mannequin dressed in an oversized cream-colored sweater and trendy pants the color of dark chocolate. Accenting the outfit was an earth-toned scarf and a cute little cap.

Jill noticed a saleswoman and motioned to her. "Excuse me. My sister loved that outfit on the mannequin over there. Could you help me find everything for it?"

The woman's eyes lit up with the prospect of the sale. "Absolutely. What sizes do you need?"

"Let's go with a medium for the sweater. Probably a size four or six for the pants."

"Did you want the accessories too?"

"That would be great. Thanks."

The woman nodded. "I'll be right back with those."

Jill stayed where she was near the dressing room entrance, a little afraid that Reagan's obvious fear might prompt her to try to sneak out and take her chances on her own.

Sure enough, when Jill poked her head into the dressing room, Reagan was stepping out of the changing stall.

"The saleswoman is getting an outfit for you to try on. She'll be right back with it." Jill motioned her back into the stall. "Just hang out here for a couple more minutes."

"Okay."

Jill stepped back out as the woman arrived with the selections. "Thank you so much. This is perfect."

"Absolutely. Please let me know if I can get anything else for you or if you need different sizes."

"I will. Thanks." Jill turned and moved back into the dressing room, where Reagan was standing outside a changing stall. "Reagan, here. Try these on."

Without a word, Reagan accepted the offerings and ducked back into the stall to change. When she opened the door again, Jill studied her. The pants were tucked into the new boots she had decided to wear after trying them on in the shoe department, and the sweater hung past her hips. Jill stepped forward and arranged the scarf artistically around Reagan's neck and then opened up her purse and dug out some mascara and lipstick.

"Here. Let's see if we can make you look a little older." Jill carefully helped Reagan apply the makeup. When Jill stepped back, she smiled. With the light makeup and dressed in the latest fashions, Reagan no longer looked like a teenager. Unless someone really looked closely, they would guess her to be in her early twenties.

"This is great. You look ten years older." Jill took the cap off of Reagan's head. "Try to tuck your hair up into the hat."

Reagan took her long brown hair and twisted it up so it was no longer visible beneath the cap.

"Perfect." Jill stepped closer and started removing the price tags.

"What are you doing?" Reagan lowered her voice. "You aren't planning on us stealing these clothes, are you? I thought your husband was a cop."

"Don't worry. We're going to pay for this. We're just being creative about it."

Though she was obviously skeptical, Reagan pulled the tags from the hat and scarf and handed them over to Jill.

When Jill had all of the tags in her hand, she said, "Wait here for another minute. I'll be right back."

"How did those work out?" The saleslady asked her when Jill reemerged from the dressing room.

"Great." She glanced over at a trio of women walking by, all three of them carrying purses. "I think if I can find her a purse to go with it, we'll be all set."

"We have a few over here." She motioned to the display beside the checkout counter. "Otherwise, we'll need to go over to accessories."

Jill studied the half dozen styles available in the women's department, selecting one with a long strap in the same chocolate brown as the pants Reagan was now wearing. "This should work." She pulled the tag off and handed it, along with the others, to the saleswoman. "I hope it's okay, but she wants to wear the outfit out of here. Can I get a shopping bag for her old clothes?"

"Absolutely." The saleswoman handed her a bag, exchanging it for Jill's credit card.

"Go ahead and ring me up. I'll be right back to sign." Jill went back to where Reagan was waiting nervously and handed her the new purse. "Take this and come wait just inside the door here. When I tell you, we're going outside. One of Doug's friends will be waiting for us with a car."

"Are you sure this is going to work?" Reagan whispered. "What if someone recognizes me? What if Laith is here?"

"He'd probably walk right past you and never even know it," Jill said with feigned confidence. She straightened her shoulders and uttered a silent prayer, then pulled her cell phone from her purse and called Doug. "We're ready. We're in the women's department on the second floor and just need to pay."

"The minute you sign the credit card receipt, head for the elevator and go down to the first floor. Hector is waiting outside with a car. He'll hand you the keys, and then I want you to drive over to the Whitmores' house."

"The Whitmores? Why there?"

"Because they're close by, and they've got a great security system."

"Okay." Jill tried to keep her voice casual despite the worry pulsing through her. "Be careful."

"I will. You too."

Chapter 5

DOUG STAYED ON THE MOVE, weaving his way through the food court, ducking in and out of stores. As soon as Hector called and said Jill and Reagan were safely on their way to the Whitmores' house, Doug searched for the right spot to carry out his plan.

As usual, the mall was bustling with activity both in the shops and in the parking lot. He glanced down at his watch—3:15 p.m. He slowed slightly as he passed by a directory. Then he continued strolling toward one of the many sit-down restaurants, choosing one on the opposite side of the mall from where he had left Jill and Reagan.

He walked to the entrance, pleased to see it nearly empty. Besides a couple of men sitting at the bar, discussing the upcoming Redskins game, only three tables were occupied. Realizing that he wasn't going to find any place in the mall less populated on a Saturday afternoon, Doug texted his location to Hector and headed inside.

A woman stood by the entrance and offered him a smile. "Sir, would you like a table?"

Doug nodded. "I have a business associate who is meeting me here. Do you have one that is out of the way? Maybe somewhere in the back?"

"How about over here?" The hostess drew out two menus and led the way past several tables and then turned to the left and motioned to a corner booth.

"This is perfect." Doug slid into the booth and accepted the menu. Then he glanced up at her. "Can you tell me where your restroom is?"

"Right over there." She pointed at the little hallway directly across from his table.

"Thanks." Doug waited for her to leave him and then slipped his phone from his pocket. He leaned down and placed it on the floor beneath the table. He heard Hector come in and sit at a table near the entrance. Knowing that his backup was now in place, Doug crossed to the restroom and waited.

He didn't have to wait long. Not ten minutes after he had taken up his position outside of the men's room, he heard the fake social worker's voice when he greeted the hostess and asked if he could look inside for a friend he was supposed to meet there.

Doug pulled his weapon free of its holster, trying to hear the footsteps over the light music playing through the overhead speakers. Seconds ticked by, and Doug could only imagine that Brian was taking his time to search for him at the handful of tables that currently had customers.

Finally, the familiar figure stepped into view, turning the corner to the secluded section where the waitress had seated Doug several minutes earlier. Then Brian Wendall turned and froze when he saw Doug standing a few yards behind him, his gun already drawn and aimed at Brian's heart.

"Hello again," Doug said dryly. "I think you have some explaining to do."

"What's going on?" The man stood frozen, his face pale. "Why are you pointing that thing at me?"

Out of the corner of his eye, Doug saw Hector moving forward, his own gun drawn. A ten-year-old boy stood up in the booth and pointed while the two men at the bar ducked for cover. At least no one was screaming. Doug hated when that happened.

He kept his gun steady, his eyes searching for the truth in the other man's face. "Why are you following me?"

"I'm not. I just came in here for lunch."

"Lunch will have to wait." Doug kept his gun trained on the man who had claimed to be Reagan's social worker. When Hector moved into position beside him, Doug holstered his weapon and pushed Wendall up against the wall to search him for weapons. Immediately, he found the handgun holstered at the man's shoulder. "What do we have here?"

The man's jaw clenched, but he said nothing.

Doug finished searching him for weapons and then pulled his handcuffs from his pocket and secured the man's hands. After he handed the man over to Hector, he retrieved his phone and turned it off so it could no longer be traced. With a nod to Hector, he said, "Let's go. Maybe once we get to FBI headquarters, you can tell us why you're following me."

* * *

Reagan stared out the window, her hands gripped tightly in her lap. She and Jill had made it out of the mall safely enough, but she knew now that Laith was going to find her. Eventually, a time would come when Jill and Doug wouldn't be able to hide her from him. And when that happened, her life would be over.

She squeezed her eyes shut against the tears that threatened.

"Are you okay?" Jill asked, her tone soft and understanding.

Reagan didn't trust her voice, so she didn't say anything at all.

"I know this must have been frightening for you, but I promise Doug will figure out how someone was able to track us down, and he'll fix the problem to make sure it doesn't happen again." Jill turned into a neighborhood with ridiculously large houses. After making a couple of turns, she pulled into a long driveway that led up to what Reagan could only describe as a mansion.

"What are we doing here?"

"Hopefully visiting some friends," Jill told her. "If they aren't here, we'll just have to wait in the car until we hear from Doug."

Jill led the way up the front walk and rang the bell. Reluctantly, Reagan followed behind her.

Footsteps sounded inside, and then the front door swung open to reveal a tall, dark-haired woman. She was older than Jill, probably old enough to be a grandma, and her smile was instant and friendly.

"Jill. It's so good to see you." The woman stepped forward, her arms outstretched for a hug. "I didn't know you were going to be in our neighborhood today."

"I hadn't planned on it," Jill admitted. She returned the woman's hug, then pulled back, her tone apologetic. "I'm sorry to drop in unannounced, but would you mind some company for a little while?"

"Not at all." She waved them in. "Who's your friend?"

"Katherine Whitmore, this is my foster daughter, Reagan Bower," Jill said, leading the way into the house. "Reagan, Mrs. Whitmore is a good friend of mine and Doug's."

Reagan stared at Jill, shocked by her casual reference to her as a foster child.

"I didn't know you were a foster parent," Katherine said excitedly. "That's wonderful. When did this happen?"

"Just yesterday." Jill glanced at Reagan. "We were kind of thrown together through unexpected circumstances, but it's been nice having her in the house."

"Well, come in and sit down. I want to hear everything that has been going on with you lately. We haven't talked in weeks." Katherine led them into an enormous living room, one that had to be as large as the entire apartment Reagan used to live in with her mother.

Reagan's eyes were drawn to the tall, built-in bookshelves on the far wall—shelves and shelves of books. She stood at the edge of the room, unaware that she was staring until Jill nudged her forward and led her to a chair beside the sofa. On the coffee table in front of her, she saw several more books fanned out so the covers were easy to see.

A car engine sounded in the driveway, and Reagan tensed. A moment later, she heard the rumble she guessed was a garage door opening and then closing, followed by a door slamming somewhere deep in the house. Then a tall, silver-haired man walked in.

"Hi there." The man's smile encompassed all of them, and he leaned down to give Katherine a kiss before crossing to where Jill was sitting.

Jill stood and shook the man's hand. "Hello, Senator. How are you?"

"Wonderful." His eyes swept down to look at Reagan, and she could feel herself shrink back against the chair cushion.

"This is Reagan. She's going to be staying with Doug and me for a while."

"Good to meet you," the senator said, but he didn't move any closer.

Reagan remained silent, wondering absently if he was really a senator or if he was like the colonel, someone who liked to pretend to have more power than he really did.

"Where's Doug?" the senator asked.

"He had a little problem with work he needed to take care of, but we were in the area, so he suggested that he meet us here. I hope that's okay."

"Of course." He nodded. "I was thinking about throwing some steaks on the grill for dinner. Can we talk you into joining us?"

Jill hesitated briefly. "Actually, that would be great, if you don't mind."

Katherine stood. "In that case, why don't we move into the kitchen, and I can get started on a salad."

"Sure. What can I do to help?" Jill stood as well.

"Just come in and keep me company." Katherine looked down at Reagan. She must have noticed the way Reagan was staring at the books in front of her. "Reagan, do you like to read?"

"Yeah, I guess," she said noncommittally. In truth, reading was one of the few things she truly enjoyed.

"Those books on the table are ones I have doubles of. If you want, go ahead and look through them. You're welcome to take any that you want."

"Really?" Reagan heard the wonder in her voice, but she didn't care.

"Absolutely. I've read a few of them already, and they were excellent." Katherine took a step toward the doorway that Reagan assumed led to the kitchen. "And when you're done looking at those, come on into the kitchen. After Jill and I finish making the salad, you can walk with us to feed the horses."

Reagan nodded numbly. New clothes, free books, real horses. She supposed everyone should get a glimpse of a fairy tale at some point in their life. Then she swallowed hard. Maybe today was someone's idea of a bad joke. She would get to see what life could be like for lucky people. Then she would die.

She picked up the book closest to her. If she was going to die, she might as well die happy. Flipping open the cover, she started to read.

Chapter 6

QUESTIONING BRIAN WENDALL TOOK ALL of ten minutes. The man wasn't talking, and Doug was convinced that no amount of threats or cajoling would get this man to betray whomever he was in league with. Doug had run his fingerprints but found he wasn't in any of the criminal databases. According to the background check that followed, Doug learned little more than the man's name and address and that he owned a private security firm.

His story about freelancing with child protective services certainly hadn't checked out, but other than that, he appeared to be a model citizen. At least, he had been a model citizen right up until they had arrested him for attempted kidnapping. Doug hadn't found any known associations between Brian Wendall and Laith Mansour other than Reagan's mention of seeing them together, but Wendall was tucked away safely in jail just in case. Doug had no doubt Laith had sent this man to find Reagan, but how had he been able to trace Doug's cell phone?

Questions continued to roll through Doug's mind on the drive to the Whitmores' home. Where was Laith Mansour hiding? Who was the colonel? And mostly, why would anyone want Reagan dead?

Hector had offered to run a security check for Doug and make sure these guys, whoever they were, hadn't managed to trace him back to his house. Doug expected that by the time he was ready to take Jill and Reagan home, he would know whether it was safe to do so.

He arrived at the senator's oak-lined property, appreciating the elegant home with its circular driveway, and knocked on the front door, concerned when no one answered. On impulse, he followed the scent of grilled meat to the back patio, where he found Jim Whitmore dressed casually in jeans and a crewneck sweatshirt, a pair of barbecue tongs in his hand.

"Hey, Senator."

"Hi, Doug. We've been expecting you." He flipped one of the steaks. "The girls are at the stables, feeding the horses."

"How's Reagan doing?"

"She hasn't said much, but she seems okay." His eyebrows lifted quizzically. "Why?"

"We had a little scare with her at the mall today. I was just wondering how she's handling it."

"What kind of scare?" Jim asked. "And how did you end up with a teenager living with you?"

"It wasn't planned. Believe me." Feeling overwhelmed both by the run-in at the mall and the shopping marathon that preceded it, Doug wearily ran his fingers through his hair. "This has been a crazy couple of days. I don't even know where to start."

"Why don't you start at the beginning?"

Doug had already planned on talking to Jim about the possibility of a target on or around Halloween. He couldn't see any reason not to tell him the rest, so he did what Jim suggested and started at the beginning.

* * *

She must be in shock. Reagan couldn't think of any other reason she would be hallucinating like this. Or maybe she was already dead, and she didn't know it yet.

She looked across the round kitchen table at the man she now knew was a U.S. senator from Virginia, exactly the kind of man Laith and his friends would have loved to take a shot at, and this man was talking to her like she mattered. No one was treating her like some kid who didn't have an opinion or acting like she was some second-class citizen because she was a girl.

These four people were talking to her . . . and listening.

The food was yet another oddity. Steak and salad and mashed potatoes and glazed carrots. And none of it had come from one of those little plastic trays made for the microwave. And the taste. She hadn't known food was supposed to taste this good.

"What do you think, Reagan? Do you have any idea what kind of people Laith would go after?"

Reagan looked over at the senator sheepishly. She didn't want to tell him the truth, but she was afraid not to. Besides, if this wasn't real, it wouldn't hurt for her to be honest. "People like you." She felt her cheeks color at her own words. "He hates anyone in charge of anything, but he especially hates the government."

"I can't think of any kind of costume parties that would have to do with government officials," the senator said. "You're sure these guys are going to be wearing costumes?"

Reagan nodded. "They were talking about dressing up like ninjas, Star Wars characters, stuff like that."

"It's certainly clever," Katherine put in. "Halloween would be a tough time for the authorities to check everyone carrying a weapon since so many costumes use them for props."

"We'll keep checking into possible parties in the D.C. area. That will be our focus on Monday." Doug pushed back from the table. "For now, we should be getting home."

Jill stood as well. "Thank you so much for dinner and for letting us drop in on you like this."

"We enjoyed having you," Katherine said. Then she turned to Reagan. "And, Reagan, it was so nice meeting you. I hope you enjoy the books. And if you need more, come on back. You're welcome to borrow any of the ones I have whenever you want."

Stunned by the casual offer, Reagan struggled to speak. "Thanks."

They said their good-byes, and Reagan walked outside, hesitating when she looked at the two cars in the driveway, not sure which one she should get into: Doug's or the one she and Jill had come in.

"We'll take my car," Doug told her, clicking his key to unlock the door. "Hector will send someone to pick up the other one later tonight."

As soon as they were settled in Doug's car, Jill voiced Reagan's fear, the one Reagan had been too afraid to speak aloud. "Are you sure it's safe at our house?"

"Yeah," Doug said, his voice surprisingly certain. "Hector went by to make sure everything was okay, and he did a deep background check to make sure nothing could be traced to us. He's confident that our house is still safe."

"I thought you were being overprotective when you took so many precautions when we moved here. Now I'm glad you did."

"How did they find us?" Reagan asked.

"My cell phone." Doug looked back at Reagan, and she could have sworn he looked apologetic. "I didn't realize the social worker last night was a phony. He had my name and tracked me down through the GPS on my phone. Since I didn't turn it on until we were at the mall, we're sure it couldn't have given away our home location."

"We've sure been blessed through all of this," Jill said and glanced back at Reagan. "The Lord must really be watching out for you."

Reagan could only stare. Why would God care about her? He certainly hadn't cared about her before. As they made their way back to her current home, she stared out the window and wondered how long it would last. That wonder slowly turned to hope, and without her even realizing it, hope shifted into a silent prayer to the God Jill said cared about her.

* * *

"We're going where?" Reagan asked, surprise and a touch of defiance evident in her voice.

"Church," Jill told her again, clearing the last of their breakfast dishes from the table. "You can either wear that dress we bought yesterday or the skirt and one of your new tops."

"Why are we going to church?"

"We go every week." Jill knew a couple of her friends struggled with getting their teenagers to church each week, and she knew it was a stage a lot of kids went through. Of course, her friends' kids had been brought up in the gospel. She suspected Reagan had little if any experience with religion. In fact, she doubted Reagan even knew what it was like to be around people who were generally supportive and friendly. Her background clearly had been something very different from what Jill was used to. "We're leaving in thirty minutes, so you need to get moving."

To Jill's relief, Reagan didn't argue. She disappeared into her room and returned fifteen minutes later dressed and ready to go.

The moment they walked into the chapel, Jill could feel Reagan's reserve settling in. When the bishop approached them, Reagan shrank back farther, positioning herself so she was behind her and Doug, as though using them as a shield.

"Good morning," Bishop Chandler greeted them in general before zeroing in on Jill. "Sister Valdez, I don't know if you got my message, but I was hoping you might have a minute today to meet with me." Then he glanced over at Doug. "I'd like for you to be there too."

Jill glanced back at Reagan, unable to imagine leaving her alone in the foyer at church. "Today might be a little tough. We may need to leave after sacrament meeting. Could we make it another time?"

The bishop hesitated briefly. Then he said, "Of course. I'll have Brother Hawkins give you a call to set up a time." He looked at Reagan. "Who's this?"

"This is Reagan. She's staying with us for a while."

"Good to meet you." The bishop extended his hand. Reagan looked up at Jill as though silently asking if this man was safe. Jill gave her a little nod, and Reagan reluctantly shook his hand.

As soon as the bishop moved on to greet someone else, Jill led the way to the padded pew on the left side, where they normally sat, and then motioned for Reagan to slide in first, leaving Jill between her and Doug. As soon as Jill settled into her seat, she reached out and took a hymn book from the holder in front of her. As an afterthought, she drew out a second book and handed it to Reagan.

The prelude music continued as other ward members filtered into the chapel and took their seats. Jill noticed a family with several teenage girls sit in the long pew in the center, each of the girls carrying that light with them that showed they knew their family and those around them loved and accepted them. Jill glanced over at Reagan, immediately wondering how different her life might have been if she had been given this gift for her whole life.

In Reagan's lap, the hymnal lay open to the first hymn, and her head was bent as she read the words.

Warmth spread through Jill as a simple thought popped into her mind. Reagan had the gospel now. She might not know it, but the simple act of reading that hymn was giving her a glimpse into the truth that the Lord knew who she was. She was safe and protected for the first time in her life. For as long as this lasted, Jill prayed that she could make Reagan feel loved.

Chapter 7

DOUG SAT ON HIS COUCH early Monday morning and listened to Hector give him the latest details on this case that had been dropped into his lap. Brian Wendall, the man who had been following him at the mall, still wasn't talking, and no one had made any progress with anything that might help them find Reagan's stepfather. The search of the nearby cabin where Laith Mansour had been staying with the girl had given them few answers and had created a lot more questions.

Doug had been relieved that the forensics team hadn't found any sign of bomb residue, but they had found a number of spent shell casings. Further analysis revealed the casings had been from several different guns, all of which were M16 assault rifles.

"The signs definitely suggest this could be some sort of militia group," Hector said with a shrug. "Or it could be a bunch of guys who like guns and have a distorted view of reality."

"Either way, someone was shooting at Reagan the other day."

"That's another thing," Hector said. "The slug we pulled out of the tree near the cabin you were staying at wasn't from an automatic weapon."

"I could have told you that," Doug said. "It was some kind of handgun."

"Yeah. Ballistics said it was a 9 mil, probably fired from a Beretta."

"You know, there's one thing I don't understand."

"What's that?"

"After Reagan's mom died, why did Laith want to keep her around?" Doug asked, considering. "He doesn't have any blood relation to her. It would have been easy enough to hand her over to social services and walk away."

"That's a good question. Maybe he was worried she already knew too much and would talk," Hector said. "After all, he did try to kill her."

"Again, why wait? If Laith had wanted her dead, he could have gone after her weeks ago. Why now?" Doug heard the slight movement in the hallway and turned in time to see Reagan jump back out of sight. "Reagan?"

Doug didn't hear anything, but he suspected she was still standing just out of sight. "Reagan, I know you're there. Come in here, please."

She peeked around the corner, eying Hector as though trying to overcome some unspoken fear.

"It's okay, Reagan. This is Hector Flores. He works with me at the FBI. He only wants to help."

Apparently his words swayed her, and Reagan slowly came into the room, stopping several feet from them.

"You heard us talking?" Doug asked. He could tell by the look in her eyes that she had likely been eavesdropping for several minutes. "Maybe you can help us understand why Laith picked the other day to come after you."

She pressed her lips together. "It was because of the colonel."

"I don't understand."

"Laith wanted me to go to some hotel with them. He wanted me to deliver a package." She drew a breath as though trying to clamp down on her emotions. "When I found out the package was a bomb, I said I didn't want to go."

"Is that when you ran away?"

"Laith told me I had to do what they said, but I said I didn't want to. He hit me, but he knew I wasn't going to change my mind." She shrugged as though the physical abuse was nothing new. "Then the colonel said that I knew too much. The way he was looking at me scared me, so when they were loading up the guns in the colonel's truck, I ran."

"You said the colonel was wearing a military uniform. Do you know which branch he was with?"

"He's a marine," Reagan said with certainty. "And he isn't really a colonel. He had those stripes on the sleeve of his uniform. Colonels don't have those."

"How did you know that?"

She rolled her eyes, and for the first time, Doug caught a glimpse of the girl behind the seemingly reserved exterior. "I watch TV."

Doug tapped a few keys on his computer and pulled up the images of the various rank insignias. "Can you tell me which one of these was on the colonel's uniform?"

Reagan looked at the screen without moving closer. She studied the images for a moment, then pointed. "I'm pretty sure it was the second one."

"So we're looking for a marine staff sergeant with brown hair and brown eyes." Doug considered for a moment. "Any idea what kind of car he drives?"

She nodded. "A black pickup truck. A big one."

"New? Old?"

"It was pretty shiny. I guess that means it's new."

"Any idea what state the license plate was from?"

She shook her head.

"That's okay. This will help," Doug told her. "I'm going to try to access the Marine Corps' personnel database to see if I can run vehicle registrations against rank. A sketch artist is going to come over later to see if you can help us identify the men who were at the cabin. In the meantime, I'd like for you to look at some pictures of hotels. Can you do that for me?"

She nodded obediently. "Okay."

"Great." Doug grabbed one of two rolling chairs beside a long desk in the corner. "Let's get started."

* * *

Jill walked into the living room and found Doug sitting in front of the computer at the desk in the corner and Reagan sitting in a chair beside him, where she could see what he was displaying on the screen.

Since Reagan was the key to a possible threat to national security, Doug's boss had given him permission to work from home so he could fulfill the dual role of making sure she stayed safe and trying to uncover new leads. Hector would work from the office and give Doug any support he needed, as well as provide Doug with the latest updates.

Her heart warmed as she listened to Doug patiently guiding Reagan through photos, his voice gentle and filled with quiet understanding. Jill shifted the tote bag on her shoulder. It was filled with work she had brought home from school with her the previous Thursday, the last day she had worked before she and Doug had taken their short vacation together. It was hard to believe it had been only three days since Reagan had entered their lives.

She knew more about her now, even though Reagan still didn't offer more than basic facts. Reagan had turned thirteen two weeks after her mother died, just days after her stepfather had moved them to the secluded cabin in the woods.

From what Jill had gathered, either Reagan's mother or stepfather had decided to home-school her the previous year. Jill suspected that someone at her middle school had noticed the early signs of abuse or had at least realized that something wasn't right at home, which likely caused the adults in her life to hide her away from any possible prying eyes.

Jill set her bag on the couch. "Good morning."

"Hi, honey." Doug shifted and waited for his usual good morning kiss. "Hey, I forgot to tell you the bishop called last night."

"Oh, I forgot to call Brother Hawkins back to let him know when we could meet with the bishop. He called earlier, but I was hesitant to set up a time since things are so crazy right now."

"Should we be worried that Bishop is calling us himself?" Doug asked.

"Probably. Sounds like one of us is getting a new calling." She thought about the possibilities and the fact that she'd been teaching Relief Society for only a few months. "It must be you." Then she grinned mischievously. "Maybe you're going to be the new early morning seminary teacher."

"You're the teacher in this relationship, not me. I don't think the bishop would trust me to teach anyone over the age of ten." Doug smirked back at her. "Besides, he said you were the one he wants to meet with."

"I guess we'll find out as soon as we talk to him."

"I guess so." Doug dismissed the topic and motioned to the kitchen. "There are some doughnuts in the kitchen if you want one."

"Doughnuts?" Jill looked over at Reagan. "That doesn't sound like a very healthy breakfast."

"Hey, beggars can't be choosers. I asked Hector to pick something up for me on his way over this morning. That's what he showed up with."

"Hector was here? Before eight in the morning?"

"Yeah, he left a few minutes ago." Doug motioned at the computer screen. "Reagan and I are going to figure out which hotel she saw a picture of so we can narrow our search of Halloween activities."

"Are you sure you don't want me to take work off today?" Jill asked hesitantly. She was already worried that if she turned her back on Reagan for too long, Reagan would disappear. She wasn't sure how she felt about leaving the girl's care entirely up to Doug so soon.

"We'll be fine," Doug assured her.

"Okay." Jill hefted her bag again and settled it on her shoulder. "I'm going to grab some breakfast and head out. Call me, though, if you have any problems."

"We will," Doug promised. Then he gave her a wicked grin. "And I saved you a Bavarian-cream-filled."

Jill grinned. "It's times like these I really love you."

"Yeah." Doug gave her a smug look. "I know."

⋆ ⋆

Reagan didn't know how she felt about being left alone with a man, even if it was a man who carried a badge. She knew he also carried a gun, and her experience with men and guns hadn't given her any positive memories. Still, Doug seemed okay so far. He kept showing her one photo after another of hotel buildings, usually several pictures of the same one to make sure they didn't miss something.

They spent the morning looking through nearly all of the hotels in D.C. Then they took a break and made sandwiches for lunch. Now they were back at it.

Once they'd exhausted the list of D.C. hotels, Doug started showing her hotels in Virginia that might also have a view of the Washington Monument.

Reagan sat up straighter in her seat when a new photo loaded. "That's it. That's the picture I saw."

"You're sure?"

She nodded. "It was this same picture. It was hanging up on the big project board in the living room for at least a month."

Doug shifted, and his dark eyes pinned her. "What else was on the project board?"

"A bunch of stuff."

"Like what?"

"Pictures of guns. Little boxes with words in them."

"Could you draw what it looked like for me?"

"Maybe." Reagan rolled her shoulders restlessly.

Doug was quiet for a moment. "We've been at this all day. What do you say we get out of here for a little while?"

Reagan didn't know what to say or even what he was offering.

"Have you ever shot a gun?" Doug asked.

Her eyes widened, and she shook her head.

"Do you want to learn?"

"Laith said girls aren't supposed to use guns."

"I think we've already established that Laith is an idiot," Doug said without any heat. "Go put some shoes on. There's a shooting range not far from here, and it's pretty empty this time of day."

Afraid to argue, Reagan did as she was told. Twenty minutes later, she found herself standing at the edge of a wide field while Doug instructed her on the basic safety of firearms.

He demonstrated each aspect of using a handgun until, finally, he told her to put on the funny ear coverings that he said would protect her hearing. Then he showed her where to line up, and he handed her a loaded weapon.

Her first thought was that it was heavier than she had expected it to be. Then she lined up with the target and squeezed the trigger the way Doug had told her. She felt the jolt from the kick of the weapon and a terrifying rush of power.

Wide-eyed, she looked over at Doug, and a look of understanding passed between them.

"Scary, huh?"

She nodded.

"It's okay," Doug assured her. He put a hand on her arm to make sure the gun was pointed toward the target. "Just make sure you remember what I told you. Square up with your target, keep your arms steady, and don't forget to breathe."

Her heart beating rapidly, Reagan followed his instructions. She drew a deep breath, fired again, and, for the first time in her life, found a glimmer of what it was like to feel in control.

Chapter 8

DOUG WAS SURE HE WAS going to go cross-eyed any minute. He had been staring at photographs, background reports, and traffic video feed for more than a week. Reagan had spent countless hours with him, examining pictures of marine staff sergeants assigned to Virginia as well as the D.C. area. So far, all they had managed to do was eliminate a lot of possibilities in their search for the colonel.

Reagan had literally looked at the photos of every marine staff sergeant currently assigned to D.C., Maryland, and Virginia twice. They had expanded their search to include other sergeant ranks in case she had been mistaken about the exact insignia on the colonel's sleeve, but that was unsuccessful too. Now they were going to widen their search even further to include North and South Carolina.

Doug sighed. It was going to be another long day.

He thought of how many hours Reagan had already spent helping him. She was a trooper. He had to give her that. She hadn't complained once about anything he'd asked her to do, not even the detailed sketch he'd had her draw of Laith's project board or working with the sketch artist to try to identify the men she'd seen at the cabin. In fact, he found her to be helpful in general. She had been good about assisting Jill with basic household chores and had seemed to enjoy helping Jill grade papers for school.

The idea that Reagan should be in school had crossed his mind, but he wasn't willing to take the chance that Laith might be able to find her through the transfer of school records. Reagan also wasn't a candidate for the Witness Protection Program at this point since it appeared that once Laith was captured, she would be safe.

Jill had offered to take some time off to spend it with Reagan, but Doug insisted she save her leave. He knew the day would come eventually when he would have to work somewhere that he couldn't take Reagan with him. He definitely wasn't about to leave Reagan home alone.

Admittedly, it was odd watching his wife leave for work each morning while he remained behind with a timid thirteen-year-old who was more than a little wary of men. Still, he thought they were making progress. She no longer waited for him to tell her she could eat breakfast or lunch; she now recognized that if she was hungry, she could find something to eat for herself.

She also seemed more capable of entertaining herself than when she'd first arrived; she was content to read books or watch television, and she even seemed to enjoy raking leaves and doing simple yard work. He couldn't be sure if she was getting more settled or if he was getting more used to having her around now.

They had been to the shooting range together a half dozen times now, and he took some pride in knowing she was turning into a pretty good shot. She still didn't express her opinion or talk about her feelings, but he supposed that was normal for a kid who was trying to find out where she belonged. Doug could admit that he had wondered what would come next for her. It would be odd when this case ended and she could be placed in a foster home.

A knock sounded at the door. Relieved to have a reason to step away from the computer, he pushed back from his desk and crossed the room. He leaned forward and looked through the peephole before opening the door to Hector.

"Come on in." Doug waved him inside. "Anything new going on?"

"Actually, yes." Hector handed him two files and then sat down on the couch. "We finally found a link between Laith Mansour and the military."

"What's that?" Doug sat in the chair across from him.

"Apparently, Laith was a wannabe Navy SEAL. His aptitude scores were high enough that he was given an out-clause. If he washed out of the SEALs, his recruitment would be nullified."

"I gather he washed out?"

"Oh yeah." Hector nodded. "He didn't even make it through the first day of hell week."

"That gives us a tie to the military but not to the marines."

"It's possible that the sergeant we're looking for is with one of the recon units out of Camp Lejeune in North Carolina. That's the marines' version of a Navy SEAL. From what I understand, the two units could cross paths in some of the specialty schools."

"It's a long shot, but we might as well check it out. Can you dig up the personnel photos for Camp Lejeune? Let's not limit ourselves to recon though."

"I already did. I e-mailed you a link, but that blue file has the printouts of the staff sergeants. I thought it might make it easier for you if Reagan could look at those without tying up your computer."

"Thanks. I appreciate that," Doug said. He set the file down on the arm of the chair and then leaned forward and rested his elbows on his knees. "Anything new on the hotel?"

Hector shook his head. "The hotel manager said they don't have any events scheduled for Halloween, and they don't have any kind of costume parties planned for the weekend before Halloween."

"Reagan said the colonel wanted her to take a package into the hotel. There has to be a specific reason for these guys to pick that location to plant a bomb." Doug hesitated a moment, and Hector's words caught up with him. "Wait a minute. You said the hotel manager told you that there isn't a costume party this weekend. Do they have any other events scheduled?"

"I don't know. He didn't say."

"Find out."

Hector nodded, pulling his phone from his pocket. He scrolled through phone numbers and made the call. Doug listened to the one-sided conversation, seeing by the light in his partner's eyes that something indeed had been missed.

"Well?" Doug asked as soon as Hector hung up.

"You were right. The hotel manager doesn't know specifically what the event is that's planned, but the banquet facilities have been reserved for Saturday night."

"Who reserved it?"

"The Department of Defense."

"Any chance the manager gave you a contact name?"

"He's looking it up and said he'd get back to me, but get this"— excitement laced his voice—"the manager mentioned that the convention center across the street has a huge anime convention the same weekend. That will be going on the Friday and Saturday before Halloween."

"Anime convention?"

"Yeah, you know, those Japanese cartoons?"

"Like Pokémon?"

Hector nodded. "A good number of the participants dress up like their favorite characters, and they flood that part of the city."

"Which means anyone in costume would blend right in, and no one would look at them twice."

"Exactly."

"Let me know when you get that contact info for the event at the hotel. Let's see if we can figure out if these guys have a specific target in mind or if they're just trying to strike out at the DoD in general."

"You got it."

* * *

Jill debated whether she should call the Young Women president and cancel. Several weeks ago, she had agreed to help out with their Wednesday night activity this week when she found out the bishop was going to be out of town for business and several of the Young Women leaders had conflicts.

Selfishly, she wanted to stay home to spend time with Reagan. She felt like she'd had far too little time with the girl so far, and she found herself envying Doug and the bond he seemed to be forging with Reagan. Realizing that Reagan would probably benefit from being around some kids her own age, Jill walked into the living room, where Reagan was watching television. "Hey, why don't you go get some shoes on and come with me?"

Reagan looked at her skeptically. "Come with you where?"

"The youth in our church are having an activity tonight. It'll be a lot of fun."

Reagan immediately shook her head. "I don't want to go. I want to stay here."

Jill hesitated, not sure if she should press or let Reagan get her way. She had hoped to introduce Reagan to some of the girls from church the previous Sunday, but Reagan had been just as wary at church her second time attending as she had been during her first. When Doug had whispered in Jill's ear, suggesting that they not push her to stay, Jill had reluctantly agreed.

She could understand Reagan's resistance, but she also knew it would be easier on her to meet some of the youth in a social setting where Jill could stay right by her side rather than in church, where she would have to go into a class by herself.

"Just come with me," Jill urged her. "It will be fun. I promise."

"I don't want to go," she repeated with a slight whine.

Jill took the whine as a good sign. Finally, Reagan was starting to sound like a typical thirteen-year-old, right down to balking at going to an event with a bunch of strangers. "Don't you think it's about time you meet some kids your age?" Jill asked.

A pained expression crossed Reagan's face. "I wouldn't know what to say."

"Saying hello is always a good place to start." Realizing that social settings were probably foreign to Reagan, Jill gentled her voice. "Reagan, you can stay with me the whole time if you want. I just really want the chance to spend time with you. It's hard going to work every day when I'd much rather be here at home with you and Doug."

"I thought you liked your work."

"I do," she said. "But I like you and Doug better."

Surprise reflected in Reagan's eyes before her lips curved up slightly. "I guess I can go with you."

"Thanks. I promise it'll be fun."

* * *

Reagan decided that Jill needed to seriously rethink her definition of fun. Two dozen teenagers were gathered along the curb in the quiet neighborhood, several of them with rakes in hand.

She looked over at Jill suspiciously. She had neglected to mention that the activity she was dragging her to was a service project at some older couple's house. "What exactly are we supposed to do here?"

"Nothing too strenuous. We'll rake up the leaves in the yard, harvest the last of their pumpkins, and then turn their garden so it's ready for spring."

"Why don't they just do this stuff themselves? Or hire someone?"

"They used to have their kids help, but they've all grown up and moved out of the area. And they don't need to hire someone, because we can do the work for them." Jill climbed out of the car. "Come on."

Reluctantly, Reagan followed. They were halfway across the leaf-covered lawn when two girls about Reagan's age crossed toward them.

"Sister Valdez!" The tall blonde girl bounded toward them, reaching her arms out for a hug as soon as she was in reach.

To Reagan's surprise, Jill hugged her back and then turned to give the other girl a hug too. "How are you girls doing?"

"Good," the shorter brunette replied.

Then the energetic blonde spoke again. "I'm so glad you're here."

"Me too." Jill stepped back and put a hand on Reagan's shoulder. "Reagan, this is Amber and Jasmine."

The two girls greeted her just as some lady across the yard motioned for everyone to gather around. Jill nudged Reagan forward, and Reagan was surprised when all of the chatter ceased and everyone folded their arms for a prayer.

As soon as the prayer concluded, Amber turned to her. "We're supposed to be picking pumpkins. Want to come with us?"

Surprised by the invitation, Reagan looked back at Jill. As though she knew Reagan wasn't sure what to do, Jill stepped forward and said, "That sounds fun. I'll come too."

Amber led the way to the field in back of the house. Reagan's eyes widened when she saw the rows and rows of tangled vines, pumpkins in various sizes visible at random intervals. Two wheelbarrows were parked on the side of the garden next to an older man who was holding several pairs of scissors and some kind of clippers.

The man handed out the various cutting utensils and then showed them how to harvest the pumpkins. Reagan followed Amber and Jasmine's lead, cutting pumpkins from the vine and loading them into the wheelbarrows. Jill helped for a few minutes, but then one of the other grown-ups pulled her aside.

At first, Reagan worked in silence a few yards from the other girls. Then Jasmine started working in the row beside her. "So do you live here now?"

Reagan didn't quite know how to answer, nor did she want to explain that she didn't really live anywhere. Keeping it simple, she said, "Yeah. For now."

"Where did you move from?"

"I moved around a lot."

Jasmine tried to lift an enormous pumpkin but couldn't quite manage it. "Hey, Reagan, can you help me with this one? It's seriously heavy."

"Sure." Reagan shifted and grabbed one side of the pumpkin. Together, they carried it to the wheelbarrow.

"Are you coming to our ward's trunk or treat? It's a week from Saturday."

Reagan thought of what was supposed to be happening on that particular Saturday, what Laith and his friends had planned. "I don't think so. I think I have to help Doug with something."

"Bummer." Jasmine considered for a minute. "Maybe you can come out trick-or-treating with us on Halloween."

"You go trick-or-treating? I thought that was just for little kids."

"Not around here." Jasmine shook her head. "Halloween is pretty much a big party in our neighborhood. All of the adults hang out in their cul de sacs to give out candy, and everyone from babies to teenagers dress-up and trick-or-treat. It's a lot of fun. You should come."

Reagan let herself wonder for a moment where she would be two weeks from now, desperately hoping she would still be here, that she could make plans for something as silly as trick-or-treating. Not that she had a costume, but it might be fun to walk around with Jasmine and see what everyone else did for the holiday.

When Reagan didn't answer right away, Jasmine continued. "Jill has my number. I'm sure she would be cool with it."

"I'll talk to her about it."

"Great."

Chapter 9

DOUG'S EYEBROWS LIFTED WHEN HE heard the door open and laughter ring out. Reagan's laughter.

"I've never heard anyone scream so loud," Reagan said with a giggle as she walked into the room.

"Well, she did have the head of a scarecrow land right on top of her." Jill grinned back at her.

Doug looked at them and found himself grinning. "Can I assume you had fun?"

"I think so." Jill looked over at Reagan as though looking for confirmation. Reagan nodded, but her smile faded slightly.

"Reagan hung out with Jasmine and Amber tonight," Jill told him.

"Those two will talk your ear off," Doug commented humorously.

Reagan seemed to muster her courage and then blurted out, "Jasmine wants me to go trick-or-treating with her."

"That sounds like fun," Jill said without missing a beat. Then she turned and gave Doug that look, the one that silently pleaded for him to back her up.

Doug was quick enough to understand there was a lot more going on here than a simple request. Halloween was two weeks away, but it was also after the threat Laith posed. Reagan wanted to know if she was staying with them that long, and Jill was asking for him to let her.

He wasn't sure exactly how he felt about extending Reagan's stay, but he had to admit he was kind of getting used to having her around. He considered for a moment. "I don't see why you can't go out. I'm sure Jill can help you figure something out for a costume."

"Really?" Hope lit Reagan's eyes.

"You can call Jasmine tomorrow afternoon and let her know," Jill suggested. "For now, you need to get to bed and get some sleep."

Obediently, Reagan started toward the hall and then turned back. After a brief hesitation, she moved toward Jill and gave her a hug. Jill looked up at Doug, a look of surprise and wonder in her eyes. Then she pulled Reagan closer and pressed a kiss on the top of her head.

"Good night, sweetie," Jill said softly.

"Good night." Reagan pulled away and took an awkward step back. Then she looked at Doug and repeated, "Good night."

"What was that all about?" Doug asked as soon as Reagan had left the room.

"I don't know." Jill smiled, and she closed the distance between them to wrap her arms around his waist. "But I like it."

* * *

Reagan spread the stack of photos out on the kitchen table again. She had been staring at pictures of marine sergeants for so long that she was beginning to think that she could pick one out of a crowd from fifty yards away. Unfortunately, she had yet to find a picture of the colonel.

A sigh escaped her when once again she failed to find anyone who resembled the man she had seen so often at Laith's cabin. None of these men had that cold look in his eyes or that heavy brow that made him look like he was always concentrating.

She picked up the pictures and carried them into the front living room, where Doug was sitting at the desk doing something on the computer. He was muttering to himself, but that wasn't anything new. He always seemed to do that when he was concentrating. And worrying.

Doug didn't have to tell her how worried he was. She might not know him that well, but it didn't take a genius to realize he was stressing out. So were the guys who came by the house to talk to him about Laith and the colonel. They were running out of time, and everyone knew it. Whatever Laith was planning was supposed to happen a week from Saturday.

She waited for the muttering to stop before she stepped forward and handed him the latest pictures.

"You didn't find him?"

Reagan shook her head. "Do you have any more for me to look at?"

"That was the last of the sergeants who are stationed around here." Doug took them from her, and his brow furrowed. "What are the chances that this guy is a former marine?"

"I don't know. When he came over, I always tried to get out of his way."

Sympathy or something like it flashed on Doug's face. He was silent for a moment. Then he asked, "Was he always in uniform when you saw him?"

"Yeah." Reagan nodded. "Always."

"That's odd." Doug turned to his computer and started punching keys. "Most military guys I know are more than happy to put on regular clothes when they're away from work."

"I'm pretty sure he was still working somewhere because he kept bringing these files with him to the cabin."

"What kind of files?"

"I don't know, but they all said 'top secret' on them."

"Are you sure?"

She nodded.

"Did they say anything else? A file name or something like that?"

"Yeah." Reagan struggled to bring the image forward, the manila folder with red stripes across it. "Bluebird. That's what it said on the top."

"Do you know what *Bluebird* stood for?"

She shook her head.

Doug picked his phone up off of the desk. "I'll call Hector and see if he can dig anything up. Why don't you go put some shoes on, and we'll go out to the shooting range."

"Okay." Reagan walked out of the room, but she stopped as soon as she was out of sight so she could listen to Doug's phone call.

She heard him greet his partner and tell him about the Bluebird file. Then she heard her name mentioned. "Reagan finished going through the rest of those pictures you brought over. We still haven't found the guy."

Doug paused, obviously listening to Hector say something. "She's already looked through the pictures twice. That kid is a trooper, and she's obviously really bright. Considering what she's been through, I'm surprised she's been able to remember as much as she has."

Reagan stood in the hall, frozen in place. Doug and Jill had been nice to her over the past week and a half, but Doug's words surprised her, especially since they were offered in such an offhanded way when he didn't even know she was listening.

After another moment of silence, Doug continued his side of the conversation. "I asked her about that. It sounds like he's still active duty. I think we need to stop limiting our search. Ask Max if he can send over one of our office laptops for me. I want to have her start searching the military database. We've got to figure out who this guy is, especially since we didn't get any hits on facial recognition for him or the other two guys Reagan told us about."

Reagan waited another second until she heard Doug saying his good-byes. Then she hurried to her room to retrieve her shoes.

"Are you ready?" Doug asked as soon as she reappeared.

"Yeah." Reagan zipped up her jacket.

Doug glanced down at his watch. "Tell you what. Let's swing by and pick up some sandwiches at the deli. We can take lunch to Jill at the school before we go to the range."

"I get to see where Jill works?"

"Sure." Doug glanced at the computer and the stacks of photos and papers beside it. "We both deserve a little downtime before we dive back into this case."

* * *

Reagan carried the white paper bag from the deli in one hand and a soda in the other as she followed Doug through the elementary school hallway, her shoes squeaking on the white vinyl floor. Various art projects decorated the walls, the personalities of both the students and the teachers evident outside each door.

Doug slowed near a doorway, and Reagan could hear Jill's voice coming from inside. "Everyone, it's time to line up for lunch."

Doug moved through the doorway, sidestepping the rush of kids who were now crowding the entrance to the classroom. He looked back at Reagan and motioned for her to follow. Reagan followed him inside, instantly feeling the curious stares of the seven-year-olds who filled the room.

"Hi there," Jill greeted them, excitement and surprise in her voice. "What are you doing here?"

"We brought you lunch," Doug told her.

"Thank you." Jill waved toward the table in the corner. "Go ahead and sit down. I'll be back after I walk them down to the cafeteria."

"Okay." Doug set the two drinks he was holding on the table as Jill ushered her students out into the hall.

Reagan heard one of the little girls ask, "Who's that?"

"That's my husband and my foster daughter," Jill told the girl. Then without breaking stride, she spoke to the boys at the back of the line. "Peter and Jalen, keep your hands to yourselves."

Reagan absorbed the little jolt she felt at hearing herself referred to as Jill's daughter, even knowing that the word *foster* meant it wouldn't last.

Jill had called her their foster daughter before, and Reagan could only wonder if she would ever be more than that to anyone again. Until she'd met Jill and Doug, she hadn't really thought about her lack of family or that her life wasn't quite normal. Now she thought about it all the time.

She put the sandwiches down on the table and turned to look around the room. Colorful posters hung on the walls, along with charts partially filled with colorful stickers. The class rules were prominently displayed by the door. Reagan read the first one. *Be Kind.* She wondered what life would have been like if the adults in her past had lived by that one.

"Does it seem weird to be in an elementary school again?" Doug asked.

"Yeah." Reagan lowered herself onto one of the chairs beside the table. "I was bummed when Laith said I couldn't go to school anymore."

"Once we find Laith, we'll make sure you can go again," Doug said.

Reagan wanted to ask where she would go to school and if Doug was planning on letting her stay with them, but before she could muster up the courage to ask the question, Jill came bustling back into the room.

"So what did you bring me?" Jill asked, taking a seat beside Doug.

"Turkey and avocado."

"That sounds perfect." She dug her sandwich out of the bag. "So much better than the peanut butter and jelly I had packed from home."

"We figured you wouldn't mind if we brought you something."

"Definitely not." Jill started unwrapping her sandwich, and Reagan followed suit. Jill took a bite, chewed, and swallowed before asking, "What else are you two up to today?"

"We're about to head out to the shooting range."

Jill looked over at Reagan. "Do you like going shooting?"

Reagan rolled the question over in her mind. She still wasn't used to people asking how she felt about things, and she took a moment to consider her answer. Did she like shooting? She did like the rush of power that pulsed through her every time she fired a weapon and the sense of freedom that came from being out among the trees. "Yeah. I like being outside and stuff."

"Doug tried to teach me how to shoot when we first started dating."

Doug lowered his voice and leaned closer to Reagan. "Don't let her fool you. She knows how to shoot just fine."

Reagan heard the humor in his voice and found herself pleased that she recognized the dry sarcasm for what it was. Her lips twitched up into the beginnings of a smile.

"I've spent enough time around you that it would be hard not to know the basics," Jill admitted. She took a sip of her drink and picked up her sandwich again. "Any chance you two want to swing by the grocery store on your way back from the shooting range? If you can pick up some chicken, I'll make some stir fry tonight."

"We can do that," Doug agreed easily.

Reagan looked down at the food in front of her and thought of how different things were now. Two weeks ago, she'd been lucky if she could manage a few scraps of food for herself after Laith and whatever friends he had working with him each day had eaten whatever she'd microwaved for them. Now she had real food in front of her with the promise of another meal in a few hours.

She drew a breath, and a plea echoed through her mind—*Please let this last.*

Chapter 10

JILL DIDN'T HAVE TO ASK Doug how the case was going. She could feel by the tension in the air that he and his coworkers hadn't made any progress in the past couple of days. She had arrived home on Friday night to find a sketch artist working with Reagan again in an effort to identify the man Reagan referred to as the colonel as well as the various men she had seen visiting Laith at the cabin.

She hoped a few hours in church would help Doug find some peace and maybe even the inspiration he needed to break through the challenges he and his coworkers were facing. She also hoped Reagan would be willing to stay for the entire three-hour block of services rather than just sacrament meeting.

They took their seats in the chapel, and Jill felt a little lift when Jasmine walked by and greeted Reagan. Jill motioned for Jasmine to stop and talk to her, hoping to ease Reagan's transition.

"Jasmine, would you mind taking Reagan to Sunday School and Young Women's with you today? She doesn't know where her classrooms are."

"Sure, no problem," Jasmine said enthusiastically. "You can sit with me and Amber."

"Thanks," Reagan said, even though she looked a little overwhelmed.

"Don't worry," Jill assured her. "All of the girls are really nice. They're the same ones who were at the activity on Wednesday night." When Reagan continued to look at her warily, she added, "Besides, I'm sure someone will make sure everyone hears about Melissa and the scarecrow."

Humor lit Reagan's eyes. "That was so funny."

Jill put her arm around Reagan and gave her shoulders a friendly squeeze. "I'm really glad you're here."

Surprise replaced the humor on Reagan's face, and she gave Jill a thoughtful look. "Me too."

* * *

Reagan had never seen anyone work so hard before. Every morning when Reagan woke up, Doug was either on the phone or doing something on the computer. Other FBI agents came by the house every day now, sometimes staying for several hours before leaving them alone again.

She thought of all of the preparations Laith and his friends had made, the conversations she had overheard. Laith's plans were always focused on steering clear of the authorities. Now Reagan knew what the other side of the equation looked like. The authorities were definitely looking for him.

Doug's friends were just as wary about talking in front of her as Laith's had been, but their way of communicating their desire for privacy was so vastly different. While Laith had shouted or used the back of his hand to send her scampering into the other room, Doug and his friends just asked her to give them some time alone. They even said *please* most of the time.

When Reagan thought of the men who had paraded through her mother's life and, by extension, through her life, she found herself wondering why her mom had never been able to meet anyone like Doug and his friends.

She supposed deep down she knew the answer. It was because of the drugs. She doubted someone like Doug would sit around and watch someone take so many pills that they were passed out more often than not. Reagan didn't know if anything could have changed what happened to her mom, but she did know she didn't want to live like that again.

Reagan finished getting dressed and went into the kitchen in search of breakfast. She smiled a little at the certainty that the refrigerator and pantry were well stocked and that she was allowed to help herself to the contents.

When she turned the corner, she saw Doug buttering a piece of toast and Jill standing behind him, her arms wrapped around his waist.

"If there's anything I can do, just tell me," Jill was saying. "I can take some leave if you want to go into the office."

"No." Doug shook his head and put the butter knife down long enough to pat Jill's hand. "Reagan's been a big help, and some of the guys are coming to meet me here this morning."

"Okay." Jill stepped back and motioned to the refrigerator. "I made some chicken salad last night, and there are still some cookies in the cookie jar." Her tone changed a little when she added, "Make sure there are some cookies left when I get home."

"I won't let Reagan eat them all," Doug said without missing a beat.

Reagan stepped forward. She thought he might be joking, but she wasn't sure. She saw the humor in Jill's eyes when Jill turned and saw her, and Reagan let herself say what she was thinking. "You do know that Doug's the one who eats all of the cookies, right?"

Jill gave her a knowing look. "Of that I have little doubt."

"The problem with being the only man in the house is that I'm outnumbered," Doug said.

"You love it, and you know it." Jill reached up and kissed him. "I'll see you both tonight."

Reagan felt that familiar warm glow move through her when Jill gave her a quick hug before collecting her things and heading out the door.

"Since you told on me, I guess it's your turn to clean the kitchen."

"It was my turn yesterday," Reagan retorted.

"Yeah, but I'm older." Doug took a step toward the living room and then turned back to give her a wicked grin. "And make sure you don't eat all of the cookies."

Reagan fought back the grin trying to form. Barely.

* * *

"Thanks for meeting me here," Doug said the moment his boss, Max Barnett, walked into Doug's living room, followed by Hector. "I'm still leery of going into the office until Laith Mansour and his buddies are in custody."

"Where's the girl now?"

"In her room," Doug said. "Were you able to convince DoD to cancel or relocate their event?"

Max shook his head. "I don't know exactly what's going on at this thing, but I get the impression that there's more to it than meets the eye."

"What do you mean?"

"The contact name and number were a front. The woman didn't know any details other than that she needed to make some basic arrangements with the hotel," Max told him. "According to the hotel manager, a large block of rooms was reserved, but there wasn't any link established between it and the banquet hall reservation."

"That's odd," Doug agreed. "What do you think is going on?"

"I don't know. Maybe it's really CIA or DIA holding something. Until we figure it out, we can't talk to the people in charge, much less warn them."

"I'll see if I can work on that angle." Doug led them into the kitchen, where the sketch Reagan had helped him create was laid out on the table.

"What's this?"

"Reagan told me Laith kept a project board in his cabin. This is what we've been able to reproduce from what she remembers." The sketch Reagan had originally drawn had been crude, but it had given him enough details for them to create something a little more usable.

"Is this supposed to be the hotel here?"

"Yeah." Doug nodded. "From what I've been able to piece together, Reagan was going to deliver a bomb disguised as a delivery for the conference in the hotel. It would likely have been disguised as a floral arrangement or a box of educational materials."

"What are these four guns supposed to represent?" Max pointed at the sketches of weapons that were located on the paths near the two main entrances into the hotel.

"Shooters."

"You think we have four shooters?"

"We think so now that we have Wendall in custody."

"Then why would they need a whole case of weapons?"

"Reagan said their costumes all had hidden pockets sewn inside of them."

"She thinks they were going to hide extra guns there?"

"There and maybe in and around the hotel." Doug nodded. "With the anime convention starting on Friday, I think they'll probably try to stash several around the grounds. It's possible they might have even planned to rent a room so they could have direct access on the inside."

"Then we could have even more shooters than the ones shown here on the outside."

"I asked Reagan how many people she could remember coming in and out of Laith's cabin. She recognized Wendall, the guy who was looking for her at the mall. Then there was Laith, the colonel, and two others."

"That gives us four who still aren't in custody," Hector commented. "Even knowing where they're planning on positioning themselves, this isn't going to be easy."

"Reagan has been working with a sketch artist. We're trying to use the composite sketches to help us ID the man she calls the colonel, along with the other two men."

"We're running out of time. The anime convention starts in two days," Hector said. "And the vendors will start setting up tomorrow."

"I've got some undercover agents working at the convention center, hoping to find these guys before Saturday," Max told him.

"I don't know how we're going to find them, especially since they'll be in costume."

"I can find them." The voice came from the doorway.

"Reagan." Doug looked at Max apologetically before speaking to her. "I told you to stay in your room while I was in my meeting."

"I can find them," she repeated. Her eyes were dark and determined. "I can help you stop Laith and his friends before they shoot people."

Max looked over at Doug, clearly considering the possibilities. "You know, she is the only one who has seen the costumes, and she's more likely than any of us to recognize these guys from a distance since she's seen them before."

Doug shook his head. "It's too dangerous."

"Doug, if we don't find these guys before Saturday, we may not have a choice. We can't sit by and watch a mass shooting take place, not without using every available resource to stop it."

Doug knew Max's words were true. Hadn't he agreed to take Reagan into his home as much to gain information as to protect her? He looked over at her now. She was no longer the terrified stranger who had appeared at their cabin, nor was she simply an informant who needed to be kept safe. Something had changed over the past few weeks, something that left worry churning through him at the thought of putting her in harm's way.

A sense of panic rippled through him, but he nodded. "Just understand, having Reagan there is our last resort."

Max's eyes met his. "Agreed."

Chapter 11

Doug didn't waste any time following their few remaining leads. Max and Hector were barely out the door before Doug made a quick phone call. Call waiting beeped, and he saw that the bishop was calling again. This was at least the fourth time in the past couple of weeks that he had called their house. Not able to deal with whatever he might want at the moment, Doug finished up on the phone and ushered Reagan out to the car.

"Where are we going?" Reagan asked, pulling on the hooded sweatshirt Doug had insisted she take with her to ward off the cool weather.

"The Whitmores' house."

Reagan's eyebrows drew together. "How come?"

"Because I think the senator can help me piece together some of the information we're still missing."

"Why would the senator know anything about Laith?"

"He wouldn't, but he might know about Bluebird. Or he might know how we can find out about it." Doug climbed into the car and waited for Reagan to take her seat beside him. After reminding her to fasten her seat belt, something he still hadn't managed to drum into her head, he put the car into gear and started toward Great Falls.

When they knocked on the Whitmores' front door, it was Katherine rather than the senator who answered.

"What perfect timing," Katherine said with a smile. "I was just going to go out for a little ride. Any chance Reagan has time to come with me?"

Reagan's eyes lit up with both wonder and a hint of trepidation. "Me? Ride a horse?"

"Absolutely. My daughter's horse would love to get out of the pasture for a while." Katherine shifted her attention to Doug. "Is that okay with you? Jim seemed to think that the two of you might need a while to talk."

Doug could tell by the expression on Reagan's face that this would be a new experience for her. "Reagan, do you want to learn how to ride?"

She hesitated for only a moment. Then she nodded.

"Okay, then. Just be careful."

"I'll take good care of her," Katherine promised, motioning for both of them to come inside. She waved toward the study to their right. "Jim is in his office. You can go on in."

"Thanks." Doug watched Katherine lead Reagan toward the back door before he crossed to Jim's office and knocked.

Jim looked up from the papers spread out on his desk. "Come in."

"Thanks for seeing me on such short notice."

"It sounded important."

"I think it is." Doug nodded. "I'm hoping you can shake loose some information. This thing with Reagan has led us to a roadblock of red tape, and we don't have a lot of time to untangle it."

"In that case, tell me what you know, and we'll see what I can do."

* * *

Reagan fetched pads and saddles and bridles, carrying whatever gear Katherine needed but not daring to get too close to the horses. Once Katherine had both of their horses saddled, Reagan followed Katherine's directions, standing on the left side of the horse and placing her foot in the stirrup. Awkwardly, she swung herself up into the saddle, grabbing on to the saddle horn for balance when the animal beneath her sidestepped.

"It's okay." Katherine's voice was soothing, and she patted the horse on the neck. "Here you go. Sit up straight in the saddle, and hold on to the reins."

Reagan took the leather straps Katherine handed her, not sure she was ready to try this without someone right by her side. But before she could protest, Katherine swung herself into her saddle and nudged her horse so she was right beside Reagan's mount.

Very patiently, Katherine instructed her, slowly walking with her around the pasture, teaching her the basics of riding and how to steer and stop her horse.

She was just starting to get the hang of it when Doug and the senator appeared. The senator waved at his wife, and she guided her horse to the fence, where he was waiting for her.

"Doug and I have to go to a meeting. Is it okay if Reagan stays here with you?"

"Absolutely. I think she's about ready to hit the trail."

"Okay." The senator stepped back. "Have fun."

Doug offered Reagan a wave before disappearing back down the path toward the house.

"What do you mean 'hit the trail'?"

"I mean you know enough that you're ready to leave the pasture and go out for a trail ride." Katherine gave her a look of confidence and challenge. "Are you ready?"

Reagan's heartbeat quickened. "Do you really think I can do this?"

"Absolutely." Katherine gave her a definite nod. "And I'll be right there with you."

Anxiety and anticipation twined together and spurted through Reagan as one emotion. She took a deep breath. "Okay. Let's go."

* * *

Doug followed the senator and their escort through CIA security. He was both relieved and concerned that Jim had identified the agency overseeing Bluebird—relieved because he now knew who had the answers he was looking for and concerned that the CIA project manager might resist giving him those answers.

The fact that they had to come to CIA headquarters instead of talking over a secure line cemented the fact that this was a highly classified project, one the CIA had clearly gone to great lengths to protect.

They were shown to an elevator and then taken to a reception area in the original headquarters building. After a couple of minutes, the secretary showed them into a private office.

A man who looked to be around fifty stood and circled his desk to offer his hand to the senator. "Senator Whitmore, I'm Simon Keaton. I appreciate your coming in to meet with me."

"Thanks for fitting us into your schedule," Jim said and motioned to Doug. "This is Doug Valdez from the FBI."

"Please, sit down." Simon moved back to take his seat behind his desk while Jim and Doug lowered themselves into the chairs across from him. "I understand you were inquiring about Bluebird."

"That's right." Doug nodded. "We have reason to believe this project may be the target of a potential terrorist attack."

"There must be some mistake." Simon shook his head. "Besides being highly classified, this project isn't likely to be of high value for a potential terrorist."

"The fact that we're aware of the project proves that the secret is already out," Jim said before Doug could demand that they share information.

Simon acknowledged that with a nod. "Just understand that what I tell you here can't be shared with anyone unless they are cleared by this agency."

"I understand," Doug said.

"For some time, the military has become increasingly concerned with individuals within their ranks trying to breed dissidence in the name of religion."

"You're talking about Jihadist extremists."

"Yes. The Fort Hood shooting proved that the military's concerns were warranted," he said. "This agency has been involved in a joint operation to try to identify any individuals who are communicating with terrorists overseas."

"What does Bluebird stand for?"

"Bluebird is an undercover operative the military planted within those ranks. He is a practicing Muslim, one who has served this country diligently. Three years ago, he informed his superiors that a member of his unit tried to recruit him in helping with their movement, one that encourages violence against anyone who doesn't share their beliefs."

"Bluebird is the code name for him?"

"That's right."

Doug turned this latest piece of information over in his mind, trying to fit this piece of the puzzle in with everything Reagan had told him. "By any chance, is he involved in some meeting this Saturday night in Arlington?"

Simon's face paled. "How could you know that?"

"Because I have been working on the threat assessment of a suspected attack, likely a mass shooting on Saturday at a hotel in Crystal City," Doug told him. "We believe that the shooters are going to use an anime convention as cover so they won't be noticed carrying around weapons."

"The convention is exactly the reason we chose this location. We knew it would be an easy way to put our people in disguise without anyone being suspicious." Simon shook his head. "What else do you know?"

"Our information suggests that one of the men involved is a marine sergeant, and at least one other is a civilian."

Simon stood and moved to where a heavy black filing cabinet was located in the corner of the room. He pulled open the second drawer and retrieved a file. He then flipped it open, perused the contents for a moment, and plucked out three photographs.

"Do any of these match the description of the sergeant you're looking for?"

Doug took the photographs from him and studied the top one. He shook his head and then flipped it over. Although he hadn't ever seen the man, the face staring back at him fit the composite the sketch artist had done from Reagan's description.

"This could be him. I'd have to show it to my witness to be sure." Doug checked the third photo, now convinced that the second one was likely their man. "Who is he?"

"Rafi Abba. He's assigned to a unit out of Camp Pendleton, but he's been working here in the D.C. area for the past three years. He's the man who tried to recruit Bluebird."

"Somehow, he knows Bluebird is feeding you information."

"How did you find out about Bluebird? Who is your witness?"

"A thirteen-year-old girl named Reagan. Her stepfather is Laith Mansour. From what Reagan has told us, it sounds like Mansour is not only Abba's accomplice but is likely one of the masterminds behind the attack."

"Are you sure you can trust her?" Simon asked skeptically.

"She doesn't have any reason to lie," Doug said, instantly defensive. "They were planning on using her to deliver a bomb to the hotel. When she refused, they tried to kill her."

"Where is she now?"

"I have her in protective custody." Doug held up the photo again. "Can I get a copy to show her? If you want, you can even do a lineup sheet."

"That won't be necessary. I don't think any of us doubt that this is the man behind the planned attack." He shook his head. "The question is how do we proceed? Since we're talking about a threat on U.S. soil, obviously, the FBI will take the lead, but I do want my people involved."

"With this happening in three days, we can use the help," Doug said.

"In that case, let's compare notes and figure out how we can stop this thing."

Chapter 12

Jill walked into her bedroom and found Doug sitting up in bed, a notepad in one hand, a pen in the other, and a scatter of notes on his lap and bedside table. "I thought you said you weren't going to bring your work to bed with you anymore."

"I'm not." Doug glanced up at her. "As soon as this case is over."

"Do you want to talk about it?"

Rather than answer her, he asked, "How was Young Women's? Did Reagan have fun?"

"She did." Jill kicked her shoes off. "Jasmine has been really sweet to make sure Reagan is included, and the other girls seem to be pretty accepting of her. It's nice to see."

Doug looked at her suspiciously. "You sound like you're getting pretty attached."

Jill turned to face him, her eyebrows lifting. "Aren't you?"

"What do you mean?"

"I mean, you take her out shooting nearly every day, and you spend all day with her."

"Yeah, because she's our main source of information on the people trying to create terror two days from now," Doug said edgily.

Jill ignored his defensive tone. "It may have started out that way, but you can't fool me. You care about Reagan, and not just because of what she knows about your case."

"Of course I care. She's a good kid." His shoulder jerked up. "But that doesn't mean I'm ready to parent a teenage girl."

"I think you already are," Jill said. She dressed for bed and climbed in next to him. "What's going on with this case? Can you talk to me about it?"

"I can't tell you much. This case took a turn I hadn't expected." He seemed to consider for a moment. Then he laid his notebook down and sighed. "It looks like the whole bombing and mass shooting is really a front. We think Laith and the colonel are going after a specific target. We know who the target is now, and we can keep him safe without these guys knowing we're onto them. We fully expect they'll go forward with their plans."

"You still haven't found Laith?"

Doug shook his head. "He hasn't been seen since the day Reagan ran away from him."

Jill put a hand on Doug's arm and said sympathetically, "You're worried."

"If we can't find these guys before Saturday, Max wants me to bring Reagan up to our temporary control center so she can help us try to identify the players."

"You can't let them take Reagan up there." Jill sat up in bed and shifted to face him more fully. "If Laith or the colonel finds her, they'll try to kill her."

"I know." Doug let out a frustrated sigh. "We'll take every precaution, but Max is right. She may be the only person who can help us find the men we haven't yet identified."

"I don't like it." Jill shook her head. "She's finally starting to feel safe. I don't know if she can handle facing these men again, even if she only has to see them on video."

"I agree, but she volunteered."

Jill's jaw dropped. "What?"

"She's determined to stop them." His statement held pride. "Like I said, she's a good kid. We just have to pray we can find these guys before they have a chance to strike. That way she won't have to face all of these demons from her past."

"I've definitely got the praying part covered."

"I figured you did." Doug leaned forward and pressed his lips to Jill's. "I love you, you know."

"Yeah, I know." Jill reached for his hand and gave it a squeeze. "And I think you love your new daughter too."

Doug shook his head. "Jill, don't do that. I'm not ready to think about what happens next, not until we get through this weekend."

"Just promise me you'll consider letting Reagan stay," Jill said, a flutter of excitement rippling through her. "I'm starting to think that maybe she's one of the answers to our prayers."

"You seem to have forgotten that we weren't exactly praying for the same things before Reagan showed up."

"We're praying for the same things now," Jill said softly. "Please at least promise you'll think about it."

"I'll think about it." Doug's eyes met hers. "Later."

* * *

Reagan heard the doorbell, followed by Doug's footsteps heading for the entryway. Quietly, she slipped out of her bedroom and made her way to her usual spot in the hall so she could hear what was going on. She hated not knowing what was happening, and she suspected something had changed yesterday when she hadn't been around.

Doug's stress level had been steadily rising for the past week, but his meeting with the senator yesterday afternoon seemed to have left him even more on edge. She had been so focused on her ride with Katherine and the new books Katherine had sent home with her that she hadn't noticed the extra tension until they'd started their drive home. Then the silence had been nearly unbearable.

Reagan had even dared to ask Doug if something was wrong, but he had just said he had a lot on his mind. That had ended the conversation.

She had to admit that she had been relieved to get out of the house with Jill last night for the Church activity. It was nice spending that hour or two pretending her life was normal, pretending she didn't know what was about to happen.

Before she had gone with Jill the first time, Doug had made her promise that she wouldn't talk about what she knew with anyone. Not that she would anyway. After all, who would believe her? She was still amazed that Doug and Jill believed everything she had told them, that they trusted her to tell the truth.

She recognized the lowered voices now, both Doug's and Hector's. She edged closer to the doorway.

She had a feeling Doug knew she was always listening, but he hadn't ever told her to stop. Besides, she wanted to make sure she didn't miss anything.

"We're all set," Hector told Doug. "We have two rooms in the hotel where the shooting is expected to take place. One is on the second floor just up the stairs from the banquet hall. It's one of the rooms the CIA had reserved for Bluebird. If anyone comes looking for him there, our agents will be ready."

"And the second room?"

"Because of the anime convention, the only other room we could get was the presidential suite. That's where we'll be setting up our taskforce headquarters."

"Are the surveillance vans in place?" Doug asked.

"Yeah. We have one disguised as a maid service van inside the parking garage near the elevator. Then we have two more at opposite corners of the building. The imagery is feeding up to the equipment in the presidential suite," Hector told him. "We also have agents interspersed throughout a two-block radius to keep an eye out for any of our suspects."

"What about Bluebird?"

"The CIA wanted to put him in a safe house, but he refused. He said he wants to be there to help identify these guys. He's already moved into our hotel suite, and he'll stay there until we get through this."

"That's gutsy," Doug commented. "I would have thought he'd want to stay out of the line of fire, especially since we think he's the real target."

"I thought so too, but this guy is determined to help us stop this attack before anyone gets hurt. Besides, no one will know he's there. If anyone looks for him, they'll go to the room on the second floor, where we have people waiting for them."

"Still no sign of any of our suspects?"

"Not yet. If we're right, they'll show up sometime today. The vendors have already started setting up, but so far, we haven't seen anyone in costume," Hector told him. "According to the event coordinator, attendees can start picking up their passes at seven o'clock tonight. The lines for the actual event usually start up around four in the morning."

"Great," Doug muttered. Reagan could hear him shuffling papers before he continued. "According to the CIA, the Bluebird meeting was scheduled for seven o'clock on Saturday night, and it was expected to last for several hours." He paused for a moment again, and Reagan strained to hear to make sure she wasn't missing something. Then she heard Doug's voice again. "Logically, these guys would make their move a little after the meeting is scheduled to start. That way they'd be sure Bluebird is already there."

"I agree. They would also have an easy time blending in around then since that's dinnertime and plenty of the convention goers will be walking around town, going out for something to eat," Hector said. "We have our undercover guys in place with the hotel staff. No one besides our agents and the hotel manager will have access to the conference room, so we'll know if they try to plant any kind of explosives."

"Have our guys already done an initial sweep to make sure something isn't already planted there?"

"They should be finishing that up now," Hector told him. "Are you ready to head up there? Max wants you on scene."

"Let me call Jill. I'll see if she can get a substitute teacher so she can take off the rest of today. I don't want to leave Reagan here alone."

"Okay. Let me know if you have a problem. Otherwise, I'll see you over there in an hour or so."

Reagan heard the two men walk to the front door. Then she heard Doug walking back toward the kitchen.

"Reagan, you can come out now."

She froze, not prepared to go out and face Doug and the truth that she had been spying on him. Mustering her courage, she emerged from the hall and gave him a sheepish look.

Doug just stared at her, his eyebrows lifted in that cocky look of his. "I'm assuming you heard all of that so I don't need to tell you what's going on."

"Why can't I come with you today?" she asked. "I might be able to help."

"Honestly, I'm hoping we can find these guys before Saturday so you won't have to go to the hotel at all." Doug picked the house phone up off of the kitchen counter. "This isn't fun and games. It can be dangerous."

"I know that," Reagan said, even though she didn't want to think about that part. She just wanted to stay with Doug, where she felt safe. "But I want to help."

"You can help by staying where I know you're safe." Before she could object further, Doug said, "One of the reasons I'm going to Crystal City today is to check out the layout of the hotel to make sure we can get you inside without putting you in danger."

Resigned, she watched Doug call Jill and listened to him work out the logistics of how soon Jill could come home. As soon as he hung up, Reagan said, "You're going to be careful, right?"

He reached over and gave her arm a squeeze. "Kiddo, I'm always careful."

She took a deep breath and let it out. "I was just checking."

Chapter 13

"ZOOM IN ON THAT GUY." Doug pointed at the computer screen, where the surveillance video was visible. The man known only as Bluebird stood beside him, watching the screen as well.

Aaron Lithcombe, the computer tech, did as he was asked, zooming in on the image Doug indicated. Before Doug could comment, Bluebird shook his head. "That's not one of them. He's too short."

Doug shifted his attention to the bulletin board situated on an easel in the corner of the room. On it were four sets of images. Using the composite sketches that had been created with Reagan's help, the CIA and Bluebird had identified the remaining suspects.

Except for Laith, all three of the other suspects were currently serving in the military. One of them, Ferran Sarabi, was Naval intelligence and had been involved in supporting Bluebird in his intelligence gathering efforts. No one was quite sure if he had already been involved with Jihadist extremists when he'd started with the operation or if he had been converted sometime in the past couple of years and then had started feeding information to Laith and his co-conspirators. Regardless, they were quite certain he was the source of the leak.

"Wait. Back that one up," Bluebird said, his voice taking on a sense of urgency.

Doug turned and looked at the screen. The tall man walking along the sidewalk was dressed in some sort of dark-colored robe, making him look like a cross between the grim reaper and cartoon royalty. Doug's focus narrowed when he saw the thick staff gripped in his right hand. "That prop is long enough and thick enough to hide a weapon, but with his mask on, there's no way to be sure who he is."

Bluebird nodded. "Look at the way he's walking though. Everyone else is checking out the other costumes, and most of them have those badges for the anime convention hanging around their necks."

"Our guy doesn't have one." A sense of anticipation hummed through him.

Aaron zoomed in on the man's staff. "He could just be going to the costume party down the street. We know there's one at the Hyatt tonight."

Doug shook his head. "He looks like he's checking out the area rather than the people."

Aaron shifted in his seat to look at Doug. "Do you want me to have one of our units pick him up?"

Bluebird shook his head before Doug could respond. "If we pick him up and the others notice, there's no telling what they might do. We need to bring him in without them realizing we're onto them."

Doug agreed with his logic, but he was also anxious to put this guy in custody, where they could be sure he wasn't a danger to anyone. The last thing he wanted was for this investigation to stretch out another night. If they couldn't identify all of the players tonight, he knew Reagan would end up sitting here with him tomorrow. "Do you have any suggestions?"

"I bet we could come up with something." Bluebird nodded.

Doug noticed someone stop a girl dressed as Pikachu and then point down the street. "I think I have an idea." He looked at Aaron. "Have our guys track him, and tell Hector I need him up here. We'll need a few minutes."

"Okay. You got it."

* * *

"I look ridiculous." Hector gave Doug a pleading look from beneath a wide-brimmed straw hat. "Please tell me I don't have to go out in public like this."

Doug fought back a grin as Alicia, another one of their agents, leaned down to cuff the bright blue pants of the anime costume she had prepared for just such an emergency. The red shirt wouldn't have been so bad, but set against the bright yellow sash tied around Hector's waist, it made him look like he could have stepped out of a pirate cartoon.

Alicia stood. "Stop whining," she said, stepping back to admire her handiwork. She glanced over at Doug. "I think that's as good as it's going to get."

"Why do I have to be in costume?"

"Because." Doug didn't offer any explanation beyond the single word. "Are you ready?"

Hector let out a long-suffering sigh. "Let's get this over with."

"Okay." Doug looked over at Alicia and asked, "You know what to do?"

"I've got this." She nodded and held up her hand to show a miniature tranquilizer dart fastened to the palm of her glove. She moved toward the hotel room door. "Come on, Hector. Let's see how convincing you can be."

Hector followed her but turned and looked at Doug before opening the door. "Just know, you are going to pay for this."

"Have fun, kids," Doug said sarcastically. He watched them leave, ignoring the exasperated look Hector shot his way, and then shifted to stand beside Bluebird to watch the current images. "Do we still have our guy in sight?"

"Yeah. He walked by our hotel, and now it looks like he's circling around again." Aaron looked up at Doug. "Maybe this guy really is just someone who's lost."

"Where's his staff?"

"What?" Aaron zoomed in to reveal that the character in question was no longer carrying any props. "He must have stashed it somewhere."

"He really could be involved. We figured these guys might use today to plant weapons in preparation for tomorrow."

"Hector is asking whether you want them to proceed," Aaron said.

Doug looked over at Bluebird, seeing the same determination in his eyes that he was sure his own mirrored. "Proceed."

Two minutes later, Alicia appeared on the edge of the screen when she took her position several yards behind their suspect. Then Hector stepped into their suspect's path. The robed figure tried to step around him, shaking his head when Hector spoke to him. Even on the screen, Doug could sense the man's nervousness, an emotional overreaction to someone asking for simple directions.

As planned, Hector blocked his path and continued to try to engage him. He succeeded in slowing him down long enough for Alicia to close the distance between them. When she was only a few feet away, she appeared to stumble and slap a hand on their suspect to keep her balance. The tranquilizer dart hidden on her glove did its job, and a few seconds later, the man fell to the ground.

* * *

"You can't let her go with you." Jill crossed her arms and straightened her shoulders. "Doug, it's too dangerous."

"You think I'm happy about this?" Doug's voice took on an edge. "I don't have a choice. We only managed to identify one suspect yesterday, and he's not talking. That leaves three more unaccounted for, three more people who pose a serious threat."

Jill's chest tightened. She understood that Reagan had come to live with them because of the past she had suffered, because she knew things these potential gunmen didn't want her to know. But that logic paled behind Jill's protective instincts and her overwhelming desire to keep Reagan close. "She's just a kid."

"No, Jill. She's not just a kid. She's the girl who might just be able to stop a mass shooting before anyone gets hurt." Doug raked both hands through his short, dark hair. "I don't like this any more than you do. If there were another way, I'd jump at it. Unfortunately, I don't have a choice in the matter. Max said I have to bring her in."

She recognized the weariness of Doug's gesture and realized he was as conflicted as she was. Jill also knew her concerns weren't just for Reagan but for Doug as well. For their entire marriage, she had faced the reality that someday Doug might walk out of their house and never come home again. She tried not to think about it, but today, she couldn't stop the worst-case scenarios from racing through her mind. Today, she had so much more to lose.

Biting back the swirl of emotions, she wrapped her arms around his waist. "I'm scared."

"I know." Doug pulled her close, and Jill suspected his emotions were in as much upheaval as her own. "I'll keep her safe."

"Keep yourself safe too."

"I will." He edged back and looked down at her. "I'll call you as soon as we're on our way home."

Jill clung to his waist, not quite ready to let him go. Doug indulged her, keeping his arms around her while a minute stretched into two. Then she tipped her head back, reached up, and kissed him. The kiss was meant to soothe, but she could feel a tangle of underlying emotions swirling through both of them.

When she pulled back, she reached down and squeezed his hand. "I'll be praying for you tonight."

"I appreciate that," Doug said. "I'll take all the help I can get."

Chapter 14

"I DON'T LIKE THIS," DOUG said, worry curling uncomfortably in his stomach. He had done what his boss had demanded and brought Reagan into FBI headquarters to prepare for the stakeout this afternoon. Reagan had told him Laith was planning to strike on a Saturday night, but he never imagined she would end up personally involved in helping prevent it. Unfortunately, with every minute that passed, he felt more pressed to shield Reagan from anything that might put her in danger.

Max gave him a knowing look. "None of us are thrilled that we weren't able to stop this before now."

"There's got to be a way we can do this without Reagan there. She should be home, where she's safe."

"She doesn't have a home," Max reminded him. "And she isn't going to be safe until Laith and his co-conspirators are in custody."

Doug instantly thought of Reagan's bedroom in his home, of the jacket hanging on her doorknob, the shoes on the floor, and books on her bedside table. For the first few days after she'd arrived, he might have still considered that room a guest room, but somewhere along the line, it had become Reagan's room, and his home had become Reagan's home.

Max must have sensed the turmoil and concern swirling inside him because his tone held understanding when he continued. "Doug, you know as well as I do that we need her. There's no way we're going to be able to identify these guys without her. She's seen all of the players, and she knows what the costumes look like. She's our best chance of stopping this thing before it turns deadly."

"It's possible they changed the costumes after Reagan ran away."

"Which is even more reason that she might be the only one to recognize them."

Even though his protective instincts urged him to protest further, he knew Max's words were true. He gave a resigned nod. "I know you're right." He considered for a minute. "I want her to wear a vest though."

"I doubt she'll need it since we'll keep her in the hotel suite, out of sight, but Alicia is taking care of it. We're taking every precaution we can think of."

"I still don't like it."

"None of us do." Max gestured toward the door.

Doug turned to see Alicia leading Reagan into the room. He wouldn't have recognized her had he not been living with her for the past few weeks. Alicia had outfitted her with a costume to help disguise her in case Laith or his friends caught a glimpse of her. She wore dark pants and a white dress shirt, black tie, and teal blazer. Her hair was tucked up under a short black wig.

He tried to fight the unsettled feeling that wouldn't go away. "Are you all set?"

Reagan nodded. She was good at hiding her emotions, and he could tell she was trying hard to keep everyone from seeing her fear. But he saw it.

"You don't have to do this, you know."

"Yeah, I do." She drew a deep breath and gave him a long, level look. "You said yourself that I'm your best chance of finding these guys."

Doug put a hand on her shoulder and gave her a reassuring squeeze. "This will all be over soon."

"Let's get this show on the road," Max said.

* * *

"We're almost there. Keep an eye out for anyone who looks familiar," Doug said as they passed the Pentagon City mall.

Reagan looked over at him, noting that he was wearing the clothes he normally wore to church. "How come you aren't in costume?"

"I'll be staying up in the command center with you, so I don't really need to blend in with the street scene."

"Yeah, but Laith might recognize you." A flash of concern sounded in her voice. "You did shoot at him."

"I doubt he would be able to pick me out of a crowd. He never got close enough to get a good look at me, just like I barely saw him through the trees."

"I guess." Reagan stared out the window, noticing the Halloween decorations on the various homes and businesses they passed. A fake graveyard had been set up in one yard, complete with creepy figures hanging from the tree behind it. Another yard had jack-o-lanterns lining the sidewalk, the odd-shaped faces flickering with candlelight.

Doug turned another corner, and suddenly, the sidewalks seemed flooded with people in costume.

Six teenagers dressed up like anime characters crowded the sidewalk as they spoke excitedly. A couple in their early twenties dressed as some kind of samurais tried to push past them.

Two more people dressed as Star Wars characters, complete with masks, posed outside a restaurant while someone snapped a picture of them.

"This isn't going to be easy," Doug muttered, but Reagan couldn't tell if he was talking to her or to himself.

"How are we supposed to find them with all of these people around?" Reagan asked.

"We have surveillance vans around the hotel, and we're tapped into the hotel security cameras. You'll have a lot of video feed to look at in the hotel room, but you won't be the only one searching."

"I just want this over with so we can go home," Reagan admitted.

"That makes two of us," Doug agreed. He drove slowly as they passed the parade of pedestrians. He stopped at a red light, and Reagan continued to stare out the window, overwhelmed by the crowds.

"Anything?" Doug asked.

"I don't think so."

Doug's phone rang, and he hit the button to put the call on speaker. "Valdez."

"Doug, we've spotted one of the suspects. Ferran Sarabi is dressed up like a ninja, and he's a half block from the hotel."

"We're only three blocks away."

"Sarabi is near the front entrance. If you drive around the back of the hotel to get to the parking garage, you'll miss the action."

"Got it." Doug turned on his blinker to make a right turn. "Call me back when you have him in custody."

"Will do."

Doug ended the call and gave Reagan a hopeful look. "That's one down. Only two more."

"Laith and the colonel," Reagan said, stating the obvious.

"Yeah." Doug nodded. "Laith and the colonel."

* * *

Doug shook his head in frustration. Dozens of federal agents littered the area, and somehow, their suspect had managed to escape them.

"They're still in pursuit," Max said as Doug pulled into a parking spot three rows away from the elevators leading to the hotel. "Is Alicia with you?"

"She just pulled in behind me."

"Let her know what's going on. I'll get back to you as soon as I know anything."

Doug turned off the engine and climbed out of the car. Reagan followed suit and stood awkwardly while Alicia parked beside them and then approached Doug.

"What's going on?"

"Our guys spotted one of the suspects, and they're in pursuit," Doug told her. "Can you take Reagan upstairs? I'm going to make sure no one followed us here."

"Sure."

Doug nodded at Reagan. "Go with Alicia. I'll be up in a minute."

Wordlessly, Reagan let herself be led through the cars toward the elevators. Doug shifted his attention, alert for any movement. He noticed an older couple heading for their car, the man taking the time to open the door for his wife before circling around to get in.

Doug worked his way along the rows of cars, glancing back when the couple's sedan started toward the exit. That's when he caught a quick blur of movement.

For a second, he thought he'd imagined it, but as he continued staring, he saw it again, along with a flash of color moving toward the elevators, where Alicia and Reagan were now standing.

"Watch out!" Doug shouted just as the man known as the colonel emerged with a gun in his hand.

At the shouted warning, Alicia whirled to face the colonel, but she was still in the motion of drawing her weapon when the colonel struck his hand out and knocked her to the ground.

Reagan screamed, the colonel now turning his gun toward her.

Doug rushed forward, unable to take a shot of his own because of the concrete pillars standing between him and the colonel.

He saw Alicia kick, knocking the colonel to the ground, the colonel's gun skittering across the concrete floor.

Then, to his amazement, Reagan reached down and picked up the weapon, aiming like he'd taught her right at the man who had a moment before been threatening her life.

The elevator doors slid open, and Reagan stumbled back into the open elevator car. Doug couldn't tell if she was trying to escape or just trying to put some distance between her and the man trying to kill her.

Regardless, she continued to aim the gun at the colonel, leaving him frozen in place long enough for Alicia to regain control of her weapon and the suspect.

The elevator doors slid closed before Doug could stop them.

"Go!" Alicia jerked her head toward the stairwell door. "I've got him."

Doug didn't have to be told twice. He pushed the door open and raced up the stairs.

* * *

Reagan would have felt ridiculous standing in the elevator, dressed like a cartoon character, but she was too scared to care at the moment. Every one of her nerves burned inside of her, and she felt like she couldn't even see straight. She didn't realize she was still aiming the gun at the elevator doors until they slid open on the first floor and the two girls dressed like Sailor Moon characters took one look at her and screamed.

Reagan could feel her cheeks flush, and she lowered the gun to her side. The elevator doors started to slide closed, and she instinctively put a hand out to stop them. She didn't know where she should go now, but she was sure she didn't want to go back downstairs to face the colonel.

She looked at the buttons on the elevator, realizing that this one didn't go any higher than the lobby. She could see the bank of elevators just across from her that presumably led upstairs, but she wasn't sure how to get to the suite Doug had told her about, where the FBI was set up.

She could feel tears threatening as emotions bubbled up inside of her—fear, adrenaline, and so many others she couldn't name.

She drew a deep breath and then another. Surely Doug would come find her. He would know that she needed him to keep her safe.

With a great deal of effort, she forced herself to take a step forward and then another. She would wait in the lobby until Doug came. And then everything would be okay.

Chapter 15

Doug burst through the stairwell door onto the first floor and raced toward the lobby. Across a wide hallway, he saw Reagan emerge from where he knew the elevators were located. She still clutched a gun in her hand, but her arm was hanging by her side.

His sense of relief lasted only for a heartbeat because as he took in the rest of the scene, he spotted a man in a delivery uniform, a package in one hand. The man would have looked harmless enough if his face hadn't been so familiar. Less than twenty yards away stood the man he had been searching for, the man he had sworn to keep away from Reagan.

Laith Mansour didn't notice him or anyone else in the lobby. He was too busy staring at Reagan, a look of stunned rage on his face.

The next few seconds could have come straight out of Doug's worst nightmare. Laith set the box down on a chair in the lobby, and then his right hand disappeared beneath the jacket he wore.

Doug surged forward when he saw that same hand whip out, a gun now gripped in it. He shouted at the room in general, but his eyes stayed focused on Reagan. "Get down!"

Reagan didn't drop. She simply froze, her eyes wide, the gun gripped in her own hand remaining by her side.

A silent prayer raced through Doug's mind. His hope that the dozen civilians in the lobby would simply drop to the ground and give him a clear shot didn't materialize. Instead, he was faced with a mad chaos as people screamed and scrambled between Laith and him.

Aware that he wouldn't be able to reach Laith in time to prevent a shot, he sprinted toward Reagan. He knew Reagan's vital organs were protected by body armor, but Laith wasn't aiming at her heart. He was aiming at her head.

Laith's shot sounded just as Doug lunged in front of Reagan, one of his arms hooking around her waist so he could pull her to the ground. An instant before they crashed to the floor, his body jerked where a bullet impacted his own bulletproof vest, pain shooting through his chest.

He struggled to lift his weapon to take aim at Laith before he could fire again, but before he could manage it, another shot rang out, and Laith dropped to the ground. Standing a short distance away was a brightly dressed pirate, a straw hat on his head and a gun in his hand.

Hector rushed toward Laith, disarming him and checking for a pulse.

Doug lowered his weapon and let himself lie back on the floor. He turned his head to see Reagan staring at him, her eyes wide, her breathing rapid. Though it pained him to do so, he reached out and grasped her hand. "Are you okay?"

She didn't answer at first, as though her mind was still trying to catch up with what had just happened.

Before Doug could repeat his question, several of his fellow agents rushed into the room. Out of the corner of his eye, Doug noticed the bomb squad enter, their attention solely on the package Laith had been carrying, while other agents began evacuating the civilians. Max was the first to make it through the crowd to where Doug and Reagan were still on the floor. "Where are you hit?"

"I took one in the chest." He winced when he tried to take a deep breath. "It hurts like mad, but I'm okay."

"How about you?" Max asked Reagan. "Are you hurt?"

Reagan looked bewildered now, her eyes shifting from Doug to Max. "He jumped in front of me." The knowledge that Laith had nearly succeeded in killing her was reflected in her eyes. "He got shot for me."

"I'm okay, Reagan." Despite the throbbing in his ribs, Doug forced himself to sit up. "We're both okay now."

Max gave Doug a hand and pulled him up to a stand. He then did the same to Reagan. "The other suspect is in custody. Jerry is taking him in now."

"That's good news," Doug said with relief.

"Is it over?" Reagan asked, her voice teary. "Can we go home now?"

"Yeah." Doug nodded. "We can go home."

* * *

Jill peeked into Reagan's room to see her burrowed in her blankets, her body relaxed in sleep. She still couldn't quite visualize what had happened the night before, not because she hadn't been given the details but rather because the images were so terrifying that she didn't want to let them form.

Doug's boss had insisted he make a stop at the local emergency room before allowing him to come home. Thankfully, he hadn't broken anything, though Jill suspected the bruising and stiffness would bother him for the next week or two.

Reagan whimpered in her sleep and then rolled over, pulling her blanket firmly beneath her chin once more. Jill's heart swelled with love. A mother's love.

She wanted to soothe, to protect. She wanted to help this girl learn how to leave the nightmares behind and find the courage to face the future. Mostly, Jill wanted to be part of that future.

She loved the idea of watching Reagan expand her interests and friendships, of standing on the sidelines of whatever activities she might choose to participate in. Mostly, though, she wanted moments like this one, when she could simply enjoy knowing that she could be part of a child's life.

With a sigh, Jill pulled Reagan's door shut and started down the hall. She hadn't quite figured out how to broach the subject with Doug about adopting Reagan. She knew he wasn't thrilled with the prospect of adoption in general, but surely his feelings had changed over the past few days. She had seen how sensitive he had been to Reagan's needs last night when they'd returned home and the way he'd gotten up every couple hours to make sure she was okay.

Jill walked into the kitchen and started lining up the ingredients she would need to make french toast for breakfast. She was just putting the first pieces on the hot griddle when Doug stumbled into the kitchen, a day's worth of beard shadowing his face, a look of pain in his eyes.

"Did you take any pain meds yet?"

He shook his head. "I wanted to get something in my stomach first."

"This will be ready in a few minutes."

Doug opened the refrigerator and grabbed the orange juice. He poured himself a glass, guzzled it down, and then filled the glass again.

Even though Jill was anxious to talk to Doug about their future with Reagan, she bided her time, waiting until he had a plateful of breakfast in front of him and had downed a couple of his over-the-counter pain pills.

She finished making the french toast, setting some aside for Reagan and fixing herself a plate while waiting for the pain meds to take effect.

Then she put her plate on the table and slid into her seat next to Doug. "I want to talk to you about Reagan."

Doug finished chewing the bite in his mouth and gave her a nod. "Yeah, about that."

"Yes?"

"She's been pretty traumatized through this whole ordeal. I don't know that it would be good for her to go into foster care right now."

Hope bloomed inside of Jill. She took a breath and reached over to put her hand on top of Doug's. She waited until his eyes lifted to meet hers before she dared to speak. "Doug, I don't want her to go into foster care. Ever."

He was silent for a moment, his eyes dark and unreadable. Then he drew a deep breath and said, "You want to keep her."

"Yes." Jill squeezed his hand. "I want to keep her."

He stared at Jill for a long moment, but she didn't see resistance in his expression like she had expected. Instead, she saw uncertainty followed by a glimmer of anticipation. The corner of his mouth twitched as though he was trying to keep from smiling, and he tugged on her hand to draw her closer as he stood to face her. "In that case, congratulations, Mrs. Valdez. It's a girl."

"Really?" Her excitement was uncontainable. "You're okay with us adopting Reagan?"

"I am." The smile he had been suppressing broke free, and Jill was amazed to see the elation she felt evident on her husband's face too. "Of course, that's assuming it's what she wants."

Then, to Jill's surprise, Doug turned toward the hallway. "What do you think, Reagan? Are you ready to be an official part of the family?"

Jill looked at him, confused. "She's still sleeping."

"No, she's not." Doug tilted his head toward the hall, a smug look on his face.

To Jill's surprise, Reagan peeked around the corner, her expression caught somewhere between embarrassment and delight.

Jill looked from Reagan to Doug and back again. "You were spying on us?"

"She's pretty good at it," Doug told her before Reagan could respond. "So what do you say? Can we be your new parents?"

"I can be a Valdez?"

"Absolutely." Jill crossed to give her a hug. "Welcome to the family."

The doorbell rang before Reagan could respond, though the delighted wonder on her face said it all. Doug pushed back from the table. "I'll get it."

A moment later, he reappeared with the bishop.

"Bishop Chandler. What brings you by?" Jill asked.

"I wanted a chance to talk to you and Doug before church. I've been wanting to meet with you for the last few weeks, but our schedules haven't lined up."

"Is everything okay?" Jill asked.

"Yes, but I have a calling I want to extend." He looked over at Reagan as though noticing for the first time that she was in the room.

"You remember our daughter, Reagan, right?"

"Your daughter?" The bishop looked from Doug to Jill, confused.

Doug nodded, a hint of a smile evident on his face. "We'll start the official adoption paperwork this week."

"Congratulations." The bishop's shoulders seemed to relax slightly. "In that case, this new calling may work out better with your schedule than I thought." He paused for a moment, focusing on Jill. "Sister Valdez, I would like for you to be our new Young Women president."

"Me?" Jill's eyes widened, and she looked at Doug to gauge his reaction.

Doug held up both hands. "Don't look at me. It's your decision."

She looked back at Bishop Chandler. "Are you sure about this?"

"There are only a few times when I've been absolutely certain about who should be in a calling," the bishop told her. "This is one of those times."

Somewhat bewildered and clearly overwhelmed, she looked at Doug once more. He shrugged and said, "I'll support whatever you decide, but I'm sure you would do a great job."

Then Reagan stepped forward. Her words were tentative, but there was a smile on her face. "Don't worry, Mom. I'll help you out."

Jill blinked back the tears that welled up in her eyes. Her heart bursting with joy, she reached out and pulled Reagan into a hug. Offering the bishop a watery smile, she said simply, "In that case, we accept."

About the Author

ORIGINALLY FROM ARIZONA, TRACI HUNTER Abramson has spent most of her adult life in Virginia. She is a graduate of Brigham Young University and a former employee of the Central Intelligence Agency. Since leaving the CIA, Traci has written several novels, including the Undercurrents trilogy, the Royal books, *Obsession*, the Saint Squad series, *Deep Cover*, and *Chances Are*.

When she's not writing, Traci enjoys spending time with her family and coaching the local high school swim teams.

THE DEATH HOUSE

◆ GREGG LUKE ◆

To my brother, Lemar,
an all-around great guy

Acknowledgments

As with all my works, I have a few choice individuals who are brave enough to risk emotional duress and possible brain damage by slogging through the first drafts of my mindless wanderings. *The Death House* is no exception. I'd like to thank Tom and Brooke Ballard, Melissa Duce, Dawn Bergesen, Jacob Luke, and Juliana Luke for helping me make the story work. I'd also like to sincerely thank the editors at Covenant whose meticulous diligence helped craft this into a much better story. Written in first person with a YA tone, this novella is different from anything else I've written but still carries my bizarre flavor of suspense. I hope you enjoy trying to figure out what haunts the Death House.

Chapter 1

EVERYONE WHO KNEW ABOUT THE old Collier mansion called it the Death House. I could see the creepy, rundown manor from my bedroom window some two hundred yards away. But that meant it could see me too. The stare down began July, 30, 2012, the day after we moved here. And I knew it wouldn't end until one of us was destroyed.

In spite of its name, the Death House wasn't a mausoleum, nor was it a place where the state of Nevada carried out capital punishment. It was just a big, abandoned house where a gruesome, still-unsolved double death had occurred. Almost everyone said the place was haunted. Some people said it was cursed. That's why everyone stayed away from it—especially at night. And that's why I decided it was up to me to find out what had really happened there.

The truth was, I wasn't convinced the manor was anything other than a dilapidated old house. But until I explored it, I couldn't be sure. It was more than simple teenage curiosity; my fascination with the Collier mansion bordered on obsession. For reasons I couldn't explain, I felt compelled to explore it, drawn to it by some unseen, unrelenting force, as if it were up to me to solve the murders and prevent them from happening again.

"I think you're criminally insane," wrestling captain Shane Memmott said, sneering.

He probably meant *certifiably* insane. I hadn't committed any crime— by reason of insanity or otherwise—but I didn't want to argue the point. With Shane, it rarely did any good.

Eight of us sat around a peninsula at the Rexall drugstore's '50s-era soda counter. We met there every Wednesday and Saturday evening. Shane made his flawed diagnosis to the group after my announcement that I'd be exploring the town's infamous haunted house.

"Anyone goes in the Death House and they're *corpus crispy*. That's Latin for 'burnt meat.'"

In addition to being wrestling captain, Shane was also a self-proclaimed know-it-all. However, like most know-it-alls, he actually knew very little. The idiotic nonsense he continually spewed baffled me. He claimed he was going to Harvard Law School someday. Fat chance. Yet, because his biceps were bigger than his brain, no one ever told him he was wrong.

"No, it doesn't. Corpus Christi is a city in Texas," I explained with only a hint of a snicker.

The other teens gawked at me, apparently shocked that I'd corrected the big guy.

"Besides," I added quickly, "I'm not afraid. It's just a dusty old house. I don't believe in ghosts or curses or anything like that."

Shane barked out a laugh and slapped the countertop. "I got a dollar says Smut won't go in the Death House." He called me Smut because my real name is Smoot. His derivation was only one of a thousand I'd heard over the years. It didn't faze me.

"Wow. A whole dollar, huh?" I scoffed.

"Yeah, because I know you won't do it."

"Have *you* gone in there?"

His smug expression faltered. "'Course not. I ain't stupid, stupid."

"Then how do you know it's haunted? Have you seen the ghosts?"

"Well, no. But a lot of people around here have. And we've all heard the noises and smelled the smells."

Murmurs of concurrence came from six of our group. The seventh was a stout Paiute Indian boy we called Bug. He wore thick glasses that made his eyes look like an insect's. Always content simply to sit and listen, Bug rarely said anything.

"Have *any* of you been inside?" I asked.

They all found sudden fascination with their soft drinks. Not even Bug made eye contact.

"No? Great, then I'll be the first."

"And the last," Shane said with another sneer.

"Dude, that place has death written all over it. You couldn't pay me to go in," a pudgy boy we all called Bucky said. His real name was Buckthorn, or something equally humiliating. His twin brother went by Rocky. It was less painful than Throckmorton. Why do parents do that to their kids?

"Seriously, man, that place freaks me out," Rocky said.

"Nah, he's just joking. You—you're just joking, right, Adam?" Earl said in a high, shaky voice. Pasty-faced and twitchy, Earl always seemed to be on the verge of a full-on panic attack. Talking about ghosts and haunted houses didn't help any.

"Nope, no joke," I said confidently. "I'm gonna check it out next Wednesday night instead of coming here. Anyone in?"

The idea of merely approaching the Collier mansion turned everyone's faces as pale as Earl's. The soda pop fascination intensified.

"There's something more going on in there than ghosts and goblins," I said.

"Yeah, murder," Stephanie said darkly. Stephanie was a tall, pretty blonde. I think the only reason Shane came to our gatherings was that she was sometimes there.

"Actually, from what I've read, a killer's never been identified, so it's not officially a murder," I argued. When no one responded, I continued. "Come on, guys. You've all lived here a lot longer than I have. You all know the story. October 13, 1912, Mr. and Mrs. Collier's severed heads were found in their pumpkin patch. Their eyes were missing, their skin was blistered, and their hair was singed off. Searches were made, but they never found their bodies."

"Or their eyes," Bucky added in a sinister voice.

Earl groaned, holding his stomach. He looked ready to throw up.

"Yeah. But what's really cool is Mrs. Collier's glass eye was still in her face," Rocky said, matching his brother's sinister tone. "Her real one had been chewed out."

Earl grimaced and placed his hands over his ears. Frankly, I'm surprised he stuck with our little gang. Perhaps he stayed because there was nothing else to do in our small desert town.

"It was *missing*, not *chewed out*," I corrected. "The point is they never found either body. So . . . what happened to them?"

"No one knows," Bucky and Rocky said in unison, grinning at each other with mischievous eyes. I worried about those two.

"And no one with any brains cares," Shane cut in, leaning his face uncomfortably close to mine. His breath smelled like Froot Loops. *Fitting.*

"Why do you want to go in there anyway?" a bob-haired brunette named Traci asked. "The place is way creepy. And I'm pretty sure it's considered trespassing."

I hesitated. I couldn't very well tell them I was *drawn* to the place, that I *needed* to find out what had really happened; that somehow I felt *responsible* for preventing it from happening again. "I'm merely curious, that's all. Look, haven't you guys ever wanted to explore the place? I mean, it's totally cool on the outside. Imagine what it looks like inside."

No one responded. The soda-staring resumed.

"I still say you're criminally insane, Smut," Shane mumbled. A few awkward chuckles followed his lame remark.

"Fine. I'm outta here," I said, raising both hands in surrender. "If you guys change your minds, let me know. See you all Monday."

Walking out of the pharmacy, I wrestled with my bullheaded determination. On the surface, I wanted to change my mind and *not* go in the derelict mansion; but deep down, I knew I would forever regret it if I didn't. It felt as if my soul was playing a dangerous game with my mind. *Some game!* It was the cruelest of ironies: I didn't *want* to go in; I *had* to go in. And the last thing I wanted to do was go in alone.

Chapter 2

OUR TOWN, SNAKELEG, NEVADA, WAS a sleepy, ex-mining town. With barely eight hundred permanent residents, it was surprisingly large for being so isolated. Located in the southern Nevada wasteland, we were a hundred miles north of Las Vegas and a few more west of St. George, Utah. In other words, the middle of nowhere. Most of the residents worked at the school, but there were just as many retired ranchers, die-hard desert dwellers, and people just hiding from humanity. My parents fell into the last category. They were doomsday preppers, fortifying against an imminent apocalypse.

Our school, Snakeleg Municipal, was a collection of mobile bungalows randomly placed around an old, three-story brick building that had once housed the Lincoln County courthouse. The placement of bungalows had no sense of balance or functionality. I guess no one really planned on the school getting as big as it did, so they simply kept wheeling in new bungalows whenever the student body grew beyond capacity.

On Monday, the school was buzzing with gossip. Rumor had it that a new family had moved into town over the weekend—a dad, a mom, and two kids, a girl and a boy. No one knew their ages, but that didn't matter because our school was the only public school for forty miles in any direction. They taught grades one through twelve there—maybe two hundred students or so. If the new kids weren't home-schooled, we'd see them sooner or later.

It ended up being sooner; they both showed up at lunchtime that afternoon. The younger students, including my little brother, had barely finished their lunch period and were exiting the cafeteria. When I walked in, I noticed a new young boy sitting by himself toward the far wall, seemingly unaware of the fact that his lunch period was over. He looked to be about eight or nine—the same age as my little brother—with a head full of unruly hair. And he looked scared to death. I quickly grabbed a meal selection and sat next to him. "Hey, you must be the new kid. Welcome to Snakeleg, man. I'm still kinda new here too. My name is Adam." I kept my tone light and casual. I know how frightening going to a new school can be. Because my parents were always looking for a safer bug-out location, this was the third high school I'd attended in as many years. *Thanks, Mom and Dad.*

The boy said nothing. He kept his eyes riveted on his meal tray.

"Listen, I have a brother about your age. His name is Zeek. He's pretty cool, even for a little brother. Maybe he can help you find your way around—"

I stopped midsentence when the cafeteria suddenly went deathly silent. Everyone was staring at a girl who'd just walked in. She looked to be about seventeen, was tall and slender, and had pale eyes and the most lustrous, dark-copper-colored hair I'd ever seen.

A meteor slamming into the middle of the cafeteria wouldn't have made a bigger impact. The guys in the cafeteria stared with mouths agape, clearly homing in on the new target. The girls all offered fake smiles while checking out her clothing and accessories. They clearly did not appreciate the new competition.

The new girl looked over the lunchroom crowd with a neutral expression, zeroed in on me and the new kid, then went to the food service window, picked up a tray and utensils, and made a meal selection.

Urgent whispers spread through the cafeteria like wind-whipped wildfire. I heard snippets of conversations around me. "Who is she?" "Her hair is so fake." "She seems stuck up." "Did you see her eyes?" "She looks bulimic." "I bet she's a slut"—this from one of the girls. "I get first dibs"—this from one of the jocks.

With a tray partially loaded with food—or what the lunch ladies *claimed* was food—the new girl made her way through the maze of tables and sat next to the boy across from me. She whispered something in his ear, then tousled his hair. The boy got up and ran from the cafeteria.

She watched him go, then frowned at her tray, and asked, "So is any of this edible?"

I didn't answer her question because I was totally dumbstruck. It was her eyes. They'd looked pale from a distance, but now that she was directly across from me, I could see how eerily colorless they were. I guess you could call them green, yet they were such an ashen, washed-out khaki-green that they were barely darker than the whites of her eyes. Were it not for a thin, dark olive ring framing each iris, they would have blended right into the whites. They really creeped me out—but in a cool, what-planet-are-you-from kind of way.

"Hello, kid? You speak-a English?"

I shook my head, loosening my brain cramp. "Uh, yeah. Of course. Sorry. I don't mean to stare, but . . . well, you've got the most—"

"I know," she interrupted with a pained sigh. "I've got strange eyes or an angel's eyes or the devil's eyes or they're hypnotic or beautiful or weird or bizarre. You name it, I've heard them all."

"I was going to say 'mesmeric.'"

She cocked her head to one side. "All except that one. I'm impressed." Her lips parted in a slight smile. "So . . . about this food?"

I shrugged. "It's pretty safe as long as you don't actually swallow. But don't expect any flavor."

The skin around her eyes crinkled with her smile.

"And if you do accidentally ingest some," I continued, "I know where you can get some ipecac to make you barf."

The smile faded, her shoulders drooped, and she casually toyed with the straw in her orange juice.

Her unfavorable reaction shattered my fragile confidence. Normally, my tongue refused to move when I tried to talk with a pretty girl. I interacted with a number of them at school—in our Rexall gang too—but rarely one-on-one. I did much better in a group. Maybe this situation had been different because *she* seemed so different. And then I let fly the *ipecac* remark. What if she really *was* bulimic? I gave her tolerance of me about three more seconds before she bolted—just like the young boy had.

But instead of leaving, she took a sip of her orange juice and said, "I hoped you'd be an okay guy."

Was that a compliment or criticism? "Uh, thanks, I think. So . . . was that your little brother?" I asked, referring to the young boy she'd whispered to. It was obvious he was; I guess I didn't know what else to say.

She didn't answer my question. Instead, she frowned, took another sip of OJ, and began picking through her meal. Feeling very uncomfortable with her nonresponse, I took a sip of water, picked at my own food, and mentally rehearsed everything I'd just said—just to make sure I hadn't offended her. *Maybe it* was *the ipecac remark . . .*

"Mesmeric," she finally said as if musing aloud. "That's a pretty big word for . . ."

Ugh! Not again!

I knew what she was going to say: that I was too young to know words like that. I got that a lot. Although I was almost sixteen, I looked like I was about thirteen. And it didn't help that I hadn't even started to shave yet. A strong breeze could blow off any mustache I could ever hope to sprout.

Wanting to validate my choice of words, I began rambling. "I have a pretty big vocabulary because I like to read. Actually, I like to read a lot. I remember a lot too, but I'm not a know-it-all, you know? Well, maybe a little. And I write for the school newspaper. One day I hope to publish a novel. Got one almost finished already. Would you like to read—uh, never mind. Sorry. You were going to say, 'For someone so young,' right? That I 'used big words for someone so young'? That's okay. It happens a lot. My mom says I look young for my age, 'cause I have an innocent face—"

Ugh. Did I actually just quote my mother?

I felt blood rush to my cheeks. Someone once told me diarrhea of the mouth indicated constipation of the brain. And there I was spewing a verbal deluge worthy of Noah, proving I suffered from severe mental impaction.

I averted my eyes and toyed with the orange putty that was supposed to be mac and cheese. "So anyway . . . that's why I know a lot of words."

"Got it," she said, grinning. "So you're basically a brainiac."

I paused a moment, if only to organize my thoughts. I didn't want to sound stupid again. "You can say 'nerd' if you like. Honestly, I'm one of the few guys in this town not offended by that label."

"If that's what you prefer." She then pushed her tray to one side and leaned back. "My name is Eve, by the way."

"Mine's Adam."

She huffed and rolled her eyes. "Oh, *that's* original."

"It's also true."

Her colorless orbs bored right through me as if trying to determine my level of honesty. "Adam."

"I swear. My name's Adam."

Her brow furrowed. Then slowly, she leaned forward. "Okay, Adam. Since you know so much, tell me, how did this town get its bizarre name?"

"Snakeleg?" I shrugged. "No one seems to know for sure. Some say an old miner found a rich silver ore vein, then got drunk in celebration, and claimed to have seen a snake with legs dancing by his campfire. Others say it's a direct translation from some Paiute Indian legend. Then there's one that claims one of the major legs of silver ore from the Comstock Lode snakes under this town."

"Really? Which do you believe?"

"Haven't really thought about it."

"Uh-huh. So what's your last name?"

"Smoot. It's Scottish. Why? What's yours?"

Her eyes narrowed for a moment. Then she nodded. "Okay. You were honest with me, so I'll be honest with you. My real name is Eventide Mudswallow. The Mudswallow part I can't help; it's from Yorkshire, I think. But Eventide? Seriously, I hate that name."

"An old family name?"

"An old church hymn: 'Abide with Me; 'Tis Eventide.' Mom claims it was going through her head when she was giving birth to me." Eve hummed a few bars, which I sort of recognized. "Anyway, Mom starts singing the first verse of the song, and right when she gets to the part, 'Behold, 'tis eventide,' *plop*, out I come. So she named me Eventide. Get it? Behold, it's Eventide?"

I tried not to snicker. "Well, it *is* original."

She huffed again. "Original, corny, and just shy of cruel and unusual punishment."

"Yeah, I've never understood why parents do stuff like that to their kids."

"Me either." Glancing at her watch, she seemed suddenly preoccupied with a more pressing concern. After a minute, she said, "Well, it was nice meeting you, Adam Smoot."

"Yeah. You too, Eve."

She stood and leaned over her uneaten food toward me. "And in case you get such a crazy notion, if you ever tell anyone what I just told you, or if I ever catch you picking on that little boy, I'll kill you." She smiled with a tilt of her head, but her pale eyes said all too clearly that she was serious. "Thanks for letting me sit with you."

I swallowed hard. "Um, you're welcome?"

She whipped her hair back with a snap of her head, took her tray to the dish counter, and left the cafeteria.

I didn't see Eve or her brother the rest of the day. But boy was I suddenly popular with the jocks.

"Dude, what's her name?" "Where's she from?" "Hey, nerd, did you get a phone number?" "Dude, does she like cage fighting?"

The only thing I revealed was that her name was Eve. But I made it sound like I'd learned so much more, just to keep them guessing. The trouble was *I* was the one just guessing.

Chapter 3

Eve DIDN'T SHOW UP AT lunchtime Tuesday or Wednesday. I wondered if she was even at school those days. I didn't see her brother either. Since I wrote for the school paper, I knew how to get information other students weren't privy to. If I could find out her class schedule, I could arrange an "accidental" meeting.

The administration office had a tiny bell above the door that tinkled whenever it opened and closed. I entered and, seeing no one around, walked directly to a computer in the bullpen. I tapped the screen awake, sat down, and pulled up current school records.

"Exactly what do you think you're doing, young man?" came the hawk-like shrill of Ms. Galinsky. She was standing in the principal's doorway, glaring at me over horn-rimmed glasses. She must have heard the bell. Galinsky was a hard, unforgiving woman who ran the school like a penal colony. I should have smelled her coming. She wore an eye-watering perfume that could set off smoke detectors. Rumor had it she bought it in five-gallon drums.

"I'm looking up some information for a piece in the *Herald*."

"Did you get permission first?"

"Would I be sitting here, right in front of you, accessing the school's computer files, if I didn't have permission?"

She stared at me with bloodshot, protruding eyeballs. Set in a disturbingly narrow face, they always seemed on the verge of falling out.

Without waiting for a response, I turned back to the computer and resumed typing. By answering her question with a question, I gained a small window of time. But it'd be very small. She'd figure out my ruse in a matter of seconds.

I typed in the name *Mudswallow*. The search brought up two names: Eventide and Simon. A box listed their address, phone, and birthdates. Eve was sixteen; her brother, Simon, was nine. The cool thing was that Eve's birthday was one day before mine; the uncool thing was that she'd forever be one year and a day older than me. I didn't bother writing the information down; I'd remember it. I quickly reviewed Eve's former schools and addresses and her academic transcripts. There were a lot of them. A whole lot. *That's interesting...*

Right as I got to Eve's current class schedule, I saw Galinsky's scowl reflected in the monitor. Her neck craned to see what I was doing. Her hands grappled her protruding hips, her fingers thrumming. I quickly brought up a file listing the school almanac and current statistics.

"Precisely what are you looking up, young man?" she demanded.

"Just some stats," I said on the fly. "Did you know that this is the first year we've had over two hundred students at Snakeleg Municipal? And according to these records, 60 percent of those are male."

Right then, her perfume hit me like the concussive wave from an explosion. I've never smelled poisonous gas before, but if I had to guess, Galinsky's fragrance came close. I held my breath to limit my exposure.

"Why's *that* so interesting?" she asked. "Is that what you're going to write about?"

I could have simply said yes and left, but I hadn't reviewed Eve's schedule yet. Besides, the smart-aleck know-it-all in me had to say something that would stall Galinsky a bit longer.

"I might. Get this: Forty percent of the students are female, and only 78 percent of girls graduate. And yet, that's still higher than the male student body graduation percentage. A two-proportion, Z-significance analysis, with a P-value indicating a statistical ratio at an alpha-level of 0.05, reveals that the female nongraduating 22 percent are still smarter than males. Wouldn't you agree?"

She continued to glare at me, her neck still craning. Then, grunting as if she were choking on a rodent, she turned on her heel and stormed into the principal's office.

I switched back to Eve's schedule and checked out her classes. A moment later, the door chime tinkled, and Shane walked into the office, holding a yellow slip of paper. I recognized it as a truancy citation. He glared at me as harshly as Galinsky had. "What're you doing back there, Smut?"

I logged off the computer and stood. "I'm just helping out a bit because I can type ninety words a minute. How fast can you type?"

He hesitated. "Uh, only wusses can type."

"Oh. Is that why your wrestling coach also proctors the computer lab?"

He responded with a deer-in-the-headlights look.

"You want me to help you record that unexcused absence ticket?" I asked, pointing to the paper in his fist.

"How the—? You're not supposed to know about that," he said, ramming the yellow slip into his pants pocket. His face glowed red with anger. "You've been spying in school records, haven't you? That's against the law! That's a violation of my privacy! I could sue you for defecation of character!"

I was about to correct his terminology but figured he wasn't actually that far off the mark.

"Fine," I said, holding up my hands and averting my eyes. "I didn't see a thing."

Having obtained the information I wanted, I left the office without further comment. The tinkling of the bell mixed with a fresh batch of caustic words from Shane as I exited the office.

I told myself my interest in Eve was purely academic—something to fill my mind, to take it off of what was to come only hours from now. It was partly true. But after having just found some pretty unusual information on Eve, my curiosity was piqued. That was good. I wanted to keep my mind busy. I *needed* to keep it busy—if only to take it off the fact that it was Wednesday.

Tonight was *the* night. The Death House was waiting.

Chapter 4

AFTER SCHOOL, I WENT HOME, did my homework, read for an hour, played a mindless game with Zeek, then ate dinner. Mom had prepared another of her learning-to-survive-on-anything meals. This one was jambalaya loaded with tiny crickets.

"They're high in protein, no saturated or trans-fats, and they add a nice crunch to the meal," she said, beaming with pride.

"Dig in, son. Someday soon, bugs will be all that's left to eat in this world," Dad added in a confident tone. "They're nutritious and delicious. What's more, they're readily harvestable in nearly every environment in the world."

Dad chowed down with gusto. Zeek followed suit. I had a small helping and tried thinking of the crickets as lumps of undercooked rice. It helped. A little.

Afterward, I excused myself to go "meet with friends to study at the Rexall."

"Be vigilant out there," Dad said every time I left the house. "The end of the world will come when you least expect it."

Since my dad expected it daily, I wondered what he meant by "least."

Night comes quickly in the high desert in October. It wasn't unusual for twilight to linger until ten o'clock, but when night fell, it dropped like a guillotine. That evening, I wished the twilight would last much longer. I dreaded what was to come. My watch read nine o'clock. The sun had set, but the western sky continued to bleed a disturbing crimson glow.

As I stared at the Collier mansion, a tremulous chill slithered up my spine. The Death House loomed in the red twilight, its sagging eves and black windows staring at me as if in challenge.

I swallowed a dry lump in my throat and made a snap decision to delay my quest.

Instead, I rode my bike to the Mudswallow family's address. To my surprise, it ended up being a ramshackle trailer in a rundown trailer park about two miles from my house. A weathered sign leaning to the side outside the park read *Shangri-La Mobile Estates*.

Mobile *estates*? Who were they kidding? Parking my bike, I frowned in confusion. Eve lived in a trailer park? I'd expected someone as well put together as her to come from a well-to-do family that lived in an elegant home—of which there weren't many in Snakeleg. My curiosity was on overload.

The Shangri-La boasted twenty slots for hookup, but only nine were filled. The U-shaped tract was deathly quiet. The trailers along the loop were in various states of disrepair. Eve's trailer ended up being one of the worst: a beat-up single-wide set on cinder blocks, surrounded by dried-up grass and shrubs and a lone cottonwood tree in serious need of pruning. I double-checked the address. It was correct.

Melding into moon shadow, I cased their yard. Wanting to remain unseen before I knocked on her door, I moved with utmost caution. But it was difficult. Gravel and dried grass crunched under my shoes.

I wondered why her parents would buy such an embarrassing domicile. Unless . . . unless they couldn't afford anything better. Considering *that* possibility made me think twice about knocking on the door. If they *were* dirt poor, Eve might be embarrassed by my visit. Still, I was honestly concerned about why she hadn't been at school the past two days. Something didn't feel right.

The bluish glow of a TV flickered against the curtains covering the picture window at the front of the trailer. An incandescent bulb in a tiny window midtrailer cast a sour yellow wash on the trailer next door. A porch lamp was the only exterior illumination, but it was presently unlit. I was about to check out the back of the trailer when a movement on the small porch caught my attention. The stoop was barely big enough to hold a folding lawn chair and a withered potted plant. Someone was sitting on the chair. I couldn't make out much of their shape, but whoever it was, was small.

I moved behind the cottonwood and crouched. Had he or she seen me? I pushed that thought aside and waited.

After a few minutes, the porch-sitter slid out of the chair and stepped into the moonlight. It was the young boy from the cafeteria—Simon.

He carried something in his hand. It looked like . . . a walkie-talkie? He adjusted a knob on the unit, spoke into the mouth piece, and then held it skyward. I wasn't very far from him, but I didn't hear any radio static or hiss. Maybe he had it turned way down.

As I leaned forward, he looked in my direction and urgently whispered something else into the mouthpiece. I shrank back, again wondering if he'd seen me.

Two new questions flooded my mind: If Simon held one walkie-talkie, who held the other? And had *that* person seen me too?

Simon stepped down from the small porch and climbed onto a large rock next to the trailer tongue. That put him even closer to my hiding place, and yet, he didn't look in my direction again. He spoke into the walkie-talkie and again held it skyward. That seemed odd. Wouldn't he want to hold it to his ear to hear the other person? I wished I was close enough to hear what he was saying. *Maybe if I lean in a bit more . . . ?*

Just then, a car entered the trailer park and headed toward us. I quickly rounded the cottonwood as the wash of headlights lit my hiding place. I crouched motionless, barely daring to breathe. I was in Simon's direct view, but I hoped the bright backlighting from the headlights would conceal me. Without a word, he shielded his eyes with his hand, hopped off the rock, and scurried back onto the porch.

To my surprise, the car pulled into the Mudswallows' parking space. It was a trashed Toyota Echo. It was too dark to see much detail, but I could tell it was a light color and was cankered with rust spots.

I assumed it was Mr. Mudswallow returning from a hard day's work; my mouth fell open when the cab light came on and Eve stepped out. My jaw dropped a fraction farther when I realized she was wearing a Denny's waitress uniform. My surprise wasn't that she had a part-time waitressing job; it was that the closest Denny's was thirty miles away. It was far, but not far enough to warrant missing two whole days of school.

"Simon! You know you shouldn't be outside," Eve said sharply, though a tinge of weariness laced her words.

"I was talking to Mom and Dad," the boy said.

In a panic, I looked around. His parents were nowhere in sight. Perhaps his mom and dad had the other walkie-talkie inside the trailer home. But then, why hadn't I heard any of the conversation?

Eve stopped short. I couldn't tell if she was mad or not, but after a moment, she withdrew a Styrofoam carton from her car, locked the door, and walked to the stoop to give Simon a warm hug. "It's late, little man. Come on," she said, taking his hand and leading him into the house. "I brought you a piece of chocolate cream pie. We'll share a treat, then it's bedtime."

I looked at my watch. It was already past ten. I'd been out a full hour? I had to get moving. I still needed to explore the Collier mansion like I said I would.

I decided to talk to Eve at school the next day—that is, if she was there . . . and if I was still alive.

Chapter 5

As I made my way home along the sparsely lit streets, my thoughts filled with evil portents. Our house was one of seven on a long, dead-end street. The first six houses sat close to each other, three on each side at the beginning of the street. They were all built in the sixties, with white gravel roofs, small bedrooms, huge living rooms, and small yards surrounded by chain-link fences. The seventh house was the Collier mansion.

Having nothing between our house and the abandoned manor wasn't a good thing. It was one of the reasons I felt so drawn to it. It was as if the mansion exuded a magnetism that pulled me toward it. I'm sure other people felt the exact opposite; they were repulsed by it. Perhaps that was why no one ever wanted to get close to it. Perhaps that was also why my dad got our home for such a low price. It'd been on the market for twenty years. Go figure.

When I turned down our street, the Death House loomed in the pale moonlight. The night sky was mostly clear. Only a few dark tufts of cloud obscured the stars like cancerous dark blotches. The mansion's hunched roofline, bristling shingles, and canted eves made it look like a beast poised for attack. In the daylight, it was scary enough; at night, it seemed downright demonic.

Gathering my courage, I pedaled on, passing my house and heading straight to the mansion. I paused at the manor's wrought-iron gate to study it from a safe distance. I could swear it was studying me just as intently. But I couldn't back out now. Tonight was the night, the night I'd sworn to begin my exploration into what really happened within its slowly decomposing walls. I had to keep going.

A gust of wind so dry it abraded the skin coursed along the street, carrying with it a few dead leaves, jagged sections of tumbleweed, and ghostly dust devils. I sucked in an arid breath and tried to walk boldly toward the mansion. I was surprised at how much effort it took. All my senses screamed for me to turn and run.

When we first moved here, I'd had no problem strolling right up to its wrought-iron perimeter fence to gaze at the crumbling architecture. Of course, that was before I'd heard it calling to me—and before I'd heard about the curse. Even though I didn't believe in ghosts or hauntings, the more I learned about the Collier mansion, the less I wanted to go near it. Still, I knew uncovering its almost hundred-year-old secrets was up to me.

Even now, as I stood gathering nerve to tread the cracked walkway, it felt as if someone else was controlling my legs, pulling me forward. The crumbling steps and dusty veranda beckoned to me with a thin wail. The wind picked up, whistling through the blistered balustrades lining the wide porch. Was that what I was hearing?

Placing my hand on the gate, I expected the heat of the day to still radiate from the metal. Instead, the ironwork was ice cold, like the frost-covered walls of a steel meat locker. I tried to pull my hand away, but the metal stuck to my flesh, biting it, refusing to let go. It felt as if my skin would shred if I pulled too hard.

Suddenly, the wind shifted and blew directly from the mansion. At first, all I felt was the hot, dry air. Then came the smell—a fetid, repulsive odor that reeked of sulfur, decay, and rot. I didn't know if the scent was carried from somewhere behind the house or from the house itself, but its putrid funk gagged me, churning my stomach.

Then there was the voice. More than a squall soughing through a small opening or whishing around a soffit, the sound was too mournful, too pleading to be the result of a gust of wind. As I listened, it gradually, deliberately shaped itself into a word—a word I didn't want to hear and certainly did not want to obey.

"Come . . . cooomme . . . *coooommme!*"

Yanking my hand free and crying out from the pain, I turned and ran for home, leaving my bike behind. I could get it later. I don't remember my feet hitting the ground, but I found myself tearing up our walkway, crashing through our front door, and flying up the stairs to my bedroom. I may have called out "Hello" or "I'm home," but I honestly couldn't remember.

In my room, I approached my window from a sharp angle, hoping the Death House wouldn't see me. I twisted the rod, adjusting the slant of my blinds, until I could no longer see out—but more importantly, until the Death House could no longer see in.

But I knew it was there. Watching. Waiting.

Chapter 6

I saw Eve in the hallway after first period the next day and followed her to her locker. I needed to ask her an important question.

"G'morning, Eve," I said, trying my best to sound confident yet calm.

"Hey there . . ."

"Adam."

"Yeah, Adam. How could I forget?" She sounded tired, like she was trying to win a losing battle with fatigue. She probably hadn't forgotten my name; she just had other stuff on her mind.

"Right. So how are things going? Are you adapting to SM okay?"

She considered me with narrowed eyes, which I still found a little creepy. I couldn't tell if she was confused or angry. "SM?"

"Snakeleg Municipal."

"Oh. Yeah . . ." she said, fumbling. "It's fine, I guess."

Hoping I wasn't being too pushy, I said, "It's just that you're obviously a transfer student, right? So adapting to a new school can be confusing, especially when trying to work out which class credits transfer and which don't. You know?"

"Yeah," she said, focusing again on her locker combination.

She wasn't very talkative, but she wasn't shutting me out either. I decided to continue. "So how about this desert air? It takes some getting used to, doesn't it?"

"It's dry," she agreed, opening her locker.

"How does Simon like it?"

She whirled on me, quick as a rattlesnake strike. Any friendliness I'd seen in her eyes had vanished. Now there was nothing but cold, steely indictment. "How do *you* know his name?" Even her words seemed full of venom.

I opened my mouth, but nothing came out. My tongue suddenly felt as large as a baked potato. I almost gagged trying to form a reply. She took a step toward me, shoulders back, fists balled, eyes seething. I tried to step back, but the flow of students in the hallway made retreat impossible.

"Well?" she hissed.

"I-I work for the school paper, remember? I get updates from the office all the time. I-I think I saw his name on a memo?" My answer wasn't totally a lie. I *did* get the information from the office—just not from a memo. Besides, I was with him for a few minutes at lunchtime the other day. He could have told me then.

She searched my eyes. It was hard not to look away but just as hard to keep staring at her pale irises. They reminded me of a zombie's eyes— at least the ones I'd seen in movies.

Finally, she turned back to her locker, pulled out a backpack, and slammed the door shut. "I'm late for class."

Watching her power-walk away from me, I felt like I had shot off my big toe and stuck my whole foot in my mouth to nurse the wound. I wasn't sure what I'd said to offend her, but I'd clearly stepped on a nerve.

Confused, I scratched my head. I'd thought we were friends. Well, maybe not *friend* friends, more acquaintance friends. She'd said I was okay. I knew that wasn't much to go on, but it was more than I ever got from any other girl I'd known. Particularly a pretty one.

My intention—after the small talk—had been to ask her if she'd heard anything about the Collier legend or the spooky mansion at the end of my street. I was hoping to tell her what I knew before she became jaded by other opinions and then perhaps ask her to explore it with me. I knew it was a long shot, but I lived by the saying "If you don't ask, the answer will always be no."

I turned around to head to my class—and bumped into Shane. He was leaning against the lockers, grinning at me in his slimy, smug way.

"You really think you have a chance with a girl like that, Smut?"

It took a few seconds to get my bearings. "Excuse me?"

"The new girl. Duh. Don't play stupid, stupid. I saw you talking to her. She didn't seem very happy when she left, which proves you're a dork when it comes to girls." His grin filled with lust. "Perhaps I should go comfort her."

"I don't think that's such a good idea. She doesn't like jocks." I wasn't sure if that was completely true, but I didn't care.

"No, she doesn't seem to like scrawny dorks like you. Once she learns I'm going to Harvard Law School, she'll be all over me."

"You haven't even met her, and I already know she's over you."

My play on his words zinged right past him. Ignoring me, he gazed longingly upward as if experiencing a divine manifestation. "That hair, those eyes . . ."

Heaven help me, he's going to wax poetic.

"She also possesses a very astute brain," I told him. "She always gets good grades."

"No, it's more than that, dork. She's like . . . like Hermaphrodite, the Greek goddess of love."

"Um . . ." *Nah.* It was better to let that one slide, if only in hopes of seeing him call her that *and* seeing her response. "Listen, Shane, she's different from other girls. Trust me."

He barked out a laugh. "Trust *you*? I can't even trust you to cover a bet."

Cover a bet? Now what was he talking about?

Right as I was going to ask, the bell rang. We were both late to class, but I guessed only one of us truly cared.

He punched my shoulder. "See you Saturday, loser. And don't forget to bring your dollar."

My dollar?

I shook my head and ran to class.

At lunchtime, I sat at the table where I'd first met Simon. He wasn't there. And Eve never showed up either. That concerned me, especially after the way we'd parted. Was she eating lunch elsewhere, or did she go home early? If she had to go to work, I wondered what her parents thought of her skipping school. Or did they even know? And why had she gone ballistic when I'd asked about Simon?

* * *

That night, I rode my bike to Eve's home again. It looked exactly the same as before. Eve's car was gone, but the flickering, bluish hue still danced against the curtains in the picture window. After making sure no one lurked in the shadows (besides me), I crept close enough to hear the show on the TV. I caught only snippets of dialogue, but it sounded like *Fairly OddParents*.

I figured I'd just sit in the shadows until Eve came home because I was too chicken to meet her parents by myself, then I'd talk to her about the Death House. However, I soon grew weary of listening to random snatches of the cartoon, so I decided to explore a bit. I snuck around to the back stoop. It looked very rickety, and I didn't dare step on it for fear of it breaking. Instead, I slinked back to the front and stood on the large rock, trying to peek through a split between the curtains. It was a creepy thing to do, but curiosity overrode common sense. The living room was pretty dark, but I could see back to the kitchen. *That's interesting.*

The mess on the kitchen table revealed that dinner had been Lucky Charms. The milk and cereal box were still out. Since it was almost ten o'clock, I assumed Simon was in bed and Mr. and Mrs. Mudswallow were watching TV. But *Fairly OddParents*? If they *were* watching it, they definitely were odd parents themselves. I knew that drill—I had honest-to-goodness odd parents myself. They considered the television socialism's mouthpiece.

A noise from the mobile home next door stopped my heart. I jumped off the rock and scrambled under the Mudswallows' trailer. The neighbors' door opened, and an overweight, bearded man stepped outside carrying an overstuffed trash bag. He wore only a tank top and rumpled boxer shorts. As he dumped the large bag into a larger can, a woman stepped out onto the landing. She had roughly the same characteristics as the man—minus the beard—and wore only a ratty nightshirt and a head full of pink, spongy hair-curlers.

The man seemed shocked that she'd joined him. He spat some very colorful curse words, then said, "Dang it, Mabel. Don't come outside dressed like that. Show a little dignity, for crying out loud."

The woman expelled a few choice words of her own, then stepped back inside the trailer. The man followed her in, slamming the door behind him.

Charming neighbors.

I didn't leave my hiding place, figuring I could simply listen for the creaking of floor boards or the plodding of footfalls above me to indicate movement inside. It was better not to risk exposure until then. I closed my eyes and focused on the sounds above me.

* * *

I don't know when I fell asleep, but the headlights of Eve's car woke me with headache-inducing intensity. They stopped a few feet from my face. I prayed she hadn't seen me under their mobile home. When the car door opened, Eve slowly got out, placed her hands on the small of her back, and stretched with a pain-filled groan. I could swear I heard bones pop. She then shut her car door, locked it, and went inside.

As I inched my way out from under the trailer, I glanced at my watch. *What the*—? I rubbed my eyes and looked again. 12:32 a.m.

Ugh!

Not bothering to listen for Mr. and Mrs. Mudswallow greeting their daughter after a grueling evening shift, I hightailed it home. I was able to sneak in the back sliding-glass door and up the stairs without detection. That's quite a feat considering my parents have an alarm system worthy of Fort Knox. Luckily, I knew all the codes. Even the ones they thought I didn't.

As I lay in my bed, I felt overwhelmed. Not only was I supposed to solve the mystery of the Collier mansion, but now I also had another conundrum to unravel. What the heck was up with Eventide Mudswallow?

Chapter 7

OUR GANG GATHERED AT THE Rexall a little earlier than normal that Saturday. Rain was expected that night, and we all wanted to be home before it fell. I didn't know why. It was so miserably hot I knew most of the water would evaporate before it even hit the ground.

Everyone wanted to talk about Eve. Traci and Stephanie said they'd each seen her in a class, but neither had had a chance to talk with her. They said she always sat in the chair closest to the door. She rarely said much of anything. She was apparently pretty smart—she was able to answer all of the teacher's direct questions, but she never volunteered an answer. She only spoke when spoken to.

"Some of the girls think she's too stuck up to talk to anyone," Stephanie said.

"No way. She's just playing the shy, new girl," Bucky said. "That's how they get attention, you know. Every girl does that at first: plays the shy, innocent type. Then after a couple weeks, you can't get 'em to shut up."

I cringed in his behalf. Everyone knew you *never* threw out a negative generalization about girls in front of girls.

"They do not," Traci scoffed.

"You're an imbecile, Bucky," Stephanie said.

Rocky laughed at his brother's expense. "She pegged you, Bucky."

"You're even worse, Throckmorton," Traci added.

"I object, Your Honor," Shane cut in with a lame, stuffy accent. "There's actually some truth to that claim about girls."

At that point, I left to get a root-beer float. No way was I going to be involved in that ill-fated debate. When I returned, all eyes were on me.

"Fess up, Adam. We saw you talking with Eve at lunch on Monday. The next thing we know, you don't show up for Wednesday's posse. Did you two go on a date?" Stephanie asked with raised eyebrows.

"I went to her house," I said with a shrug.

"Really?" Shane, Bucky, and Rocky all said at once. Traci and Stephanie gawked at me. Earl and Bug merely sat there sipping their sodas.

"Yep."

Shane crumpled up a napkin and threw it at me. "You did not, you dork."

"Yeah, dude, no way you went to her house," Bucky said.

"Yeah, nice try, moron," Rocky said.

"So why *did* you go?" Bug asked.

Everyone stopped and stared at the bespectacled Paiute.

"Huh?" the twins asked in unison.

Bug looked down at his glass of root beer. "I wondered why Adam went to her house."

After a lengthy pause, Shane spoke up. "Bug, he was joking. He didn't really go. I mean, he doesn't even know where she lives, right?"

"Snakeleg's not that big, Shane," Traci said. "And you can find almost anyone on the Internet through public records."

Shane waved her off. "And even if he *did* go, it was probably just to help with homework or something lame like that. It's the only thing Smut knows how to do with a girl."

I smirked, choosing not to comment on his sophomoric innuendo.

"I think he wanted to ask her to go into the Collier mansion with him," Bug said softly.

All eyes turned back to the Native American. Even mine.

"What makes you say that?" I asked, forcing a chuckle.

He shrugged. "Because no one here is brave enough to go with you."

A moment of awkward silence filled the air.

"Yeah, like *anyone* wants to go get killed in the Death House," Rocky scoffed.

The silence continued. Earl was paler than he'd been a minute ago.

"I ain't scared of nothin', dweeb," Shane finally grumbled. "And you still owe me a dollar."

I frowned. "For what?"

"'Cause last week I bet you a dollar you wouldn't go to the Death House, and now we know you didn't because you said you went to Eve's house instead. Ha!"

"Oh, snap," the Dumb Brothers cheered, giving each other a high five.

I didn't hedge. "In that case, *you* owe *me* a dollar, because I went to Eve's place *and* the Collier mansion that night."

"I ain't giving you nothin', Smut," Shane spat. "You got no evidence."

He was right. But he had no proof that I didn't go either. I decided to call his bluff. "Okay then, Mr. Know-It-All, go with me tonight, and we'll get some evidence on what really happened there."

His face blanched for a second. Then he snorted. "Don't waste my time, dork. I already know what happened."

"Really?" I said in mock awe. "Tell me, then. Fill me in on all the gory details."

Earl moaned pitifully.

Shane didn't flinch. "There's nothing to fill in. The police already determined it was a murder-suicide. The case is officially *ad nauseam*. That's legal speak for 'case closed.'"

"No, it's not, you imbecile," I said before I could stop myself. Shane gave me one of his *you're-dead-meat* glares. "*Ad nauseam* basically means 'to the point of throwing up,' which is exactly what you guys make me want to do with all your silly ghost stories."

That was a total lie, of course. The mansion terrified me. But I couldn't very well tell *them* that.

Trying to divert the focus from me, I said, "Look, the place was searched after the bodies disappeared, right?" A few nods confirmed my query. "I looked it up. Local and regional newspapers state that the county sheriff ran a multi-countywide search, called in the territorial marshal, and everything, but they still came up empty. No evidence of foul play. No suicide note or last will and testament. Nothing. Not even a claim on Mr. Collier's life insurance policy."

"What is this—a stupid history class?" Shane muttered, still scowling at me.

"It just doesn't make sense, man. The place has been empty for nearly one hundred years. Why is that?"

"Dude. Because everyone knows it's haunted," Bucky said.

"Yeah, the basement's probably filled with dead bodies," Rocky added.

"Can we be done now?" Earl said, lowering his head to the granite countertop.

"That's a bunch of bunk, and you know it," I said. "I want to know why the bank just lets it sit there rotting away instead of selling it to some out-of-towner."

"I don't think the mansion's for sale," Stephanie said. "My dad works at the bank. He says they turn down all purchase requests on it. It's in some kind of untouchable trust or something."

"Even after one hundred years?"

She shrugged.

"So you're telling me no one's been inside after the original investigation was closed?"

"You don't listen very good," Shane said bitterly.

Ignoring his bad grammar, I went on: "Come on. Surely some curious trespassers or looters have crept in from time to time. Haven't you guys heard of anyone doing that?"

More silence enveloped our little group. Bug looked directly at me but didn't speak. His eyes seemed to register some kind of understanding, some kind of hidden knowledge.

"I heard of one guy who went in searching for jewelry and stuff," Earl said with his face still on the countertop. I wasn't aware he was still listening, but I welcomed his input. "He got out . . . but he was messed up pretty bad in his head."

"Yeah, dude, I remember that," Bucky said enthusiastically, snapping his fingers. "He kept talking about scary noises and bad odors. He ended up killing himself. Soaked the inside of his car with gas, then got in and lit a match. *Ka-boom!*"

"Yeah, they said you could feel the blast clear in Mesquite, man," Rocky confirmed. "The only way they could ID him was through dental records."

"And his teeth were scattered all over town," Bucky said, finishing the tale.

Nods of affirmation circled the stone peninsula. Earl groaned, clearly sorry for bringing up the story. Bug continued to stare at me with hooded eyes.

"And *you* want to go in there," Shane said in his condescending tone.

"Yes, I do," I lied. I didn't *want* to go in; I *had* to.

Chapter 8

I DON'T KNOW WHY IT took me almost four months to figure this out, but it came to me the next morning: perhaps the kids I hung out with were not the best source of information on the history of Snakeleg or the Collier mansion.

I'd noticed a grisly old cowboy sitting at the opposite end of the counter a time or two when I'd been at the Rexall with the gang. Perhaps he'd lived in town long enough to have more accurate information on the mansion.

"Hey, does anyone know anything about that old guy?" I asked at our next meeting, nodding toward the senior citizen.

"His name's Dee," Traci said.

"He's a tough old geezer who hates everybody," Shane grumbled.

"Really? Why?" I asked.

"Don't know," Bucky said.

"Don't care," Rocky said, finishing the thought.

I wondered if those two were connected some way other than genetically. "How long has he lived here?"

"Years, I'd guess," Traci offered.

Bucky stole a glance in Dee's direction. "Probably from the start. I mean, just look at him, dude. He's got one foot in the grave—"

"And another on a banana peel," Rocky said.

Only Shane snickered at their inconsiderate duet.

"Have any of you ever talked to him?"

"Get real, Smut," Shane sneered. "No one talks to him because he literally doesn't talk to no one."

"Why? Is he mute?"

"No, he hears just fine," the big guy said, annoyed.

"No. I said *mute*, not *deaf*. If he can't talk, how does he communicate?"

Shane looked confused. "Who said he can't talk?"

"You did. You said he *literally* doesn't talk to anyone."

"Yeah. So?"

Ugh. "Never mind."

I should have known better than to take Shane's use of *literal* literally.

If Mr. Dee never spoke to anyone, then perhaps he had something to hide. Determined to find out what it was, I went directly to the Rexall the following Monday after school. I walked up to the barstool next to him and sat. Since he always wore a sweat-ringed cowboy hat, a faded western shirt, roughed-up blue jeans, snakeskin boots, and a week's growth of beard, I came dressed in a wrinkled collared shirt, my oldest pair of jeans, a ball cap, and hiking boots. There wasn't much I could do about the beard.

The old-timer favored me with a sideways glance, issued a grunt of disdain, and returned to staring at his creamy fountain drink. I sat mutely, waiting for the waitress—a middle-aged lady named Ethyl.

When she asked what I wanted, I jerked my thumb at Dee's beverage, and in my best western accent said, "I'll have whatever he's having."

"You . . . want an egg cream? You sure?"

"Of course I'm sure," I growled, knowing I probably sounded as stupid as I looked.

She shrugged and stepped away.

Dee cast another sideways glance and muttered, "Dang kids."

So he isn't mute. I'd guessed as much.

I snorted in response to his two-word chastisement, then shouted to Ethyl, "And make it a double." Then, resting my elbows on the counter, I mumbled, "Most kids chug them energy drinks that wire 'em up on so much caffeine it makes 'em plum crazy."

I'm not sure why I was talking like a hick. I guess I figured it might give me an edge in breaking through Dee's crusty shell. But knowing I sounded like an idiot, I was pretty sure my attempt would be an epic fail.

Dee huffed and took a pull on his egg cream. A line of thick foam clung to his mustache.

Ethyl brought me a frothy drink in a large mug. I had no idea what an egg cream was, but it looked pretty much like old cow's milk. If it was anything like eggnog, I'd be in trouble. The traditional holiday drink was way too mucilaginous for me. Gathering my courage, I tipped the mug, took a mouthful, and was pleasantly surprised. It tasted like a high-end cream soda, only made with real cream and extra vanilla. If there was real egg in it, I couldn't tell, but it was incredibly rich. And even though a third of it was foam, I doubted I'd be able to finish half the mug.

"Mighty tasty," I said, smacking my lips and wiping them on my sleeve.

"Yep," Dee mumbled before taking another pull on his drink.

I offered my open palm over the countertop. "Name's Adam."

He stared at my hand, and his jaw flexed rapidly, and his lips pursed. After what seemed an agonizing mental debate, he took my hand in a quick shake. I made sure to squeeze his hand as firmly as I could. His skin felt like sandpaper. We didn't make eye contact.

"Dee," he said right before blowing out a windy belch.

"Just moseyed into town a few months back," I said, still trying to sound like I was fresh off the cattle drive. "You lived here long, pard?" *Ugh. That was a definite fail.*

He didn't answer. I was pretty sure I'd overstepped my bounds. So I mimicked his work-worn posture and attitude: leaning against the counter, not letting my eyes drift more than a few inches from my egg cream, taking an occasional sip, issuing an occasional grunt.

By the time I'd finished about half of my drink, I was feeling kind of sick. I could usually pound down a half brick of ice cream without blinking an eye. But I'd met my match with this stuff.

Ethyl slid my tab in front of me. "Anything else, son?"

I rummaged through my pocket for change. "Not today, thanks."

She gathered my money and walked away.

I figured Dee and I would spend the rest of the evening in silence unless I said something. I wasn't sure if he was buying my cowboy act—I know I wasn't—but I still needed information from him.

Taking a chance, I mumbled, "History books say this used to be a mining and ranching town."

Dee grunted.

"Seen evidence of mining," I continued. "Ain't seen no cattle, nowhere."

He grunted again.

"They all die off?"

He took a sip of egg cream. "Most run off."

Wow, I got an actual full sentence from him!

Thinking the cows had run off because of work around the mine, I chuffed with disdain. "Dang-nab Colliers."

He turned to look at me through eyebrows so bushy it'd take an army corps of engineers to trim them. "T'weren't the Colliers, boy."

I frowned. "It wasn't?"

"T'weren't the Colliers," he repeated softly.

"You don't say." I figured that was a safe statement. "What happened, then?"

He didn't say.

As it turned out, he didn't say *anything* the rest of the time I was there.

After thirty minutes of painful silence, I knew my interview with Dee was over. My egg cream was half finished, but regrettably, my information on the Colliers and their mine was still near empty.

Chapter 9

"IS THIS SEAT TAKEN?" EVE asked me the next day at lunch.

I was sitting at my usual table along the far wall. She must have snuck in when I wasn't looking because I didn't hear any reaction to her entrance. Either that or the student body had already gotten used to her.

"Nope. Go ahead and sit if you don't mind being seen with a brainy type who always seems to say the wrong things at the wrong time."

She ducked her head shyly. "Sorry I had a meltdown the other day. You didn't say anything wrong. I'm just overprotective."

I shrugged. "Nothing wrong with that."

She sat down, then reached across the table and took my hand. "Thanks for understanding. And for being nice to Simon. I owe you."

I froze. All my efforts at being suave and debonair went right out the window at her touch. Even playing the *I-don't-really-care* game no longer worked. I wasn't even sure I was breathing right then. Her hand was warm and comforting. But it also felt a little rough, a little work-worn.

She must have sensed my uneasiness because she smiled, gave my hand a quick squeeze, and withdrew her touch.

"So what's new in your world?" she asked, opening a small carton of orange juice. "Are you working on a project for the school paper or finishing up your novel?"

I couldn't believe she remembered that. I had to swallow several times to work up enough spit to make speech possible. "I'm always working on something."

While that was a true statement, the newspaper articles I wrote were hardly Pulitzer material, and most of them were severely culled by the editor. My novel, on the other hand, was always a work in progress. I quickly took a bite of my spaghetti to make speaking socially unacceptable.

Eve opened a cup of yogurt and ate a dainty spoonful. She continued to hold me captive with her eyes. I tried not to squirm but couldn't stop myself.

"Is something bothering you?" she asked.

I chewed and swallowed as fast as I could. "No, not really."

Her eyes narrowed in on mine. "You're lying, Adam. I hate liars."

How the—? I shook my head. "I'm not really lying, per se . . ."

"'Not really?'"

I looked around. A few people stared at us, but in a noisy, overcrowded cafeteria, it didn't matter. We were ostensibly alone. "Well, actually I *am* involved in a project of sorts. But it's not for school."

Her eyebrows slowly rose, accompanied by the vaguest of smiles.

I fidgeted and scratched the back of my head. "I'm trying to figure out what really happened at the Collier mansion on the night of October 13, 1912."

"The Death House?"

"You learn fast," I said. "Yeah, that's what the locals call it. Do you know anything about it?"

"Just what I've heard around the area. You know, that it's been abandoned for one hundred years or so," she expounded. "A lot of locals say it was something supernatural, like a demon spirit or some curse. They say the place is haunted."

"That's what I've heard too."

She leaned forward. "I've also heard the Collier mine unearthed an ancient Indian burial site."

"No kidding?" Now, why hadn't any of my gang told me that one? Especially Bug?

"Have you seen the place?" Eve asked, seeming to gather excitement.

I smiled broadly. "I live next door."

Her eyes widened. It was a truly eerie look. "Please tell me you're lying."

I leaned back and folded my arms. "Nope, no lie."

She inched forward a bit more. Her voice dropped to an anxious whisper. "Have you gone inside yet?"

This was too good. Maybe my luck was changing. "No. But I want to. I want to figure out what really happened before next Friday."

She seemed enthralled. "Why next Friday?"

"Well, it's the hundredth anniversary of *the* Friday the thirteenth. More than that, I . . . I feel like I *have* to, like it's my responsibility, you know? Maybe because I live next door. Like, if anything happens, my family is next in line. My family's weird, but I'd hate to see anything happen to them."

Holding me in her gaze, she slowly leaned back. A full minute passed without conversation. The rumbling chaos of the cafeteria seemed to be miles away. I wanted to say something, but I could think of nothing, nor could I look away.

Then Shane's voice broke through my trance. "What's going on here? You two having a staring contest?" Laughing at his own banal humor, he sat uncomfortably close to Eve.

She scooted away, frowning. "Do you mind? Ever hear of personal space?"

"Hmm, let's see," he said, stroking his square chin thoughtfully. "No, I don't mind, and yes, I have heard of personal space. I'm just wondering what a gorgeous lady like you is doing in Smut's personal space."

Her frown deepened. She flashed me a questioning look.

"He calls me Smut because my last name is Smoot."

She faced the know-it-all jock. "Really? Name calling? You're kind of big to still be in the fifth grade."

I had to bite my lip so as not to laugh.

Shane flinched as if he'd been punched, but his grin stretched from ear to ear. "Oo, ouch. This one's got a bite," he said to me. When I didn't respond, he turned back to Eve. "So tell me, Eve—that *is* your name, right? Eve?"

Her eyes smoldered with contempt. She said nothing.

"Ha! I knew it. See? I got my sources, doll face. You need to know anything in this town, you ask Shane."

"Okay. Who is he?" Eve asked, tilting her head to one side.

Shane laughed loudly, totally full of himself. "That's me, baby. Ain't that right, Smut?"

Like I was going to help him. I busied myself in my spaghetti, saying nothing.

"Oh? I thought your name was Buzz," Eve said with surprising innocence.

"I'll answer to anything you want, babe. If you like Buzz, I'll be Buzz."

"Oh, goody. Do you want to know what your new last name is?"

Shane slouched forward, resting his elbow on the table, his cheek in his palm. "You bet, angel eyes."

"It's Off."

"Off? That's . . . kinda different. But if you like it, I like it."

What an idiot. "Say the whole name out loud, Shane," I suggested. He did. It still didn't register. How obtuse could someone be?

"So is Smut here bothering you?" Shane asked her.

"Not at all," Eve said, standing. "In fact, he just asked me out."

I did what? I'm sure my face registered as much shock as Shane's did. I'd like to say the big guy was at a loss for words, but plenty spewed from his mouth. The whole sentence isn't worth repeating, but it ended with "kidding me?"

"Nope, no kidding. And I said I'd love to," she responded, looking at me as she uttered the remarkable statement. Her stare bored into mine again, answering much more than a simple yes to a question I hadn't actually asked. Not yes, she wanted to go out with me but yes, she wanted to go explore the Collier mansion with me.

I grinned at the irony. In a potentially fatalistic way, our first date could end up being our last day alive.

Chapter 10

I MET EVE AT HER locker the next morning. She looked more refreshed today. Perhaps she didn't have to work at Denny's last night. Since it was Wednesday, I invited her to our gang gathering at the Rexall. She accepted my invitation.

At seven o'clock, Bucky, Rocky, Traci, Earl, and Bug walked into the pharmacy. Eve had yet to show up. No one knew where Shane and Stephanie were.

"They're probably making out somewhere," Bucky said, prodding Rocky a few times with his elbow.

"I doubt that," Traci said. "Steph's working at the thrift store tonight. That's probably where Shane is too. Now that Adam has a girlfriend, he's trying extra hard for Stephanie."

I choked on my root beer. "Wh–at? What girlfriend?"

"Miss Freaky Eyes," Traci said. "Since you're the only one who's ever talked with her for more than three minutes, everyone assumes she's your girlfriend."

"Well gee, Traci, I've talked with you for hours," I pointed out. "What does that make us?"

Bucky and Rocky burst out laughing. Earl joined in, but it was clear he didn't know why. Bug merely sat there.

"You know what I mean," she said with a huff.

"Well, trust me, she's not."

The conversation shifted to the upcoming Harvest Moon dance. As Bucky and Rocky tried to out-gross each other—and Earl—with graphic descriptions of the latest slasher movie they'd seen, I chanced a look toward the far end of the soda counter. Sure enough, there sat Dee. I wasn't in my western attire, so I thought it best not to approach him. We'd had a moment between us the other day. He'd think I was simply another annoying kid today. But I couldn't stop thinking about what he'd said to me. And—more significantly—what he *hadn't* said. He seemed very adamant when I asked about the mine. *T'weren't the Colliers.*

Then what was it? Did he know?

"So, Smut, you ever gonna go into the Death House or what?" Rocky asked snidely.

I refocused on our group. "Yep, still am. I scoped it out the other night. Didn't see much that scared me." Which was true. I'd *heard* and *smelled* and *felt* some things, however, that I hoped to soon forget.

"Well, when you stop showing up here, we'll know you finally went in," Bucky said.

"Because you won't come back out," Rocky finished.

"Alive," Earl said in a squeamish voice.

We all stopped and stared at the anxiety-ridden kid. Had he really joined the Dumb Brothers' repartee? Or was he truly in fear for my life?

"Whatever." I chuckled. It didn't sound as brave as I'd hoped.

I glanced at my watch. It was now eight thirty, and Eve was still a no-show. Did she stand me up on purpose? Or had she been called in to work?

It didn't matter. I had to make another trip to the Collier mansion—with or without her. I needed to get closer this time. The compulsion was still there, like a smoldering ember waiting to burst into flame inside me. Each night in my bed, I could sense the old place calling for me, pleading for me, reaching for me.

October thirteenth was fast approaching. Tonight, I had to show the Death House I was not afraid.

Chapter 11

I LEFT THE REXALL AT nine o'clock. We liked to stay until Ethyl kicked us out at ten, but as usual, I had things to do.

I first went to Shangri-La Mobile Estates, keeping in the shadows as much as possible. Eve's car was missing. *Aha.* She *had* been called into work . . . which meant she didn't stand me up. I was really hoping she'd go with me to the Collier mansion tonight.

I loved the way she'd given Shane a triple slam: first, by telling him to buzz off; second, by saying I'd asked her out; and third, by happily accepting. I hoped it would give Shane a whole new respect for me. But I wasn't going to hold my breath.

Satisfied that Eve hadn't spurned me, I made my way back home. Pausing at the corner of our lot, I stared at the mansion for a few seconds to gather courage. *You can do this,* I told myself. *You* will *do this.*

Next thing I knew, I was standing at the mansion's wrought-iron gate. Darkness had fallen, and the evening breeze had picked up. I gingerly touched the gate, tapping it a few times to check its temperature. It felt pretty normal; the metal gave no frigid bite or scalding heat. I unlatched the gate and pushed it open. The long-unused hinges screeched in complaint. I paused and looked around, though I didn't know why. No one ever came down this dead-end road. Steeling myself, I pushed the gate wide open. The wail from the hinges sounded like a dozen cats set ablaze.

I marched up the uneven cobbled walkway to the steps of the porch. The front door was blocked with a warped section of plywood, the bottom half of which had broken away due to weather and dry rot. The door behind the plywood had a large, beveled-glass front. I got down on my hands and knees and peered into the vacant house. It was dark inside. A small porthole window at the top of a staircase channeled a column of moonlight across the landing. Cobwebs abounded. Dust motes hovered on stagnant currents of air. I couldn't make out much else.

I checked the street once more to make sure no one was watching, then made my way around the side of the mansion. Because the house was set on a gradual slope, I had to scramble up an incline to reach the back. The result was that the front of the mansion was taller than the rear. All of the lower-level doors and windows were boarded up.

A wide, multipaned sunroom extended some sixty feet along the middle of the back. Twin wrought-iron trellises rose along both sides of the sunroom to a second-story balcony. At some point, they were probably covered with vines or climbing roses, but now they stood in skeletal relief against the weathered brick exterior. Iron ultimately rusts and deteriorates, but in these dry desert conditions, the process takes eons. I tested the strength of one by standing on the bottom lattice. It held my weight. I climbed a few more rungs and shook it. Metal grated against brick, but it held to the wall. Good.

I continued up until I was at the balcony level where the windows were all exposed. With the greatest of care, I stepped from the trellis to the balcony. As I did, a cloud obscured the moon, making an already dark night even darker. I misjudged my landing and stumbled, skinning one knee and both palms. The balcony's surface was made of rough-hewn granite slabs and was littered with dust, dead leaves, and guano. As fearless as I wanted to be, I was admittedly trembling with fright.

Pausing there on all fours, I closed my eyes and tried to clear all unpleasant thoughts from my mind. *Isn't this fun? Isn't it an adventure?*

As soon as I felt a bit calmer, I stood and brushed myself off. As I did, the cloud passed from the moon, illuminating the deck with the bleak pallor of a neglected graveyard. Turning toward the tall windows, I saw a young man staring back at me. My heart slammed against my chest, and I staggered back, sucking in a gasp so fierce it hurt my lungs. I bent over and placed my hands on my knees, then took several smaller, calming breaths. Who the crap could be in there?

I slowly pried my eyes open, cringing the whole time. Dead leaves and bone-dry dust cavorted around my feet. With agonizingly slow movement—and with eyes still lowered—I stood. Taking a deep breath, I raised my eyes to look back into the eyes of the mysterious guy.

As it turned out, to look at my reflection.

I blew out a lungful of frustration and embarrassment and made a few quirky movements just to confirm the reflection was not some malevolent doppelganger. Luckily, he wasn't.

The breeze picked up again, and the house began making its infamous ghostly sounds. But they weren't only coming from outside the house this time. Evil sounds now seemed to be coming from within its crumbling walls.

It was then I felt a powerful urge to step closer to the window. Someone inside still awaited my recognition. They were right in front of me, directly on the other side of the glass pane, mere inches away. But the harsh glare of moon glow prevented me from seeing into the room beyond.

Screwing my eyes shut, I refused to look inside, refused to acknowledge whoever was in there demanding my attention. And yet, there was no option, no other choice but to obey. And whatever awaited me inside did not have my best interests at heart—of that I was sure.

Squinting, I took another deep breath and stepped up to the window. Then I saw him—Mr. Summerdale Collier himself—staring at me with such loathing that I shrank from his gaze. With unmoving lips, he seemed to be conveying a message no one ever wants to hear. I swear I heard him speaking. But I wished I hadn't. His words pierced my soul: *You're a dead man.*

I knew I was simply staring at a portrait hanging on the far wall, but the image seemed so real—as did his message!

Chapter 12

BACK IN MY ROOM, I cowered under my blankets. I rehearsed in my mind what had just happened, and at the same time tried to wipe the images from my memory. What had happened seemed impossible. Mr. Collier's portrait could not speak to me. It was an inanimate object. It wasn't staring at me; it was simply a layering of oil paint and brush strokes on stretched canvas. It *couldn't* stare at me.

But it had.

I forced my mind to think of other things, pleasant things that would make me smile. It took considerable, concerted effort, but I was finally able to calm down and relax. And then my alarm clock went off.

What? Time to get up? I hadn't even gone to sleep yet.

I went to school in a mental fog. It was all I could do to stay awake in my classes. At lunch I got two cans of Mountain Dew, which barely got me through my afternoon classes.

Opening my locker at the end of the school day, I found a folded piece of paper someone had slipped through the vents in the door. The note read:

We need to talk. Meet me at the Rexall Friday night. —Eve

I blinked a few times and read it again. How Eve knew where my locker was wasn't nearly as vexing as why she wanted to meet with me. The question bounced around in my head, giving me a headache.

When I got home, I went straight to bed. Mom asked if I was feeling okay, and I told her I was simply tired. To admit I wasn't feeling well to my mother was intentionally subjecting myself to a battery of tests most lab animals wouldn't survive. And I could forget about leaving her presence with my dignity intact. I learned long ago that unless I couldn't stop the bleeding or I was seeing a light at the end of a dark tunnel, it was best to tell Mom I felt fine.

I awoke when she called me down for dinner. My head still pounded, and my thoughts whirled aimlessly, but at least my body felt somewhat better.

After a dinner of freeze-dried something-or-other, I retired to my room again and stared at the Collier mansion until midnight. It didn't speak to me again. Perhaps my close encounter had drained it of evil portents for the moment. Or perhaps Summerdale Collier had already said what needed to be said.

My sleep was fragmented.

* * *

Friday felt about the same. I knew I talked to people and they talked to me, but I couldn't remember a thing we talked about. Eve's note was tucked deep in my pants pocket. Tonight we'd meet at the Rexall. To what end, I could only guess.

That evening, I put on my pseudo-western attire and rode my bike to the Rexall. I wore my western garb in case Dee was there, but my main focus was Eve. Hopefully she wouldn't stand me up again.

Entering the pharmacy, I saw Dee in his usual spot. A middle-aged couple sat at the peninsula. Eve wasn't there. *Just my luck.* I moseyed over to Dee and ordered a Mountain Dew. I needed the caffeine to stay awake, and I didn't have the stomach to tackle another egg cream.

Dee snorted disapproval of my beverage choice.

"Sometimes a man's gotta do what a man's gotta do," I said in my hardest voice.

He thought for a moment, then raised his egg cream in a toasting gesture. I clinked my glass against his and took a few generous swallows.

"The Colliers," he mumbled to his drink.

"The Colliers?" I echoed.

"Stupid."

"You got that right."

"Plum ridiculousness."

"Yes. Yes, they were."

He grunted.

"Building a mansion in the middle of the desert," I ventured.

Another grunt.

"It *is* a bit ostentatious."

Dee frowned. I heard a growl somewhere deep in his throat. Apparently, he didn't like my choice of words. "It's . . . showy," I corrected.

He sipped his egg cream. "It's wrong."

"Oh yeah. Stupid thing's *way* too big."

He frowned again, this time glaring right at me. The growl made it out of his throat, ending in some foamy gunk at the corners of his mouth. "You got wax in your ears, boy?"

"No, sir."

"You a dunderhead, then?"

"A dunderhead?" Right as I asked, it occurred to me I may have confirmed his assumption. "No, sir, I'm not a dunderhead. Just curious."

"Stupid."

Did he just call me stupid? I took a guess. "The mansion."

"Yeah."

"How so?"

"It's the wrong place."

"It's in the wrong place?"

"Not *in*. On."

"Would a smaller house have been better?"

He slammed his mug to the counter, splashing egg cream over the granite surface. "Jumpin' Jehoshaphat, boy, you been kicked in the head by a mule? I'm telling you they built that house *on* the wrong place."

That was probably the longest set of words he'd assembled in a decade. The insult didn't faze me because I finally understood what he was saying.

Maybe I *was* a dunderhead.

Then a girl's voice directly behind me asked, "What was on that location before?"

I spun around to a pair of pale, almost colorless eyes. Eve didn't acknowledge my presence other than leaning on the counter to see past me. Dee frowned deeply at her, his jaw flexing under bristling whiskers, dribbles of egg cream clinging to his chin. The staring contest lasted almost a full minute. I sat mutely, not wanting to interfere with whatever mind melding was going on between them.

"Girl, what in tarnation is wrong with your eyes?"

"I'm a witch," Eve answered plainly.

Dee's eyes narrowed. After a moment, he grunted, nodded, and turned back to his drink.

Really? He went for that?

"Is that where you wanted to take me? To the Collier mansion?" she asked me.

"Take you? I never said anything about taking you anywhere."

She looked shocked, but I knew her look was in jest. "Yesterday at lunch, the large jock with the small mind couldn't believe you asked me out either. But I'd love to go explore this mansion with you."

Dee gave us a hard look at her declaration but said nothing.

"What's with him?" Eve whispered.

I shook my head and mouthed the word *later*.

She didn't like that answer. Leaning forward—almost on top of me—she asked, "Excuse me, old timer. What's all this about the Collier mansion? Is it really haunted? Is that why you were saying it's a bad place?"

He eyeballed the two of us coldly. "Never said no such thing," he grumbled.

Eve gave me a glance—her face embarrassingly close to mine. I tried not to squirm. "He simply doesn't want us going near the mansion," I explained. "Dee here seems to know more about it than anyone else in town."

She edged forward a bit more. "Is that right, Dee? Do you know what's going on in there?"

He took a long pull on his egg cream but didn't say a word, didn't even acknowledge he'd been spoken to. Apparently, Eve had gone too far. He'd closed up again. But she wasn't ready to quit.

"Why do they call it the Death House?" she asked him.

He acted like we weren't even there.

She reached over and touched his sleeve. "Hey."

His face snapped toward her, and he hissed. He really, truly hissed, exposing crooked yellow teeth coated with egg cream. It was a deep, throaty hiss accompanied by a generous salvo of creamy droplets. It was equally disgusting and frightening. Eve sat back quickly, probably to avoid the spit. I was surprised she didn't fall off the barstool.

I hurriedly jerked my head, indicating we should leave. Regaining her spunk, she huffed but stood to leave.

I tipped my cap to the old guy. "Dee."

He grunted.

Eve tipped an imaginary hat to him. "Old timer."

"Witch."

Exiting the Rexall, I chanced one last look at Dee. He was still scowling at his egg cream, but in his eyes, I thought I detected a flicker of a smile.

Chapter 13

WALKING MY BIKE DOWN MAIN Street, I rehearsed the history of Snakeleg and the Collier mansion to Eve. She listened intently, nodding occasionally, flashing looks of skepticism frequently.

"And you live next door to this place," she stated.

"Sort of. Ours is the last house on the row, but the street doesn't dead end for a couple hundred yards or so. That's where the mansion sits."

She smirked. "So the Death House sits on a *dead* end."

"Yeah. Kind of cliché, I know."

"And you're trying to find out what really happened in there because . . . ?"

And there it was. She'd asked *the* question, the one I wasn't sure how to answer myself. I stopped and looked into her pale eyes. They were even more bizarre in the dimly lit streetlights. They looked . . . *void*, as if they had no depth and yet went on forever. My mouth opened, then closed. How could I explain the unrelenting power I felt from the place? How could I describe the tugging on my soul that drew me to the mansion, that demanded I solve the riddle of the Colliers?

"I'm not sure. It's like this . . . well . . . this . . ." I shoved my hands in my pockets, feeling frustrated and weak. "Maybe it'd be easier to explain if you saw it," I said hopefully.

She tilted her head to one side and smiled. "See, you *did* want to take me there after all." She slipped her arm in mine and said, "Lead the way."

It was all I could do to move one foot in front of the other. She was touching me again, causing instant paralysis over my entire body. Why did I react that way? She was just being friendly, right? It wasn't like the evening was going to end with a kiss. Heck, it wasn't really even a date, because I hadn't really asked her out. But she was acting as if I had. And then she went and cast some spell on me with the touch of her hand. Maybe she really was a witch.

Using all my concentration so as not to appear as awkward as I felt, I led the way back to my house in silence. By the time we got there, it was almost ten o'clock. I parked my bike along the side of our house. "So . . . what time did you tell your parents you'd be home?" I asked casually.

A flash of hesitancy crossed her face. "Oh, they don't care."

"Then it's also a good thing you didn't have to waitress at Denny's tonight," I said before I could stop myself.

Her expression turned in an instant from open companionship to an animal poised for attack. She removed her arm and spun me around to face her. "Okay, Smoot. You've got ten seconds to explain how you know that," she snarled, poking her finger in my chest. "And don't give me that working-for-the-school-paper crap. How do you know so much about me?"

I ducked my head. "It's . . . complex." I shuffled my feet a bit, thinking. "Let me show you something first, okay?" I led her to the street, where we had an unobstructed view of the Death House. "There it is," I said, pointing.

The weak moonlight painted the mansion with mottled patterns of gray, casting a subtle, foreboding pall across the dead space between it and us.

"Oh . . . my," she said in a breathless whisper.

"It all started the day after we moved here," I said softly. She turned as if to speak, but I held up my hand. "Please hear me out. And please don't laugh."

I finally told her about how I felt drawn to the place, how I knew something more had transpired there than the local gossip revealed. I explained how I knew I had to go inside, to explore the place until I had solved the mystery, and how I had to do it before Friday the thirteenth.

"Why? Are you superstitious or something?"

"No. It's because something bad is going happen *on* that day."

Expressions of curiosity and dread crossed her face. "What?"

I shrugged. "I wish I knew."

"And how do you know it'll be something bad?"

"I wish I knew that too."

"So . . . how does all this relate to me?"

Lowering my eyes again, I kicked a pebble at my feet. "Basically, I'm too chicken to go in there alone."

She caught on instantly. "And none of your friends will go because they're also too scared."

I nodded.

"Even the big guy?"

"Shane."

"Yeah, him. He won't go either?"

"Nope."

"And you were hoping I would."

I smiled sheepishly and shrugged again.

She frowned, then took a good long look at the shadowy mansion. In a word, it looked *evil*. "Is it speaking to you now?"

"No. I think it said all it wanted to last time I was there."

"That you're a dead man."

"Yeah."

"You're a dead man if you go in, or you're a dead man if you don't figure it out before the thirteenth?"

That was an excellent question. "I . . . I'm not sure."

"I see." She paused a moment, chewing on her lower lip. "Okay, Adam. This is all fascinating, but it still doesn't explain how you know I'm a waitress."

My hands slipped back into my pockets. How could I tell her I was stalking her without sounding like a creepy pervert? Deciding to simply plunge ahead, I said, "The school has records of your address and such. Since you only occasionally show up to school, I went to your place to see if you wanted me to bring you your homework."

The look on her face told me she only half believed me.

"Okay, honestly, I went the first time to ask you to explore the mansion with me—just like you guessed. And then when you drove up, I saw your Denny's uniform, and I . . . I chickened out."

"And now you know everything about me." Her voice held no accusation this time. Instead, it was filled with a tone close to remorse. Her colorless eyes held more than sadness; they also held shame.

"No, not everything," I said firmly. "I only know that you seem a lot braver than I am and a lot more confident. That's why I want you to go in there with me." It was a hard admission to make for a young man wanting to impress a young lady, but I felt a huge weight leave my shoulders when I did. "Look, I'm not sure what we'll find in there. Maybe nothing. Everyone in town says the house was thoroughly inspected during the initial investigation. But . . . well, I think they may have missed something crucial."

"Something that will happen this Friday the thirteenth. Something dangerous?"

"I suspect so."

Eve studied my face for the longest time. The sadness in her eyes was slowly replaced with a look of compassion and understanding. She glanced at her watch. "Okay, listen, it's almost eleven. I have to work tomorrow morning. Can you come over to my place tomorrow after three? I think we can make a deal."

I couldn't believe my ears. Did she really ask me to go to her place? I felt elated and horrified at the same time. What would Simon think? Worse, what would her parents think? And what would they think about my plans to trespass in a haunted house with their only daughter?

"Okay," I said with only the slightest quaver in my voice. "What deal?"

"Tomorrow. After three," she answered. "Now, walk me home."

Chapter 14

SATURDAY MORNING DAWNED EVEN MORE overcast than Friday. That shouldn't have surprised me, knowing what we had planned for later in the day. Even nature was conspiring to make this a spooky experience.

I did my Saturday chores with robotic numbness. My mind was totally preoccupied with the things Eve and I would discuss that afternoon. Luckily, most of my chores took place in—and *under*—our garage, so I didn't have to look at the mansion. Our yard was xeriscaped with desert plants, gravel, and large boulders, which meant very little yard work. Instead, my tasks included inventorying, rotating, and generally maintaining our fallout shelter supplies.

Our two-car, double-deep garage was big enough to store four normal-sized cars. My dad cut through the cement in the back, dug out the foundation and a couple tons of dirt and rock, installed a reinforced fallout bunker that was better furnished and stocked than our house, then repoured the garage floor. He'd been a hugely successful general contractor before retirement, so he had little difficulty getting everything exactly the way he wanted it—and in record time.

But my thoughts were not on the doomsday my parents incessantly prepared for; instead, I was focused on my own imminent judgment day. During my tasks, I made note of several items I should probably take with me when I entered the Death House.

I finished my chores early and tried to interest myself in an Orson Scott Card sci-fi novel. It didn't work. The book, on top of the gloomy day, seemed an all-too-accurate portent of the activities of the coming afternoon. So instead, I took a nap, hoping my dreams wouldn't hold the same ill-fated promise I was sure the day held.

I awoke precisely at three—which meant I was already late. I leaped down the stairs two at a time and ran to the garage. I hopped on my bike and sped to Shangri-La Mobile Estates. Eve's car was there, making the characteristic ticking sounds most cars do as they cool down. Good. Perhaps I'd timed it just right.

I parked my bike against the cottonwood tree and knocked on the door. Her little brother answered.

"Hey there, Simon. Remember me?"

The young boy gave me a frown filled with mistrust.

"My name is Adam. I go to the same school as you and Eve."

His frown deepened. Perhaps Eve hadn't explained that I was coming over. He seemed intensely leery.

"It's okay, dude. She wanted me to meet her here," I explained. "Is your sister home?"

He shook his head.

No? No, what—she wasn't there, or she didn't want to meet me? "Can you at least tell her I'm here?"

He slowly began to close the door. It was then that I noticed he was carrying his walkie-talkie. It was only a toy. No wonder I didn't hear any static coming from it the other night. "Whoa, cool walkie-talkie, man. Is that yours?"

He paused and looked at it.

"I used to have one just like it when I was your age. Where's the other one? Does Eve have it?"

Simon shook his head and held up the toy so I could see it better.

"Is this the only one? Well, that's okay. Man, it's so cool. Who do you talk to on it?"

"Our mom and dad," Eve answered from behind the boy.

Simon scurried off into the depths of the trailer home. She stepped away from the threshold, pulling the door open, and motioned me inside.

"Thanks," I said, feeling a strange sense of trepidation.

As my eyes adjusted to the interior darkness, I noticed a surprising lack of furnishings. There was a ratty couch, a recliner covered with a bed sheet, a small, cheap entertainment center, and a pile of kids' DVDs. Everything was clean and orderly; there just wasn't much of it. And it all screamed thrift store hand-me-downs.

Eve sat in the shrouded recliner. "Since you already know *some* things about me, let me fill you in on the rest. Then we'll make a deal."

I nodded, more than a little curious. Her voice had that resolute yet defeated sound to it. She was still in her Denny's uniform.

"Okay."

"Simon and I moved here because it's the middle of nowhere. We've lived like this for about two years now, moving from one middle-of-nowhere to another. We have to leave when people find out too much about us."

The confused look on my face drew out a sympathetic smile on hers.

"Apparently you *don't* know everything about me. That's good, in a way. It means no one else does either."

"Know what?" I asked, again taking in the sparse interior.

She followed my gaze. "Quite the posh setup, huh? Honestly, it's all I can afford. You see, truth is, it's just Simon and me. My parents died skydiving two years ago. It hurt me, but it devastated Simon. He totally closed up, wouldn't speak or eat or even sleep much. I really worried about him. The state wanted to put us in separate foster homes. Simon's always been a unique child. He's not mentally challenged, but his emotions run deeper than most people think. To separate us would kill him. I'm sure we have cousins somewhere, but we've never met any."

"Ah," was all I could think to say.

"My parents were 'free spirits'," she said, making quotation marks in the air. "We were on the road a lot, traveling wherever the wind took us." She gave a harsh scoff and shook her head. "What that really means is that we never had the chance to make friends our own age. So after news came of the state's plans for us, I grabbed the keys to the van, and we hit the road. I sold the van the next day and bought that gutless wonder outside."

I sat there and gawked. If she was making this up, it sounded pretty convincing. But then, why would she make up such a depressing story?

"I've learned a few tricks of the road since then," she continued. "And I've always looked a lot older than I am, so I've been able to get things and make up excuses to keep nosy people off our backs. I travel from one job to the next . . . but I worry about Simon. I'm all he's got. I know it's important to keep him in school, if only for the interaction with other kids his age. I've found it's easier if I can be in the same school so I can keep an eye on him. That's why we stick to these small towns, where the grade levels are integrated."

She paused and wiped at her eyes. "Trouble is, I have to work so much to make ends meet that I end up spending too much time away from him. That's why I miss school a lot. I can't get a sitter because they'd find out we don't have parents and then 'do the right thing'"—she used her quotation marks again—"and call social services. So I just do what I can. I wish I could afford proper counseling for him, but that's never going to happen. So when people get wise to us, we move to another town."

When she looked up, I could see the wetness now covering her cheeks. I never heard any waver or shudder in her voice, but it was obvious she was crying. Perhaps her emotions were so scarred that tears came without anguish.

"I won't tell anyone. I swear it."

Simon ran back into the room, waving his walkie-talkie. He handed it to me, then snuggled next to Eve. She smoothed his hair and kissed the top of his head. "That's his security blanket. He uses it to talk to Mom and Dad. He believes it gets through to them in heaven. But he doesn't understand why they never answer."

My eyes were stinging now. I tried to swallow away the tightness in my throat. "So . . . what's the deal you wanted to make?" I asked, not knowing what else to say.

"Help me keep an eye on Simon."

"You mean, like, at school?"

"And other times."

I figured that wouldn't be too difficult. "Sure, but . . . well, why me?"

She shrugged. "Because you're trustworthy. When I saw you sitting with Simon, I knew you were okay. In fact, you seemed to be the only one in the cafeteria that first day who wasn't judging me."

"Oh, I wasn't," I said, shaking my head. "And I am . . . very trustworthy," I rambled, switching to a vigorous nod. "Your secret's completely safe with me."

She held my gaze for a minute, considering, contemplating, as if trying to read my thoughts, my body language. I saw her shoulders drop ever so slightly—whether in disappointment or gratitude, I couldn't tell.

"Look," I said firmly. "I don't care where you're from or what your history is. So you had a weird family life. I'm living in one of those right now. Trust me, when you meet my parents, you'll understand. I think Snakeleg is a perfect town for you. It is for me too."

"Except for the Death House," she said.

I rubbed the back of my head, stalling. "Something is going to happen there, Eve. I don't know why it's so important for me to find out what, but I know it truly is. Call it a premonition. Let me figure it out, then when the thirteenth has come and gone, we can work together to figure out how to fix your mess."

She flinched. "You think I'm a mess?"

I smiled, hearing some of the old fire in her voice again. "Yes, I do. But I also think you're handling it better than most adults would. *And* because I'm in on it now, let's call it *our* mess."

It took only a moment for her to match my smile. "I like that."

I did too. But there was one more thing that concerned me. "So Simon stays here by himself when you're at work or . . . on a date?"

She stroked his hair again. "He knows the rules. We have one of those single-use cell phones so he can dial 911 if he has to. We've covered what's a real emergency and what's not. And sometimes he'll stay overnight at a friend's house. He knows not to talk too much about our parents." She kissed the top of his head again and looked up. "As far as dates—I don't."

Really? "But—but you must get asked all the time. I mean, well, you're gorgeous."

Her smile was full of mischief. *Oh no.* "Why, Adam Smoot, was that a come-on?"

I felt the blush ignite my face. "You know what I mean."

"Yes, I do," she said, smiling. "Sorry for teasing you. I've just learned to avoid the truth by joking about everything."

She then whispered something to Simon. The little boy scooted off the couch, retrieved his walkie-talkie from me, and ran down the narrow hallway.

"But I'll still go with you to the mansion. If you're going to help me, then I'm going to help you."

My mind was whirring with ways to help this enigma of a girl, but the thoughts were tangled with the issues concerning the Collier mansion. How could I put the astounding Eventide Mudswallow at risk by dragging her through that place—especially now that I knew she was the sole provider for Simon? How could I tempt her fate and mine by selfishly picking up the gauntlet thrown by a century-old dead man?

"I hope you have a good flashlight," Eve said, bringing me out of my wonderings.

I grinned broadly. "You have no idea. I've got several really good flashlights. I told you my parents are weird? They are doomsday preppers; we've got about every survival knickknack you can think of and then some. Plus, I have a brother about Simon's age. You can bring him over when we go explore the mansion. He can stay the night or go back with you when we're done. It's perfect. We moved here only a few months ago, so my kid brother is still aching for friends. He'll love it."

I watched a light grow in Eve's pale eyes; they went from dim and reticent to bright and full of hope. "That's perfect, Adam. I'll drop him off, then we'll check out the mansion. But . . ."

"But what?" I asked, wondering what flaw she could see in my brilliant plan.

The mischievous smile was back. "Do your weird parents have anything that protects against ghosts?"

"I doubt it." I chuckled uneasily. "Do you believe in ghosts?"

"I didn't used to."

Remembering my last visit to the Collier mansion, I said, "Yeah. Me too."

Chapter 15

As it turned out, the soonest night Eve had off was October twelfth. I wasn't happy about it, but it was still *before* the doomed Friday, so I agreed.

The night was oppressive. Eve arrived with Simon right after suppertime. I'd warned her about our meals, and she'd opted to feed Simon before coming over. *Good call.*

My parents loved Eve after about one second, probably because she was the only girl I'd *ever* brought home to meet them. I dreaded the introduction, knowing the kind of welcome she'd receive.

"I always knew this day would come," Mom blubbered as if we'd just announced our engagement. "But you're so much more beautiful than we expected."

"Thank you, Mrs. Smoot," Eve responded, flashing me a glance that said she understood Mom's unspoken message.

Yeah, thanks a lot, Mom.

"I'm proud of you, son," Dad said, embracing me in a one-armed hug so as not to display too much emotion.

Happily, Simon and my brother hit it off immediately. We got the boys settled in Zeek's room and then gathered a bunch of things from our fallout bunker. I tried to think of every contingency without packing everything we owned. Fortunately, I was able to fit it all in my backpack—a waterproof, fireproof, lightweight, high-tech marvel of modern camping.

The wind whipped at our clothing as we headed out. I led Eve to the back of the mansion, saying very little. As we climbed the rose trellis to the second-story balcony, my stomach churned with angst. The minute my feet hit the pavestones, I felt like we were not alone. I looked around the balcony, but I couldn't see anyone.

I helped Eve onto the pavestones, and we stood for a moment to catch our breath. The wind blew even harder there, moaning and howling like a chorus of lost souls.

"It feels like someone's watching us," were Eve's first words.

"I feel it too," I confessed. "Come on, let's get this over with."

We approached the tall windows and cupped our hands around our eyes so we could see inside. I immediately saw a pair of eyes staring back at me. And they weren't a reflection or a painting this time. They were blinking, real human eyes—staring at me through thick glass lenses. I cried out and fell back.

Eve helped me up. "What's the matter? Did you see something?"

"Yeah. Someone's in there. A boy, I think."

She glanced back at the dark sunroom. "Who?"

"I don't know. I didn't see any other details."

"How did he get in there?"

I scanned the length of the glass wall and saw that the vented portion of one window had been wedged open. "Come on," I said, heading toward the opening.

We crawled through the narrow gap and stood in the musty great room. The large, open space was two stories high and smelled of dust and rot. Nineteenth-century, hand-painted tapestries hung from the walls; moth-eaten bed sheets covered the assorted furniture; disintegrating, braided area rugs littered the floor. The portrait of Summerdale Collier hung in the center of the back wall, his menacing scowl bearing down on us. It sent a chill up my spine that made me shudder.

Eve stood behind me, her hands gripping my shoulders. "There— below the portrait," she whispered.

Standing in a dark pool of shadow directly under the dour visage of Mr. Collier was the vague shape of someone about my size.

"H-hello?" I stammered.

"Hi," the shape said, stepping from the darkness.

I nearly ran until, to my relief, it turned out to be Bug.

"How did you get in here?" I asked, feeling the panic drain from my body.

He pointed to the open window vent we'd just crawled through.

Ask a dumb question . . .

"I mean, *what* are you doing here?" I persisted.

"There is something you should know," he said in a steady voice.

The wind lashed the windowpanes with blasts of sand, adding a serpentine hiss to the constant howling. It felt as if something wanted to prevent Bug from speaking to us. We hunkered on the floor.

"What should I know?"

"This is a bad place."

"Why hasn't anyone looted this place?" Eve asked, looking around.

"Because of the curse," Bug answered. "Anyone who has tried has disappeared."

That didn't make sense. "Wait. If a random looter breaks in and disappears, how do you know he was even here? Most looters don't announce they're going to loot a place beforehand."

Bug wasn't fazed. "Many people come to town, ask about the Death House, then disappear."

"How do you know they didn't just leave town?" Eve asked.

"We know," he said cryptically.

"Some Indian sixth sense?" she teased.

"No. Paiute legend."

"Oh yeah. The one no one talks about," I said.

He nodded.

"Shane said no one really knows the legend anymore, it's so old."

"Shane is an idiot." For some reason, it sounded extra funny coming from Bug.

"Do you know the legend?" Eve asked.

He nodded again. "It is said the greedy man did too. Mr. Collier. But he built his house in the wrong place anyway."

"'The wrong place.' That's what Dee called it."

"He knows this spot is cursed. It is a wrong place, a bad place."

"Why?" Eve asked. "What makes it wrong?"

"Evil has always been here."

"Really?" I asked, glancing around.

"Not here," he said, gesturing to the room. "Here," he said, pointing straight down. "This place is wrong. This place has bad energy. Animals always go crazy here. People always disappear. You should not be here too long, or you will disappear."

"Animals go crazy?" I asked.

He tapped the side of his head. "Their mind becomes empty. Not stupid empty, like Shane, but crazy empty. Not in control. Makes them do evil things."

"Evil things? Like being possessed by an evil spirit?" Eve asked.

He nodded grimly. "Since before the time of my grandfather's grandfather. Cattle come here to drink, they go mad and run off cliffs. Snakes and lizards here act strange, bite themselves, have strange babies."

"Strange babies?" Eve asked.

"Snake babies have two heads, sometimes three. Many have legs and claws."

"Snakeleg," I whispered.

He nodded again. "It is not something we speak of," he said, explaining why he hadn't mentioned it earlier.

"So the story of the miner who got drunk and saw a snake with legs is true?"

"Yes."

"Do you know *why* this place is cursed?" Eve asked.

Bug closed his eyes and drew a deep breath through his nose. "The legend is the origin of the Paiute people. The legend tells of a giant named Tse'nahaha who killed people by looking at them. One night, a group of people were playing a game in a house built here. They were having a good time. They set a woman outside to watch for Tse'nahaha. After a while, she heard the giant coming. He was talking to himself and singing. The woman tried to warn the people inside that the giant was coming, but they would not listen to her. Tse'nahaha was getting closer. The woman became frightened, jumped into a pit, and pulled a basket over herself.

"She heard Tse'nahaha come to a stop. He stooped down and crawled into the doorway of the house. Twice he made a sucking noise with his lips. When the people in the house looked at the giant, they turned to ash at once. Only a little baby was left inside, sleeping in a box. Tse'nahaha then went away.

"When it was almost daylight, the baby started to cry. The woman left the pit and went inside, but she did not look at the dead people. She called to the baby and said, 'Let us go away.' She set the house on fire, took the baby, and went away."

"What a terrible story," Eve said.

"It is the story of Shivwits."

"The Shivwits?" she echoed, failing to hide a smile.

"That is our tribal name. Look it up if you do not believe me."

"We believe you, Bug," I said, cutting in. "Is your tribe descended from the baby, then?"

"No, from the woman. The baby was later eaten by another giant named Pu'ihi."

"*Ack*. That *is* a terrible story," Eve said.

"But what's it got to do with this house?" I asked.

He again pointed to the floor in between us. "This is the location of the woman's house. That is why it is considered a bad place—or the wrong place to build a house. Anyone who spends too much time in this place dies. It is cursed because of the giant Tse'nahaha. Even now you can smell his rotted breath."

Eve stood and swept the beam of her flashlight across the tapestries.

"What are you looking for?" I asked.

"All legends stem from something real that the people of the time could not explain. If the Paiute legend says she hid in a pit, then there has to be a pit somewhere. Maybe one of these tapestries shows the location."

"Why is finding the pit important?" I asked, standing.

She favored me with a look of annoyance. In the partial illumination of the flashlights, her eyes looked even freakier than before. "Because I bet you anything that's where we'll find the answers to this one-hundred-year-old mystery."

The tapestries showed various scenes of formal hunting excursions, fields of wheat, or old, English-style gardens. Only one of them showed the mansion, and the detailing was exquisite. There was no question it'd been painted right after the mansion was built because everything appeared brand-new.

"Man, this thing's amazing," I said with unmasked delight. "It even has the pumpkin patch off to the side."

Eve stepped closer. "I wonder when this changed."

"What?"

"This entrance. See? It looks like a large coal chute or a delivery bay where the sunroom now stands. It seems to drop into the basement."

Staring closely at the century-old artwork, I asked, "Hey, Bug, does this place have a basement?"

When he didn't respond, I turned my flashlight to where he'd been standing. He wasn't there. "Bug?" I called out.

No answer.

Eve swept her beam around the room. The place was empty. "I think he left us."

"I can see that. But . . . why?"

Chapter 16

FASTENING VELCRO LED LAMPS TO our foreheads, we made our way down an elegant staircase to the main foyer. *Ostentatious* didn't come close to describing the place. Hardwood and marble abounded—as did dust and cobwebs.

We didn't waste time searching through each room. We knew our destination lay *beneath* the mansion. Finding a stairway in a back room, we descended on treads that complained with each step. The stairs seemed to go on forever, angling back and forth, and before long, I was certain we'd dipped well below ground level. At the base of the stairs was a stone room about twenty feet square.

"The pit?" Eve proposed.

"Maybe," I replied.

Shelves lined rough-hewn, sandstone walls. On the shelves lay an assortment of archaic mining tools, including some hard hats with candlelit headlamps. In the center of one wall, a wooden door hung skewed on one rusty hinge.

"Are we going in?" I asked.

"Do you want to solve this mystery?"

As I pulled the old handle, it crumbled in my hand. Rocking back, I lunged at the door with my shoulder. Much to my delight, it gave way with a loud crack. The sound of the thick door hitting the ground echoed into the blackness of a narrow passageway beyond. A strong waft of sulfuric air assaulted our noses.

We looked at each other, unable to hide expressions of worry. The stench was horrible.

"The giant's breath?" Eve whispered. I could have done without the correlation, but she was probably right.

I rummaged through my backpack and pulled out two state-of-the-art, collapsible gas masks. When Eve flashed a questioning look, I said, "No respectable doomsday prepper leaves home without one."

The masks featured a plastic face shield connected to a class-one HEPA respirator that strapped at the back of the head. You could talk while wearing the mask, but it made your voice sound like Darth Vader.

The long passageway was roughly five feet wide and was littered with debris, crumbled stone, and decades of dust. A large room at the end of the passageway joined with three tunnels of similar dimensions. The tunnels were chiseled from solid sandstone; the pickaxe marks were plainly evident, gouging down each wall in uniform striations.

"Which way?" Eve asked, indicating the three tunnels intersecting at the chamber.

I held up a cigarette lighter and flicked it to life. Moving to the mouth of each tunnel, I held the lighter steady. Only one of the paths bent the flame.

"This one," I said, pulling a chemical glow stick from my pack, snapping it to life, and setting it at the tunnel entrance to mark our direction of travel. The fluorescent glow illuminated the chamber in a sickly, bile-yellow hue.

As I took a step, Eve asked a question that stopped me cold. "Adam, what exactly are we looking for?"

I wasn't sure. Would there be evidence in these catacombs that proved the Collier legend a hoax? Would we find something that made sense out of all the mystery? Or would we run into a real giant—finding something that put our lives in jeopardy, perhaps even killing us?

"I don't know," I admitted. "I guess we're looking for anything that might explain what really happened to the Colliers or why the mine closed."

Eve nodded. "Okay." Her voice sounded funny—more so than the gas mask would cause. I couldn't tell if she was frightened or excited. I freely admitted I was terrified.

The air was close and heavy in the tunnel. Taking a calming breath, I noticed that even with the HEPA filter, the air still tasted old and tainted.

Our flashlights converted from an intense single beam to a bright lantern with the sliding of a sleeve. I switched my flashlight to lantern mode for a fuller illumination and moved forward. The tunnel was tall enough to stand in, but there were a few places where I had to duck and a few where I had to shimmy sideways because it was so narrow. The stone floor tilted steadily downward.

Before long, we came to another small chamber that served as an intersection for four more tunnels, two of which had been sealed with rocks. If this pattern continued we'd soon have too many options to navigate in one evening. Pulling out a compass, I tried to get my bearings. With dread, I saw that most of the tunnels led toward town. Did they actually extend that far? Or farther?

"Which way now?" Eve asked.

I held up my lighter again but couldn't distinguish which way the draft blew. Examining the floor, I could tell one tunnel had seen more traffic than the other one. Directly inside the tunnel sat an old wooden crate about the size of a breadbox. A faded label on the top read PENNIMEN'S EXTRADYNAMITE.

"What is it?" Eve asked.

"Explosives. Dynamite."

I picked up a rock and prepared to strike the rusty padlock securing the lid.

"Wait! Is that safe to do?"

"I think so. This says it's '*extra*dynamite,' which means it's made with ammonium nitrate instead of nitroglycerin. It's a lot more stable than Nobel's original stuff."

She shook her head. "Geez, you *are* a nerd."

"Pretty much."

I used the rock as a hammer, and the padlock fractured with a single strike, dropping to the floor. I cautiously opened the lid.

"Sweet," I exclaimed, removing a faded stick of dynamite. Its fuse was still attached. "They probably used this to seal these tunnels."

"Is it still good?" Eve asked.

"I don't know. It's a hundred years old, so probably not. But you never know."

"How much is there?" she asked, leaning in.

The box was nearly empty; five sticks of dynamite were all that remained. "Just five."

"What are you going to do with them?"

"Bring them along, of course. You never know when you'll need a stick of dynamite." I stuffed them into my backpack. "This way," I said, heading into the tunnel.

Eve followed without comment.

A bend in the tunnel led us to a chamber lined with several more intersecting passages that'd all been sealed off.

"Oops," Eve said. "Guess we should've picked the other path."

I wasn't so sure. "Wait a sec. You gotta wonder *why* they sealed these off. Was there no silver in them, or were they trying to hide something?"

I went to the entrance of each passageway and kicked up puffs of dust. They all settled back to the ground—except one. The dust clearly drifted away from one of the rubble blockages.

Without another word, we began removing the rocks and dirt with our hands and could soon feel a steady breeze against our skin. But the stench coming through was horrific. The gas mask seemed of little use as the smells of decay, sulfur, and ash wafted past us.

As soon as a hollow appeared, I switched my flashlight back to a beam, shined it into the emptiness, and saw . . . nothing. It was as if the chamber behind the stone wall was a black hole, sucking in everything, including light.

The feelings I'd had compelling me to explore the mansion suddenly turned to warnings of imminent danger. And death. I felt a very strong urge to turn and run. "I don't think we should go this way," I said slowly.

"Why not?" Eve asked.

I couldn't explain it, other than to say I was having bad premonitions. "I just don't."

"Nonsense," Eve said climbing past me and peering into the darkness. "Ugh—what a stench."

"That's one reason," I said.

Without looking at me, she said, "Hey, I work at Denny's; I've smelled worse. Let's go find out what the Colliers were hiding."

With nervous resignation, I agreed. We soon came to a second closure, this one not so complete. As we rolled away enough rocks to make an opening big enough to crawl through, my mind screamed for me to stop. Yes, going on might provide the answers I sought, but would they be answers that led to our demise?

I pushed the thoughts aside and shimmied through—and immediately plunged headfirst down a steep embankment of loose rubble and scree. I backpedaled with my hands, but my efforts only kicked up blinding clouds of dust. The faster I scrambled, the more speed I seemed to pick up.

I heard Eve scream my name.

I clawed with my fingers and dug my toes into the loose surface but to no avail. I was heading face-first into a black void at a relentless speed.

Then I felt nothing, as if the ground had suddenly vanished beneath me.

It had.

I was falling.

Chapter 17

I LANDED HARD ON MY side. The air burst from my lungs; my gas mask flew from my face. I heard the brittle snapping of bones but felt no significant pain. A shower of pebbles and dust rained down, pelting me for almost a full minute. I covered my head with my arms. When the downpour ceased, I rolled to my back and sat up. My backpack hung loosely off one shoulder.

Eve's light showed faintly above me, yet all around me was a strange darkness. Not as black as night but much like the subdued, reddish glow that accompanied an encroaching twilight.

Fumbling for my flashlight, I switched it on, praying it hadn't broken. Luckily, it blazed to life. A hollow scraping and crunching accompanied my movements, the ground shifting under me with each effort. It sounded like I was atop numerous sticks of blackboard chalk. I pointed the beam to where I sat—and stifled a gasp. The shifting, brittle sounds came from hundreds of bones. From the skull staring back at me between my kneecaps, I knew they were human bones.

"Adam, can you hear me?" Eve's voice filtered down.

"Yes," I yelled. "Don't go any farther. There's a steep drop-off."

"Are you hurt?"

"No. I'm okay."

"Can you see anything down there?"

"Yeah. Bones. Human bones. A lot of them."

Silence followed. She probably thought I was joking.

"Just stay put," I called up. "Let me get my bearings."

I clambered awkwardly to my feet. Suddenly, my head was spinning. I swallowed and grimaced. My throat was on fire, and while I couldn't remember screaming, it felt like I'd been doing so for hours. A headache raged behind my eyes, pounding so fiercely it was hard to concentrate. The air was pungent, thick, and I couldn't breathe without it searing my lungs. *My gas mask!*

Slipping my mask back on my face, I took some deep breaths to clear my lungs. Almost immediately, my thoughts began to sharpen. As my head cleared, I saw that a large room stretched out before me. It was almost a perfect circle, about seventy feet across. The ceiling—pitch black and sagging—was covered in soot. The rim from which I'd fallen extended at least thirty feet above me. I was at the edge of the circle, atop a tall pile of bones, gravel, and other debris: metal hardhats, a lantern, arrowheads, pickaxe heads, pottery shards, metal boot soles, shovel heads. Everything was old and warped; most articles looked like the ceiling, blackened as if by fire.

Looking back up the gravel slope, I knew I couldn't scale it. For every foot gained, I'd most likely slide back two.

"Adam! Say something," Eve yelled down. She had to have removed her gas mask to get such volume.

I lifted my mask briefly. "Put your mask back on. I'm okay. Just give me a minute to figure things out."

The floor of the cavern was uneven, fissured, and scorched. I could feel heat pulsing up through the fissures, accompanied by a strongly caustic smell, a sulfurous odor with the acidic bite of burnt things. A faint glow emanated from deep within the crevasses.

I focused my beam on them. It was then I realized I was sweating profusely. It was hot down here. Very hot. Muffled hissing sounds also rose from the dimly glowing crevasses, sounding very much like snakes issuing a warning. The moment I asked myself where I was, the answer hit me like a freight train.

I was in an old lava tube, perhaps in the caldera itself. And it was still active!

That's what the premonitions were about! Something bad *was* going to happen. It hadn't happened in a hundred years. The last time it had, it burned up hundreds of miners. That was why Summerdale Collier had closed the mine. He hadn't wanted anyone knowing he'd tunneled into an active volcano. He'd tried to conceal it by backfilling the tube and building a house on top of the mine, but his greed had stopped him from sealing the mine altogether. He'd still wanted more silver or something, so he and his wife had continued to dig until it killed both of them.

This was the pit Bug had told us about. This exact location *had* to be the origin of the Paiute legend. The giant that killed the men in the house was the toxic, burning gas from the lava flow. That was the "sucking noise" the woman had heard. Nowadays, experts called it a pyroclastic surge. It also explained the rotten, sulfurous smells and strange sounds coming from the old mansion.

Somehow, I'd sensed the event was about to repeat. Just like Old Faithful in Yellowstone, this lava geyser was ticking down to another eruption—an eruption that could wipe out our entire town. And I was sitting in the middle of the caldera!

Chapter 18

"Adam?" Eve called again. "What's going on?"

I took a breath and pulled the mask from my face. "I'm in some kind of volcanic pit." I didn't want to tell her the complete truth. Not yet, anyway. "I'm okay. But don't come any closer."

"Why not?"

"There's no way back up the slope. Oh, and there's poisonous gas down here."

I heard her cry out. "Then put your mask on and stop talking!"

"Then stop asking me questions!"

After donning my mask, I began sweeping the walls with my flashlight, looking for hand holds or some way to climb out. I wondered how high the lava had risen in the past. Since there were bones and artifacts under my feet, it couldn't have totally filled this chamber. Molten rock was so hot it could even melt . . . well, rock. And while pyroclastic gas wasn't hot enough to melt rock, at 800-plus degrees, it did incinerate pretty much everything else. That would explain why solid things like axe heads, hard hats, and arrowheads were left behind but soft things like wooden axe handles and human skin and muscle would fry.

Across the chamber, I spied a skinny iron ladder running up the far wall, almost to the height of where I'd fallen in. It was my only way out. But to get to it, I'd have to tightrope walk between the crevasses. That wasn't very appealing for several reasons: One, the rock forming the ridges was sandstone, which had been pockmarked and eroded by pyroclastic flows and eons of extreme heat. I had no idea how crumbly they'd be or if they'd even support my weight. Two, the crevasses were deep, so deep my beam couldn't reach the bottom. Falling into one would be fatal. And if the fall didn't kill me, the extreme heat down there would. And three, even though the thin ladder reached up to an adjoining tunnel, I had no idea where that tunnel led. It could be a way out or a dead end. But it was my only choice.

My head was getting woozy again, and my vision blurred in and out. My gas mask may have initially saved my life, but it wouldn't keep the threat at bay for long. I probably had only a matter of minutes before I succumbed.

I took a breath and called up, "There's a ladder on the other side. I'm going to climb it to get a better look at the situation."

"Be careful," Eve called back.

Using a pickaxe head, I poked at a foot-wide ridge between two smoking fissures. Shards of stone ricocheted noisily into the glowing depths on either side, but the ridge itself seemed solid enough. I took a tentative step onto it and gave it all my weight. It held firm.

The crest made a few jogs and dips, but it went all the way to the far side of the tube. I adjusted my backpack and gas mask, secured my headlamp, and took another step. Using the pickaxe head as a balance, I continued my trek with a cautious, steady pace. Sweat was pouring into my eyes, making a precarious journey even more hazardous.

When I was about halfway across, Eve called out, "What's that strange red glow?"

I wasn't about to stop to answer her. She was smart; she'd figure it out. I knew the answer to her question, but I didn't want to voice it. Seeing the glow meant the magma was rising. That wasn't a surprise; I'd known it was going to do so anyway. It'd be just my luck for the thing to erupt early. I took another step and heard a low rumble from deep within the bowels of the earth. Not good.

"Did you hear that?" Eve called with a shaky voice.

Duh!

I took another step. Another deep rumble belched up the crevasses.

"Adam?"

I took a quick breath. "Yes, I heard it. There must be an active vent line that runs through this area."

Right then, the ground gave a sudden jolt. I slipped and stumbled and fell. Still holding the pickaxe, my hands shot upward. A harsh screeching made my ears ring, and my descent suddenly stopped. Both tines of the pickaxe head had gouged into opposite sides of the fissure. My feet dangled into the nothingness below me.

"I'm okay," I yelled, though I doubted she heard me through my mask.

Looking up, I saw that I'd fallen only about six feet before scraping to a halt. Using the roughness of the crevasse walls, I was able to chimney crawl around the axe head and out of the fissure. The rock was hot, but it didn't burn me. Standing on the narrow ridge again, I took only a moment to catch my breath. The earth growled angrily, as if upset that it had missed a fresh meal.

I staggered quickly to the opposite side of the chamber and leaned against the far wall. I felt my strength waning quickly. My head pounded madly, and I knew my HEPA filter was failing. The toxins down here were simply too concentrated. Still, I wondered if that even mattered. If the ancient volcano down here was still active, it could destroy the town of Snakeleg in a single blast. Either way, I'd be dead.

Eve was shining her light on me, though at that distance, it did little good. Once more, the earth groaned and trembled to the point of causing small landslides into the cavern.

The bottom rungs of the iron ladder were warped and corroded, and a few were attached only on one side. The first rung was about three feet off the ground. I tugged on it and was able to bend it without much effort. That wasn't encouraging. As I grabbed the next one up, a loud wheeze came from the grotto behind me. The giant was drawing a huge breath. There was a brief pause before plumes of gray-white smoke rocketed from the fissures. I grabbed a full rung at about head level and hopped onto the bottom half rung. The ladder quivered and shrieked, but it held to the wall. Like the stone below, the metal was hot to the touch but not enough to burn.

I ascended the rungs quickly, being careful to put my hands and feet close to the side rails, which were stronger than the middle. When I'd climbed about twelve feet, the hissing geyser belched with a deafening squeal. I turned in time to see flecks of glowing lava fall from the plume of smoke. The heat in the chamber rose exponentially. I couldn't hear Eve, but I was certain she was screaming at me to climb—as if I needed the encouragement.

I made my ascent with less caution, more speed. As I neared the top, the plume of smoke suddenly ceased, as did the noise. An eerie echo bounced down the tunnels leading away from the junction. Again, I wondered where they led. This was an abandoned mine, after all. Maybe there *was* still some silver down one of the tunnels. Or was there something even more valuable?

"Adam, get out of there! This place is going to erupt!" Eve yelled.

I knew she'd figured it out.

I scrambled over the top rung and sat on a ledge with my back against the wall. Looking down, I was able to see the bottom of the chamber more clearly. The fissures continued to softly hiss, gurgle, and belch with pent-up urgency. Pulses of white and yellow flashed from deep within the recesses. The earth grumbled faintly and steadily. We didn't have much time.

"Adam!"

I stood, took a huge breath, and removed my mask. "I know! Get out of here now!" I yelled across the chasm. "Go back through the mansion."

"What are you going to do?"

"I'm going to find another way out."

As I stood, the strange shape of the bulging ceiling again caught my attention. Having gone spelunking with my dad, I was familiar with many cave formations. From my perch on the rim, I clearly saw a one-foot gap between the ceiling and the roof of the cavern, like a stubby, upside-down mushroom, indicating an enormous hanging shelf. It was roughly the same diameter as the cavern and circled the entire perimeter of the ceiling. And it was only about fifteen feet away.

"Adam, what are you waiting for? Go!" she yelled.

"I think I've found a way to stop this thing from erupting," I yelled back.

"Are you crazy? You can't stop a volcano from erupting!"

"Maybe not. But maybe I can at least divert it."

"How?"

I shrugged my backpack from my shoulders, pulled out a stick of dynamite, and held it up. "Dynamite."

"Are you insane?" she screamed. "You'll kill us both!"

"That's why you need to go. Now! Go back through the mansion and get out. I have no idea if this will work, and you need to get Simon and my family away from here!"

A loud steam geyser rocketed from a fissure, drowning out our voices. Finally, Eve straightened, blew me a kiss, pointed at her watch, and went back up the tunnel.

I didn't know if she was requesting enough time for her to exit or if she was indicating that I didn't have much time. Either way, I wanted to wait as long as possible, hoping the volcano would comply.

But it didn't.

The shaking of the ground, the increases in heat and steam, and the unrelenting noise indicated eruption was beginning. And there I loitered with a backpack full of dynamite.

Maybe I *was* insane.

Chapter 19

My INTENT WAS TO DROP the hanging shelf right on the caldera, thereby plugging it. In doing so, I hoped to shunt the pressure to other vents—with any luck, some deeper in the mountainside and away from town. But there was no telling if it would work. I could instead trigger an eruption that would wipe Snakeleg from the map . . . which was about to happen anyway.

There was only one way to find out.

I turned to look at my escape route. The tunnel was scorched black, but I could see several streaks of yellow flowstone through the pitch. That meant the avenue wasn't totally blocked. I ventured a few yards into the narrowing shaft, getting a feel for where I'd be running.

Around the first bend, I came to a fork in the tunnel. One path angled up, the other down. Which way to go? I figured the best way was toward the surface, so I decided to follow the path that ascended. I knew pyroclastic flows usually followed the path of least resistance, so there had to be a vent of some kind ahead of me. It was an extremely dangerous path to follow, considering the volcano was seconds from fully erupting, but to intentionally choose a dead end would not be smart either. I was between a rock and a hard place, in more ways than one. And time was no longer running out; it was gone.

The vent tube I hoped for was just beyond the tunnel entrance. It stood about waist high and angled off from the tunnel. Sticking my head inside, I saw a faint pinpoint of light. That was good enough for me.

I ran back to the open pit and took out a stick of dynamite. The red paper wrapping was corroded and flaky. Would it explode? Would the fuse even light? Would my aim be good enough?

I knew that explosions on a flat surface didn't cause much damage. But put the same explosion in a confined space and the results were devastating. I needed to get the dynamite into the one-foot gap between the huge hanging ceiling and the roof. And there was only one way to do that.

I yanked the fuse from the stick and lit it. It sparked and sputtered but finally caught and burned slowly to the end. That was good. A fast-burning fuse would prevent my escape. I grabbed the fuseless explosive, cocked my arm back, took aim, and hurled it at the gap. The dynamite flipped through the air . . . and bounced off the roof before it even reached the gap. It only then occurred to me that a miss meant the dynamite would fall into the red-hot fissures below. Cringing, I curled into a ball and held my breath. A second later, a loud explosion knocked me on my back. I waited for a pyroclastic surge to follow, but luckily, none came. The single stick of dynamite hadn't been enough to accelerate the eruption. But would I be so lucky the next time? I couldn't risk another practice throw. I had to go for broke. I hoped Eve had already made it out.

I took out two more sticks of dynamite and bound them together with some string from my kit. I then donned my backpack, twisted back, and lit both fuses at the same time. When they sputtered to life, I launched them at the ceiling. Fortunately, my aim was much better this time. The explosives flipped through the air and disappeared into the blackness between the hanging ceiling and the roof.

I turned and ran. I expected to be thrown to the ground again, but the fuses took their time burning. Either that, or they'd burnt out . . .

I slowed my pace when I saw the vent tube I hoped would be my escape. Just as I stooped to crawl inside, a concussive boom surged up the narrow tunnel, slamming into my side. The air burst from my lungs as I was thrown against the rough-hewn wall. I fell to my knees, ripping my jeans and scraping the flesh from both kneecaps. Grimacing against the pain, I got to my feet and took a step forward—then stopped. Something wasn't right. The dynamite had exploded, but nothing else seemed to have happened. There should have been a lot more noise. Apparently, the blast hadn't been strong enough to separate the hanging shelf from the cave ceiling. I briefly considered going back to try again. I still had two more sticks of dynamite.

I removed the remaining sticks from my backpack and ran back to the pit. Steam filled the cavern; I couldn't see a thing. Quickly lighting the fuses on the remaining two sticks, I hurled them toward where I estimated the stone ceiling still hung. Then I turned and ran again.

I'd barely made it halfway back to the vent tube when I heard another explosion, accompanied by a deafening crack from the caldera. The bass rumble of rending stone and crushing rock followed. The ground shook ferociously. Once more, I was knocked to my hands and knees. Blinding pain caused me to cry out.

Taking in a huge breath, I clambered to my feet and staggered the rest of the way to the narrow vent. I thrust my upper body in and saw the faint pinpoint of light again. The tube was big enough to crawl through—but just barely. Good thing I was skinny. I switched off my flashlight to make sure I wasn't imagining the light. Claustrophobic blackness threatened to envelop me, but there was definitely a light. My escape. Maybe. The implications of traveling toward a light at the end of a dark tunnel played an evil game with my courage.

As I removed my backpack and switched on my headlamp, something in the tunnel directly beyond the vent caught my eye. It glinted dully off my light. Not having time to examine it, I simply crammed it into my backpack, and then I tied the straps of my backpack to one ankle and lunged into the narrow vent. As my feet cleared the lip, a massive explosion ripped through the tunnel. The entire vent tube jerked violently to one side. I smacked my head against the wall, tearing my mask from my face. As I regained my focus, a surge of blistering air blew past me, burning my sinuses.

The giant, Tse'nahaha, had returned. Even if my attempt to plug the caldera had succeeded, a pyroclastic surge could still fill these side tunnels. Knowing I had only seconds, I wriggled as fast as I could, but the steep angle and confining dimensions made a speedy climb impossible; the backpack dragging behind didn't help either. I scrambled up the coarse, volcanic rock, ignoring the tearing of my flesh.

A steady rain of pebbles, dust, and dirt cascaded down from the opening above me. I soon reached the pinpoint of light, but grime matted my eyes, and I could barely see. I could barely breathe. Hot air swirled around me, noxious and suffocating. As another explosion shook the small tube, blistering gas rushed past me, causing my shoes to smolder and carrying with it the stench of melting rubber.

Following another cascade of dirt, the pinpoint of light widened into a narrow, harsh beam. A few scraggly roots clung to clumps of dirt and rock. The sunlight burned my eyes. When had it become daytime? I didn't think we'd been underground that long. With gut-wrenching awareness, I knew that meant today was *the* day: Friday the thirteenth.

Reaching the opening, I pushed against the remaining blockage of dirt. It moved but not by much. I had no idea where it exited, but I knew it was my only chance of escape. Fresh wisps of air filtered in, giving me strength to keep trying.

Another explosion rocked the ground. A hiss of steam shrieked past me, burning my exposed flesh. I gritted my teeth and pushed harder against the dirt over my head. It moved one or two inches, no more. Steam continued to spew from the vent tube, scalding my lungs. But the moisture in it also softened the dirt and roots. The more I pushed, the more they gave way. My head was throbbing, my chest pounding, my skin burning. The noxious fumes were debilitating. I felt my strength failing with each passing second. I knew moments counted. I had to get out. Now!

Clenching my jaw till it hurt, I gathered all my strength and gave one last heave against the clot of earth—and broke through. But freeing the blockage also freed the pressure behind me, and I was jettisoned into the air like a wad spit from a straw. I flew maybe ten feet before hitting the ground with a jolt. The air burst from my lungs, making breathing impossible for a few seconds. I curled into a ball, fighting for each lungful of oxygen, drawing in huge gasps of air.

The ground raged in a pinpoint earthquake. The caldera was directly below me—Tse'nahaha was angry.

I rolled to my knees, squinting against the daylight. I almost smiled, wondering if I was in the same place the heads of Summerdale and Ethelred Collier had been found that fateful Friday-the-thirteenth night one hundred years ago.

Untying the backpack still strapped to my ankle, I staggered to my feet. The mansion swayed drunkenly. Shingles and siding, bricks and trim fell from the building in a constant rain. I was surprised the structure hadn't collapsed already. The noise was thunderous. Screeching, wailing, hissing sounds rent the air. Smoke billowed from broken windows and gaps in the roof. Anyone in the mansion would be toast.

Eve! Was she still inside?

I stumbled to the street and saw her standing at the wrought-iron entrance. She was fixated on the front door, probably expecting me to walk through at any moment. The look of concern on her face emboldened me. I jogged toward her, smiling.

"I wouldn't stand there too long," I called.

She gasped and spun around. Tears sprang to those mesmeric eyes. "I don't believe it," she cried as she wrapped her arms around me.

The added pressure stung my burnt skin, but I wasn't about to say so. I wasn't stupid. Eventide Mudswallow had her arms around me, squeezing me affectionately. I only wished Shane was watching.

Chapter 20

IT TOOK ONLY A MINUTE to run to my house. The whole street was trembling. Dad was waiting at the garage door. He'd already gathered the family and Simon into the fallout shelter.

"Get in quickly," he urged. "I'm going to seal it off."

Right then, a chest-thumping boom came from the mansion, knocking us back a step. The ground under the Death House heaved, buckled, then collapsed into a large sinkhole. The hillside behind the property immediately destabilized, and a massive landslide filled in the hole. It was like some fantastic magician's trick: one minute the house was there, the next minute it was gone. The giant had just swallowed the old mansion whole.

"Let's go," Dad ordered.

We climbed down into the fallout shelter. My mom, Zeek, and Simon, all with gas masks on, sat around a small table. It looked like some alien séance. Simon and my brother also wore large, black plastic trash bags down their backs as superhero capes.

Seeing Eve, Simon stood and held his hand out clawlike toward his sister. In a low, ominous voice, he said, "Do not underestimate the power of the dark side."

I couldn't help but laugh. *If he only knew . . .*

I explained to my dad what I'd done in the abandoned mine. He immediately powered up his short-wave radio and tuned to one of his apocalypse-watch stations. Reports of tremors were coming in from as far away as Groom Lake and St. George. But here in our underground, steel-reinforced, concrete bunker, all was eerily still. The ground had stopped shaking, and the hissing and booming from the pyroclastic surge had silenced.

"Papoose Lake is boiling," someone said over the radio.

Dad smiled at me. "Apparently, your diversion worked."

"The vent tubes go that far?" I asked, astonished.

"This whole area is an ancient volcanic basin, but I had no idea it was still active!" he said in shock. "Luckily, the Collier volcano appears to be a small one—thank goodness. Still, I wouldn't be surprised if tremors are reported a hundred miles from here."

"Imagine what this will do for the Paiute legend," Eve said with a smirk.

"Imagine what Papoose Lake coming to a boil will do for Area 51," I replied.

Mom tended to my wounds as we talked about what we'd seen in and under the Collier mansion. I marveled at how little I was seriously injured. My knees were pretty gashed, but the damage to my skin only felt like a really bad sunburn. Fortunately, my fireproof backpack had worked as a damper in the vent tube. My eyes were sore but functioning, and I could finally breathe normally. Even better, Eve seemed no worse for wear.

After about three hours, an all-clear was announced over the airways. Wearing a full bio-containment suit and holding a toxic-gas detector, my dad cautiously emerged from the fallout shelter. After a few minutes, he returned and helped us out.

Looking around, it was clear that my efforts *had* paid off. The mansion was gone, but the rest of my neighborhood and the town were relatively unharmed. The main force of the volcano *had* gone elsewhere.

For a multitude of reasons, Dad suggested we all keep my involvement in the eruption a secret. I reluctantly agreed. Every kid wanted to be a hero; but as long as Eve knew, I was happy.

People were already gathering on our street to gawk at where the Death House used to be. Whispers of ghosts and demons and Indian legends took a frenzied journey through the crowd. There was mention of volcanoes and sinkholes and government experiments, but all conversations came back to the same conclusions: the Collier mansion had been built on a bad place.

Eve took my arm, and we walked away to find some privacy. "So do you think the Colliers are finally at rest?" she asked.

"I'd like to think so."

"I still can't figure how their heads ended up severed."

"You weren't in that vent tube," I said with a snort. "If there was a pyroclastic surge, it would have burnt them to a crisp. Perhaps the pressure in the tube detached their heads and shot them out like a potato cannon."

She grimaced. "Your imagination worries me."

"Well, at least it's plausible," I said, glancing back at the empty, steaming hillside.

She gave a wan smile, dropping her gaze and shuffling her feet. "I bet this town has a lot more history to discover. I only wish I was going to be here to help."

I unlinked our arms so I could face her. "What do you mean?"

She looked at me with true remorse. "With all this excitement, it won't be long before someone finds out about Simon and me. They'll want to take Simon away and—" She choked on the words, unable to finish her thought.

I put my arm around her. I couldn't believe I had guts enough to do it. "Look, my parents fell in love with Simon the minute they met him. I bet you anything they'd be willing to be his foster parents."

"But . . . but he needs so much. He's been hurt, Adam, and I haven't been able to give him everything he requires. Your parents would be taking on a lot—more than I can ask. I told you he needs professional counseling. I can't pay for a psychiatrist, and I certainly can't ask your parents to pay for one."

"Oh, I think you can afford anything you want."

Her amazing eyes narrowed in a questioning look.

"Follow me," I said with a grin.

Returning to our garage, I lifted my backpack. "Here. Open it."

She took the pack and drew back the flap. Reaching inside, she pulled out the translucent lump of multicolored rock I'd found in the mine. "What in the world is this?"

"I'm no gemologist, but it looks to me like a fairly high-grade chunk of opal."

"Opal?"

"Yeah. You sometimes find it in silver mines. I've read that some opal goes for thousands of dollars an ounce. We'll have to have it appraised, but as far as I'm concerned, it's all yours."

She wrapped her arms around me again. It felt amazing. Before I could think about what other miraculous events might happen this day, she took my face and pulled me into a knee-weakening kiss. I could swear the ground started shaking again. But this time, I knew the only one feeling it was me.

The death of the Death House was big news for a while. Several reporters from Las Vegas and St. George showed up with cameras, and local experts and a number of geologists petitioned the BLM for rights to study the area. An appeal was even submitted by the Shivwits tribe to declare the land off-limits due to its sacred nature. But the media frenzy was short-lived, and the scientists headed out after they determined that extensive mining had caused a minor breach in the earth's crust, which had led to the Collier mansion's demise.

Eve's opal turned out to be the real thing, with high ratings in clarity, color, density, and weight. She sold it to a gem shop in Las Vegas for an enormous amount of money. I never asked how much; I really didn't need to know. But apparently, it was plenty because I never saw her wear her Denny's uniform again.

Eventually, the small town of Snakeleg, Nevada, fizzled back into near obscurity. That was fine with me. And as far as Eve was concerned, the more obscure the better.

About the Author

GREGG R. LUKE, R.PH., WAS born in Bakersfield, California, but spent the majority of his childhood and young adult life in Santa Barbara, California. He served an LDS mission in Wisconsin then pursued his education in natural sciences at SBCC, UCSB, and BYU. He completed his schooling at the University of Utah College of Pharmacy.

Gregg currently practices pharmacy in Logan, Utah. He and his wife, Julie, have three children and live in Cache Valley, Utah. He has been published in *Skin Diver* magazine, the *Oceanographic Letter*, and the *New Era* magazine. Gregg has also written six novels, five of which were Whitney Award finalists.

Visit him at www.greggluke.com.

OTHER BOOKS AND AUDIO BOOKS
BY GREGG LUKE

Altered State

Do No Harm

The Survivors

Blink of an Eye

Bloodborne

Deadly Undertakings

HAUNTING REMINDERS

◆ STEPHANIE BLACK ◆

To Stanford and Kathleen McConkie, with love and gratitude

Acknowledgments

THANK YOU TO MY WONDERFUL friends Traci Abramson and Gregg Luke—it's an honor to be part of this project with you! As always, thank you to the talented staff at Covenant Communications, particularly editor Samantha Millburn for her skill, patience, and encouragement.

For their help with the manuscript, thank you to Megan Anderson, Amy Black, Shauna Black, Lora Cinelli, Susan Fredrickson, Rebecca Hall, Azariah McCarthy, Stan McConkie Jr., Sue McConkie, and Jonathan Spell. I really appreciate your feedback, insights, and information.

Chapter 1

JAMIE MCKENZIE LEAPED OVER THE low stone fence separating the parking area from the back lawn of the Treasure Chest and rushed across the grass, dampening her shoes with morning dew. She couldn't believe she'd slept through her alarm, but that was her prize for staying up until 2:00 a.m. piecing together new spring lanyards. If owner Edward Allerton came to check on his store and Jamie hadn't arrived yet, what would he do? Maybe he'd turn to his Puritan ancestors for inspiration and commission the building of a wooden pillory so Jamie could serve time on the town green. Or maybe he'd give her a stern, fatherly look and say, "This is disappointing. Your mother was never late, and I'm sure she taught you the importance of punctuality. I do not tolerate tardiness in my employees. Especially not in my manager."

The morning sun and cloudless blue sky made the leaves overhead so vibrantly green that Jamie's desire to stop and gaze almost derailed her need to hurry. Even though she hadn't endured this year's New England winter, she still reveled in the awe-filled joy of spring. How had she survived five years in Phoenix—a place where trees were an endangered species and *spring* only meant the temperature was climbing toward a hundred degrees?

It was *so* good to be home in Britteridge, Massachusetts—*so* good to be at the Treasure Chest again. Jamie tucked the box of new lanyards under one arm and stuffed the lanyard holding her car keys into her purse. After a moment of digging around, she pulled out the matching lanyard holding her store keys. She'd discovered that wearing one of the spring-flower lanyards around her neck at work was good advertising.

She slid her key into the store's lock. As she opened the door, she inhaled, loving the familiar smells: old wood, mingled with wood polish and new paint, tinged with the cinnamon-apple-citrus-floral scent from the candle section, and touched with wood smoke. It smelled like her childhood— like afternoons in the upstairs book room reading at the antique desk while her mother worked downstairs, like helping out in the kitchen frosting cookies for the town spring gala, like sneaking a few minutes between customers to scan a few pages of the AP U.S. History textbook stuffed under the counter when she worked here as a teenager.

Footsteps tapped on the brick path behind the Treasure Chest, a path Jamie was starting to wish she'd used. The wet grass had reached over the tops of her leather flats and soaked the trouser socks she wore in obedience to Allerton's *Employees must wear socks or stockings at all times* rule. She turned to see Melinda Brennan striding toward her. Except for the streaks of gray in her brown-sugar hair, Melinda looked exactly as she had five years ago when Jamie had left.

"Good morning," Jamie said.

Melinda raised her eyebrows. "Just getting here?"

Jamie held the door open for Melinda. "Don't tell Mr. Allerton."

"I doubt Ed will question me about your habits."

Ed. At twenty-eight, Jamie could probably consider herself a full-fledged adult and address Edward Allerton by his first name like middle-aged Melinda did, but it felt too disrespectful. She'd known Allerton since she was a toddler, and the thought of now addressing him as Ed felt as insolent as greeting Queen Elizabeth II with "Hey, Lizzy."

Melinda hung up her jacket and took her cranberry-red apron off the hook near the back door. "I'll open the upstairs rooms."

"Thanks," Jamie said.

Melinda had sounded matter-of-fact, but the situation embarrassed Jamie. She should have prepared the rooms already, and Melinda usually had little patience for slackers who created extra work for others. Jamie had been back for only a month, and she wanted to make a good impression on the employees, not make them wonder if Allerton had offered her the manager's job out of respect for her mother's two and a half decades of work at the Treasure Chest and not because Jamie was competent.

Melinda headed along the hallway and slipped past the decorative screen that separated the public areas of the Treasure Chest from employee-only areas. Jamie hastily tied her own apron, sparing an affectionate glance at the Treasure Chest logo her mother had designed for the aprons: an embroidered chest spilling gold coins and flowers, along with candlesticks, picture frames, and other knickknacks.

Hurrying, she unlocked the safe, filled the cash drawer, and carried it to the register in the main downstairs room. Through the bay window at the front of the room, she saw a customer approaching. *Six minutes until opening.* Jamie switched on the sound system tucked under a table displaying hand-painted baskets filled with silk tulips. Soft classical music started playing—Copland's "Appalachian Spring." She ran back to the office, grabbed the box of lanyards, and went to refill the nearly empty display from yesterday.

Three minutes left, and the customer was standing on the sidewalk outside the window, looking at the display Jamie had spent a solid eight hours designing and creating. Jamie hustled into the crystal room and switched on the lights, then readied the playroom. The handmade wooden toys were in their bins, and the beanbag chairs were stacked against the wall.

It was still one minute until ten, but close enough. Jamie didn't like keeping a customer waiting. She unlocked the front door and smiled a greeting at the slim blonde woman standing there, arms folded.

"Good . . . morning." Jamie managed to keep the words *almost* steady but felt her eyes bulge and her heart rate jump. Robin Graham. Isaac's mother.

No big deal. She'd known she'd run into the Grahams at some point. "Robin, my goodness, hello! It's so good to see you again." She stepped forward to hug Robin. Robin returned the embrace but so stiffly that her arms barely touched Jamie.

Disconcerted, Jamie stepped back. Maybe Robin hadn't expected such an affectionate greeting after five years—especially given the circumstances of Jamie's departure, after Isaac had dumped her two weeks before their wedding and married Hannah Stokes three months later.

"Hello, Jamie." Robin sounded edgy. "How are you doing?"

"Wonderfully, thank you. Loving being back in Britteridge. I can't figure out how I survived being away so long. Come in." Jamie held the door for her.

Robin walked into the entryway. "How are your parents doing?" she asked, her gaze focused on the antique cherrywood side table and the swirled glass bowl holding Treasure Chest business cards.

"Getting settled in their condo and loving it. Mom said she plans to watch the weather reports here and send me smug e-mails every time we get snow."

Robin smiled, but it was a polite twitch of the lips, not a warm expression. "Yes, Louisa never liked snow. She'll love Florida, if she can endure the summers."

"Can I help you find something?" Jamie decided to skip asking Robin about her family. Considering how uncomfortable Robin appeared already, Jamie didn't want to bumble onto awkward ground. She *had* wondered if some people—particularly the Grahams—might be uneasy with her return to Britteridge, but that hadn't worried her too much. Given time, they'd realize Jamie had been totally over Isaac for years. "We have a darling new batch of summer yard decorations that Niall Flanagan delivered last night."

"That's charming." Robin gestured at the lanyard around Jamie's neck, where tiny wooden violets, daisies, and forget-me-nots lined the woven strip of fabric.

"Thank you." Jamie wondered if Robin's compliment was sincere. She'd never known Robin to shop at the Treasure Chest, but she didn't know if Robin shared her son's view that it was a "kitschy nightmare." *I can't believe I almost married a man who called my home away from home a nightmare.*

Melinda trotted down the stairs. "Oh, hello, Robin," she said. "We missed you last week."

Robin smiled—a more genuine smile than she'd given Jamie. "I'm not sure I qualify to be in your company. But that's not why I canceled. I had a migraine."

"I'm sorry. Not fun." Melinda glanced at Jamie. "Robin has joined my quilting club," she explained.

"Wonderful! Then you've already seen Melinda's fabulous harvest quilt in the linen room upstairs," Jamie said.

"Yes, I saw her working on it. Lovely. I'm just a beginner, but Melinda is very patient."

"I'm always happy to help another quilter. Jamie, unless you need me here, I'll go unpack the rest of the boxes my father brought last night," Melinda said.

"That's fine; thank you."

When Melinda had exited, heading toward the storage room, Robin drew a postcard out of her purse and held it out to Jamie. "I wonder if you've seen this before."

Jamie looked at it. A view of downtown Britteridge. The postcard was homemade, printed on cardstock.

"I'm sorry, but we don't carry postcards. The bookshop on Main Street has a great selection—"

"That's not what I meant." Robin flipped the postcard over. In the message space in plain black font, it read, *You have something of mine. I've come to take it back.* The card was addressed to Hannah Graham. Isaac's wife.

Puzzled, Jamie took the card and studied it. "What is this supposed to mean?"

"It was mailed locally to Hannah, as you can see by the postmark."

No signature or return address. "I don't understand." Jamie handed it back to Robin. "You don't know who sent it?"

"How *could* we know who sent it?"

Jamie opened her mouth to ask why Robin was asking *her* about this, but realization made her hesitate. *You have something of mine.* Did Robin think the message referred to Isaac . . . and Jamie had returned to Britteridge in hopes of stealing him from his pregnant wife?

Robin couldn't possibly think something that crazy. Robin *did* get offbeat ideas sometimes, but she was an intelligent woman who knew Jamie well; she loved Jamie and had been crushed when Isaac had broken the engagement. Robin would never accuse her of something like this. Jamie must be misunderstanding her.

"I'm sorry, but I know nothing about this," Jamie said. "I don't know what the message means, and I don't know who sent it."

Robin slid the card into her purse, her expression as icy as the surface of Britteridge Pond in the winter. "What else *could* it mean? You moved back here just a month ago, and now Hannah has received this card. It rattled her, and I hate to see her upset at such a sensitive time."

"A . . . sensitive time?"

"She's expecting a baby. I assume you knew that."

"Yes, my mother told me. I'm so happy for them. I know it was a long road."

Robin gave her the look Jamie remembered as her "mining" gaze— eyes that could blast through rock, extract confessions, and send them to the surface in broken bits. "The last thing I want now is for Hannah to get stressed by anything," Robin said.

Jamie resisted the urge to duck behind the showpiece treasure chest on its carved pedestal. "Is she having difficulty?"

"The pregnancy has been normal, but, of course, we want to take as good care of her as possible. Something like this message is worrisome. Very dangerous for her."

Because, according to the best of doctors who got their degrees in 1882, pregnant women are as fragile as frayed thread, Jamie wanted to say, smarting over Robin's accusation. But she held back the petty words and nodded sympathetically. When Isaac had dumped Jamie for Hannah, Robin had been furious at Hannah, but plainly, she'd bonded with her daughter-in-law over the past five years. Which was *good*. Jamie carried no grudges, not anymore. She *wanted* Hannah to have a good relationship with her mother-in-law.

"I'm so sorry I don't know anything that could help," Jamie said. "If I hear any rumors of who was responsible, I'll let you know."

Robin's shoulders squared beneath her white cardigan. "For goodness sakes, Jamie. What else could it be but a reference to Isaac, and who else besides you would think they had claim on him? I know he hurt you—devastated you—and I can't blame you if you're still hurting, alone in your life while he and Hannah are happy and having a child, but this type of nonsense is *completely* out of line. If you think Isaac would *ever* betray his wife and child, you have lost your mind."

The words Jamie wanted to say boiled in her head: *If you think I would ever pursue a married man, especially the jerk who pretty much left me at the altar, then you've lost* your *mind.* But she *could not* lose her temper here. Her mother would be mortified, and Edward Allerton would be appalled if he knew Jamie had spoken rude words within the peaceful, quirky walls of the Treasure Chest.

I'm sorry you think I'd do something like that, but you're mistaken. She tried to bring the courteous words to her lips but could only stare at Robin. If she spoke, anger would gush out.

Breathe deeply. Calm down.

"I'm sure this was a fluke," Robin said coldly. "I know you'd normally never do something so tasteless and cruel, and I'm sure you won't again." She turned and marched out of the shop.

Chapter 2

AT LEAST, JAMIE THOUGHT, SHE'D accomplished a lot today. Energized by anger and humiliation, she hadn't been able to hold still, except when standing behind the cash register ringing up customers, and in her free moments, she'd dusted every item in the store, polished wood, rearranged displays, worked on orders, and jotted dozens of to-dos on her list for the town spring gala coming up in three weeks.

How *dare* Robin accuse her of sending that postcard? Maybe Jamie seemed like the obvious culprit, but that was only because Robin, and probably Hannah, had jumped to that conclusion instead of analyzing anything. If Hannah thought about it hard enough, she'd recognize another meaning for the postcard. Maybe someone was irked over something as mundane as a borrowed book and was trying to be funny about it. Maybe Hannah had a friend with a strange sense of humor.

How many people had Robin or Hannah—or Isaac—told about the postcard, blaming it on Jamie? Had word leaked to the Britteridge YSA ward Jamie planned to attend? She hoped not, or it would be interesting walking into church on Sunday. She hadn't attended church in Britteridge since moving here. The first week, she'd gone with her parents to her aunt's ward in Springfield; the second week, she'd been sick; the third week, she'd gone to church in New Hampshire with her old college friend Angela and Angela's husband and twin two-year-old girls. But now it was time to attend church locally. On Sunday, she might be facing a building full of people who thought she was a lovelorn creep.

As Jamie locked up the Treasure Chest, she couldn't endure the idea of returning to her condo. Sit and stress or pace and stress—those were her two choices if she went home. She needed to do something to distract herself. She'd go someplace fun, a place she'd missed when she was away from Britteridge, a place that would stir happy memories that predated her relationship with Isaac.

Newton's Clam Hut. Yes, she'd been there with Isaac. Of course she'd been there with Isaac; she'd been everywhere in Britteridge with Isaac, and he loved Newton's scallops, but she'd been there with family and other friends countless times too, so she didn't associate it with Isaac specifically.

Clam strips and french fries. A cup of chowder. Chattering patrons and creaky, unpolished floorboards. It sounded like heaven on earth. Her enthusiasm rising, Jamie strode along the tree-lined brick path that led from the Treasure Chest to the smaller house in back, nicknamed Junior, that had been converted into a reception hall. Just before Junior, the path veered left to the parking area. Jamie climbed into her car and headed for Newton's.

It hadn't changed at all, and Jamie smiled as she sat at a wood-topped table, waiting for her order and scanning the fishing photos on the unpainted board walls. She remembered every one of these photos. How many times had she come here in high school and college after football games or basketball games or before a movie? She belonged here. It felt *right* to be back.

She glanced at the counter to see if her order was up, and a blitzkrieg of horror wiped out her nostalgia.

Handsome, blond Isaac Graham was standing in line, waiting to place an order. Behind him stood Hannah—tall, dark-haired, slim everywhere except in her adorable pregnant belly. Next to Hannah stood a man Jamie didn't recognize, wearing a fedora, a bowtie, and a tweed jacket.

The girl at the counter leaned over the microphone. "Jamie, your order is ready!"

Isaac, Hannah, and the fedora man all glanced at each other—then glanced around the room.

Jamie wanted to sprint from the restaurant minus her clam strips, but that would make her look like an idiot—a guilty idiot to boot. She'd pretend she didn't notice the Grahams searching to see if the Jamie of the clam strips was the Jamie of the postcard . . . oops, too late. Isaac's gaze had found her.

Jamie forced herself to stand, walk to the counter, and pick up her tray. She smiled at the Grahams.

"Hey," she said. "It's good to see you again."

"Hello, Jamie." Isaac's voice was cool. Hannah averted her gorgeous green eyes. The man in the bowtie and fedora raised one dark eyebrow, scrutinizing Jamie.

Jamie had no idea how to appear unflustered when her face had heated like the interior of her car on a Phoenix summer day. They all thought she'd sent Hannah that postcard. They thought she wanted to steal Isaac.

Calm down. Act normal, and they'll realize they're wrong. "I couldn't wait to get back to Newton's," she said blithely. "Best clam strips in the nation. When I was in Phoenix, you wouldn't believe how many times I was tempted to call them and ask if they'd FedEx me a basket or two."

Isaac's brow furrowed, and Hannah kept looking away. Clearly, they wouldn't deign to play the game of polite conversation with a wannabe husband stealer.

Several new groups of people had gathered behind the Grahams and were waiting to place their orders. If Jamie wanted to deny guilt, she'd have to do it in front of an audience. From the heat in her face and the hammering of her pulse, she knew she wouldn't be able to maintain her composure. At best, she'd cry. At worst, she'd yell.

She'd deal with this another time. She faked another smile at the silent Grahams, grabbed her tray, and headed for the door, walking as fast as she could without crashing into anybody. She shoved the door open with her hip and was halfway to her car before she realized she hadn't ordered this meal to go. Instead of being packaged in boxes and a bag, her clam strips and fries were in plastic baskets, her chowder was in a bowl, her drink in a hard plastic cup, and she was carrying a Newton's tray.

Stumped by confusion and embarrassment, she stood in the parking lot, wind blowing her hair. It was too chilly to eat outside, but she was *not* going back into the restaurant. She wanted to slam the tray to the ground, drive away, and hide.

Footsteps sounded behind her—another patron heading for their car. Blinking away tears, Jamie carried the tray toward her car. She'd eat there, then return the dishes to the outside drop-off on the patio.

If she *could* eat. If the clams didn't end up sticking to her dry tongue or choking her.

"Jamie?"

At the sound of a male voice calling her name, Jamie jerked around, slopping lemonade onto her fries.

It was the man in the fedora. "Hello." He removed his hat. "I don't think we've met. I'm Julian Stokes, Hannah's brother."

His courtesy in removing his hat while introducing himself would have struck Jamie as delightfully chivalrous at any other time, but she was so mortified to be caught by one of the Graham party that all she could think was that Julian Stokes would do well to keep that hat firmly on his head. His curly dark hair, bushing on top and flattened on the sides, gave vivid meaning to the term "hat hair."

"If you've come to accuse me, save it," Jamie said.

"May I hold that for you while you unlock your car?" Julian reached toward her tray. Jamie shoved it at him.

"Go dump it somewhere. I don't want it anymore." She turned away, fumbling in her purse for her keys. She couldn't find them. Had she put them in the outside pocket? Why was her stupid purse so big? She didn't need a purse this size. What did she think she needed to haul around in it—a Rottweiler?

"I didn't come to accuse you." Julian spoke calmly.

Jamie found the flowered lanyard that held her keys, yanked it out, and unlocked her door. "I didn't send that postcard. Tell Hannah I did *not* send it. I am *not* chasing her husband. I would sooner drink platypus venom than spend five minutes alone with Isaac Graham."

She slid behind the wheel, slammed her door, and drove away, leaving Julian holding the tray of clam strips.

* * *

Jamie tried to soothe herself by designing the store flyer for the spring gala, but she couldn't concentrate and stayed up until 1:00 a.m. scowling at different fonts. How could she have acted so immature, so ridiculous . . . so volatile? Those were top-notch clam strips she'd abandoned. *Temper tantrum equals ramen for dinner.* How many goals did she have to set about not losing her temper before she got that character flaw under control? She'd done all right with Robin this morning, but seeing the Grahams at Newton's, followed by Julian Stokes's approach . . . What had he wanted from her? He'd been polite—much more polite than *she* had—but he was Hannah's brother. Chances were, he'd come to try to convince her to stay away from Isaac.

Whatever he wanted from you, he thinks you're nuts now. Platypus venom? That's what you get for watching Animal Planet while you were making lanyards last night.

What a horrible coincidence that Isaac had decided to come to Newton's at the same time she had. She should have picked some icky chain restaurant, not a place the whole town, including Isaac, loved.

It had felt so weird to see him again. When she'd come to Britteridge to visit her parents, they'd always spent the weekends with her aunt, so

Jamie hadn't ever risked encountering Isaac at church. He hadn't changed physically in five years, at least as far as she could tell from her embarrassed glances at him. His hair was a little shorter than it used to be, but that was the only difference she'd noticed.

How much had *she* changed? While brushing her teeth, she studied herself in the mirror. She wore her chestnut-brown hair a little shorter too, cut to shoulder length. She was wearing glasses at the moment; she'd already taken out her contacts. But she didn't look any older, did she? No wrinkles or gray hair. She tried to stay in good shape; she hadn't gained weight. Okay, she was a *little* curvier—she'd been very skinny at twenty-two, but she wasn't going to stay *that* skinny forever. She was a woman, not a kid, and she was perfectly healthy, not at *all* overweight—

Good grief, why was she gawking at herself, analyzing her skin and hair and figure like some vain bubblehead who thought a zit or an extra pound was the end of the world? Who cared if she looked a little older? She *was* older. She wasn't fresh out of college and head-over-heels for the first boy she had a crush on, her junior prom date, the missionary she'd written.

Deep breath. And another deep breath. Time to go to bed. Tomorrow, she'd have a better perspective on the situation.

When she woke the next morning, she was exhausted. She hadn't slept well, but she'd known she wouldn't, so she'd put several craft magazines next to her bed for perusing when she got sick of tossing and turning. Even with inadequate sleep, she felt far less stressed. Everything would blow over. Hannah would figure out the postcard referred to something else, or if someone *had* sent it as a spiteful practical joke about Jamie's return, Hannah would see that Jamie showed zero interest in pursuing Isaac, and she'd know the postcard was a hoax.

At church, Jamie quickly felt comfortable, and she even recognized a few faces. She'd worried about feeling like a grandma among all the Britteridge College kids—after all, she was only three years short of aging out of the ward—but there were plenty of older YSAs in addition to the eighteen-year-olds. No one mentioned Isaac, and Jamie's spirits grew lighter and lighter until she turned around to respond to a greeting from a woman sitting behind her in Sunday School and saw Julian Stokes on the back row.

He wasn't looking at her, but humiliation still made it difficult for Jamie to focus on her conversation with the girl who wanted to trade info on mutual friends.

Julian was in this ward? No bowtie today—he wore a regular necktie, along with a three-piece suit. He'd ditched the hat, and his curly hair stuck out on either side of his center part, making his sharply carved face look somewhat triangular. A center part? She'd seen a couple of guys with long hair part their hair in the center, but on Julian, the style made him look like a time traveler who'd disembarked in the wrong century.

She owed him an apology. Even if he'd come to the parking lot last night to tell her to leave Hannah alone, he *had* been courteous about it, whereas she'd been an etiquette train wreck.

When church ended, Jamie hurried out of Relief Society to hunt for Julian. If she couldn't catch him here, she'd have to call him, and that was worse. *Might as well get it over with.* To her relief, she met him heading along the hall toward her.

"Jamie," he said. "Welcome to the ward. I want to apologize for last night."

"Me too," she said, surprised. What did Julian have to apologize for?

"I'm sorry I was so rude. I must have seemed crazy."

"Not at all—though surrendering Newton's clam strips without a fight *has* been used in court as evidence that the defendant is *non compos mentis*, so I understand your concerns about your behavior."

Jamie nearly grinned. "Believe me, I regret it. I hope you ate them instead of dumping them."

"I did. And I didn't follow you to accuse you; I was making sure you were all right."

"Which I apparently wasn't." She lowered her voice, not wanting anyone else in the hallway to notice the conversation. "I had nothing to do with that postcard."

"Do you mind if we walk?" Julian touched her elbow, gracefully guiding her in the direction of the exit. When they were strolling along the sidewalk with no one in earshot, Jamie repeated, "I had nothing to do with that postcard. I've never been so mortified in my life as I was when Robin Graham came accusing me yesterday. Okay, actually that was the *second* most mortifying moment of my life. The worst moment was seeing Isaac and Hannah at Newton's, then acting like an idiot in front of you."

"Please don't worry about that. It's not my intention to embarrass you. I'm embarrassed about the entire situation. Robin told Hannah she'd talked to you, which we all viewed as jumping the gun. But Robin couldn't figure out who else could be responsible and wanted to 'head things off.'"

"I have no idea what I've *ever* done to make Robin think I'm capable of a mean-spirited trick like that."

"Nothing, from all I've heard about you."

"You've heard about me?"

"I've met your parents. And I know friends of yours, including, of course, the Drakes. President Drake is who I first heard mention that you were coming back to Britteridge, and he spoke highly of you."

"Aww, he's the best." Jamie thought of the soft-spoken, brilliant founder of Britteridge College, her former early-morning seminary teacher, and stake president. "How are the Drakes doing?"

"Very well. Josh left on his mission a couple of months ago. Scotland/Ireland mission."

"Nice!"

"Trevor is now assistant director of admissions at Britt and has a serious girlfriend, so everyone is keeping their eyes peeled for a diamond on her finger."

"Oh, I'm so happy for him! Trev's such a nice guy."

"Rachel is married to a man from Idaho and working hard at her wedding planning business. It's going well, I hear."

"I'm glad to hear that." Marriages and more marriages. The wind blew Jamie's hair into her eyes and billowed her ankle-length skirt in front of her. "Julian, I promise you, I would never do anything to threaten Hannah's marriage *or* her peace of mind. It melts my brain that Robin thinks Isaac is *anywhere* on my radar, let alone that I'm a home-wrecker. I thought she liked me!"

"I'm sure she did, enough so that she wasn't fond of Hannah at first. Frankly, I was disappointed in Hannah myself. Getting involved with an engaged man is an ugly game, and Hannah should have been better than that. She does regret her ill-timed actions, if that provides you any comfort."

Julian's speech matched the three-piece suit—and the hat and bowtie. A little formal, a little offbeat, a little anachronistic. He *did* look good in that suit; it complemented his lean body perfectly. "I don't need any comfort," Jamie said. "It was a long time ago. Water under the bridge. I hope Isaac and Hannah are happy, and I'm glad Robin and Hannah have grown close, though I wish that didn't translate into Robin's attacking my character."

"I think Robin is uncomfortable at the way she treated Hannah at first, so she overcompensates. Plus, she's always fussing about her future grandchild."

"Does *Hannah* think I sent the postcard?" Maybe it was only Robin.

"Hannah won't commit to any accusations, but I know she's worried."

"Should I talk to her?"

"That's up to you." The wind whipped Julian's dark hair into a poodle-ish mess on his scalp, and Jamie had to bite her lip to keep from grinning. Standing next to him, she could see he'd tried to gel it down, but the gel didn't have the muscle to fight the wind.

"This will all fade away," Julian added. "Whoever pulled this prank has had their fun. It's over." He extended his hand. "Thank you for talking to me."

"Thank *you*." Jamie shook his hand. "It's good to meet you. So you live in Britteridge?"

"I moved here a year ago. I teach at the college."

"What subject?"

"Dance. Ballroom."

"You teach dance? That's awesome." It was easy to imagine him dressed like a character out of a Jane Austen novel, waltzing with a woman in a Scarlett O'Hara skirt. No, wait, she was mixing her eras. And her continents.

"Do you dance?" he asked, drawing Jamie's thoughts back from where they'd wandered to trying to remember what Mr. Darcy's formalwear looked like.

"I love going to dances," she said. "I know how to line dance. I'd love to learn ballroom dancing. Does any of that count?"

"It definitely counts." He bowed slightly. "Thank you, Jamie. I wish you a peaceful week."

"You too." Bowing? *What a character*. Jamie had never known Hannah Stokes more than superficially; Hannah had moved to town to begin a graduate program at Britteridge College a month or two after Jamie had gotten engaged, and Jamie had left town a few weeks after the breakup—*fled* town, more accurately—to live with her sister in Phoenix and nanny her niece and nephew until she found a job in graphic design. But from what little Jamie knew of Hannah, she never would have used the words *quirky* or *eccentric* in connection with her. She'd seemed quiet and elegant. Julian must be the oddball in the Stokes clan. Or maybe Hannah was.

Jamie drove home, contemplating talking to Hannah Stokes Graham. It unnerved her how much the idea . . . unnerved her. At the time of the breakup, she'd never had the slightest interest in confronting Hannah. What was the point? Would berating Hannah for stealing her fiancé bring Isaac's affections back to Jamie? Besides, she didn't know how much Hannah had instigated things and how much Isaac had. Not that Hannah was innocent no matter what the situation. She *could* have told Isaac to get lost.

Not that Jamie cared now. But maybe it *was* time to talk to Hannah. From what Julian had said, Hannah—rightfully—felt guilty about the way she'd acted, and maybe that guilt had mutated into insecurity when Jamie showed up in Britteridge. Jamie ought to go talk to her and reassure her that she held no grudges and carried no torch for Isaac.

As tempting as it was to let Hannah worry.

Nice. I thought you said you didn't hold any grudges. She'd call Hannah tonight.

Jamie pulled into her designated parking spot in front of her condo and headed for her second-floor unit.

Isaac stood on her doorstep.

Chapter 3

JAMIE WAS *NOT* GOING TO lose her cool like she had last night. "Hello, Isaac," she said courteously as she reached the landing. She almost added *I didn't send that postcard*, but Julian would have already delivered her denial when he'd returned to Newton's carrying Jamie's tray. No point in repeating her protests now.

"May I come in for a moment?" He sounded friendly, which surprised her. Maybe she'd imagined the coldness in his voice last night. Maybe it *was* just his mother who thought Jamie was on the hunt.

Jamie studied his familiar features—dark blue eyes, a dimple in his cheek, a jawline and nose so perfect that if Disney animators needed a model for the next Prince Charming, Isaac ought to apply for the job. Good grief, did he have to be so handsome? Looking at him stirred memories, drawing her toward the past. She didn't like the sensation, so she focused on his striped red tie instead. "I think it would be better if you didn't come in. For propriety's sake." *Propriety*—there was a formal word. Julian Stokes would use it.

"Don't worry about that." Isaac shifted his briefcase to the other hand. Jamie recognized that briefcase. She'd been with him when he bought it. She'd persuaded him to get the soft-sided cinnamon-brown leather instead of his first choice of a black, hard-sided attaché case that looked like it should contain top-secret documents and a complimentary spy kit. Isaac had taken good care of the case through the years. It looked only a little worn.

"Does Hannah know you're here?" Jamie asked.

"No. I don't want her to worry. But there's something I want to say to you where people can't overhear."

Jamie wound the flowered lanyard around her hand and jingled her keys. "E-mail it."

"It's important."

"This is not a big town." Jamie kept her voice quiet. "Even if you didn't tell Hannah you were coming here, that doesn't mean she won't find out, and the fact that you didn't tell her is going to make her worry ten times as much. If you want to talk to me, bring your wife along. I don't invite solo married men into my condo."

"I don't want to embarrass you in front of Hannah. I want to talk to you before this gets out of hand."

"If this is about the postcard—"

"You know it's not about that."

"Uh . . . I don't know *anything*."

One floor down, the door opened, and Jamie heard her neighbors' voices. Isaac grimaced. "Could we talk in private?"

"*Fine*, but keep it short." She unlocked the door. "And when you get home, *tell* Hannah you were here."

She closed the door behind them and waved toward the couch. "Have a seat."

Isaac settled on the couch, sitting stiffly. He eyed the throw pillow embroidered with a scene of three owls perched on a branch, and Jamie wondered if he was afraid her eclectic tastes might contaminate him. He was certainly in danger, surrounded by the owl pillow, the faded red-and-blue bear's paw quilt folded over the back of the couch—one of Melinda's earliest quilts that she'd given to Jamie's mother—and the white-oak coffee table Jamie had painted with a starfish and seashell motif.

Jamie sat in the old rocking chair she planned to refinish if she ever found some free time. "What do you want?"

"Jamie . . ." Isaac focused on his spotless black loafers. "First of all, I want to apologize for last night. I was so startled when I saw you that I didn't know what to do. I'm afraid I embarrassed you. I'm sorry."

Mollified, Jamie relaxed into her chair. "It's all right. We were both caught by surprise."

He met her gaze. "Listen . . . I know it's years too late to say this, but I also owe you a much bigger apology."

Jamie gawked at him. He *had* apologized at the time, repeatedly. As if the words "I'm sorry" could be any comfort in that disaster. "You did apologize. It's all past."

"I know I tried, but I didn't handle it well."

"How *can* you handle something like that well? You can apologize for a ship hitting an iceberg, but it won't keep it from sinking." Afraid she'd sounded like it still bothered her, Jamie smiled and said, "Isaac, it's fine. We moved past it. Why are you worrying about this now?"

He flipped the owl pillow over so it was positioned correctly; Jamie had absentmindedly tossed it on the couch upside down. "I feel like I never explained myself."

"It was self-explanatory. I'm sorry if my moving to Brittcridge has been uncomfortable for you, but I want you to know I don't hold any grudges and will never do anything to bother you or Hannah. I'll just live my life, and you live yours. Sound good?"

"It . . . really wasn't Hannah," he said, eyes averted. "She wasn't the reason, I mean. She's not the one who made me realize I was making a mistake. I knew that already. I was already scared to death. I'd realized . . . no matter how much I loved you, we weren't a good match. Our interests were so different . . . our personalities . . . You're such a fun person, all energetic and . . . vivid, and I'm just . . . quieter. I was afraid that after awhile, we were going to drive each other crazy."

Vivid? Jamie thought.

"But everything was going forward with the wedding . . . I hated the thought of hurting you and causing a tidal wave of gossip . . . It would be so awkward." He sighed. "Being with Hannah finally brought things into focus. Gave me the courage to keep from wrecking your life and mine."

"In that case, I owe her a thank-you note," Jamie said evenly. "You don't need to say these things. I *know* we weren't right for each other. I'm over it. Thanks for worrying about me, but this isn't necessary."

Isaac opened the flap of his briefcase and drew out something flat wrapped in white tissue paper. "I brought this back," he said. "Hannah never saw it. Jamie . . . this really surprises me. It's disturbing. Promise me you won't do anything like this again. It won't change things between us."

"What are you talking about?"

"Thank heavens I found this before Hannah saw it." Isaac set the white package on the coffee table. "I know I'm to blame. I was too clumsy in how I handled things—didn't give you any resolution. Closure. No wonder you feel like things are unfinished."

"Closure! We *closured* things five years ago! You married Hannah! End of story!" Jamie regretted the way her voice rose. She was *not* still upset about this. Why was she getting riled?

"Explain this, then." Isaac unfolded the tissue paper covering the package and set it on the table. It was a framed picture—a cheap, generic wood frame, Jamie noticed, *not* from the Treasure Chest. Under the glass was a photograph and what looked like a wedding announcement.

Jamie stood and picked it up so she could get a better look. The photograph of Isaac and her was the picture from their wedding announcement. But the cream-colored, embossed announcement wasn't theirs . . . Wait . . . What on *earth*—

It *was* their announcement—her name, Isaac's name, their parents' names—but she could have sworn their announcements had been white, not cream, and that was the wrong font.

Wait—*huh?* The wedding date listed was not five years ago. It was a year in the future. Next May.

"This fantasy is troubling," Isaac said gently. "I understand that you're having a hard time, but this isn't a healthy way to deal with it. You need to talk to a counselor. You're a very active person, and when something's bothering you, you do something about it, but you've chosen a destructive way to cope with your feelings. You think that by fantasizing like this, you'll feel better and maybe even . . . set the clock back. But you won't. You're only hurting yourself."

Jamie clenched her teeth to avoid asking how many pop psychology websites computer-geek Isaac had scoured to find his analysis of "her" actions, because those weren't Isaac-style words. No . . . he hadn't Googled her alleged issues. He'd talked to his mother. Those were Robin-style words. "I did *not* create this phony announcement. It must be some kind of awful joke. Like the postcard."

Isaac reached into his pocket and drew out a folded piece of paper. "I knew you wouldn't want to just pick someone out of the phone book, so this is the name and number of a terrific counselor who helped Hannah awhile back when she was struggling. He's the best." He held the paper out to Jamie.

Oh my word. "I'm glad he helped Hannah. But I do not need a counselor at the moment. Will you please *listen* to me and stop making ridiculous assumptions? I have no idea who sent you that postcard and wedding announcement."

"Will you stop playing dumb?" Isaac's voice began to harden. "This is a silly game, Jamie. Things are *over* between us, no matter how many lovey-dovey pictures of us you leave on the hood of my car or how many intimidating postcards you send Hannah. I'm *married*. I have a child on the way!"

Frying in humiliation, Jamie snapped, "I did *not* leave this on your car, and I did *not* send Hannah that postcard."

"Give me a break. Who else would have done it?" He rose to his feet and dropped the phone number on the table. "I *tried* to be nice about this. But you are *not* going to harass my family and upset my wife. You've crossed the line into stalking."

"*Stalking*? Are you kidding me?"

"I don't want to call the police. Just leave us alone, and we'll leave you alone."

Jamie slapped the framed announcement on top of the tissue paper. "I can't *believe* you are narcissistic enough to think I'm still in love with you. You think I'm *chasing* you? You vain, self-centered *idiot*. Get out of here."

Isaac wheeled around and stomped out the door, and Jamie slammed it behind him.

* * *

By Monday morning, Jamie's anger had subsided to where she could think instead of rant to herself. The more she analyzed everything Robin, Isaac, and Julian had said, the more she realized she had no clue what was happening. Who would want to upset Isaac and Hannah so much that they'd send a taunting postcard and go to the work of creating a fake wedding announcement? Jamie didn't have any idea. She hadn't lived here in five years—over five years, actually five and a half. How could she possibly know who had a grudge against the Grahams or who was twisted enough to think poking them with the memory of Jamie was funny?

With twenty minutes left until the store opened, Jamie meticulously dusted the gilded wooden treasure chest studded with glass jewels and thought about how much she'd love to confront the jerk using her as part of a prank or a harassment campaign. Not that the culprit would care about Jamie's humiliation. Anyone cruel enough to haunt Isaac and his pregnant wife with the specter of an old fiancée wouldn't care if Jamie was collateral damage in their attack.

The click of a key in the front door lock made Jamie look up. At the sight of the familiar balding head and dark-rimmed glasses visible through the glass panes, Jamie rushed to open the door. "Good morning, Mr. Allerton."

"Hello, Jamie. You look at home here. Like your mother always did."

"Thank you. I feel at home." Jamie hoped she didn't sound nervous. This was only the second time Allerton had stopped in since she'd started working as manager, and she was still getting accustomed to her role as the person he would hold responsible for any issues in the store.

Allerton unbuttoned his brown cardigan and scanned the entryway, his gaze keen. Jamie knew he was looking for anything out of place, anything that would make the ambience of the shop less than perfect. Edward Allerton was a kind man but a *very* particular one.

Jamie followed him as he headed into the main room. She hoped he wouldn't find anything worthy of his mild-mannered chastisement, but inevitably, he would.

"The petunias in the front window boxes look colorful and healthy," he said. "You must have your mother's green thumb."

Jamie smiled. Actually, she'd just replaced the petunias on Saturday, since the previous ones had started to look ragged.

Allerton paced slowly around the rooms, checking shelves, nudging merchandise. Jamie kept pace with him. She knew from her mother that he wanted his manager next to him when he did these impromptu inspections so she could note any instructions.

"You have too many chickens." He pointed to a shelf of carved wooden animals. "It looks crowded. Take out a third of the roosters, a third of the hens, and a third of the chicks."

Jamie scribbled a note in the fabric-covered notebook she kept in her apron pocket. "I'll take care of that."

"Main room looks good overall. Glad to have you here. I worried when your mother told me she planned to retire—hated the idea of turning my store over to a stranger. I thought of you immediately, of course. Best young employee I ever had."

Jamie smiled. Allerton had already told her this—a couple of times—but clearly he enjoyed repeating his thought process in hiring her.

He adjusted two pottery bowls, pushing one a little closer to the back of the shelf and the other a half inch to the right. "People tried telling me a successful young woman like you with a good job on the other side of the country would never come back here to manage my Treasure Chest, but I hoped you'd consider it, so I took the gamble and called you. I knew you loved this place."

"I do love it, and your offer came at the perfect time. I'd gotten restless doing most of my creating on a computer. I like to *hold* projects. And I wanted to get out from behind a desk."

Allerton nodded. "I figured you must have kept us in mind all these years, since you shipped us your handicrafts even while you were gone. Your work always sells well. You have talent, Jamie, and you have the brains and the organizational skills to run this place. Having you here feels right."

"Thank you. I'm thrilled to be back."

He gestured toward the display in the bay window. "That's cluttered. Remove a few things. Highlight the pieces; don't give them claustrophobia."

Jamie made another note. "I'll do that."

"You'll get the hang of it," he said. "You're doing great."

"Thank you." Jamie drew a slow, silent breath, trying to fend off feelings of inadequacy. Allerton had just told her she was talented and doing great. Why was she feeling self-conscious at his corrections? She couldn't expect to get everything arranged perfectly to his taste without practice.

"When people enter the Treasure Chest, they want to feel homey and comfortable, not busy and crowded. This is far more than a craft boutique or a gift shop. It's an important part of our community, a place people want to linger. That's why we have the playroom for children— not simply so parents will spend more time and more money here but so children will enjoy the Treasure Chest as much as their parents. That's why we encourage customers to relax in the book room and read. The more opportunity they have to enjoy the atmosphere, the more they'll want to return. Tasteful displays, unique merchandise at reasonable prices, and a smiling manager and clerks who take the time to remember names and preferences—all of this is part of our appeal. In a small town like this, you personally become part of the store's reputation."

"Yes, sir." In her notebook, Jamie made a habit of scrawling names, descriptions, items purchased—anything to help her remember a customer for the future. She'd been good at it when she'd worked here before, and she was getting back into the swing of things.

"How are the employees working out for you?" he asked. "Melinda doing all right?"

"Of course. She's wonderful. I can rely on her for anything. Kayla is great too—she's so cheerful, excellent at charming the customers. And Wes is learning quickly."

"Everything decided for the spring gala?"

"Getting there." Jamie had always loved the Treasure Chest's role in the town spring party and admired how generously Allerton donated money to support it. "Still working a few things out with the food. Would you like to see what I have so far?"

"Don't have time this morning, but I'll check in later." Allerton headed into the crystal room and carefully examined the displays of breakables, then inspected the playroom. Upstairs, he reviewed the linen room and book room while Jamie took notes.

"I'm glad you're back in Britteridge." Allerton patted her shoulder, and they headed toward the stairs. "Especially after the sad circumstances that sent you away."

Jamie hoped Allerton didn't notice her cheeks reddening. Her mother had mentioned many times that Allerton had been furious with Isaac's behavior and had sympathized deeply with Jamie. "Thank heavens it's all past," she said.

Melinda was emerging from the back of the house as Allerton and Jamie reached the entryway.

"Good morning, Melinda," Allerton said. "How is Niall coming on the gala treasures?"

"Fine," Melinda said brusquely. "He's painted about half of them."

"Wonderful. Your father is a genius craftsman, and his work ethic is world class," Allerton said.

"Yes, he's amazing." Melinda's tone was still curt, which surprised Jamie. She would have thought Melinda would be pleased to hear Allerton compliment Niall so effusively.

"Good day, ladies." Allerton exited.

After the door closed, Melinda asked, "What did Ed find to pick on this time?"

Jamie knew Melinda disliked Allerton's habit of ignoring the store for long periods, then popping in to criticize things. "Oh, nothing much. He was positive overall. Just felt a couple of the displays are too crowded. I need to do some rearranging. I'm going to get a box."

She headed into the basement to fetch a box and packing material. When she returned, Melinda came to help her stow the items Allerton wanted removed.

"How's . . . Kevin?" Jamie was embarrassed that it took her a moment to recall Melinda's husband's first name. She didn't know him all that well, though they'd met many times over the years. He was a quiet man—polite, but not someone who enjoyed small talk.

"He's good," Melinda said. "Tired of the commute into Boston. Wishing it were time to retire. How are things with you?" Melinda's hands encased a rooster in bubble wrap, but her sapphire eyes focused on Jamie. Melinda had strikingly beautiful eyes—brilliant blue with dark lashes.

"Things are fine." She liked Melinda, but in no way was she inclined to confide in her about the trouble with Isaac. Especially since Melinda knew Robin Graham. Jamie picked up a wooden chick.

Melinda bent to put the rooster in the box, then straightened up, tucking her graying hair behind both ears. Jamie liked the way Melinda wasn't bothered by the gray streaks in her hair; she was apparently immune to the compulsion most older women felt to keep dumping dyes on their heads. She didn't slather on the makeup, and her nails were never polished, which Jamie also appreciated. Jamie never did her nails either—why bother when she perpetually had paint or glue staining her fingertips? She wondered if she'd have the guts to gray naturally like Melinda. Maybe she should ask for tips on building confidence in her inborn beauty.

Melinda picked up a brown-and-white hen. "I'm sorry if it's in poor taste to mention this, but I thought you'd want to know that I heard Isaac Graham was at your place this weekend."

Jamie squeezed the wooden chick in her hand, its miniature talons digging into her palm. *Small town. You knew this would happen. You warned Isaac.* She wrapped the chick in bubble wrap and placed it in the box. She had no idea what Melinda's informant had seen, but if they'd witnessed Isaac stomping out and Jamie slamming the door, she couldn't pretend Isaac had dropped by to volunteer his ward Boy Scouts to gather trash off the Treasure Chest lawn after the spring gala.

She glanced at Melinda. Melinda was watching her, her brow furrowed. At least she looked anxious, not disapproving, which made Jamie feel a little better. Had Robin said anything to Melinda about the postcard? Probably not, because Melinda would be blunt enough to bring it up.

"There was a misunderstanding." Jamie picked up another chicken. "He was angry at me for something he thought I'd done—which I hadn't—so he came to talk to me. It wasn't a friendly talk. I'm sure he won't be around again."

"That's good, because it would look strange if people saw him at your place." Melinda started wrapping the hen. "Not that I think you'd do anything, but you have to be careful about rumors."

Did Melinda feel obligated to lecture Jamie since Louisa McKenzie had left the state? Jamie rolled her eyes. "You're not old enough to be my mother."

"But I am your mother's good friend, and she asked me to keep an eye on you. You haven't been here for a few years, so you might have forgotten, but Ed doesn't like anything associated with his store to be questionable.

Remember that high school girl . . . Addy, wasn't it? Ed found out she'd been busted for underage drinking at a party, so he fired her. Said her behavior wasn't consistent with the family atmosphere here. She got mad and said pretty much every other kid in town was doing it, it had nothing to do with her job, and she'd never done anything wrong during work hours, but he didn't care. He still didn't want her at the store."

Jamie's face burned. "I didn't do anything questionable! Isaac and I talked for all of ten minutes. Who told you about his visit, anyway?"

"I have a friend who lives in the same condos you do. She saw Isaac. I'm not criticizing you. I'm trying to watch out for you, like your mother wanted me to do."

Jamie made a mental note to call her mother and report that diligent Melinda was taking what had probably been a casual, fluff request way too seriously. "I appreciate that, but trust me, Isaac will never be back."

"Okay. I apologize if I sounded bossy. I just don't want you to get on bad footing with Ed."

"Me neither." They continued wrapping chickens while Jamie debated between developing high blood pressure and developing an ulcer. Melinda *did* have a point. No matter how much Allerton had sympathized with Jamie when Isaac had dumped her, if he thought Jamie was stalking Isaac and Hannah, he'd fire her immediately.

Chapter 4

HER DOORBELL RINGING AT EIGHT o'clock in the morning surprised Jamie. She set down the hair dryer she'd been about to switch on and went to peer through the peephole. Two people stood on the doorstep: a very tall, thin man in a suit and a uniformed female police officer.

Jamie yanked the door open, her heart pounding. Her parents—had there been an accident? If that occurred, would she get a visit from the local police? Or a call from the police in Florida?

Calm down. More likely, it was something to do with the Treasure Chest. It couldn't have anything to do with Isaac. Even if he'd decided to call the police over that wedding announcement left on his car, Jamie doubted the police would take his report seriously.

"Jamie McKenzie?" the man asked.

Jamie nodded.

"I'm Detective Aaron Powell, and this is Officer Christy Hallstrom." Powell showed his badge. "May we speak to you for a few minutes?"

"Yes, of course. Come in." She waved them into her condo and closed the door behind them. "Would you like to sit down?"

"Thank you." Powell waited until Hallstrom was seated before sitting next to her on the couch. He looked to be in his forties and had wiry dark hair and a gaunt face that made Jamie think of Abraham Lincoln. Hallstrom looked young and friendly. She smiled at Jamie. Her congenial demeanor reassured Jamie; whatever was happening wasn't life-or-death serious.

"Miss McKenzie, I understand you've recently returned to Britteridge," Powell said.

"Yes. I grew up here but have lived elsewhere for the past several years. Did something happen at the Treasure Chest?"

"No, everything is fine there. I understand you manage the store for Edward Allerton, taking over for your mother."

"That's right." She was grateful there hadn't been a burglary or vandalism. Not that those crimes were common in Britteridge, but you never knew.

"We understand the circumstances under which you left Britteridge five years ago were painful ones." Powell's voice was gentle.

Oh no. This *was* about Isaac. He'd been so angry at her reaction to his visit that he'd told the police she was stalking him.

Why hadn't she stayed calm when Isaac had talked to her? Isaac had *wanted* to handle things quietly. He disliked confrontation and argument. When they were dating, Jamie had been a lot more likely to pick a fight than he, but Isaac was stubborn. If he got mad, it took him awhile to let it go.

Jamie was careful to make her tone matter-of-fact as she answered Powell. "It was a hard time, but it's long past."

Officer Hallstrom gave her a sympathetic look. "Coming back here must have stirred a lot of memories."

Embarrassment was about to strangle Jamie and leave her dead on the rug. "Good memories mostly. Let's cut to the chase. Did Isaac Graham tell you I'm bothering him?"

"Mr. and Mrs. Graham are concerned," Powell said. "They're afraid you may be having difficulty coping with your memories of Mr. Graham."

She had to give Powell credit for diplomacy. He looked compassionate and understanding, and Hallstrom looked so approachable that Jamie wouldn't be surprised if the officer threw her arms around Jamie with an "Oh, girlfriend, I am *so* sorry for what that creep did to you. No wonder you're upset enough to go all crazy stalker on him." Then Jamie would confess, and they'd arrest her. If you could arrest someone for putting a fake wedding announcement on a car, which seemed unlikely.

"Okay," Jamie said. "Let me make something clear. I have *no* idea who is bothering the Grahams. I've been told Hannah received a postcard and Isaac received one of our engagement photos and a fake wedding announcement, but I *did not* give them either of those things. I am *not* upset by memories of Isaac, and even if I were, I would never bother him or his family. The Grahams need to look elsewhere and figure out who might have a grudge against them or a sick sense of humor, because it's not me."

"Miss McKenzie, I understand how uncomfortable this is," Powell said. "When strong emotions influence us, we can do things we regret."

For instance, I regret ever getting involved with Isaac. Jamie kept the words back; they'd sound like sour grapes.

Powell's face became grim. "This morning, Mr. and Mrs. Graham reported they had a visitor in the middle of the night—a woman dressed in a wedding gown and a long white veil. She was walking outside their bedroom window, tapping and scratching on the glass, wailing Isaac's name."

Jamie goggled at Powell. A ghostly bride?

"Naturally, this was upsetting," Powell said.

Jamie swallowed. The scenario was so ludicrous that she wished she could laugh, but getting blamed for stalking—even overacted, melodramatic stalking—wasn't funny. "Did they actually *see* the bride's face?"

"Her face was obscured by the translucent veil, but . . . from what they could see, she was a dark-haired woman. Tallish. Average build."

In other words, they could tell the ghost bride wasn't a four-foot-tall child or a two-hundred-fifty-pound linebacker, and their imaginations filled in the blank with me. "It wasn't me. I didn't leave home all night. Feel free to search my house for a wedding gown or my shoes for mud or whatever you want. Feel free to search my computer for evidence of creating that wedding announcement."

"This was found outside the Grahams' bedroom window." Powell took a plastic bag from his pocket and set it on the table. It contained a flat, thumbprint-sized wooden violet. "Do you recognize it?"

"Of course I recognize it. It's a flower from the spring lanyards I'm selling at the Treasure Chest, and good grief, what an obvious attempt to plant phony evidence. Why in the world would a ghost-bride costume include a lanyard—except to create a connection with the Treasure Chest and me?"

"You carry your keys on a lanyard like that, I believe?" Powell asked.

Jamie knew what he was implying: even ghost brides need getaway cars, and maybe Jamie had pulled her car keys out when it was time to run and dislodged the flower. "Yes, I do. I have two lanyards, one for my store keys and one for my personal keys. Let me get both of them, and you'll see I'm not missing any of the decorations."

"Not necessary," Powell said.

Jamie gritted her teeth. Powell was saying it didn't matter: if Jamie had noticed a piece missing, she could have easily attached a new violet or swapped her lanyard for a fresh one. And her fingerprints *would* be on the violet in Powell's evidence bag; Niall had carved the flowers, but she'd painted and assembled all the lanyards herself.

"The Grahams don't want to make trouble for anyone or press charges," Officer Hallstrom said. "They just want these problems to stop."

They can't press charges anyway, Jamie thought. *Where is their proof?* The flower from the lanyard wasn't proof that Jamie had been there. She had sold dozens of lanyards. "I have no control over whether or not these problems stop, since I'm not the one creating them." A threatening postcard? A mysterious wedding announcement and an old picture? A ghost bride? What *was* this? A gothic novel? A Scooby-Doo episode?

Hallstrom leaned forward. Jamie was glad she wasn't sitting any closer; she figured Hallstrom would have laid a sisterly hand on her arm if she could have reached her. "You must feel so isolated trying to get settled here. Coming back to a familiar place is hard, I think, because you expect things to be the same, but you find out they've changed so much it doesn't feel the same at all. It was like that for me when I came home from college."

"I didn't expect things to be the same."

"Still, it's disconcerting," Hallstrom said. "It might help to talk to someone about it."

It took all of Jamie's willpower to rein in her frustration. Powell and Hallstrom obviously thought she was emotionally disturbed, just as Isaac did, and there was nothing she could say to change their minds. But they couldn't arrest her either, so it was time for them to leave.

Jamie stood. "I'm sorry to hear someone is bothering the Grahams, and if I hear any hints of who is responsible, I'll let you know."

"Thank you." Powell rose to his feet. "I hope things will be quieter now. In order to avoid even the appearance of trouble, I suggest you don't go anywhere near them."

"Good advice," Jamie said shortly.

* * *

How could Isaac think she was vindictive enough and/or troubled enough to haunt him as a ghost bride? The question clawed at Jamie's mind all day as she worked at the Treasure Chest. Isaac hadn't even seen the ghost's face. He'd seen a blowing veil, dark hair, a female form in a white gown, and thought, *Must be Jamie. Haunting the place is exactly the type of stunt she'd do.*

With her dust cloth, Jamie swiped viciously at a spider web in the corner of one of the planter boxes near the front door, the chilly evening breeze raising goose bumps on her arms. At least the police had come to her house, not to the Treasure Chest. If Allerton learned the police thought she was stalking Isaac . . .

She thought of Melinda's warning—Melinda, who apparently had a gossipy friend living near Jamie. Had that friend seen Powell and Hallstrom visiting her? Jamie stepped back from the store and looked up at the gold-and-black sign on the spacious, old, two-story home that Allerton's father had transformed into the Treasure Chest half a century ago. The letters and treasure chest of the logo were masterfully carved on the wooden sign; the gold leaf gleamed. She *adored* this place. Managing it was her dream job. If Isaac got her fired because he was stubborn enough to—

At the tap of footsteps approaching, Jamie swiftly turned and put on her business smile.

Julian Stokes strode toward her. "Jamie."

Jamie clenched her jaw to keep herself from exploding into a defensive rant. She was finished making an idiot of herself in public. But she was sure Julian knew what had happened; Hannah must have told him. Why else would he come here?

She stared at him, trying to read if he'd come to accuse. She found his green eyes studying *her*, his expression thoughtful. He'd gotten a haircut—his trimmed dark curls were short enough that they weren't thrashing around in the wind, just rippling a little. Today's only eccentricity was a blue tartan scarf worn with a wool pullover sweater. Not that there was anything odd about a scarf. It just wasn't typical May attire; though given the fact that it was all of fifty-three degrees and cloudy out here, it was a wiser choice than Jamie's light cotton blouse.

"Come inside." She marched into the store, followed by Julian. It was empty except for employee Kayla Gomez, who was wandering around, straightening merchandise.

"Thanks, Kayla," Jamie said. "Would you vacuum the playroom before you go? Some kid was eating saltines in there."

"No problem." Kayla zipped cheerfully out of the main room. She was a cutie, Jamie thought, with that glossy, cropped brown hair and sparkling brown eyes. Kayla always seemed happy at work, and Jamie enjoyed working with her—except when Kayla mentioned Isaac, which happened about twice a week. Kayla had met him at Britteridge College, where Isaac helped keep campus computers running. "Oh my heck! He is *so* hot! I couldn't believe it when your mom told me you used to be engaged to him. He totally broke your heart, right? Is it awful having him nearby?"

Jamie repeatedly lectured herself about not condemning nineteen-year-old Kayla for immaturity and thoughtlessness but did hope Kayla's Isaac-worship would fade soon. At least she didn't seem to know about his visit to Jamie's condo. Melinda wouldn't tell her; Melinda wasn't prone to gossip.

As soon as Kayla was out of earshot, Jamie spoke quietly to Julian. "I assume Hannah told you what happened. I absolutely *did not* pull that haunting stunt last night, nor have I done anything else to Hannah and Isaac, and so help me, Julian, if Hannah sent you here to—"

"Take it easy," Julian said. "She didn't send me. I came to check on you. To see how you are faring."

"Really?"

"Yes. I'm concerned about you."

"Concerned I'm a psycho threatening your sister's marriage?"

He arched an eyebrow. "Is that the impression I've given you when we've spoken before?"

"No. I'm sorry. That was unfair. I'm just . . . furious!" Jamie slapped her dust cloth on the counter near the register. "The police came to me today to tell me about the ghost bride thing and to warn me to leave the Grahams alone. *The police!* I got a visit from the *police*! They think I'm a stalker!"

The front door opened. Jamie waited a couple of seconds, giving her anger-tensed face time to relax before she turned to greet her customer, a young woman with a baby in a front pack. Julian moved graciously away and spent his time examining a display of stone eggs until the woman had purchased a set of picture frames, chatted with Jamie about the upcoming spring gala, and exited.

Kayla stepped back into the main room. "Done with the playroom. I'm going to vacuum the book room now. Someone was eating popcorn in there."

Someone sneaked in with popcorn? Jamie had apparently been slacking today on enforcing the "no food or drink" policy. "Thanks, Kayla."

Kayla headed upstairs. With the clock reading six minutes after eight, Jamie locked the front door, relieved to be done with business for the day.

"I just cut off your easiest escape route," she said to Julian once the sound of the vacuum ensured Kayla couldn't hear her. "You should be terrified because it's well known in Britteridge that I'm so obsessed with Isaac that I've lost my mind. What's next on my list? A wedding dress covered in blood representing my shattered heart? The ghost of Jamie McKenzie's ruined dreams walks Isaac's property, shrieking her anguish to the night sky while the mud of despair clings to her boots . . . I'm sorry. I do sound crazy, don't I?"

"Nonsense. You sound like you're writing a paranormal country song. But your lyrics are somewhat illogical. How can your 'ruined dreams' take ghostly form when you're still alive?"

Jamie laughed. "The *dreams* are dead, not *me*. And I didn't mean to trap you. I can let you out the front, or you can go out the back."

"I'll stay a minute, if you don't mind."

"You're welcome to hang around."

Why was Julian here? Was he really concerned about her, or was he spying for his sister—whether or not Hannah had actually sent him? He seemed like a nice guy, but he probably was spying. He'd barely met Jamie; it was hard to believe he would come to the Treasure Chest just to check on her morale. But his spying was fine with her. The more he learned, the more he could testify that Jamie had said and done *nothing* to hint at guilt.

Jamie went to take the cash drawer out of the register. "The police told me to keep away from Hannah and Isaac, but you know what? I'm going to visit them. Because we *have* to talk. They're not even *thinking* about this. They're assuming anything weird that happens is me. I'm not going to put up with this garbage. They have zero proof, but they're accusing me right and left. Do you have any idea what Mr. Allerton—the owner of this shop—would think if he heard rumors that I was stalking Isaac?"

Julian frowned. "Please think about it before you confront them. Isaac is livid. He wanted to call the police in the middle of the night and have them arrest you, but Hannah calmed him down."

Hannah calmed him down? That surprised Jamie. "There is no way Isaac is more livid than I am. And he'd need a lot more to get me arrested than 'There was this ghost outside our window who might have been a woman—I didn't see her face, but can you go arrest Jamie McKenzie because I think she's obsessed with me?'"

"Maybe he was hoping the police could catch you still wearing a wedding dress."

"Then I wish he *had* called the police. They would have found me in bed with no wedding dress in sight, no dew on my shoes, and a cold car that plainly hadn't been driven for hours. Could you wait here? I need to go take care of the money."

"Certainly."

Jamie headed into the office. When she finished counting and stowing the money in the safe and Kayla had clocked out and headed home, she returned to the main room, where Julian was standing in front of the local souvenir section, fingering a wooden carving of Town Hall. "The detail on this is astounding," he said, holding it up.

"That's Niall Flanagan's work. Any wood carving that looks too amazing to be real is Niall's."

"Ah. I've heard his name before." Julian carefully replaced the carving on the table. "So has the tedious counting of coins and bills cooled your determination to confront Isaac?"

"I have to talk to him and Hannah. Otherwise they'll keep blaming me. Either someone is after them—and only they could have any idea who that is—or Hannah or Isaac is setting this whole thing up."

"Setting it up! Why would you say that?"

"Maybe Hannah is worried about my being back in town, so she's trying to make me look—" *Oops.* Blaming Hannah in front of her brother wasn't a good idea. "I'm sorry. I have no justification for suspecting Hannah. I'm just angry and frustrated."

"Maybe you should take a day or two to calm down—and let Isaac calm down—before you confront him."

"Don't worry. I won't yell at him. I promise to stay calm. But I can't wait. Things keep happening. If we don't talk this out *now*, who knows what nasty thing will happen tomorrow? Sooner or later, rumors will spread or this is going to hit the newspaper." *If it hasn't already*, Jamie thought bleakly. "I'm going there now."

"Let me come with you, then," Julian said.

"As referee?" Maybe that was a good idea. Julian seemed far more rational about this than Isaac, and Isaac would be less likely to fling accusations in front of his brother-in-law. "Do you believe I'm innocent? Or are you being nice in the hope that it will . . . uh . . . cool my rage and my longing for Isaac?"

"Shall I be candid?"

"Yes, but if it's bad news . . . at least make it poetic."

He smiled. "I don't know what pain lingers in your heart over Isaac. But if you did want to pursue him, why would you do it in a childish, vindictive, theatrical way guaranteed not to attract him but to infuriate him and stir revulsion toward yourself?"

"*Thank* you. But what if I thought attracting him was futile and I wanted to punish him?"

"If your goal was to punish him, I still have difficulty believing you'd do it in such a foolish, self-destructive way, making him an innocent victim and you a spiteful lunatic in danger of an unpleasant visit to a courtroom."

"Thank you for thinking about this a lot harder than Isaac has. And the answer to the lingering pain question is none. I am *over* Isaac. I loved him once. I don't anymore. And I'm *not* bitter. I forgave him long ago." Jamie smiled grimly. "Let's go tell him—calmly—how much I appreciate his siccing the police on me."

Chapter 5

JULIAN OFFERED TO DRIVE JAMIE to Hannah and Isaac's house. Jamie nearly declined; if conversation escalated into confrontation and she lost control of herself, she wanted to be free to rush out without asking Julian to take her home. But showing up with Julian, in his car—him escorting her to the door—that was a *much* better scenario than showing up on her own. It would be clear that Julian supported her desire to talk to Isaac and Hannah, as opposed to his following her there because he couldn't stop her, so he'd come to protect his sister from this jealous banshee.

Calm. Logical. No matter what Isaac says to you, you won't lose your composure. You can do this. You'll convince them. Isaac's usually a rational person. Once they truly think about what's happening, they'll see it isn't you.

Julian pulled into the driveway of a gray Cape with black shutters. So this was where Hannah and Isaac lived. The house was small, but the lot was huge, separated from neighbors by wooded areas. A ghost bride could creep in, do her haunting, and slip out without disturbing any neighbors. Too bad there weren't likely to be witnesses who had seen the bride.

"Are you ready for this?" Julian asked.

"Are you? You might get in trouble with your sister for escorting me in there."

"I've already told Hannah and Isaac that accusing you of stalking them makes almost no sense and they should hunt for other culprits."

Almost no sense. Did Julian 100 percent believe she was innocent? No. How could he believe in her without even a fragment of reservation when he'd just met her—regardless of what nice things old friends had told him about her? But he was objective, helpful, and kind, and Jamie was glad he'd accompanied her as her chauffeur and sidekick. "You still might get in trouble with Hannah. Doubting my guilt is a bit less extreme than actually bringing me here."

"If I think you're innocent, why shouldn't I assist you in making your case?"

"It's just more . . . actively supportive. That might bother them."

"I'm not a fan of passivity. Hannah knows that. She won't be surprised." Julian stepped out of the car. Jamie picked up her purse and started to reach for her door handle but stopped. Both on Sunday and today, Julian had stepped forward to open doors for her, and she figured he'd be courteous enough to want to open her car door as well. She liked that. She could use some chivalry in her life.

Julian swung her door open and offered his hand. Jamie reached for it; she certainly didn't need help climbing out of Julian's Subaru, but she enjoyed the gallant gesture anyway.

He led her to the front door and pressed the bell. "If you don't mind, let me speak first. That will raise the probability of admittance."

"Good plan." Jamie moistened her parched mouth and listened for approaching footsteps.

The door opened. Isaac glared at Julian and Jamie.

"I stopped by the Treasure Chest to check on Jamie," Julian said smoothly. "She wanted to come speak to you, and I offered to bring her. May we come in?"

Isaac's lips pinched together. "She can't come in," he said after a moment. "It will upset Hannah. If Jamie would like to talk to us, she can talk through her lawyer."

Face burning, Jamie wanted to snap that if Isaac didn't quit acting like an idiot, he *would* hear from her lawyer when she sued Isaac for slander. Of course, that would involve *finding* a lawyer and *paying* a lawyer . . .

"I don't think legal counsel is necessary at this point," Julian said. "An open conversation would be more productive."

"Julian, you have good intentions, but this is none of your business. Take Jamie home." Isaac slammed the door. The lock clicked.

"You know," Jamie said, "maybe I *will* come haunt him tonight. And put a ghostly brick through his window."

"Don't give up yet." Julian drew his phone out of his pocket and texted rapidly.

"Who are you texting?"

"Hannah." He lowered his phone. "It'll just take a moment . . ."

From inside the house, they heard footsteps, voices, more footsteps. A moment of silence. Footsteps approached the door.

The lock clicked, and the door opened. Isaac shot Julian a steely look from behind the screen door. "Come in. You have fifteen minutes to present your case. Then she leaves, or I'm calling the police."

Jamie inhaled, trying to focus on the fresh evening air and the scent of lilacs instead of her desire to snarl at Isaac. *She* leaves—Isaac wouldn't even address her directly.

Stay calm. You promised yourself and Julian you'd stay calm. "Thank you," she said. Her voice wasn't as smooth as Julian's, but at least she sounded composed.

Julian pulled the screen door open and held it for Jamie as she walked in. Isaac watched her warily, clearly ready to shove her out the door if she whipped out a veil and started wailing his name.

Hannah stood in the hallway. She looked pale—maybe it was the contrast with her black dress and long, straight black hair. She led the way into the living room.

"Please sit down," she said.

Please? Hannah was a lot more polite than her husband. Jamie had always perceived Hannah as aloof or even snobbish, but at least she wasn't slamming doors in Jamie's face.

Jamie sat in a blue-striped chair. She couldn't help scanning the room, curious about what Isaac's home looked like. Cherrywood furniture in classic Colonial styles. Cream and navy-blue fabrics, accented by a few red throw pillows. A navy rug under the coffee table. Matching brass lamps. A wedding photo in a crystal frame. Few knickknacks—there was plenty of empty space. It looked like an upscale version of Isaac's student apartment. Apparently, Isaac and Hannah shared a taste for simplicity, tradition, and no clutter.

Hannah and Isaac sat together on the couch, with Isaac's arm around Hannah's shoulders. Julian settled in a wingback chair that matched Jamie's.

"Thank you for hearing me out," Jamie said.

Isaac checked his watch.

Jamie squelched another burst of anger. Trust Isaac to throw her out midsentence once the fifteen minutes expired. She'd better get to the point. "I apologize for losing my temper with you the other day. I was rude, and I'm sorry."

Isaac said nothing. Hannah avoided Jamie's eyes and toyed with her wedding ring.

So much for hoping that an apology might release some of the tension. "I am not your stalker," Jamie said. "If you're ever going to figure out who's bothering you, you need to quit assuming it's me and start figuring out who wants to upset you."

"We didn't jump to conclusions," Isaac said icily. "We've discussed this extensively, and you are the *only* person who'd have any motive for doing these things. We don't have enemies. We haven't offended anyone. Everything was peaceful until you moved back to Britteridge, and all of a sudden, we're under siege."

"Isaac, we've known each other since fourth grade. Have you ever—*ever*, in all our lives—seen or heard of me doing *anything* that would make you believe I'm capable of this type of behavior?"

"I *knew* you," he said. "I don't know what you're like now."

"Are you assuming that in the five years since I left Britteridge, I've become vindictive and warped?"

"I have no idea what's happened in your life."

She kept her tone even. "But you assume it's been so empty that I had nothing better to fill my mind with than the desire to come back and wreak revenge on you?"

Isaac rested a hand on Hannah's bulging belly. "All I want is for you to leave us alone."

"That's all I want too," Jamie said. "But it's difficult when every time I turn around, your mother or you or the police are in my face accusing me of stalking you."

"There is no one else who would have any reason to—"

"I know neither of you saw the face of the ghost bride," Jamie interrupted, but calmly. "If you had, Detective Powell would have told me."

"We saw enough." Isaac was patting Hannah's belly now, almost drumming his fingers on it, and his neck was flushed. Was he nervous, Jamie wondered? She'd thought he was just angry.

"You saw a dark-haired woman with her face obscured by a veil," Jamie said.

Hannah spoke quietly as she laid her hand on Isaac's fidgety fingers. "Yes. That's what we saw."

"If you're asking if we could testify in court that it was you, then no, we couldn't," Isaac said. "But we don't want this to go to court anyway. We want it to end. You leave us alone, and we'll pretend it never happened."

"The only way this will end is if we figure out who's responsible for it. Think about it. Even if I still loved you—or hated you—why would I do this? How does it benefit me?"

"I'm not going to try to psychoanalyze your motives."

"You were psychoanalyzing my alleged motives the other day. You're assuming you understand my motives, or you wouldn't assume I was responsible." Proud that she still sounded in control of herself, Jamie said, "This could only hurt me. I assume you've confided in people—definitely in your mother, probably in friends as well. Obviously the police. Word will start to spread. What do you think that will do to my reputation?" Picturing Edward Allerton's stern face made it hard for Jamie to keep her voice from rising. "What will it do to my job? If it continues, it will get me fired. I didn't quit my old job and pack up and move to Britteridge so I could destroy myself by pursuing a grudge. I'm asking you to please stop making accusations without proof. I am *not stalking you.* I would *never* do that to anyone. If that's all you're willing to see here, you're never going to solve this problem."

Isaac opened his mouth, but instead of speaking, he frowned, brow wrinkling and neck stretching forward as though he wanted a closer look at her. She recognized that expression. Isaac was evaluating, thinking hard. *At last.*

After a silent moment, he spoke. "Are you desperate for money? Are you hoping we'll pay you to leave us alone? I'll bet your old job didn't pay very well, and I'm sure that tourist trap where you work didn't pay your moving expenses. Are you in bad debt?"

Jamie gaped at him. Isaac finally gave it deep thought, and *that's* what he came up with?

Disgusted, she gave up on him; she wouldn't deign to share that Allerton had paid her moving expenses, and though her salary hadn't been great in Phoenix, her living expenses had been low, and she had been frugal enough to save enough for a down payment on her condo. She focused on Hannah. "Hannah, please think about this. It can't continue—it's hurting all of us. I have no idea who'd want to torment the two of you. You need to answer that question."

"Who do you think we are?" Isaac dropped his arms from around Hannah and rose to his feet. "Mobsters who ticked off the boss? Black-mailers? Drug dealers? We don't have enemies! I'm an IT guy at Britt! Hannah is an accountant! We live in a little New England town! The only crazy thing to ever happen here was a couple of years ago when that old lady wanted revenge on the Drakes and got her niece to kidnap Rachel. Otherwise, the worst that ever happens is college kids getting busted for smoking weed."

"Will you sit down? My fifteen minutes aren't up."

"This is a waste of time, and you're stressing out my wife. You've caused enough trouble—"

"I'm all right, Isaac." Hannah grasped Isaac's hand and drew him back to the couch.

"I'm not asking you to look for mob-boss-style enemies." Jamie tried not to sharpen the words, but it was getting more and more difficult to sound composed. "The things that have happened are cruel pranks, not threats to your lives. Can you think of anyone with a twisted sense of humor? Anyone who might think it was funny to stir up trouble—"

"We've already been through this!" Isaac said. "I'm not going to dissect the personalities of my friends and associates for your entertainment."

Fighting her anger was starting to feel like squashing a lion into a grocery sack. "You made the point that you don't know what I'm like now. Apparently, I don't know what *you're* like either, because I've never known you to be such a pigheaded jerk."

Isaac's voice stabbed her eardrums. "Get this straight. If *one more thing* happens to us, we will prosecute you to the fullest extent of the law."

"Good *luck*. To get me charged with anything, you'll need evidence, and you don't *have* any evidence beyond your ego telling you I have no life without you, so I'm putting on my dusty wedding dress and scratching on your window at night. You know what, Prince Heartthrob? I don't *have* that wedding dress. I sold it on Craigslist three weeks after you dumped me and used the money for yoga lessons, craft supplies, and a set of *Harry Potter* audiobooks in Spanish. If you think—"

"Forgive me for interrupting," Julian said. "We're getting off track. Hannah, do you agree with Isaac that there's no point in searching for other culprits because Jamie must be guilty?"

Isaac glowered at Julian. "Don't pester Hannah with idiotic questions. She's been through enough. The only reason she allowed Jamie in here was as a favor to you, though why you've sided with Jamie, I can't imagine. Is studying her psyche some wacky new hobby of yours? Did you get bored with learning to play the banjo?"

Jamie ground her teeth.

"I haven't sided with anyone." Julian sounded irritated. "I've sided with learning the truth. Have you?"

Isaac glanced at his watch. "Fifteen minutes are up. Get her out of here, or I'm calling Detective Powell."

Chapter 6

AFTER THEY LEFT THE GRAHAMS, Jamie spent the first mile staring out the windshield in silence. After she didn't respond to Julian's "Are you all right?" he got the message and stayed quiet as well. She *did* want to talk to him, but not yet. If she didn't have to speak—or even breathe very often—she might make it back to the Treasure Chest, where her car was parked, without having a meltdown in front of Julian.

The effort didn't last. Before they were halfway to downtown, her fury and hurt erupted, and she started bawling, quoting nasty things Isaac had said and rambling incoherently about how long it had taken her to sell all the decorations meant for the reception—they'd only kept some star-shaped candleholders because her older sister thought she might want to use them—how she and her mother had had to deal with all the mop-up, including notifying the guests, and all that Isaac, champion of cluelessness, had offered to do was reimburse her for nonrefundable deposits, an offer she had furiously—and stupidly—refused but her father had stepped in to accept, seeing how it was his money, not Jamie's—she was only twenty-two and fresh out of college. And even though Isaac had been a snaky two-timer, at least he hadn't thought she was psychotic at the time. Or maybe he had, and that was the real reason he'd dumped her. And thank heavens he had dumped her; what a nightmare marriage to him would have been. She'd rather marry Voldemort; at least he was upfront about the fact that he was evil.

Julian listened, nodded, looked sympathetic, and offered her a peppermint Gibraltar from a box he'd taken from the glove compartment. When Jamie finally ran out of steam a half hour after they'd parked behind the Treasure Chest, she wiped her eyes on a drenched Kleenex and smiled weakly at Julian. "Good grief," she said. "I'm so sorry."

"Sorry for what?"

"For unloading on you like this. For getting hysterical and trapping you here listening to me weep about your idiot brother-in-law."

He chuckled. "I'm happy to be a listening ear."

"Thank you. I'm sorry to put you through that, but thank you. I feel much less homicidal. You know what's ironic? I was *proud* of the way I acted when Isaac dumped me. I thought I handled it with amazing maturity. It was awful, it was devastating, I cried gallons of tears and raged to my sisters and my mother, but I left him alone. I didn't chase him, didn't call him, didn't text him, didn't contact him in any way. And now, five years later, he thinks I'm *stalking* him? That creep! I moved on with my life. I got over him, and honestly, it didn't take too many months before I was grateful he'd broken things off. Once the hormone tide was heading out, I could see we weren't the best match and I'd be better off with someone else. And I thought I could move to Britteridge, come back to this place I love, and work at the Treasure Chest, which is almost my favorite place on the planet, and be happy here. I thought that when my path crossed Isaac's, we'd smile and be friendly and all the messiness wouldn't matter anymore. Instead, it's been a total disaster."

"I'm sorry." Julian held out the box of Gibraltars again.

"Thank you." Jamie took another one. A candy with the tagline of *First Candy Made Commercially in America* seemed appropriate for time-traveler Julian to have on hand. She ought to go visit Ye Olde Pepper Candy Companie in Salem; she hadn't been there since high school. Good thing the candy store didn't remind her of Isaac; they'd never gone there together. Isaac didn't eat much candy.

"Anyway . . . so much for getting Isaac's help in figuring out who's harassing them," she said. "And you know something else bad is going to happen—something *worse*, because the prankster keeps stepping things up—and Isaac's going to blame me, and word will get around, and I'll get *fired*. So much for my dream come true of running the Treasure Chest."

"You won't get fired."

"Yes, I will. Edward Allerton doesn't tolerate shenanigans. He's a credit to his Puritan ancestors." She nibbled the peppermint candy and glared out the windshield at the black wrought-iron lampposts lighting the parking area. "You know what I need to do? Hire a private investigator to figure out what's going on, but I don't have the money for that. Don't they charge hundreds of dollars an hour? Or is that lawyers?"

"You don't need a PI," Julian said. "Hannah will come talk to you. Soon."

"*What?* Yes, she gave me a chance to present my case tonight, but she didn't exactly disagree with Isaac's accusations."

"Hannah doesn't like arguments, nor would she want to embarrass Isaac by siding against him while you were there. But while you were dueling him, I was watching her, and I promise, you'll hear from her. She's not comfortable with Isaac's conclusions, and she's not sure you're guilty. She'll want to talk to you."

Disconcerted but hopeful, Jamie rubbed her swollen eyelids. Whatever remained of her mascara had to be black smears under her eyes. "Give me your number, so if I don't hear from Hannah, I can call you and panic."

He laughed, and they swapped phone numbers.

"I'm scared to death of what's going to happen next," Jamie said, putting her phone in her purse. "Who would do this?"

"I don't know. But may I observe that this situation is cartoonishly ridiculous? If these incidents weren't needling old guilt, it would be easier for Isaac to see the silliness of them."

"Guilt?"

Julian tucked the Gibraltars back in the glove compartment. "Isaac hurt you. I suspect that still bothers him."

"I doubt it."

"He hasn't handled this recent situation well, but he's a good man. You know that."

"Okay, yes." Jamie sighed. "I just wish he understood that I'm over him."

"Would you like me to take you home? I can bring you back to pick up your car tomorrow if you don't feel like driving right now."

"I have so much adrenaline that I could drive the Indy 500. Or coast to coast. Truth is, I don't want to go home. If I do, I'll fume and pace until I get so frustrated that I call Detective Powell and tell him to get his crew out there to take fingerprints or footprint molds or *something* to prove I'm not the ghost bride."

"Maybe a distraction would help. May I take you somewhere? I'm at your service."

"That's very nice of you, but you probably need a nap and some Tylenol after all this. I'll stay at the Treasure Chest and get some work done. I don't want to go where anyone could see me."

"In that case, come with me." Julian started the engine. "I'll take you to the college, we'll find a deserted room, and I'll teach you the foxtrot. No—the cha cha would better suit your mood."

Jamie grinned. "Seriously? You'll give me dancing lessons tonight?"

"Why not? You're buzzing with adrenaline. Let's use it productively. You told me you wanted to learn."

"I do! But . . . are you sure you want to spend more time with me after everything I've put you through tonight?"

"Absolutely."

"Are you sure you're safe with me? My emotions could explode again at any moment, and I could go all raging and murderous."

Julian reversed out of his parking spot. "If that happens," he said, "we'll switch to the tango."

* * *

Niall Flanagan set the box on the desk and removed the first bubble-wrapped item. He handed it to Jamie.

"I can't wait." Jamie peeled off the bubble wrap. "Niall, it's gorgeous!" She touched the swirling lines on the intricately carved wooden Christmas tree. "How long did these take you?"

"Hours," Melinda said, an edge in her voice. She unwrapped a second tree and held up her father's work so the morning light through the office window sparkled on the glitter. "Not that Ed will appreciate the time he poured into them."

"He appreciates my work, darling. You know that." Niall's tone was so firm that Jamie realized his words were a reprimand. She'd heard Melinda complain before that Allerton took Niall for granted, and apparently, her complaints bothered Niall. It wasn't easy to irritate good-humored Niall; maybe this was a sensitive subject for him.

Melinda set the tree on the desk and said nothing.

"Edward keeps buying my work and pays me well." Niall patted his daughter's shoulder. "That's the only thanks I need."

Melinda snorted. "If it weren't for you, this store would have folded twenty years ago. You're the only thing that keeps it from being just another overpriced gift shop. Ed Allerton doesn't know what gratitude means."

"This glitter is genius." Hoping she could guide the conversation away from Allerton, Jamie tilted the ten-inch tree in her hands, examining it from each angle. "Just a touch of sparkle, a hint of ice on the branches. These will sell out the first day I display the Christmas stock. How many did you make?"

"Ten so far, but my hands still work." Niall waved his calloused fingers. "Say the word and you'll have more."

"I'm positive we can sell as many as you can make."

Niall's blue eyes—the same bright shade as Melinda's—gleamed as he picked up the tree from the desk. White hair and a few wrinkles made him look grandfatherly, but his energy and optimism would keep him young for decades, Jamie thought. How old was he? Melinda was probably in her late forties, so Niall must be nearly seventy, at least. She hoped he'd keep wielding his carving knives and chisels for many years. Melinda was right when she said Niall was a huge part of why the Treasure Chest was successful.

At the ringing of the chime over the front door, Melinda set the tree on the desk and turned to go attend the customer.

"I'll take it," Jamie said. It was still ten minutes until Kayla was due to start her shift, so she and Melinda were the only ones there. She knew Melinda would want to stay with her father. She always stuck close to Niall when he was in the shop.

As Jamie walked, she kept hearing Julian's voice in her head, and she had to fight an impulse to dance her way to the customer *two-three-cha-cha-cha-two-three*. The improbable situation of having Julian give her dancing lessons after that horrible scene at the Grahams' had been exactly what she'd needed. Laughing with Julian, learning a new skill, tripping over her own feet, and stomping on his as she tried to get the hang of things—it had been the perfect way to cool the melodrama in her head. Julian was right. The whole situation was ludicrous.

The sight of Hannah entering the Treasure Chest gave Jamie an urge to giggle. Another point for Julian. He'd been right about Hannah's coming to talk to her.

Hannah had an inscrutable look on her face as she walked toward Jamie. She moved gracefully, and Jamie wondered if she danced. Maybe it was a Stokes family thing. Everything about Hannah—except her pregnant belly—was long and slim. Long limbs, long neck, even a long, straight nose and long hair brushed back in a smooth braid. Jamie wondered if her hair would curl like Julian's if she didn't straighten it.

As Hannah stopped in front of her, Jamie thought fast, conscious of Niall and Melinda close by. It would be awful if Hannah started accusing her while the Flanagans could hear and mortifying beyond belief if she and Hannah were in the middle of an argument when a new customer walked in. But Julian had said Hannah didn't like arguments, so she probably hadn't come to fight.

"Hello," Jamie said cautiously.

"I know you're busy." Hannah kept her voice low. "But I feel I owe you a personal apology."

Astonished, Jamie made a blundering attempt to sound gracious. "Well . . . uh . . . thanks for at least giving me a chance to talk last night. I know you're the one who made Isaac let me in. Can we . . . go for a quick walk?"

"Can you leave?"

"Yeah, I'm actually off work today. Just stopped by to take care of a few things. Hang on a minute." Jamie hurried into the back, told Melinda she was leaving, and grabbed her jacket.

"Thanks," Jamie said once she and Hannah were walking along the perimeter of the town green. Hannah's long legs set a rapid pace, and Jamie had to speed up her own gait to match. She didn't want to get left in the dust by a pregnant woman.

"I hope I didn't embarrass you by coming to your store," Hannah said.

"No, I appreciate it. I just figured if we can move the conversation somewhere more private, so much the better. If you're here talking to me, does that mean you don't agree with Isaac that I'm the ghost bride?"

"The more I think about it, the less I think you are." Hannah adjusted her scarf so the fringed ends were even. Maybe scarves were a Stokes family thing as well, though Hannah's was a light weave in spring colors, unlike Julian's wool tartan. "Besides, Julian thinks it's ridiculous to suspect you."

"I'm glad he has good people instincts." Jamie resisted the temptation to suggest that Isaac's people instincts could use some upgrading.

"He doesn't rely on instinct alone," Hannah said. "He's researched you."

"Researched?"

"If he's concerned about something, he'll look into it."

"Like someone stalking his sister as soon as I, the prime suspect, moved back to town?"

Hannah nodded. "After I got that postcard, he did some homework and concluded that you are 'highly unlikely to engage in such absurd and mean-spirited antics.'"

Jamie smiled at Hannah's affectionate mimicry of her brother. "How did he research me? I mean, I know he already knows my family. And people in the Britteridge Ward who knew me growing up."

"If Julian has questions, he'll figure out a way to get answers. Don't worry. He's careful about it; he wouldn't have said anything that could embarrass you. But he's skilled at finding connections, friends of friends, people he can talk to without making it seem awkward."

"Wait—who *has* he talked to? Do you mean, like, talking to people who knew me in Arizona, or what?"

"I'm sure he did. I don't know who he's talked to, but I know he's gathered enough information to convince him. I promise he's not creepy. He'll give you all the details of what he's done if you ask him. He just *really* doesn't like to make mistakes about people, so he'd rather risk coming across as nosy or weird than get caught by surprise. He's been burned before and doesn't want any of us getting burned again if he can prevent it."

"What happened to make him so skittish? Or is that too nosy of a question?"

Hannah smiled slightly at the dryness in Jamie's tone. "He investigated you, so you're going to investigate him?"

"Sounds fair to me."

"Sounds fair to me too. He wouldn't mind my telling you—though he wouldn't volunteer the information himself because he still doesn't like to talk about it. When he was at BYU, he taught a few dance classes as a student, and this gorgeous girl started showing up at one of his evening classes. She wasn't enrolled in the class and would say she just wanted to observe, but she'd hang around after class to talk. Then she started asking him to teach her this or that step, and of course, Julian wasn't going to turn her down. They'd dance, and she had a knack for it—very graceful, learned fast. She said she used to do ballet." Hannah paused at the east corner of the green. "Do you want to cross Main Street or circle the green again?"

"I don't care."

Hannah headed for the crosswalk and pressed the pedestrian button. "Finally, he asked her out. They ended up dating steadily. He was head over heels—first serious relationship. He'd always been great at making friends with women but had trouble getting past the friendship stage to the romance stage. He was tired of being the buddy who got an excited text when yet another female friend got engaged to someone else."

Jamie felt a little guilty, wondering if Julian truly wouldn't mind Hannah's telling her such a personal story, along with sisterly commentary. "So he thought he'd found his dream woman. I'm guessing this has a bad ending."

"Yes. A couple of months into the relationship, a guy comes up to Julian on campus. He'd seen Julian with this woman and wanted to warn him. He'd gone to high school with her and still knew her family. She wasn't a student. She used to be but made some dumb decisions, got kicked out of BYU, and was living with a guy with whom she had a year-old baby. Julian checked into it and found out that when her boyfriend worked swing shift, she would ditch the child with her parents, come up to campus, and live the unattached student life again—which included chasing Julian."

"Oh my goodness," Jamie said. "Poor Julian."

The light changed, and they started across the street. "He was crushed," Hannah said. "He couldn't get over how easily she'd tricked him and was furious with himself for being an idiot."

"He's too hard on himself. How often does anyone run background checks on seemingly eligible people we meet at college?"

"In Julian's opinion, we should. He kept saying if he'd bothered to follow up on anything about her, like talked to anyone from her alleged hometown—she'd told him she was from some tiny town in northern Utah, but she was really from Salt Lake—he could have found out she was lying before he got emotionally involved."

"So now he doesn't take chances."

"No. He no longer trusts his instincts without facts to back them up."

"I'm flattered that I passed the test. He even—" Realizing what she'd been about to say might give Hannah the wrong impression, she stopped.

Hannah studied her with a piercing look. "He even what?"

"I don't mean . . . I was just thinking, he took me to Britt last night and taught me the cha-cha. I'm glad he . . . I mean . . . after what happened . . . that he's not afraid to . . ." What was she trying to say? That after he'd been stung by a woman who'd approached him through a dance class, that she was glad he, a dance instructor, hadn't developed a phobia of teaching women to dance? "Never mind," Jamie said.

"He gave you a dance lesson?"

Jamie wasn't sure why Hannah sounded so pleased. Or was that amusement more than approval? "I'd mentioned to him that I was interested in learning, and after that scene at your house last night, he was trying to cheer me up. It was a nice thing to do." She hoped she'd made it sound more like a service project than a date, though the way she'd brought it up right after the story of Julian's romantic disaster must have made it sound like she was claiming he was pursuing her.

Embarrassed, Jamie hurried to return to their earlier subject. "Thanks for telling me where he's coming from. Given the circumstances, it doesn't bother me at all that he investigated me. I have nothing to hide. I'm guessing he's shared with Isaac whatever evidence he's found that I'm not obsessed and filled with hate, but Isaac doesn't care?"

"Isaac is . . . stressed." Hannah touched her belly. "He worries so much about me, about the baby."

"Is everything . . . going all right with the pregnancy?"

"Yes, everything's fine. It's just . . . it took us a long time. At first, I couldn't get pregnant at all, and just when we were getting ready to go for a fertility workup, I got pregnant, then miscarried early on. Then I miscarried again six months later."

"Oh my goodness, Hannah! I'm so sorry. I can see why Isaac would be worried about the baby now, after everything you've been through."

"Yes, he's *so* protective it drives me insane sometimes. The doctor reassures us that everything is normal. The baby is growing fine, I'm healthy, the pregnancy is not high-risk. I don't have any restrictions. But Isaac freaks out if I vacuum the rug or carry a basket of laundry."

Jamie knew she should say something compassionate about how if Isaac was that worried, it was natural that he'd be so upset about the stalking incidents that he'd rush to blame Jamie, even without proof. But she couldn't push the words out. Thinking of the disdainful way he'd snapped "Get her out of here" last night still smarted.

"I'm sorry he's vented his worries on you," Hannah said. "I know this has been very embarrassing for you."

"Why is he so stubborn about refusing to explore the possibility that someone else is doing this?"

"He doesn't think he's being stubborn. He thinks he *has* explored it, and he honestly can't see any other options."

"Can you?"

Hannah played with one of the shirt buttons resting against her round stomach. "I keep asking myself who would want to do this and why. It couldn't be one of *your* friends, someone still angry over the way Isaac broke off your engagement, because if they were acting out of sympathy for you, their goal would not be to make you look terrible."

"Exactly."

"But I agree with Isaac that I can't think of anyone who would want to harass us like this. Maybe someone hates us and we don't know it, but it's such a strange way of getting back at us. So the next thing I considered was that maybe we aren't the target."

"What do you mean?"

"Maybe *you* are the target. Someone isn't trying to pin this on you simply so they can bother us while the police look in the wrong direction. Their whole goal is to make you look bad. Last night you were talking about how if rumors that you were stalking Isaac got back to your boss, you'd lose your job. Maybe someone isn't trying to hurt *us*; they're trying to hurt *you*, and we're the tools."

Jamie considered Hannah's words as they passed a bakery that smelled so appealing Jamie had to fight the urge to take a detour for a cinnamon roll. "It does make some sense." She refrained from adding, *And a huge thank you to Isaac for being dim enough to play into their hands.* "Only problem is, I can't imagine who'd be out to get me. I just moved back to Britteridge. I haven't had time to make new enemies, and I'm pretty sure I don't have any old enemies who've been stewing for the past five years, waiting for a chance to ruin my reputation."

"I don't want to accuse anyone, but do you mind if I think out loud?" Hannah asked. "We can walk the path behind the library."

"Sounds good. And I'll be careful not to treat anything you say as accusation or gossip fodder."

"Thank you." Hannah went silent as they passed behind the town library and entered the trail where Jamie liked to walk on her occasional free mornings. Once it was clear that no one was in earshot, Hannah said, "I was wondering . . . what about the woman you work with? Melinda Brennan? She's been at the Treasure Chest forever. She's a lot more experienced than you are, and she must be twenty years older, but Edward Allerton brought you in to take over as manager when your mother left. If I were her, I'd resent that."

Jamie smiled. "Melinda doesn't want to manage the store. She's never wanted to work more than part time."

"Could she say that but not mean it—pretend getting bypassed didn't bother her?"

"No, she means it. My mother told me that when Melinda's sons were young, she didn't want to be away from home too much, and now that they're grown and moved away, she still likes having ample free time for her quilting. She made it clear to my mother that she would not consider taking over for her."

Hannah looked crestfallen, and Jamie realized Hannah had hoped she'd solved the mystery.

"It's a good thought," Jamie said. "But Melinda always says the Treasure Chest eats up Niall's—her father's—life and it's not eating her life too."

"That's too bad." Pinkness shaded Hannah's cheekbones, and she grimaced. "That sounded callous—being disappointed that your employee isn't setting you up. I was just hoping I'd found an answer."

"I understand. Any other ideas?"

Hannah bit her lip. "Just one. I was hoping we could find a solution without looking in this direction."

It's Isaac! He's doing this to me! Jamie's startled thought evaporated instantly. Of course it wasn't Isaac. If he was worried about his pregnant wife, the last thing he'd do would be to spook her by recruiting someone to play the role of Jamie McKenzie, Vengeful Ghost Bride.

"Who do you think it is?" Jamie asked.

"I don't know. But I do know that Isaac's mother was *very* worried about you moving back to Britteridge."

"She was?"

"I overheard her talking to Isaac. Please don't repeat this to anyone. I don't want to end up in trouble with her."

"Believe me, I won't. I'm already embarrassed enough about the situation. What did she say?"

"This was before anything happened to us, before you even arrived. She heard the news a few months ago that you were coming, and she was concerned. She said how she wondered what your *real* motives were in coming back, that it couldn't be to take over your mother's position at the Treasure Chest. Why would you quit a good job in graphic design and move across the country to manage a piddling knickknack store?"

Jamie bristled. "We sell the highest quality merchandise! The Treasure Chest is a Britteridge classic!"

"I'm quoting Robin. I admire the Treasure Chest; it's a charming downtown landmark."

"What else did she say?"

"She told Isaac that no psychologically healthy young woman would want to come back just for a job to a place where she'd suffered so much pain. You must have ulterior motives."

"Grr." Jamie ripped a handful of leaves off a tree as they passed. "She thinks I came back to chase Isaac."

"Yes. She warned him to be careful of how he acted around you, to not give you any . . . false hope. That you were single and lonely and might take even innocent actions as signs that he was interested."

"Single and lonely! What is *wrong* with her? It is entirely possible to be single and *happy*! I am not lonely. How dare—" Jamie inhaled deeply, stopping her angry tirade against Robin Graham.

"Are you okay?" Hannah asked.

Jamie breathed out. "I'm trying to convince myself to stay calm. She really thinks I came back to chase a married man?"

"Isaac *did* tell her you'd never do that."

"Back when he thought I was sane?"

"Robin was worried you wouldn't think of him as really married—that you'd think turnabout was fair play, since he was engaged to you first."

"Oh my *word*. What is up with her? I always knew she was unconventional, but I didn't think she was completely batty."

"You know how Robin sometimes comes up with unique ideas and gets stuck on them."

"Yeah." But I never thought she would . . . I guess I always thought of her ideas and campaigns as funny. "Like when she wanted to get trick-or-treating outlawed in Massachusetts because she was sure it created lifelong issues with greed. Would you believe she tried to get it on the ballot as an initiative? To no one's surprise, she failed."

"Maybe that's why Isaac still doesn't like Halloween," Hannah said. "But I didn't know Robin was opposed to trick-or-treating. I remember last fall she told me she was debating handing out fruit gummies instead of candy bars, and she asked if I thought the kids would like that."

"She probably likes it fine now. Like you said, she gets stuck on ideas. She grabs on to a cause and is positive she's right and even gets extreme about it. But eventually, she softens up and changes her mind."

"Yes. She didn't like *me* much until—" Hannah pointed to her belly. "Now that a baby's coming, she's completely flipped around. She adores me and can't wait for her grandchild, and you're the enemy—the old girlfriend who might be a threat to my marriage. As you said, she has a tendency to go to extremes. That's why I wondered if she could possibly be involved with what's happening."

Jamie figured it wouldn't be tactful to tell Hannah how grateful she was to have been spared Robin Graham as a mother-in-law. "If she's so afraid I'll try to steal Isaac, why would *she* dress up as a ghost bride and harass . . . Oh. You think she's trying to make Isaac disgusted at the thought of me *and* drive me out of town to remove any possibility of my luring Isaac away from you."

"It's just a theory," Hannah said. "The only other one I could come up with."

"Do you really think Robin would do something like that?"

"Do *you*? You've known her longer than I have."

Jamie thought about Robin and her crusades—like when she decided all desserts were against the Word of Wisdom, and if she could corner you at the refreshment table after a fireside, she'd give you an anti-cookie lecture and send you home with samples of baby carrots and flax seeds. Or when she'd decided the best way to teach kids to be reverent during Primary was to fight fire with fire; she'd sit next to talkers and talk loudly herself, making it impossible for the kids to hear the lesson or the songs and making a wreck of Sharing Time.

"It's possible," Jamie said. "Coming from Robin."

"I think her fears are why Isaac was so quick to jump to the conclusion that you're the stalker. I'm sure Robin is still fueling that."

"Thank you for telling me. I'll, uh, figure out how to talk to her."

"Please don't tell her this idea came from me. She doesn't even know I heard her conversation with Isaac. I was eavesdropping."

"Eavesdropping?"

"They thought I was taking a nap, but I couldn't sleep. When I came out, I heard them talking in the kitchen, and I kept listening."

"I would have too," Jamie said. "I won't give you away." She owed Hannah for giving her this tip; she didn't want to make trouble for her.

"I'll keep working on calming Isaac down," Hannah said. "Let me know what happens with Robin. You can call or text me. Let me give you my number." She pulled out her phone. Jamie pulled out hers, and they exchanged numbers.

"I hope you know I would never even think of pursuing Isaac." Jamie slipped her phone back in her pocket. "What happened years ago doesn't matter anymore. Honestly, it's all for the best that it worked out how it did."

Hannah looked at her, and Jamie felt unsettled at the relief in Hannah's face. Despite Hannah's rational approach to the situation, had she still worried that Jamie was angry with her or pining over Isaac?

"I've . . . always felt that I owed you an apology," Hannah said. "Even if it worked out for the best, we didn't go about it in the right way. I should have waited until Isaac resolved things with you before I was willing to see him. I told myself I was being supportive when he needed a friend, but it was inappropriate to get involved with him under the circumstances."

This apology sent Jamie's jaw falling open and stuck her feet to the paved path. Julian had told her Hannah regretted the timing of her actions, but Jamie had never imagined she'd be this candid about it.

Hannah stopped next to her. "I'm not sorry I married him, of course. I love Isaac, and we're very happy. I'm just sorry for acting at the wrong time."

"Well . . . thank you for . . . I mean . . ." Jamie wanted to say she'd forgiven Hannah long ago, but she realized that wasn't true. She'd *thought* she'd moved past everything associated with Isaac, but in her heart, hadn't she always cast Hannah as a stuck-up, conniving fiancé stealer? "I'm glad you and Isaac are happy. I'm happy *for* you, and I'm glad everything worked out like it did." She resumed walking. "I promise to be polite to Robin and leave you out of it."

Chapter 7

FOR THE REST OF THE morning, Jamie focused on preparing a creative way to approach Robin. She wanted a tactic unusual enough to jar stubborn Robin out of her warped interpretation of Jamie's return to Britteridge. Maybe Robin wasn't the culprit, but Jamie was 98 percent sure Hannah was right.

She was also 99.9 percent sure Robin wouldn't admit to anything. If Robin felt she was acting from pure motives, she wouldn't feel obligated to own up. No point in trying to coax a confession; Jamie just wanted to get Robin to stop. If she didn't do anything else to damage Jamie's reputation and Hannah calmed Isaac down, that would, Jamie hoped, be enough.

She dropped by Niall's house, collected scrap wood, sanded and painted it, and Mod Podged pictures onto the wood pieces, creating a collage of the last five years of her life. If Robin thought Jamie's life was so empty and lonely that the only thing filling her time and her mind was a compulsion to chase her ex-fiancé, Jamie would use photographic evidence to show her she was wrong. She shouldn't waste so much of her free time on the project, but she enjoyed the creativity and enjoyed looking at old pictures and choosing shots: a family reunion, a work party, a San Diego beach trip with friends. Christmas with her nieces and nephews, Jamie with the girls in her Laurel class, Jamie at a service project painting a house, Jamie volunteering at the library, teaching English, and brushing up on her college Spanish. When she was finished using the project to make her point to Robin, she could send it to her mother as a happy retirement gift—her mother would love it. Or maybe Jamie could make a collage of each child in the family and give her parents the complete set for Christmas.

In the late afternoon, she headed over to the Treasure Chest to get some work done while her project dried. At eight o'clock that evening, she linked the wood pieces together with silver chains to create a wall hanging, wrapped her project in tissue paper, and put it in a paper sack. She didn't need to look up Robin's address. She remembered very well how to get to Isaac's parents' house: a white colonial with teal shutters and a path behind it that led through the woods to Britteridge Pond. She'd strolled along that path with Isaac countless times.

She didn't call ahead—she didn't want to alert Robin that she was coming. If Robin wasn't home, Jamie would keep returning until she was.

The lit windows at the Grahams' house made Jamie hopeful. With all the adrenaline gushing through her body, she'd be climbing the walls if she couldn't confront Robin tonight. She'd have to call Julian and request samba lessons.

She rang the bell. After a few seconds, the door swung open, and Jamie smiled nervously at Isaac's father. She hadn't seen Drew Graham since moving back to Britteridge and had no idea if he shared Robin's animosity.

"Jamie!" His hair was completely gray now, but other than that, he looked the same, including the apron he was wearing that was speckled with some kind of sauce. Drew liked to cook, and from the delicious smell of roasted garlic in the air, Jamie wondered if they'd had his specialty garlic and mushroom pasta for dinner. She didn't worry that she'd interrupted the meal—the Grahams always ate at six o'clock, and it was past eight thirty.

"It's . . . uh . . . been a long time," Drew said.

Not animosity, Jamie decided. Definitely confusion. He didn't know what to think of her. "It's good to be back. I've missed Britteridge."

"Uh . . . how are your parents?"

"Doing well. Loving retirement."

"Glad to hear it. They're missed."

"I'll tell them."

Drew scratched his ear. "What can I do for you?"

"Is Robin here?"

"Uh . . . just a minute." He walked away. Jamie heard creaks from the stairs.

A couple of minutes passed. Jamie shifted the paper bag to her other hand and unzipped her jacket. Now that the sun had gone down, the air was chilly, but apprehension made her sweaty.

More time passed. Were Drew and Robin arguing about whether or not to let Jamie in? Or were they stalling because the police were on their way to arrest Jamie for trespassing? She listened for sirens and started planning what she'd say to Detective Powell if he showed up.

Finally, she heard footsteps approaching the door. "I'm sorry," Drew said. He looked down at his apron, picking at a blob of what looked like dried bread dough. "She's tired and not up to visitors right now. Maybe you could come back another time."

Had Robin realized why Jamie had come—that she suspected the truth—and was afraid to face her? Not wanting to do anything to make Drew more nervous or push him further onto Robin's side, Jamie said politely, "Thanks, Drew. I'll try her later. It's good to see you again."

"Good night." He sounded relieved, as though glad he could shut the door and lock her out.

Jamie sighed and started down the porch stairs. She'd return after work tomorrow. As she crossed the flagstones that marked a path to the street, a whispery voice startled her.

"*Jamie.*"

She wheeled around. No one was behind her or next to her or on the porch. Maybe the wind in the trees had made a strange noise and her nerves had concluded that ghosts were whispering her name.

She started back toward her car.

"*Jaaaaamie.*"

Heart pounding, Jamie whirled back around. The voice sounded like it was coming from the side of the house—maybe behind the house?

Funny, Robin, Jamie wanted to shout. Had Robin decided to entertain herself by scaring Jamie directly instead of framing her? Was that why it had taken Drew so long to return to the door—because Robin had needed time to put on her running shoes and sneak out the back? How easily spooked did Robin think she was?

A ripple of white showed near the rear corner of the house. Jamie strained to focus on it, but it disappeared. White fabric, blowing in the night breeze . . . a long white dress and veil? If Robin was dressed as the ghost bride and Jamie could catch her—

Jamie dropped the paper bag and sprinted toward the back of the house, still clutching her purse. The backyard was empty and dark. As her eyes adjusted to the faint illumination of moonlight, Jamie scanned the yard and the dark silhouettes of trees at its borders. She almost called Robin's name but decided that was dumb. If Robin heard Jamie hollering her name, she might decide to cut the haunting short and sneak away rather than risk Jamie's capturing her.

"*Jaaaaamie.*"

The voice emerged from the darkness of the trees. Robin must be on the path leading to Britteridge Pond. Jamie raced across the lawn toward the familiar path.

Moonlight lit the path well enough that Jamie could step without tripping over tree roots, but the trees on either side were blurry blackness. She reached into her purse, searching for her mini flashlight, but she couldn't find it.

With her arm up to her elbow in her purse, Jamie slowed down, irritated at how freaked out she felt. She *knew* it was Robin; she *knew* Robin wouldn't hurt her. Why did she feel like she was blundering into a horror movie?

She paused and listened, hoping footsteps could tell her whether Robin had stayed on the path or veered into the trees.

Leaves rustled in the wind, but she could hear no footsteps on the hard-packed dirt of the trail or twigs snapping or leaves crunching off to the side. She dug more desperately for the flashlight. She would clean out her purse first thing when she got home. Cautiously, she moved forward, scanning the trees around her for a flicker of white bridal gown. If Robin was out here, Jamie planned to grab her, yank off the veil, and take pictures of her as the ghost bride. Thank heavens she could at least find her phone. She always kept it in the outside pocket of her purse.

To the left, Jamie heard a crunching sound—a foot cracking a fallen branch? She stared into the trees but could see only darkness with blacker shadows. No hint of ghost bride . . . *There she is!* White fabric flapped in the darkness, a light contrast to the trees. Jamie stepped off the trail, hands in front of her so she could feel her way around trees. This woman was beyond crazy. Jamie *had* to get a picture. Or better yet, drag Robin straight to Isaac.

The moonlight was dimmer, mostly blocked by trees, and no matter how Jamie strained her eyes, she could hardly see. Even moving at a snail's pace was dangerous; she kept stumbling over rocks and scratching herself on branches. The white fabric was no longer visible, and Jamie had no idea which direction Robin had gone.

Something brushed her cheek, and Jamie shrieked and swatted at it, picturing huge spider webs and giant spiders. A branch tugged her hair, and she had to stop to free herself. This was ridiculous. She could not go on without a flashlight. She groped in her purse, feeling pens, wadded up receipts, tubes of lipstick, hand sanitizer . . . She was never going to catch Robin in the act. Robin might have already returned to the house. She knew this wooded area even better than Jamie—maybe she'd followed a path through the trees that Jamie couldn't see.

Something touched Jamie's leg, and she yelped, jumping to the side and knocking her shoulder into a tree. *Will you calm down? It was just a bush. Or an animal. A raccoon, a cat, a stray dog, a werewolf—*

Standing in the blackness, her shoulder throbbing, Jamie tensed with growing fear. What was she doing chasing a crazy woman into a forest at night? She didn't think Robin would hurt her, but if she was unbalanced enough to lure Jamie out here . . .

Following Robin had been a terrible idea. She needed to go back to the house and confront Drew to find out if he knew anything about Robin's ghost-bride activities. Isaac's father had always been a sensible man, much more sensible than Robin. He must know what Robin was up to, and he probably felt guilty about it. If Jamie pressed him, he'd crack.

She pulled out her phone. Wasn't there a flashlight app on this? She couldn't remember how to switch it on, but at least the screen provided a little light. Maybe she should use the phone right now and call the police.

Footsteps crunched behind her. Jamie swung around, holding out the phone, but the feeble light showed nothing.

The coldness in her clammy face and hands made Jamie want to turn away from the wind. Robin had lured her out here—why? Jamie had been so eager to get proof that Robin was the ghost bride that she hadn't wondered what Robin planned to do after drawing Jamie into the woods.

"Robin!" Jamie shouted. "I know it's you. Forget this stupid game. We need to talk."

No response. Just the wind . . . and were those animal noises?

"I'm calling the police," Jamie hollered. "This is *so* ridiculous—"

A dark figure lunged toward her.

Jamie screamed. She turned to run, but after two steps, she smacked her forehead on a branch. Flailing, she knocked the branch out of the way.

A whooshing noise behind her made her scream again. Something fluttered against her head and slithered over her shoulders and down her back. Jamie whirled, swinging wildly at whatever was touching her. Her arms tangled in a mass of fabric. Light blinded her.

"Frightening, isn't it?" Robin spoke from several feet away, and the beam of light lowered. Reeling, Jamie realized she was fighting with a white bed sheet.

Robin made her voice theatrically spooky. "A scary specter in the night! A scary voice crying your name! It may have seemed funny to you when *you* did it. A harmless prank. It's not funny when you're on the other end of it, is it? Now you know how Hannah and Isaac feel."

Flummoxed, Jamie wadded the sheet and threw it to the ground, squinting at the faint silhouette holding the flashlight. "What is *wrong* with you?"

"What's wrong with *me*? I was trying to get through to you, since obviously persuasion and even the police couldn't. I knew you'd chase me when I called your name—you'd be sure you could handle whoever was taunting you. You'd show them you weren't scared. That didn't last, did it? I've never heard an adult woman scream like that."

Humiliation and lingering shakiness kept Jamie's mouth shut. She didn't want Robin to hear her voice trembling.

"I hope this is a wake-up." Robin marched toward her and snatched the sheet off the ground. She wore a black ski cap, a black sweater, and dark jeans. "Now that you know how it feels, can you really keep up your horrible ghost drama, tormenting a pregnant woman and the husband trying desperately to protect her?" The beam of Robin's flashlight caught the glint of Jamie's phone where she'd dropped it while fighting the sheet. Robin picked it up and held it out to Jamie.

Dazed, Jamie took it.

"I think you've learned a good lesson," Robin said. "Sometimes learning by experience is the only thing that works. Follow me. I'll lead you back to the trail." She trotted ahead.

Not wanting to get left alone in the dark, Jamie staggered after her. This made no sense. Robin was the ghost bride . . . Jamie had *thought* she was the ghost bride . . . but if she was, what was the point of . . . ?

Once they reached the Grahams' back lawn, Robin glanced over her shoulder at Jamie. "Go home, dear. I think we've settled things."

Jamie's voice came out croaky. "You are wrong about me. I am *not* the ghost bride."

"You don't have to confess," Robin said. "Let it rot your soul if you want. But this is over. Good night." She marched up the stairs to her back patio and went inside.

Chapter 8

JAMIE SAT IN HER CAR in front of the Grahams' house, staring at the bed of geraniums illuminated by twin lampposts at the end of the flagstone walkway. Should she call the police? What could she tell them? Robin hadn't dragged her into the woods, and Robin hadn't attacked her. Was Jamie going to call Detective Powell to whine that Robin had tricked her and psychologically wiped the floor with her?

If Robin was the ghost bride, was she conniving enough to respond to Jamie's visit by grabbing a dark hat and sweater and a white bed sheet, creeping out the back door, and luring Jamie into the woods so she could solidify the point that *she* thought Jamie was the ghost bride—to the end of keeping Jamie from suspecting *her*?

My brain just imploded.

Robin's occasional quirky obsessions and her occasional decimating of good sense had been enough to make Jamie believe she could be the ghost bride, but to believe Robin would put on a show like she had tonight just to misdirect Jamie and further blame her for something Robin was doing herself . . . that was pushing it.

In fact, maybe believing Robin was the ghost bride at all was pushing it. To frame Jamie . . . lying about her, putting Jamie's job in peril, putting her in danger of getting in trouble with the law, not to mention scaring her own pregnant daughter-in-law and son . . . No matter how much Robin wanted to boot Jamie out of Britteridge, would she play so dirty?

On the other hand, if Robin truly thought Jamie was guilty, then luring her into the woods to give her a scare and topping it off with a lecture— *that* was a believable Robin stunt.

Jamie ought to text Hannah and let her know what had happened. Fingers still a little unsteady, she pulled out her phone.

The screen showed a missed call and a voice mail from Edward Allerton.

Jamie's tongue returned to panicky extra-dry. Allerton didn't usually call after business hours. Her mother had told her how thoughtful he was, preferring to leave his manager alone at night unless it was an emergency.

Clenching her teeth, Jamie tapped the button to listen to her voice mail.

"Jamie, this is Edward Allerton. Please call me as soon as possible."

He sounded calm. Solemn—maybe even grim? Jamie tossed the phone onto the passenger seat next to the paper bag holding her photo project that she'd retrieved from the Grahams' lawn. She couldn't call him back while sitting in front of Robin's house. Robin would call the police if Jamie didn't drive away soon.

As she drove home, she struggled to settle her anxiety. *Don't panic. Even if he did hear rumors about you, he's smart enough to recognize the rumors are ridiculous. If he thought you were a psycho-flake who would do something like that, he never would have hired you.*

Right?

Jamie kept swallowing, wishing she'd thought to stash a water bottle in the car. *Calm down. It's probably something else.*

Yeah right.

As soon as she was in her condo with the door locked, she crumpled on the couch, jacket still on, and, with icy fingers, pressed the button to return Allerton's call.

"Hello, Jamie," he said. "Do you have a few minutes this evening? I'd like to meet with you."

He wanted to meet with her without telling her why? *Not* a good sign. Apprehension made her cheeks burn. Good thing Allerton couldn't see her now, scarlet with what would look like a guilty blush. "Yes, of course I can meet with you. Tell me when and where."

"I'll meet you at the Treasure Chest in twenty minutes."

"I'll be there, sir."

"Thank you." Allerton hung up.

By the time Jamie arrived at the shop, she'd managed to make herself look composed, at least according to a glance in the rearview mirror. But she couldn't hide the scratches that branches had left on her face. Her hair looked tousled and staticky—she couldn't find her favorite brush and had been resorting to her backup brush. She'd thought the good brush was in her purse and had finally dumped her purse on the living room floor and searched the contents, but it wasn't there or in the bathroom or in her car. But at least she'd finally found her mini flashlight.

Her heart thudded as she stepped out of the car. She should have parked on the street in front of the Treasure Chest, but she'd headed to the parking lot behind it out of habit. Now she had to walk across the grounds to get to the back door, and that prospect gave her chills. She'd always thought the Treasure Chest grounds were beautiful, day or night, no matter what season, but tonight, they looked likely to be infested by monsters and serial killers. The lamps atop wrought-iron posts looked creepily dim, like the illumination in a spook alley, designed to make things look scarier.

She rushed along the brick path, glancing at the house at the back of the property as she hurried past. She'd wanted to have their wedding reception at Junior, but Isaac had thought it looked too 1930s—someone's great-grandmother's house with a few walls knocked out to make a larger reception room. She should have known she and Isaac were a mismatch right at that moment. Of course, tonight, everything looked so eerie that the idea of a wedding reception there felt about as comfortable as whacking a piñata in a graveyard and scrambling over graves to find scattered Tootsie Rolls.

Out of breath, she unlocked the back door and hurried around the main floor to hit light switches. The click of the back door opening made her jump. She went to meet Allerton, hoping it was Allerton and not Dracula.

"Good evening." Allerton wore a long overcoat over a V-neck sweater and wool slacks. He even wore a tie. In her jeans and fleece jacket, Jamie felt underdressed.

"Hi." Jamie smiled at him. "Cold evening."

"What happened, dear?" He waved toward her face.

Jamie's thoughts raced. Talk about a complicated, embarrassing story. "I . . . ran into some tree branches."

He frowned but didn't ask for details. "Come into the office."

Allerton took the seat behind the desk, and Jamie chose a carved chair Niall had made years ago that had ended up beautiful but too uncomfortable to sell. When a customer returned it, Jamie's mother had taken it into the office. The carved back jabbed the sitter in the shoulder blades, but Jamie didn't care tonight. She planned to sit stiffly on the edge of the chair anyway.

"Jamie, earlier this evening, I received a disturbing phone call from Mrs. Robin Graham."

Horror slapped Jamie. Robin had called Allerton? When? Since Allerton's message had been on Jamie's voice mail when she'd left the Grahams', Robin must have called before Jamie showed up.

Stay calm. Handle this. "I'm sorry the call disturbed you. I can guess what Mrs. Graham said to you, and none of it is true."

Allerton studied her through his dark-rimmed glasses, eyes keen but not accusatory. "She fears it's been difficult for you being back in Britteridge. Too many painful memories."

Jamie wished she could slow her pulse rate and control the blood vessels sending what must be half the blood in her body to her face. "I have countless memories of Britteridge, and the vast majority of them are happy, including wonderful memories of the Treasure Chest. What happened with Isaac Graham hurt at the time, but spirits—like bodies—can heal. I healed. I'm sorry Robin can't see that."

"She claims you've been bothering her son and daughter-in-law."

"She's mistaken. I know she means well"—That was more generosity than Robin deserved, Jamie thought—"but she's wrong. I am not bothering Isaac and Hannah. That is so far from anything I would even consider doing that it would be more credible to believe I can transform into a bat and commute here from my castle in Transylvania."

"You've always been a nice girl," Allerton said. "A smart girl who had a tough break."

Jamie wanted to groan. Did Allerton—like Robin and Isaac—think Isaac's dumping her had defined her life? Her mother had told her that at heart, stern Allerton was a sentimental man who had teared up on more than one occasion when discussing Jamie's dashed marital dreams. "Everyone has challenges. I've long since grown past what happened with Isaac. I hope he's happy, because *I'm* happy."

"I'm glad to hear that." Allerton tapped a pen against the desk—an experimental pen of Jamie's, painted with daffodils and decorated with a tiny clay daffodil on top. She'd decided it wasn't worth the work for what she could charge for it, so she'd only made a few. "One reason I invited you to take over your mother's position was that I knew you were a clean-cut young woman leading an upstanding life. I assumed you were the kind of manager I wanted. A person who would carry forward the strong reputation of the Treasure Chest and never embarrass it."

"I would never do anything to embarrass you or hurt your business."

His brow wrinkled. He looked sad and older than she thought he should look. "Your family has always been an asset to the Treasure Chest. Part of its good reputation."

Sweat trickled down Jamie's back. Was Allerton saying that even if she wasn't guilty, the rumors would still make her a liability? But he didn't look angry or condemning. He looked melancholy.

"Sir, there is no truth at all in the rumors, and I'll do whatever it takes to make sure people know that."

"I've always thought of you as my granddaughter," Allerton said wistfully. "I want this to work out for both of us."

"It will, sir." Jamie tried to appear confident, but Allerton's intense gaze moved over her face, from her scratched forehead to her scratched cheek, and she suspected he was wondering if she'd sustained those scratches while playing ghost bride. She *had* to explain. "I went to Robin Graham's tonight to try to convince her she was wrong and I would never do the things she's accused me of doing. She refused to talk to me." Jamie tried to give a succinct version of what had happened next, but as she talked, she wished she hadn't tried to explain the scratches. The story sounded preposterous, as though Jamie was floundering to come up with a way to excuse her injuries and, under pressure, hadn't been able to create a decent lie.

"I have no idea who's really bothering Isaac and Hannah," Jamie said. "But it's not me."

Allerton ran his thumb over the daffodil on top of the pen and said nothing.

Chapter 9

A TEXT FROM HANNAH SURPRISED Jamie as she sat in the office the following morning, struggling to focus on order forms. She'd texted Hannah last night but hadn't heard back, and she'd felt too discouraged to try again, wondering if Robin had talked to Hannah and told her of the incident in the woods, spinning things so it sounded like Jamie had more or less confessed to being the ghost bride.

She read Hannah's message. *Sorry I missed your text last night. We were at a concert, and I forgot to turn my phone back on afterward. Did you talk to Robin?*

Relieved that Robin hadn't yet turned Hannah against her, Jamie texted back. *I tried. You won't believe what she did. Too much to explain in a text. But in other news, she told my boss I was stalking Isaac.*

Hannah's answering text came quickly. *Oh no! Are you in trouble?*

I still have a job, Jamie texted. *He's not sure it's me doing those things, but he's worried about the reputation of the TC. I'm afraid if anything else happens, my job is toast. Robin is acting nuts about this. Can I call you?*

Can't talk now. I'm at work. I'll contact you later.

Jamie tried to return to her forms, but focusing on orders was like trying to stitch appliques onto one of the seasonal flags while it was already on the flagpole flapping frantically in the middle of a nor'easter. Maybe she should work on plans for the spring gala instead. The Treasure Chest's contribution to the town event had to be perfect. The last thing she needed was for anything to go wrong and embarrass Allerton. Along with the spring crafts at the library, the carnival booths at the elementary school, and the all-ages dance on the town green, the Treasure Chest's elaborate decorations, refreshments, souvenir magnets, and drawings for free merchandise were highlights of the gala. Jamie had decided on a pirate theme for Junior, where they would set up the refreshments. According to her mother's records, it had been thirteen years since they'd done a pirate's cave, and Jamie figured it was time to dust off the gold doubloons and faux jewels.

The store got busy, and Jamie exited the office to assist Melinda and Kayla. Two hours later, she slipped into the office for a quick look at her phone. Hannah had texted her.

Can we talk in person? Isaac will be gone tonight. We need to figure things out. I don't think Robin would be cruel enough to go to your boss and blame you if she was the stalker.

I agree. I can meet, but I'll be here doing preliminary work for the gala. Can you come to the TC?

No problem. I could help you. What time?

Hannah was willing to come help her with party prep? She'd seriously misjudged Hannah Stokes. *Any time after eight.*

I'll be there at eight thirty.

Park in the lot behind the TC. I'll meet you in Jr.

Thanks.

Jamie felt a little less miserable. With Hannah's help, there was still hope for getting things figured out. It amazed her that her best allies in this fiasco were Hannah and Hannah's brother.

Julian. She ought to update him. She'd texted him yesterday morning to tell him Hannah had visited, but she hadn't contacted him to report on Robin's ghost bride stunt or on her call to Allerton. She hoped she could talk to Julian without ranting or crying—not something she could have managed had she called him last night but something she could handle today.

She didn't have time to call him now, and he was probably busy teaching. She'd let him know she and Hannah were getting together tonight at eight thirty and she'd call him afterward to give him the full report. She sent a short text and returned to the main room.

Melinda was helping a mother and daughter choose between the pink and the yellow silk rose wreaths, and Kayla was monitoring the crystal room and the playroom, so Jamie headed toward the bearded man near the door, who turned out to be seeking a gift for his mother. As she led him upstairs to the linen room to show him the selection of quilts and throw pillows, she contemplated Hannah's willingness to help her. Of course Hannah had her own motives for wanting to solve this mystery—she was the one getting harassed by a ghost bride—but she could have refused to work with Jamie or, like Isaac, blamed her instead of viewing the situation objectively.

So much for the negative opinion of Hannah she'd nourished all these years.

All day, Jamie worked as hard as she could, grateful every time a customer walked through the door so she could try to focus on providing excellent service instead of obsessing about being falsely accused. She still felt anxious and absentminded, but since she succeeded in holding cheerful conversations and break any merchandise or lose her ability to count change, she figured she was doing all right. She did misplace the roast beef sandwich she'd brought for a late-afternoon lunch/dinner but finally found it on a shelf in the upstairs storage room. She must have had it in her hand when Kayla had interrupted her meal to ask if they had any more ceramic frogs.

"You're going to love this year's magnets. Simple and eye-catching," Melinda said as Jamie dusted one of the side windowsills just after closing time. Looking out the window, Jamie was glad last night's eerie feelings were gone and the new leaves rustling in the twilight looked appealingly springlike, not menacing.

"I'm sure they'll be amazing." Jamie picked up a receipt someone had dropped on the floor and nudged hay back into place in the window display. A string of clear lights twinkled in the window, accentuated by the darkening sky.

"It's unbelievable how many hours he spends carving and painting those things," Melinda said.

"I believe it. He's incredible." Niall's handmade magnets were famous throughout Britteridge. Allerton loved to sit in front of the Treasure Chest on gala night with a basket of magnets on his lap, benevolently handing them out, one per family.

"I might go over to help him tonight." Melinda squirted glass cleaner on the counter. "He needs the help. He always takes on more than he can handle."

Jamie felt guilty that she hadn't been helping Niall with the magnets. She should make time to do that, even if she was feeling overwhelmed by managing the store, preparing for the gala, and handling the mess in her personal life. If she could sort and plan the decorations for the pirate's cave tonight, that would be big progress. A productive talk with Hannah would be an even bigger achievement. Maybe if the two of them confronted Robin together, they could persuade her to retract her report to Allerton or at least get her to admit to him that she had no proof that Jamie was guilty.

Are you kidding? After her scare-and-lecture stunt in the woods, do you think she'd be open-minded enough to admit she could be wrong?

Thinking of Robin brought a blast of stress and anger. Knowing nothing useful could come from fuming, Jamie tried instead to think about pirate-cave backdrops as she went through the process of closing the store for the night. Maybe she could recruit Julian to help on the night of the gala. She could imagine him playing a swashbuckling pirate.

After Melinda clocked out, Jamie headed into the basement to start looking for the decorations she wanted. Her mother was wonderfully organized; it wouldn't be difficult to locate decorations appropriate for a pirate's cave.

The tidiness of the basement didn't compensate for its cold, dungeon-like ambience. Jamie appreciated the bright bulbs hanging from the ceiling as she checked the clipboard her mother had left hanging on a nail. Shelf #17—that was in the right corner, second shelf down—pirate costumes, gold coins and jewels, the big pirate treasure chest Niall had made years ago. Seashells . . . she'd have to order some sand.

She glanced at her watch. Hannah would be here in a few minutes. She ought to head for Junior—

A faint crash from upstairs made Jamie start. She dropped the clipboard onto a box and sprinted up the stairs. Had something fallen over? She flicked light switches on and scanned the main room. Everything looked fine there. The crystal room . . . Oh no. The blue glass vase of flowers Jamie had set on the shelf under the window had fallen and shattered. White peonies and purple irises were scattered over the hardwood floor, and a puddle of water and shards of glass reached halfway to the middle of the room. The curtains thrashed in the wind.

Fear grabbed Jamie. Why was that window open? Had someone broken in? Was there an intruder? *Oh.* She'd opened the windows herself earlier in the day to feel the gorgeous warmth of the afternoon. She thought she'd shut them in the evening when the wind had begun blowing harder and the temperature had dropped, but she must have missed this one. Not surprising, considering how distracted she'd felt today. *Wonderful.* Just what she didn't need—to act sloppy and careless at work. The whipping curtains must have knocked the vase over. Good thing it wasn't expensive crystal or one of Allerton's antiques.

Jamie raced for the janitorial cupboard. She needed to wipe that water up immediately before it damaged the old wood flooring.

With the mess cleaned up, Jamie checked her watch. Eight thirty-seven. Oops. She hoped Hannah was late. Otherwise, she was at Junior, locked out and wondering where Jamie was.

Thick clouds dimmed the moonlight, and Jamie wished she could brighten the glow from the lamps spaced along the path leading to Junior. Maybe she was still rattled after last night, or maybe she was remembering the transformation of this path into the Treasure Chest's traditional haunted lane, which she'd enjoyed every Halloween when she was a child.

As Jamie reached Junior, she saw a dark-haired woman in a pale cape heading toward the parking lot. Embarrassed that Hannah had given up waiting for her and had started to leave, Jamie called, "Hannah!"

Hannah spun around to face Jamie, then stepped backward, wobbling a little. Blood streamed from her hairline and dripped over her cheekbone. Her cape rippled in the wind.

"*Hannah?*" Jamie stared at the blood on Hannah's face. "Are you okay? What happened?"

Blood? Or makeup?

Hannah was the ghost bride?

What's wrong with you, idiot? She's wearing a white or ivory-colored cape, not a wedding dress, and she can't be the ghost bride. She and Isaac saw the bride together.

Jamie rushed toward Hannah. "What happened? You're hurt . . . I'll call an ambulance—"

"Get away from me!" Hannah shrieked, backing up. "The police are on their way."

Jamie stopped. "Hannah—"

"I *trusted* you." Hannah touched her bloodied temple, then lowered her hand, her fingers red. Blood dotted the collar of her cape. "No matter what Robin and Isaac said, I couldn't believe you'd do this. I *trusted* you."

The wail of sirens pierced the noise of the wind. "Hannah—"

Hannah wrapped her arms around her pregnant belly. "If you take one more step toward me, I will *kill* you." She staggered, stepping to the side, obviously dizzy.

Panic ripped at Jamie. "Sit down. You have to sit down, or you're going to fall. *Please.*"

"*Stay back.*"

"I'm staying back! Just sit down."

Hannah pressed her palm against a tree trunk to steady herself.

"Do you want me to call Isaac?" Jamie didn't know what else to say. What had happened to Hannah?

Hannah laughed hoarsely. "Yes, call Isaac. Tell him what you did."

"I didn't do anything! I was inside the Treasure Chest. I have no idea what . . . Please . . . You need to sit down before—"

"Who else could it have been? Who else knew I'd be here? I didn't tell *anyone*! I didn't even tell Isaac!"

Flashing red and blue lights lit the parking area. Besieged by confusion and fear, Jamie fought a terrified urge to sprint into the trees and disappear. "I don't know what happened here, but I didn't do it. Did you see the ghost bride? Did she attack you?"

At the thud of heavy footsteps on the brick pathway, Hannah turned toward the approaching police officers.

"Keep her away from me!" Hannah hollered.

Jamie's lips felt numb and her tongue dead. Even if she had known what was going on, she couldn't have spoken to explain it.

Chapter 10

SHAKING, NAUSEATED, JAMIE SAT ON a chair in the Treasure Chest office and waited, guarded by a uniformed officer standing near the back wall. At least she assumed he was guarding her as opposed to hanging around to keep her company. Tears kept stinging her eyes, but she tried to control them through fast blinking, not wanting the police to notice she was crying. She was going to be arrested. She'd lost her job for sure, and she'd go to prison.

Jamie pressed her hands over her face, wanting to scream *I didn't do this!*

Footsteps. Jamie dropped her hands and looked up to see Detective Powell entering the office. She started to stand but stopped, figuring she wasn't supposed to stand without permission when she was being detained as a suspect.

"Hello, Jamie," Powell said.

Hello again, Jamie thought bitterly. From the way Powell had talked to her last time, it was obvious he'd made up his mind that she was guilty. Tonight's attack on Hannah would confirm that.

"I don't know what's going on." Jamie's body jerked with shivers even though she wasn't cold. "I didn't hurt Hannah. I don't even know what happened. We were planning to meet here tonight; she was going to help me with the decorations while we tried to figure out who was haunting her, and I was in the basement looking for pirate stuff, but a vase broke upstairs, so I had to clean that up, and I was late meeting her, and saw her walking toward the parking lot, and she was bleeding and yelling and saying—"

"Jamie, take a deep breath. Deep, slow breath."

She tried, but it ended up shallow and frantic. "Please tell me what happened. Is Hannah okay?"

"She'll be fine."

"I didn't hurt her." Tears spilled out. "I didn't hurt her. I haven't done anything to her, I would never—"

"Jamie." Powell pulled a chair toward Jamie and sat facing her. "I want you to calm down."

"You think I attacked her, don't you?"

"How about you stop panicking and trust me to do a little investigating before I accuse anyone?"

Jamie blinked away tears. Powell had kind eyes. Pensive Abraham Lincoln eyes. Maybe he hadn't made up his mind about her. Maybe he would listen. "Okay." She yanked a tissue from the box on her desk and wiped her face. "May I tell you how Hannah ended up coming here tonight?"

"Please do."

Jamie told him about the text from Hannah, about setting up the time to meet, about their suspicions of Robin Graham and Robin in the woods last night, about Allerton, about everything that had happened tonight. Powell looked sympathetic and intensely interested. Even the way he made notes on his pad seemed reassuring, as though pencil marks validated her story.

"Did you tell anyone else Hannah was coming?" Powell asked.

Jamie sniffled and wiped her face. She hadn't mentioned it to any customers. Or to Melinda or Kayla. "Just Julian Stokes, Hannah's brother. Julian doesn't think I'm the ghost bride, and I thought he'd be happy that Hannah was so willing to help figure out the truth."

Powell wrote something on the pad. "What exactly did you tell him?"

"Um . . . well, I can show you. It was a text conversation." She drew her phone from the pocket of her Treasure Chest apron, found the conversation, and held the phone out to Powell. "You can see my conversation with Hannah as well."

Powell studied and tapped the screen of the phone for a few moments. He handed the phone back to Jamie.

An officer entered the room, carrying a clear plastic bag. Inside of it was a blue, star-shaped glass candleholder.

Jamie gasped.

"Thank you," Powell said. He held the bag in front of Jamie. "Do you recognize this?"

Jamie gawked at it. Yes, she recognized it. She knew exactly how it felt in her hand; she'd lifted dozens of them, tied ribbons around them, felt the sharp points of the stars against her fingers and palms, watched the overhead lights glittering on them as she'd envisioned them on the tables at the reception while she and Isaac embraced family and friends—

Dizziness washed through her, blackening her vision for a split second as though she'd been flipped upside down on a rollercoaster.

"Jamie?"

This is a nightmare, Jamie thought. *Things like this do* not *happen to real people.*

Powell leaned closer, holding out the bag. "Do you recognize this?"

She had to answer. Powell already knew the answer anyway because Isaac must be here by now to help Hannah, and Isaac would have recognized it. "It's one of the candleholders that we were going to use at my wedding reception. Where did you find it?" Now she was the one asking a question to which she already knew the answer. The candleholder must be the weapon that had injured Hannah.

"It appears that this was the projectile thrown at Hannah Graham." Powell leaned back and set the bag carefully on the desk. "Six candleholders were retrieved from the path or nearby. One struck her in the shoulder. One struck her in the leg. One struck her in the head, cutting her. One struck her in the back. The other two missed."

"She looked like she was bleeding badly."

"She's on her way to the hospital so they can check her out, but the gash appears superficial."

My fingerprints are all over those candleholders. I touched every one of them. Jamie watched Powell with burning eyes, dazed by how completely someone was setting her up. Who would do this to Jamie and hurt Hannah in the process?

Not Robin. It can't be Robin. No matter how much she wants me gone, she would never injure her daughter-in-law.

Then who? Julian had known Hannah would be here, but Julian wouldn't hurt his sister. And he had no motive.

"Where do you store these candleholders?" Powell asked.

"I . . . don't. I mean, I'm not the one who kept them . . ." She tried to think. "Sarah . . . my sister . . . she was going to buy them off of my parents. She loved them, wanted to use them for some event or other . . . I can't remember what. I think they ended up in my parents' garage. But my parents moved . . . This doesn't make sense. My mother would have either sold them or packed them up and taken them with her." Jamie couldn't think. Despair clogged her neural circuits.

"Do you have any idea who might have had access to them before your mother left?"

"You'd have to ask her. I'm not even sure where she would have . . . who would . . . Do you want her phone number?"

"Please."

Jamie went blank. Her mother had had the same cell phone number for years, and Jamie couldn't think of it. She groped in her apron pocket for her phone and, with rubbery fingers, tried to find the contact info.

"May I?" Powell held out his hand.

"Thank you." She tried to hand him the phone and dropped it on the floor. "I'm sorry." She bent to pick it up, but Powell beat her to it and swiftly tapped the screen.

She heard the front door swing open and new footsteps in the hall. An officer stuck his head into the room.

"Hey, Aaron, got a second?"

Powell rose to his feet and picked up the bagged candleholder. "Excuse me, Jamie."

Numbly, Jamie watched him exit. She wondered what would happen if she tried to leave the office. Could they hold her here if she wasn't yet under arrest? She wasn't sure how that worked and didn't feel like asking the officer at the back of the room if it would be all right if she went home and hid under her bed.

Wait . . . she knew him. She glanced at his nametag. Mendoza. That was Ben Mendoza, from high school. *Oh, good grief. Could this get any more humiliating?*

Yes. It could get a *lot* more humiliating if Powell told her she was under arrest for stalking and assaulting Hannah and her old AP Bio classmate had to handcuff her and haul her out to a patrol car. *Hey, Jamie. Long time no see. You have the right to remain silent—*

Ben turned his head, and his eyes met hers.

"Hi, Ben," Jamie said bleakly. "Sorry. It took me awhile to recognize you. Distracted by the nervous breakdown."

"Hi, Jamie." Rather than hold Jamie's gaze, he shifted his eyes toward the framed black-and-white picture of Edward Allerton's parents standing in front of the Treasure Chest. He was probably embarrassed to be here, wondering if straight-arrow Jamie McKenzie had really transformed into a violent, vindictive harpy.

"I didn't do this," Jamie said, knowing it was pointless repetition. Ben had already heard her wailing her innocence to Powell. "I would never hurt anyone. And if I did, do you think I'd be this *stupid* about it? I got a thirty-three on the ACT! I got a full-tuition scholarship—"

"Don't panic," Ben interrupted. "Powell's good. He'll figure things out."

"May I go wash my face and get a drink?"

"You can go wherever you want, but you'd be smart to stick close until he's done talking to you."

"I want to talk to him," Jamie said, suddenly too afraid to leave the room. What if they thought she was sneaking out to go burn evidence or scrub blood off her hands? Especially since she'd said she wanted a drink and there was a water cooler in the corner of the office, which made it a lame excuse to leave. "Never mind. I'll wait for him."

Ben walked to the cooler, filled a cup, and brought it to her. "I never could understand why you got engaged to Isaac Graham. He's an okay guy, but I didn't think he was your type."

Jamie groaned and took the water. "He's not. It just took me a long time to figure that out."

"Half the girls I knew had crushes on him," Ben remarked.

"He *is* hot, and a nice guy, and we went to the same church, and I'd had a crush on him for years, so when we started dating, I didn't really think through—" Jamie stopped herself; Ben wouldn't be interested in a detailed history of hers and Isaac's relationship. "Ben, you know me. Could you please—" Before Jamie could finish begging him to advocate for her, even though his best defense would be "She had straight A's and never cheated in high school biology," Powell stepped through the doorway. He was carrying armfuls of white, silky fabric.

Apprehension prickled Jamie's skin. Powell set the fabric on the desk and smoothed out two items: a long, translucent veil with several tears in it and a dirt-stained lacy wedding dress.

He looked at Jamie and raised his eyebrows.

"Not mine." Jamie wished she didn't sound so discouraged. "Let me guess. You found those somewhere on the property."

"Stuffed behind some bushes," Powell said. "Do they look familiar at all?"

Jamie stood to examine the dress. If she *could* recognize it . . . if she *could* scrounge up any idea of who might have worn it . . .

It didn't ring any bells. It was long-sleeved, with a high, ruffled neck. Jamie couldn't remember seeing it at anyone's reception, and she would have remembered, since a high-necked style looked positively pioneer-ish compared to the dresses most of her peers wore. The ghost bride had probably purchased it on eBay. The veil was floor-length and voluminous—Jamie had never seen anyone wear that either.

She shook her head. "I've never seen these before."

Powell picked up the veil. Two clear plastic combs were sewn to the underside of a wreath of flowers to hold the veil to the hair. Caught between the teeth of one of the combs were a few strands of dark hair.

Jamie reached eagerly for the veil, but Powell held out his hand. "Don't touch it, please."

"*There.*" Jamie pointed to the hair, feeling floppy with relief at finally locating some concrete evidence. "Take that hair and test it, and you'll see it's not mine. It's probably from a wig."

Powell used tweezers to remove the hair. Jamie was ready to rip some hair out of her head and offer it for comparison but figured there might be a procedure they needed to follow. At last, the stalker had made a mistake—

A thought jolted her. Her missing brush. What if . . . what if the stalker had taken it so she could swipe a sample of Jamie's hair—and plant it with the veil? Jamie peered at the hair caught in Powell's tweezers. It was dark, but from a few strands, she couldn't tell if it was the same reddish-brown shade as hers.

Are you kidding? How paranoid can you be? The brush probably fell under the seat of your car or got kicked under the couch. You haven't looked hard enough.

Powell slipped the hairs into a plastic bag. Jamie's mouth was dry; she needed a swallow of water. She'd had a cup of water in her hand, but now her hand was empty. What had she done with it? She must have set it down, but it wasn't on the desk.

"Did you lose something?" Powell asked.

"A cup of water." She already knew someone was setting her up. Was it a stretch to think the culprit might have swiped a few strands of her hair to help convince the police of her guilt?

She wanted to snatch the plastic evidence bag away from Powell. Hannah, attacked here at the Treasure Chest when only she and Jamie were present . . . The weapon a candleholder from Jamie's canceled wedding, covered in her fingerprints . . . and now Jamie's hair snagged in the ghost bride costume.

Powell leaned over and picked up the cup of water. She'd set it on the floor near her chair. He handed her the water, and she gulped it.

"My brush was stolen," she said, setting the empty cup on the desk.

"Your brush?"

She babbled out her fears, knowing this must sound like a pathetic, last-ditch fabrication from a criminal who knew she'd been nailed. Powell listened patiently, even when Jamie took a couple of minutes rambling about all the places she might have taken the brush and how it was sometimes in her purse and sometimes in her bathroom and occasionally in her car, and she couldn't remember when or where she'd seen it last. When Jamie finished, she asked, "Am I under arrest?"

Powell's eyes were thoughtful. "No."

She didn't need mind-reading skills to know Powell's "no" meant "We just need to confirm a few things first." Like confirming that the fingerprints on the candleholders were Jamie's, like confirming that her hair was stuck in the veil's comb.

At least she was still free tonight. The evidence they'd gathered so far must not be enough without eyewitness testimony, and Hannah—once she'd calmed down—must have conceded that she hadn't seen the face of the ghost bride who'd pelted her with candleholders.

"We'll be in touch," Powell said.

Jamie nodded. She expected him to tell her to not leave town or something like that, but he silently gathered up the wedding dress and veil.

Not that she *would* leave town. Until the door of a jail cell slammed shut, she would be in Britteridge racing the clock, trying to figure out who was framing her.

"Officer, where is Detective Aaron Powell? I need to speak with him." From the hallway came the familiar voice of Edward Allerton.

Jamie wondered if she could make it out the window before Allerton walked into the room.

Chapter 11

JAMIE PACED HER CONDO, ARMS squeezing the embroidered owl pillow. Allerton hadn't talked to her at the Treasure Chest. On learning the police were done questioning her, he'd dismissed her—"Go home, Jamie"—and remained behind, probably to get the details about what Jamie had done to besmirch the reputation of the Treasure Chest. Too mortified and drained to stay and try futilely to argue her innocence, Jamie had fled.

She kept expecting her phone to ring and Allerton to tell her she was fired, but so far, he hadn't called. Not that she needed to hear the official word to know it was true. No way would Allerton keep her around after this. She ought to go polish up her résumé . . . but what was the point of doing that now? They probably had volunteers who came to the prisons to help inmates with that kind of thing. At least her sentence would be short . . . right? Hannah's injuries were minor. A year? Could she get off with community service and a fine since this was her first—

Will you stop freaking out and start thinking? Jamie hurled the owl pillow across the room, knocking an empty glass and a knitting magazine to the floor. *Remember how you marched over to Isaac's house to demand they tell you who was harassing them because only they could know who had it in for them? So who has it in for you? Only you can answer that question.*

Jamie retrieved the owl pillow, flopped on the couch, closed her eyes, and tried to concentrate. *Be logical. What is the obvious end result of what's been happening?*

I will be fired. I will be arrested. I might serve time in prison, and when I'm released, I'll move as far from Britteridge as I can because I'll never be able to look anyone in the eye here.

So who wants to get rid of me?

Pressing her chin against the knotted fringe on the edge of the pillow, she mentally searched for names, even digging as deep as high school to figure out who might hate her this much.

Nobody. Not that everyone loved her. Sure, she'd annoyed some people in her life—by wrecking the curve on a test, for instance, or by dating Isaac, who, as Ben had pointed out, had been a popular guy in high school—but she couldn't think of any old enemy who'd resent her being in Britteridge enough to go all vengeful. Except Isaac out of embarrassment or guilt. Or Robin out of worry for her son's marriage. Or Hannah out of fear of losing Isaac. But neither Isaac nor Robin would ever hurt Hannah, so that shoved *them* off the suspect list.

Hannah herself? Had her efforts to help Jamie been a pretense? She could easily have stuffed the ghost bride costume in the bushes, clonked herself on the head, then started yelling that Jamie had attacked her. But if it was Hannah, she had a sidekick who had played the role of ghost bride outside Hannah and Isaac's window.

Jamie imagined how well it would go over if she banged on Hannah's door tonight and demanded the name of her sidekick. That would be a great way to land herself in jail. She couldn't talk to Hannah or investigate anything about her. She could only ask Powell to do so and hope he was willing.

Who else?

After a few fruitless minutes, Jamie tossed the pillow aside and stood up. If she couldn't think of any other names for her list, she needed to switch her approach. Forget who wanted to get rid of her and start with who had had the opportunity to attack Hannah tonight.

According to Hannah, she hadn't told anyone she was meeting with Jamie, not even Isaac. And Jamie had only told Julian. Julian would have to be exceedingly warped to hurt his own sister. *Could* he be that twisted? He seemed so nice—a little quirky, yes, but in harmless, charming ways. But the fact was, she didn't know him very well.

Had the disastrous relationship Hannah had told her about left Julian resenting women? Maybe his pain over his girlfriend's deceit had festered and led him to view all females as heartbreakers and troublemakers. Maybe he was lashing out at Hannah and Jamie, figuring Hannah deserved it as a fiancé stealer and Jamie deserved it for coming back to Britteridge to torment Isaac with guilty memories. Or something like that.

Covered in a dress, veil, and wig, could Julian pass for her in the dark? Maybe. He wasn't a large man—maybe four inches taller than Jamie's

5'6"—and he was trim. But with the muscles in his arms—she'd noticed his arms when he taught her the cha-cha—she couldn't believe he would fit into the long, tight sleeves on the wedding dress Powell had shown her. Would he be sneaky enough to have *two* dresses on hand so Powell would find one that plainly didn't fit him? Had it amused him to come to Jamie after the earlier incidents and pretend to be concerned about her while secretly he relished her embarrassment and anger?

She sighed. This theory of Julian's guilt was getting too elaborate. If Julian was *that* disturbed, it didn't seem likely that Hannah wouldn't suspect it. It was more likely Julian had told someone about the meeting and word had spread to the culprit.

Powell already knew Julian had been aware of the meeting; he would investigate him. But Jamie didn't want to wait to hear from Powell. If she could find out *now* if Julian had told anyone about Hannah's coming to the Treasure Chest, that would be progress.

She picked up her phone from a side table and gripped it, biting her lip. Even though Julian was probably innocent, she was still nervous to talk to him. He'd been so supportive, believing in her innocence, but would he still believe in her when his bleeding sister was telling him Jamie had attacked her?

You have to ask him. Do it. If he hangs up on you, so what?

Rallying her courage, she touched the screen, locating his number.

Voice mail. Jamie squeaked out a "Please call me" and hung up.

Maybe he was in a place where he couldn't take a call—like the hospital, with Hannah—but he could answer a text.

Too impatient to wait for him to call back, Jamie texted him. *Did you tell anyone Hannah and I were meeting at the Treasure Chest tonight?*

The phone rang. Mom! Quickly, Jamie lifted it to her ear. "Hey."

"Honey, are you all right? You sounded awful in your message."

"I *am* awful. Or rather, I'm trying to convince the police I'm *not* awful." Jamie reported on everything that had happened, comforted each time her mother interrupted with "You poor child!" "That's ridiculous!" or "My goodness, you're lucky you didn't marry that brainless boy."

Jamie finished by asking about the star candleholders. "You still had them before you moved, right? Or did you send them to Sarah?"

"I had most of them. I sent a dozen to Sarah for her party, but the others were still in the garage with my holiday decorations. I have them here in Florida. I thought of using them to make some Christmas centerpieces; they're so pretty. I hope that doesn't bother you."

Jamie gritted her teeth. Even her *mother* thought she'd be sentimental about what happened to decorations from her almost-wedding to Isaac? "I don't care what you do with them. I'm just wondering how someone got their hands on six of them."

"Hang on, honey. Let me see if I'm missing any."

Jamie waited. It wouldn't take long. Her mother would be able to go straight to the correct box and count the candleholders.

"Okay, I checked. There *are* half a dozen missing. Oh, honey, I'm sorry! I have no idea how someone could have stolen them. You'd think I would have noticed someone fishing through boxes in the garage, but I wasn't always good about keeping it locked. Crime rates are so low in Britteridge."

Jamie doubted someone had come searching for random wedding decorations to use against her. "The culprit must have known about the candleholders and swiped them before I even arrived in Britteridge. By the time I got here, your stuff was already packed up and you were living in temporary housing."

"Why would someone do this to you?"

"I have no idea." The culprit must have planned ahead, scheming from the moment she—or he—had learned Jamie was taking over her mother's position, determined to evict Jamie from Britteridge.

Why had the culprit given her a few peaceful weeks here before starting to harass Isaac and Hannah? Jamie supposed that small delay did make her guilt more credible. If she'd started planting fake wedding announcements and flinging candleholders before she'd even unpacked, that was too precipitous for belief.

"Mom, did you take the candleholders anywhere recently? Use them for decorations?"

"Well, it's been a few months, but I did take them to the Treasure Chest. I was thinking of using them in a late February window display—a blue and silver color scheme. I thought it would be a nice change after all the pink and red for Valentine's Day, and then I could sell the candleholders that Sarah hadn't taken. But when I put the candleholders in the display, it looked cluttered, so I took them out and decided to hold on to them."

Jamie jumped to her feet. "You had them at the Treasure Chest this winter? After people knew I was moving here to take over for you?"

"Yes, that's right."

"Who knew they were there? Who saw them?"

"I don't know exactly . . . Besides those of us working there, you mean?"

"Everyone."

"Well, Melinda was helping me, and I remember Kayla worked that day because she was disappointed that I didn't use the candleholders. She kept gushing about how they looked like they were made of sapphires . . . Oh, I think Niall came by with a delivery, and Edward popped in as well. I remember that because Edward complimented the display and told me to hurry up because the store was opening in an hour and he didn't want a mess scattered around. The man is such a worrywart! I'd never been late finishing a display."

"Okay. Any customers?"

"No one in the store, dear, since we were still closed, but I was working in the front window, and a lot of people paused to look in as they passed. You know how it's always an event when we swap the displays."

"How many people could have known the candleholders were from my canceled reception?"

"Oh, darling, I have no idea. I know I mentioned it to some people but can't remember who—people at work, other friends, you know, in the course of chatting, saying we'd gotten rid of everything but the candleholders. Jamie, first thing tomorrow I'm getting on a plane. I will deal with Robin Graham. We've been friends for decades, and I'm not going to—Oh! Someone's calling. It's someone from your area, but I don't recognize the number."

"It's probably Detective Powell. Talk to him. He wants to know about the candleholders."

"I'll set him straight. I'll call you back when we're done."

Jamie lowered the phone. It beeped in her hand, and she lifted it to see a text from Julian. *Sorry I couldn't take your call. I'm at Hannah and Isaac's house. I'll call as soon as I can. No, I didn't tell anyone. Hang in there.*

At least he didn't sound hostile.

And at least she now had evidence that she wasn't the only one who could have thought of using the candleholders as projectiles. According to her mother, pretty much anyone could have learned about the candleholders and stolen them to implicate Jamie.

Unfortunately, *anyone* wasn't a great starting point.

Who could have stolen the candleholders *and* known Hannah would be at the Treasure Chest tonight? Hannah and Julian both claimed they hadn't told anyone. Jamie hadn't told anyone. Maybe someone had overheard her talking to Hannah. No, they hadn't spoken about it. It had been a text conversation. Someone would have had to read it off her phone or Hannah's phone.

She had no idea who could have gotten the information from Hannah's phone, so she couldn't start there. But who had access to Jamie's phone? It had been in her purse in the office all day. It seemed unlikely that a customer could have wandered back there without Jamie, Melinda, or Kayla noticing.

What about Melinda? Or Kayla?

Jamie pictured college student Kayla. Why would she have anything against Hannah or Jamie? Kayla hadn't even met Jamie before she'd moved back, though Kayla had heard the story of Jamie and Isaac. Given the way she'd tactlessly and repeatedly mentioned how hot Isaac was, Jamie wouldn't be surprised if she had a crush on him. But talk about a stretch for a motive! Even if she had a crush on Isaac, injuring Hannah and getting Jamie fired and arrested certainly wouldn't draw Isaac to Kayla. It would be an act of jealousy. Revenge on the women Isaac had loved/did love.

Too much of a stretch. Even more of a stretch than accusing Julian. Try again.

Restlessly, Jamie fingered the fringe on the owl pillow, her thoughts moving to Melinda. Melinda, like Kayla, could have gotten access to the phone without Jamie's noticing. And like Kayla, she knew about the candleholders *and* could have stolen the brush out of Jamie's purse—if Jamie's theory about the hair in the ghost-veil comb was correct.

What motive could Melinda have for wanting to get rid of Jamie? She'd made it clear she didn't want Jamie's job. Was there any other reason the older woman might resent her? It was difficult to tell what Melinda thought of her. She was always cordial and helpful, but she was never particularly friendly. Jamie knew that was just her personality, but that reserved façade could hide negative feelings.

Melinda knew Robin; they quilted together. But even if Robin had shared her fears that Jamie had come to steal Isaac, Jamie couldn't fathom Melinda's taking it upon herself to rid Britteridge of Jamie. Why would she feel obligated to do Robin's dirty work?

It seemed absurd to think that either Melinda or Kayla would want to set Jamie up, let alone attack a pregnant woman to do so. But since they'd both had the opportunity, at least it was a place to start.

What should she do first? She could start by talking to Niall about Melinda. Subtly. Carefully. Okay, not subtly, because she couldn't endure waiting until morning. Calling Niall at ten thirty would tip him off that her call was urgent. But she could be careful how she phrased things so she didn't insult Niall by making unfair accusations against his daughter.

Niall was a night owl. It wasn't too late to call. Jamie dialed.

"Jamie! What's up, love?" Niall sounded chipper. Clearly, he hadn't heard about the ruckus at the Treasure Chest.

"Do you mind if I come over?" Jamie asked. "I want to talk to you in person."

"Ah now, am I in trouble with the management?"

Jamie forced a chuckle. "No, you're marvelous, as always. I just need to talk to you."

"You're welcome any time before one. At one o'clock, I'm raising the drawbridge."

"I'll be there in a few minutes."

* * *

"Is the open window all right?" Niall glanced over his shoulder at the fluttering curtains. "Mel always says it's chilly in here, but when I work, I sweat."

"It's fine." Jamie was sweaty too but with nervousness as she looked at white-haired Niall leaning over his workbench, sanding a snowman. "Is Melinda here?"

"No, but she said she was coming at some point to help with the magnets." Niall gestured at several shelves covered with wooden cutouts that had started out as mass-produced ovals, circles, and diamonds. Niall had carved facets into the wood and added a layer of blue, green, or red paint topped by a glitter glaze to produce "pirate jewels." "Kevin's traveling for work, and Mel said she needed something to do. She still might show up. She's a nocturnal creature, like me. I'm on the last batch of magnets but needed a break, so I switched to snowmen."

"The magnets look great." So Melinda hadn't been here yet. Jamie wondered if she had an alibi for earlier this evening when Hannah had been attacked. Maybe not, if her husband was out of town.

"What's the story?" Niall set the sandpaper down and ran his fingers over the snowman. "You sounded off on the phone. Is something wrong with the shop?"

"Not wrong with the store. With me."

"I'm sorry, love." Niall picked up a finer-grit sandpaper. "What is it?"

It sounded like he didn't know about the issues with Isaac and Hannah. Good. He wouldn't suspect why she was asking about Melinda. Jamie sat on a stool near the workbench. "This is awkward, but some things have happened lately—I'd rather not go into detail—but they indicate someone doesn't like having me in Britteridge. I'm wondering if Melinda might . . . be upset with me for any reason?"

Niall glanced over his shoulder at her. "Why would she be upset with you? You're a brilliant manager."

"Was she . . . bothered in any way when she found out I was taking my mother's place?"

Niall turned back to his snowman. "She wasn't. Why would she be? Mel has never wanted to manage the shop. You know that."

"I know, but . . . can you think of any reason why she . . . might be happier if left?"

"If she's giving you cheek, love, I'll talk to her."

"No, she hasn't done anything. I'm just trying to figure things out, and I wondered if it's hard on her in any way, having me here. If she resents me for any reason. If she doesn't, that's great. I just . . . wanted to check. Make sure I'm doing the right things so she enjoys working with me. She's wonderful; I wouldn't want to lose her."

Niall was sitting still, shoulders tense, hands clutching the snowman. It was strange to see him motionless. Usually Niall would be continually sanding, carving, painting, or at least fiddling with any object in reach. Was he bothered about Jamie's strange questions or bothered because he knew Melinda did resent her?

"Niall . . . if I've done anything to offend her, I'd like to know what it is so I can fix it."

"You haven't done anything. Everything's grand."

"Are you sure?"

"Maybe she . . . thinks Allerton favors you, love. Not your fault. Nothing for you to worry about."

"Favors me? But . . . you said she didn't *want* to manage the—"

"Ah, don't worry about it. Mel can be a silly girl." He held up the snowman. "Stripes on the scarf?"

Chapter 12

"THAT WAS STRANGE," JAMIE MUTTERED as she trudged to her car, uncertain what to do next. After trying a couple more times to lead Niall to tell her what he meant by Allerton's "favoring her," she'd given up and let him chat about paint colors.

Niall had seemed troubled—determined to divert the conversation away from Melinda and focus on the minutiae of his current project, and out of character in the way he kept stopping work, then abruptly restarting.

Something *was* going on with Melinda. Jamie didn't know whether or not it was related to the stalking of the Grahams, but there was something Niall didn't want to discuss.

She sat behind the wheel of her car, debating where to go. It was past eleven o'clock. She should go to bed, but she felt too wired. She'd go to the Treasure Chest. The police would be long gone. Allerton would be gone. Everything would be quiet. Jamie could have the chance to look around for herself and see . . .

Uh . . . see what? What do you expect to find?

She had no idea, but she started driving toward the Treasure Chest anyway. She wasn't scared to go there this late. The ghost bride had made it clear she didn't want to hurt Jamie directly; she wanted to get Jamie blamed for hurting others. Maybe Jamie could find some clue of the path the ghost bride had followed so she could map out in her mind how the assailant had reached Hannah without risking being seen by—

Jamie frowned. The ghost bride had needed superb timing to pull off her attack. If Jamie had exited the Treasure Chest at the wrong moment and Hannah had seen her approaching, Hannah would have known the wraith in the trees chucking candleholders wasn't Jamie. Lucky for the ghost bride that Jamie had been distracted by that broken vase and had been stuck inside cleaning up for several minutes . . .

Lucky?

Or was that planned as a distraction to keep me out of the way?

But the doors of the Treasure Chest had been locked at the time of the attack. Jamie and Allerton had keys—did anyone else? Maybe someone had sneaked in—

But the floors creaked, and Jamie had been in the basement; she would have heard someone walking around upstairs, knocking over the vase, and fleeing, no matter how stealthily they had tiptoed. Instead, all she'd heard was the crash of the vase.

The vase had sat near a window—that's why she'd assumed the wind had blown it over. A ground-floor window. Had someone pushed the vase over from outside? Maybe Jamie *hadn't* forgotten to close the window. Maybe Melinda—or Kayla or a late-in-the-day customer—had opened the window after Jamie had closed it for the evening.

Jamie parked in front of the Treasure Chest, took her mini flashlight from her purse, and walked to the side of the house to the crystal room window.

The wind made her shiver as she stepped near the window, careful of Allerton's azalea bushes. Leaning close to the screen, she shone her flashlight along the mesh.

A two-inch slit had been cut in the screen near the left side of the frame. Pulse throbbing, Jamie studied the damage. It would have been easy to slip a stick through that hole, push the vase over, then run around the back of the house and attack Hannah.

Should she call Detective Powell? The thought of how he'd react dampened Jamie's excitement. The slit didn't prove anything. Powell would think Jamie had made it herself to try to dodge blame.

Still, she should call him immediately and ask him to come look at it. Maybe there were footprints in the mulch surrounding . . . oops. She'd probably stomped all over any footprints that were there.

Brilliant.

She turned to step over the rock border that separated the planting area from the grass. The sight of a shadowy figure standing nearby made her yelp.

"Stay quiet." The voice was whispery, the face concealed by a dark mask. The beam from Jamie's flashlight caught the gun in the intruder's hand.

"Drop the flashlight."

He's going to shoot me. I'm going to die. Tonight.

"Drop the flashlight!"

Jamie flung the flashlight to the grass. "I don't have much money, but you can take my purse." She held the heavy bag out. In the illumination from the security lights at the corner of the house, the dark figure seemed to be dressed as a ninja. *A ninja?*

The assailant ignored Jamie's purse. "Stay quiet, and I won't hurt you." Jamie didn't recognize the rough voice. "Get in your car."

Slowly, Jamie began to walk. A tornado of fear whirled through her brain. She shouldn't go with him. If she did, she'd die for certain. She should take her chances now, run, start screaming—

"We're going to the Grahams'," the ninja hissed. "You need to leave another message."

Simultaneously horrified and relieved, Jamie continued her sluggish pace toward her car. This wasn't a random attacker who had spotted a woman alone late at night. This was the ghost bride.

Instead of framing Jamie indirectly, she had apparently decided to force her to commit an actual crime. If that's what she wanted, she wasn't likely to shoot unless Jamie made trouble. *She or he?* With the darkness and the costume, Jamie couldn't tell if the attacker was male or female, but she thought of the ghost bride as a she.

Who are you? With the ninja behind her, Jamie couldn't turn around to study her. *Are you Melinda? Why are you doing this?*

"Get in through the passenger door and climb over to the driver's seat. You're driving."

"I won't help you attack Hannah or Isaac."

The gun poked her in the spine. "If you cooperate, no one will get hurt. You're just leaving a message. Get in the car."

Jamie obeyed. Would the ninja really shoot her in cold blood if she balked? Maybe. Shooting Jamie was a quicker way to get rid of her than framing her for attacking Hannah.

But she doesn't want to kill me, or she would have done that long ago. She won't pull the trigger unless she panics and thinks that's her only option.

Keep her calm.

"Drive to the Grahams'," the ninja rasped. "Don't attract any attention. Park before the fork in the road so your car isn't visible from the house."

Jamie pulled out of her parking spot and headed for Isaac's house, glad she'd paid attention when Julian had driven her there and glad she knew Britteridge well. It would *not* be good to get lost. She could picture the ninja getting frustrated and trigger-happy, shouting, "You missed the road! I said turn left!"

Out of the corner of her eye, Jamie tried to scrutinize her kidnapper but couldn't discern anything except that the ninja was maybe Jamie's size. She sat bent low in her seat so her head wasn't visible through the windshield, but she kept the gun pointed at Jamie.

It was worth a try to attempt conversation. The more Jamie could learn, the better prepared she'd be to thwart her. "Why are you doing this?"

"Shut up and drive."

Giving up on that strategy, Jamie thought about the phone in her purse. She still had the purse next to her—she'd jammed it between her seat and the driver's door—but she couldn't think of a way to grab her phone and dial 911 without getting a bullet in the chest.

When she reached Isaac's neighborhood, she parked where the ninja instructed. Desperately, she glanced around, hoping an insomniac would be out for a midnight dog walk, but the neighborhood was quiet, and the few windows she could see were dark. The houses were widely spaced, surrounded by trees.

The ninja yanked Jamie's keys out of the ignition. "I'm getting out. Don't open your door. I'll do it for you. If you open it before I get there, I'll kill you."

Jamie wondered if the ninja was a good enough marksman to shoot a moving target in the dark, but the way she kept the gun aimed at Jamie through the windshield as she walked around the car was enough to keep Jamie from gambling.

The ninja yanked the door open. Jamie grabbed her purse to keep it from falling out.

"Leave the purse. Get out of the car."

Jamie set her purse on the floor of the passenger side and stepped out of the car. The ninja closed the door.

"Cut through the trees to the Grahams' property." She shoved a flashlight into Jamie's hand. "Keep the beam low."

"What—"

The gun jabbed her in the ribs. Jamie closed her mouth, switched on the flashlight, and started walking.

As soon as they reached the perimeter of Isaac's property, the ninja snatched the flashlight back. Some of the windows in Hannah and Isaac's house were still lit. They were awake, or at least Isaac was. Hannah was probably asleep, exhausted by the evening's trauma.

"Take this." The ninja reached around Jamie, holding something out.

Jamie took the object. A can of black spray paint.

"Go up to the house—*quietly.* I'll be right behind you, and if you make any trouble, you're dead. You're going to write *Isaac is mine* in big letters on the side of the house."

"For real?" Jamie whispered. "This is *so childish.*"

The muzzle of the gun tapped her between the shoulder blades. Obediently, she crept toward the house. What did the ninja hope to accomplish by forcing Jamie to do this herself? Did she think Powell would bring out an expert to compare the graffiti to Jamie's handwriting? Would she make Jamie touch everything in sight in hopes of leaving fingerprints? Had she planned this as the crime that finally put Jamie in prison?

Whatever the ninja's motives, Jamie figured it was better not to provoke a criminal holding a gun. She would cooperate until she could see a chance for escape. Then she'd run.

Jamie shook the can. The metal ball rattled so loudly that she flinched, worrying the ninja would punish her for the noise.

The ninja said nothing, so Jamie pressed the nozzle and started to spray-paint the message on the siding, hyperaware of the dark figure behind her.

"Good," the ninja whispered. "Now step over here. Get up on that boulder so you can reach higher and write *Hannah must die.*"

"Listen . . . I don't think this will do you any good—"

"*Quiet.* Move."

Jamie moved a few steps farther, climbed onto the decorative boulder positioned among the bushes near the side of the house, and shook the can of paint.

She was on the last letter of *die* when hands grasped her foot. The ninja wrenched Jamie's foot sideways and slammed her shoulder into Jamie's thigh, knocking her in the opposite direction from her foot.

With a scream, Jamie tumbled off the boulder and landed in a bush. Pain seethed through her ankle, flowing up her leg. She twisted, trying to escape the bush, scratching her face and hands. Her injured foot hit the ground, and pain made her shriek again. Her knee buckled, and she sprawled onto the grass.

Woozily, she looked around and caught a glimpse of the beam of a flashlight among the trees.

A door opened. Someone was coming from the house—more than one person; she could hear voices . . . Isaac . . . Was that Julian? . . . And here she was alone, paint on her fingers, a paint can beside her—

Frantically, Jamie rolled over and tried to rise to her knees, to her feet. Her limbs shook, she was going to throw up—the pain—her ankle must be broken. The ninja was escaping—

"Get her!" Jamie yelled with the pitiful volume she could manage. "Get her—ran into the trees—" She collapsed, her face hitting the grass.

Hands caught the back of her jacket and flipped her over.

"You're finished," Isaac snarled.

"It wasn't me. I mean, she forced me . . . *Get her*—dressed in black—ninja ghost bride. Don't you see her flashlight?"

"The police are coming."

Jamie tried to sit up. Isaac grabbed her shoulder and shoved her back to the grass. "Don't *move*. You're not going anywhere."

"Will someone *catch* her before she gets away? She's a ninja—" Pain funneled away the rest of her air; she couldn't talk anymore. Overhead, trees rattled in the wind.

The ninja would escape. All the police would find here was Jamie, Jamie's car, and Isaac angrily testifying that Jamie had been alone. No one would believe she'd been forced here at gunpoint.

Not a chance.

Chapter 13

"A NINJA GHOST BRIDE," POWELL repeated. He was squatting on the grass, scrutinizing Jamie.

"I can't swear it was the ghost bride. I assumed that. But it was definitely a ninja. I mean, a ninja costume." Jamie felt a tickle of despairing humor at how absurd her story sounded. She wanted to start laughing. Or crying. Or bawling in pain at the burning in her ankle.

"This is *ridiculous*," Isaac snapped. He stood a few feet away, wearing his bathrobe. "You got caught. Stop making up silly stories. You're getting arrested."

"Am I really?" Jamie fired back. "Thanks for making that clear, because I thought the police were here to cite you for exceeding the legal limit on stupidity."

"Do you have any idea who the ninja was?" Powell asked, not looking at Isaac. "Was there anything you could identify about her?"

At least he was playing along enough to ask the question. That was better than Jamie had anticipated. "I never got a good look at her. I'm not even sure it was a woman—I assumed that too. All I know is that she or he was about my size and spoke in a whisper to disguise her voice." How could she say she suspected Melinda when she had zero evidence and zero motive for her?

"You said the ninja accosted you at the Treasure Chest."

"Yes. Oh!" She told Powell about the slit in the screen and her theory of the broken vase being used to keep her out of sight while Hannah was attacked. When Isaac kept trying to interrupt, Ben Mendoza finally gripped his arm and forced him to walk away from Jamie and Powell. Hannah came around the side of the house to stand by Isaac. Red lights flashed as an ambulance pulled up to the curb.

"Did you tell anyone you were planning to go back to the Treasure Chest tonight?" Powell asked.

"No. I hadn't planned on it. It was spur-of-the-moment. I'd gone to visit Niall Flanagan, and when I left, I was too restless to go home, so I decided to poke around the Treasure Chest."

"Niall Flanagan? Why?"

In the background, Jamie could hear Isaac trying to convince Hannah to go inside and lie down, that it was over, they were safe, Jamie was no longer a danger. "Because . . . I'm grasping at straws. I was trying to think who would have had the opportunity to set me up, and I thought of Melinda Brennan. I wanted to see if Niall knew of any reason she might hate me."

Powell rose to his feet. "Was Mrs. Brennan at her father's house?"

"No."

The paramedics were heading across the grass toward Jamie. Despite the pain, she wanted to tell them to wait. She didn't want anything to cut off this conversation with Powell, or she'd probably never get another chance. He'd stamp *Case Closed* on her file and lock her up.

"Hello!" A male voice called from somewhere in the trees. "I'm bringing the ninja in. I've disarmed her. I'd appreciate it if you wouldn't shoot us."

"That's Julian," Hannah exclaimed.

Julian had caught the ninja? Heart racing, Jamie watched the trees.

Two shadowy shapes emerged, one close behind the other. Powell, Ben, and two other officers hurried toward them, one of the officers aiming a flashlight in their direction. As the bright light hit them, Jamie saw the ninja—still dressed in black but unmasked—being propelled forward by Julian.

Melinda.

Inundated by relief, gratitude, and confusion, Jamie stared at Melinda's angry face. She'd been right in her hunch, but she still had no idea why Melinda would do this.

Julian stopped as the police met him, and he pushed Melinda in Ben's direction. From his waistband, Julian pulled out a gun, keeping the barrel pointed at the ground, and offered it to Powell.

"Her gun," he said. "But I don't think it's real."

Powell took it. "Fake."

"Fake!" Jamie shouted. "I got scared out of my mind by a fake gun?"

"This was *her* idea." Out of breath, Melinda still sounded poised and credible. "She dragged me along. She gave me the fake gun to scare Hannah Graham. Said I'd lose my job if I didn't help."

Furious, Jamie rolled over and lifted herself to her hands and knees. She couldn't stand, but she could crawl across the yard to confront Melinda.

"Easy, ma'am." One of the paramedics caught her arm.

"I'll be back," Jamie said. "But she is finished destroying my reputation."

"I didn't want to do any of this," Melinda said. "And *him*"—she pointed at Julian—"I would never have let this scrawny punk bring me back here if I didn't think I'd better come explain before Jamie started blaming me."

"Excuse me?" Julian said. "Scrawny punk? Woman, I took first in cabaret at DanceSport nationals. Had circumstances required it, I could have lifted you over my head and twirled you to the police."

Melinda snorted. "Officer, you need to arrest Jamie McKenzie. She's been threatening me and forcing me to help her stalk the Grahams."

"I'm sorry, Mrs. Brennan." Powell handed the fake gun to one of the officers. "Would you be willing to come to the police department and tell me about it?"

"Of course. I'm sorry I didn't report her earlier, but I was scared, and I had no idea she'd go this far. I was hoping she'd get Isaac Graham out of her system and settle down. I knew her as a child, and I'm friends with her mother. I didn't want to get her in trouble if it wasn't necessary."

"I understand. Please come with me."

Powell's sympathetic tone appalled Jamie. Why wasn't he challenging Melinda's lies? "This is *not* true—"

"Stay calm, Jamie," Powell said. "Let the paramedics tend to your leg, and I'll be in touch soon. Mendoza"—he tipped his head toward Jamie—"talk to her." He turned and walked toward the road with Melinda at his side, followed by a couple of other officers.

Jamie collapsed full-length onto the cold grass as Ben approached. *Stay calm?* When Melinda might still get away with framing her?

One of the paramedics began checking her pulse and blood pressure while the other eased up the hem of her jeans to examine her ankle.

Julian knelt beside her. "You all right?"

"I think so." She looked at the paramedic near her feet. "Is it broken?"

"Can't tell without an X-ray. We'll splint it and get you to the hospital."

"She did it on purpose," Jamie said to Julian; he hadn't heard her report to Powell. "She grabbed my ankle, twisted it, and shoved me off the rock I was standing on. She didn't want me to run away. She was setting me up to get caught—the clincher that would put me in jail—and it apparently worked, even though you caught her. Thanks though. How did you do it?"

"I heard you yelling something about a ninja and catch her. I saw a light moving among the trees. I figured it must be a flashlight, so I headed toward it. She turned it off when she heard me coming, but I still caught up to her. I have excellent night vision, I move fast, and I don't think she could see very well out of that ninja mask."

"She's lying. I never threatened to—"

"I know," Julian said. "It was a ludicrous fabrication."

"I need a lawyer." Thank heavens Julian didn't believe Melinda, but did Powell? Jamie glanced at Isaac and Hannah, standing several yards away, Isaac's arm around Hannah. It was too dark for her to see Isaac's expression, but she doubted he was regretfully thinking he had misjudged Jamie.

Jamie glanced at Ben and wondered when he would tell her she was under arrest. Or would they wait on the formalities until a doctor had cared for her ankle? She looked up at Julian, his hair a curly silhouette in the dimness. "Hannah said you're good at figuring things out about people. Is there any way you could figure out why Melinda—"

Julian touched her shoulder. "Done."

"Don't panic," Ben said. "Just because *you* don't know of a motive doesn't mean Powell doesn't."

Jamie grimaced. "He didn't sound like he—"

Ben shook his head. "Just because he's playing nice doesn't mean he believes her. It means he wants her off guard when he interviews her."

"*Does* he know of a motive?"

"Yep," Ben said. "But I'd better let Edward Allerton explain it."

Chapter 14

In response to a knock at the back door of the Treasure Chest, Jamie grabbed her crutches and moved awkwardly along the hallway. On the back porch, she found Niall holding a large box.

"Brought the rest of the jewel magnets," he said.

"You didn't have to finish them so soon." Jamie's eyes stung. "You should take some time off . . ."

"Don't see you taking time off, love." Niall gestured at the brace on her foot.

"I'm not *really* working. I'm sitting with my foot up in the office, going through the checklist for the spring gala. Kayla and Wes are handling the shop. Wes has been great about taking on additional hours. Niall . . ." Jamie floundered. She hadn't spoken to Niall since Melinda's arrest—he hadn't returned her calls—and she couldn't just push ahead with business and avoid Melinda's name. "I'm so sorry."

"Do you want these upstairs or down?"

"Leave them up here." Jamie followed him, slow on her crutches, as he headed for the upstairs storage room. She stood in the doorway as he slid the box onto an upper shelf.

"How are you doing?" she asked.

"Grand. Yourself?"

Jamie sighed. Neither of them was all right, but plainly, Niall didn't feel like sharing his emotions. "I didn't know Mr. Allerton had planned to . . . I was shocked when he told me . . . I had no idea . . ."

"Ed is welcome to give the Treasure Chest to you. He can do whatever he wants with his property. We have no claim on it, and I told Mel that many times."

Jamie was still reeling over what she'd learned in a late-night emergency room visit from Allerton: at the time of his retirement, two years from now,

Allerton planned to deed the Treasure Chest, Junior, and the surrounding property to Jamie. Jamie knew wealthy Allerton enjoyed donating large amounts of money and surprising people with his generosity, but she'd never imagined he'd do something like this for her. She had no idea what the store and property were worth, but given their location in a prime area of downtown Britteridge, the word *fortune* came to mind.

Allerton had wanted to wait until Jamie's August birthday before giving her the news, but excited over his plans, he'd confided in Niall last winter—a conversation Melinda had eavesdropped on. Later, Allerton had overheard part of an argument between Melinda and Niall, with Melinda raging that if Ed wanted to give his property away, he should give it to Niall. Niall was the reason the Treasure Chest thrived, whereas Jamie had done nothing to earn it. She thought of the apology Allerton had given her last night: "I'm sorry, dear. I knew Melinda was envious, but she always seemed to have excellent self-control, so I thought her jealousy would pass. I never imagined she'd strike out at you."

"She wanted the Treasure Chest for you," Jamie said, focusing on Niall with teary eyes. "You definitely deserve it more than—"

"Deserve it?" Niall scowled, an expression so uncharacteristic that Jamie was surprised he even knew how to look cranky. "Are we competing for Ed's gifts? Ed pays me well for my work and bonuses on top of that, more than I need. What do I want with this place? I'm older than Ed; I don't want to run a shop. I have my own work. I was Mel's excuse for greed; her heart was on her inheritance. I'm sorry for what she did to you. I'm sorry I was a fool. Didn't see my own daughter's cruelty."

"She never meant to take it this far," Jamie said.

"She chose to cause harm. Once she got started, her greed ran away with her."

Melinda's plan had been clever, Jamie thought. If she could make Jamie appear vindictive, obsessed, and in pursuit of a married man, strict Allerton would never follow through on his plans to give her his property. He'd fire her, she'd leave Britteridge, and—Melinda no doubt hoped—he'd decide to deed the property to Niall instead.

"She's sorry now," Niall said gruffly. "She won't come near you or Hannah Graham again."

Jamie couldn't think of what to say, so she nodded. Melinda was out on bail, but Jamie wasn't worried. Melinda wouldn't dare violate the terms of her bail by bothering Jamie or Hannah. Powell had reported that once

Melinda had realized stonewalling was futile, she had confessed and cooperated, her focus shifting to how she could best minimize punishment.

Jamie could imagine how Melinda's lawyer would spin things. First-time offender, upstanding citizen, mother of two, extenuating circumstances, driven by devotion to her father. Melinda wouldn't do anything to jeopardize her chances for getting a lesser sentence. Now that she knew Allerton's money was out of reach, what did she have to gain?

Niall walked past Jamie, heading into the hallway. "I'll be back later with the first batch of snowmen."

When Niall was gone, Jamie returned to the office and sank into a chair. Niall must be hurting, but he wouldn't show it. He'd keep on carving and sanding and painting, coping with sadness through his work. She wondered how Melinda's husband was doing.

Light footsteps approached the office, and Kayla leaned through the doorway. Her cheeks were rosy, and she grinned. "Isaac Graham is here. He wants to talk to you. Is it okay if I send him back?"

That depends on whether or not he's groveling, Jamie wanted to say. "Send him back." After the way Isaac had treated her, she didn't know what to expect from him now. At least his wife had both sense and humility. Hannah had called her to apologize and had even sent flowers and chocolate-covered cranberries, which had embarrassed Jamie. Hannah had been very reasonable most of the time, and Jamie couldn't blame Hannah for accusing her after being clonked on the head with Jamie's wedding decorations.

Isaac walked into the office. He looked solemn, but it was an all-purpose solemn look that would work for either "I'm so sorry" or "If you hadn't moved back here, none of this would have happened."

"Hello, Isaac," she said coolly, but her conscience twitched. She could stand to show a little humility herself. Yes, Isaac had been a jerk, but he'd been under a lot of stress. She ought to cut him some slack. She made her voice friendlier. "How are you doing?"

"Good. How's your ankle?"

"Sore. Bad sprain. But it will be fine. Please, have a seat."

Isaac remained standing, hands resting on the back of the carved wooden chair facing the desk. "I . . . came to apologize. I'm sorry for . . . the way I acted. The things I said to you."

"Thank you." Jamie tried to sound sincere, but it still gouged deep to think how easily Isaac had believed she'd stalk his family.

"I should have known you would never . . ." He broke eye contact, and his words mushed into mutters. "Acted like an idiot . . . couldn't figure out who else could have a grudge . . . "

Jamie knew it probably didn't reflect well on her character that the more mortified Isaac looked, the more pleased she felt. "I'm just grateful Melinda didn't succeed."

"Can't believe Melinda Brennan . . . nuts the way she attacked Hannah and kidnapped you."

"From what Detective Powell said, she insisted she never planned to kidnap me. She acted out of panic, realizing how much trouble she could be in if her plan didn't work."

"Yeah, he told me that too. She'd assumed you'd get arrested after that attack on Hannah, and when you didn't, she got worried."

Jamie nodded. Melinda had come to visit Niall that night, but when she'd seen Jamie's car, she'd parked out of sight and gone to eavesdrop beneath the open workshop window, wanting to know why Jamie was there so late. When she heard Jamie asking Niall about her, she freaked out.

"She needed to do something immediately to *prove* I was guilty before I made people suspicious of her," Jamie said. "It was clever of her to think of using one of the Treasure Chest's costumes as a disguise."

"What were you doing with a ninja costume?"

"In the basement, we have a box of costumes we use at Halloween, at the spring gala, and so on. Melinda didn't have a key, but apparently, Niall did, one Mr. Allerton gave him years ago that he hung on a key rack in his utility room. She took the key, came here, changed, and planned to meet me at my apartment—then saw me driving up. I came right to her! And I can't *believe* I got fooled by our own props."

"Under those circumstances, the gun would have fooled anyone except an expert," Isaac said. "How can you think clearly when someone is threatening to kill you?"

"True," Jamie said, appreciating Isaac's tactful comment. *That* sounded more like the Isaac she'd known all her life, not the Isaac with the knee-jerk accusations.

"Um . . . so . . . Edward Allerton is giving all this to you, huh?" Isaac gestured around the room.

"I still can't believe it. I guess he was serious all those times he told me he considered me his granddaughter."

"Does he have any family?"

"His wife died years ago. He has one son and two grandsons, but I guess he figured they'll inherit enough without this."

"Congrats. I'm happy for you. I know you love this place."

"Thank you. I'm in shock, but I'm thrilled. And I think my love for the Treasure Chest is the main reason he's giving it to me. He knows I'll keep it running, not sell the property for cash. Isaac . . . I'm happy for you and Hannah. I hope now you know I mean that."

"Thanks. Jamie . . . again . . . I'm *really* sorry." He adjusted the chair in front of him with fidgety motions, then moved to the other chair facing the desk and slid it backward to line it up with the first, as though Jamie had invited him to straighten the office. If she handed him a dust cloth, maybe he'd do the baseboards.

"I was . . . scared out of my mind," he said. "I thought I was a good husband . . . taking care of my family, getting ready to be a father . . . even read a couple of books about fatherhood. Never had any interest in that kind of book before, but I wanted to be ready."

Jamie hoped they hadn't been books Robin had recommended.

"Then we got that postcard, and more weird stuff started happening. Someone out there was a threat to my family, and I didn't know what to do. I didn't know how to protect Hannah and the baby—" Tears welled in Isaac's eyes. Amazed, Jamie tried not to stare. She'd never seen Isaac cry.

He wiped his eyes with the back of his hand. "Sorry. I shouldn't have accused you without proof, but I couldn't think of anyone else who might hate us, and you'd just moved back to town . . . I'd never thought you were spiteful, but I'd hurt you, so . . . maybe you'd changed . . . ?"

"Did you feel better thinking it was me because then at least it wasn't some unknown stalker?" Jamie asked. "You knew I wouldn't really hurt Hannah—I hope—so blaming me must have felt safer than not knowing who was bothering your family."

"Yeah . . . I guess you're right . . . It did feel safer that way, but when Hannah got attacked . . ." The tears slid down his face. He pressed his hands over his eyes and stood silent.

Jamie spoke softly. "I'm so sorry Melinda used Hannah to get at me."

Isaac lowered his hands and wiped his face on his sleeve. "It's not your fault." His voice shook. "Sheesh, I'm sorry. I didn't mean to lose control on you. So . . . are you sure you're doing okay?"

"I'm fine. My mom was up here helping me for a couple of days, but she got bored when there wasn't much for her to do."

"I . . . uh . . . heard Julian has been helping you out as well."

"Yes, he brought me dinner last night. He's been experimenting with Thai recipes lately, and the food was amazing."

"Hannah was saying . . ." Isaac trailed off.

"Saying what?" Jamie attempted to sound nonchalant.

"Well, she's just . . . excited to see him . . . He's been so skittish about . . . never mind. None of my business. But he's a good guy. Glad he's helping you."

"I'm glad he's helping me too." She hoped Isaac wouldn't notice that she was turning red. "I invited him over tonight to help me finish up the leftover chicken satay."

Isaac grinned. "Have fun."

"I totally will," Jamie said.

OTHER BOOKS AND AUDIO BOOKS
BY STEPHANIE BLACK

The Believer

The Witnesses

Fool Me Twice

Methods of Madness

Cold As Ice

Rearview Mirror

Shadowed

About the Author

STEPHANIE BLACK HAS LOVED BOOKS since she was old enough to grab the pages and has enjoyed creating make-believe adventures since she and her sisters were inventing long Barbie games filled with intrigue and danger or running around pretending to be detectives. She is a four-time Whitney Award winner for Best Mystery/Suspense, most recently for *Rearview Mirror* (2011).

Stephanie was born in Utah and has lived in various places, including Arizona; Massachusetts; New York; and Limerick, Ireland. She currently lives in Northern California and enjoys spending time with her husband, Brian, and their five children. She is a fan of chocolate, cheesecake, and her husband's homemade bread.

Stephanie enjoys hearing from readers. You can contact her via e-mail at info@covenant-lds.com or by mail, care of Covenant Communications, P.O. Box 416, American Fork, UT 84003-0416. Visit her website at www.stephanieblack.net and her blog, Black Ink, at www.stephanieblackink.blogspot.com.